O9-ABI-641

The Guardian

"An entertaining thriller-cum-romance-cum-conversion story is what readers get in this fast-paced novel.... Christian readers will relish this intriguing tale."

PUBLISHERS WEEKLY

"More than an investigative thriller, this is a great romance dealing with complex matters of faith."

ROMANTIC TIMES

"Another exciting new thriller from an up-and-coming talent in Christian fiction."

LIBRARY JOURNAL

"Page-turning excitement...true spiritual conflict...romance. I can't wait to read her next one!"

HANNAH ALEXANDER, author of *Silent Pledge*

Danger in the Shadows

"Dee Henderson had me shivering as her stalker got closer and closer to his victim. The message that we have nothing to fear as long as God is in control was skillfully handled, but I got scared anyway! I highly recommend this book to anyone who likes suspense."

TERRI BLACKSTOCK, bestselling author of *Emerald Windows*

"A masterstroke!... Dee Henderson gives the reader not one but two irresistible heroes."

COMPUSERVE REVIEWS

The Negotiator

"Solid storytelling, compelling characters, and the promise of more O'Malleys make Henderson a name to watch. Highly recommended, with a cross-genre appeal."

LIBRARY JOURNAL

"Dee Henderson has deftly combined action, suspense, and romance in this first-class inspirational romantic suspense."

AFFAIRE DE COEUR

The Truth Seeker

"Another fantastic, page-turning mystery by Dee Henderson! Heartwarming romance and exciting drama are her trademark, and they'll be sure to thrill you a third time!"

SUITE101.COM

"Read one book by Dee Henderson, and I guarantee you are gonna be hooked for life!"

THE BELLES AND BEAUX OF ROMANCE

"For a complex story and profound statement on Christianity, read *The Truth Seeker.*"

THE ROMANCE READERS CONNECTION, Inspirational Corner

The Protector

"There are very few books that touch the soul and the heart while trying to deliver an inspiring message, but Ms. Henderson always manages to accomplish this feat."

BOOKBROWSER

"A riveting addition to the series!"

HUNTRESS BOOK REVIEWS

"*The Protector* is vintage Dee Henderson."

WRITERS CLUB ROMANCE GROUP ON AOL

THE
GUARDIAN

BOOK TWO—THE O'MALLEY SERIES

DEE HENDERSON

Multnomah Publishers® *Sisters, Oregon*

This is a work of fiction. The characters, incidents, and dialogues are products of the author's imagination and are not to be construed as real. Any resemblance to actual events or persons, living or dead, is entirely coincidental.

THE GUARDIAN
published by Multnomah Publishers, Inc.

© 2001 by Dee Henderson
International Standard Book Number: 1-57673-642-3

Cover images by Tony Stone Images
Scripture quotations are from: *Revised Standard Version Bible* (RSV)
© 1946, 1952 by the Division of Christian Education
of the National Council of the Churches of Christ
in the United States of America

Multnomah is a trademark of Multnomah Publishers, Inc., and
is registered in the U.S. Patent and Trademark Office.
The colophon is a trademark of Multnomah Publishers, Inc.

Printed in the United States of America

ALL RIGHTS RESERVED
No part of this publication may be reproduced, stored in a retrieval system, or transmitted, in any form or by any means—electronic, mechanical, photocopying, recording, or otherwise—without prior written permission.

For information:
MULTNOMAH PUBLISHERS, INC.
POST OFFICE BOX 1720
SISTERS, OREGON 97759

Library of Congress Cataloging-in-Publication Data:
Henderson, Dee.
    The guardian / by Dee Henderson.
        p.cm. – (The O'Malley series ; bk. 2)
    ISBN 1-57673-642-3   1. United States marshals–Fiction. I. Title.
PS3558.E4829 G83 2001   813'.54–dc21   00-011830

02 03 04 05 06—11 10 9 8 7

But truly God has listened;
he has given heed to the voice of my prayer.
PSALM 66:19

———⣿———

TITLES BY DEE HENDERSON:

———⣿———

Prologue

C an I take Mom the flowers?"

They were not allowed inside the ICU, but the nurse who had come out to the waiting room nodded anyway. Janelle knew what the boy did not, and it made her want to cry. His mother was dying. Let him take the flowers.

Marcus was such a polite young man, patiently sitting alone in the ICU waiting room for the brief visits allowed each hour. He had been coming for the last nine days. A neighbor who worked at the hospital brought him in each morning, and each evening took him home.

He had brought roses with him today, three of them, carefully wrapped with a damp paper towel around the stems, foil around that. There were grass stains on the knees of his jeans. He had told her yesterday that he was tending the rose bushes during his mom's absence.

"Can I get you something to eat? A grilled cheese sandwich maybe?"

"No, thank you."

She was positive the boy was hungry, but there had been a tirade the one and only time his father had come to the hospital and found him sharing a sandwich with an orderly. Marcus had politely refused the offers of food ever since.

"The chaplain is with her now," Janelle told him, and the boy's relief was visible.

"He prays good."

"You pray wonderfully too." She had seen him with his mother's Bible, struggling to sound out the words as he read.

"I try."

He pushed off the molded plastic chair, not tall enough for his feet to reach the floor when he was sitting down. "Thanks for coming to get me."

"You're welcome, Marcus."

She watched him walk to the glass door of the ICU, use all of his weight to pull it open.

He hadn't asked her if his mom was getting better. It was the first time he had not asked.

It was hard to breathe; her lungs kept filling up with fluid. She had rallied today, and it was with a sense of urgency she knew she had to see her son. Renee heard Marcus before she saw him and wiped away any sign of the strain, smiling toward the door. He came in escorted by the supervising nurse, carrying flowers.

Her heart tugged at the sight of him, wearing his favorite baseball shirt, washed but wrinkled, and blue jeans that would need a stain remover. He had asked her yesterday how to do the laundry right.

She hugged him, ignoring the IVs, marshaling her strength to make her grip firm. Her smile came from her heart. "You brought me flowers."

"I picked your roses. Was that okay?"

"Very okay. They're beautiful." She laid them on the blanket at her chest so she could enjoy them.

The chair scraped against the tile floor as Marcus pulled it to the edge of her bed.

He eagerly told her about the kittens at the neighbors and the way the black one with one white paw liked chasing a feather duster. She let him talk, smiling at the right places, watching him, holding his hand. Her son. The joy of her life. The doctor had told him laughter was good medicine, and he had latched on to that and taken it seriously, coming with a story each day to make her laugh.

She would ask about his morning, but in the last couple days he had started to avoid answering that question. It wasn't going well at home, and he wanted to be her guardian and not tell her. She brushed her fingers through his hair; it would need to be cut soon. She hoped he didn't end up having to do it himself. His father would not think of it.

"Mom?"

She had drifted on him; the story was over. She smiled an apology. "I'm laughing inside, honey."

"It wasn't very funny."

That drew a chuckle.

Her strength was fading and she could hear the wheeze returning.

Marcus's hand in hers squeezed tight. "Shall I get the nurse?" he asked, his voice calm but his eyes were anxious.

Two minutes with him. It wasn't enough. But the reality could not be denied. "Yes." He moved to slip his hand from hers, and instead she tightened her hold. "Before…you do. I want my kiss."

He grinned. He was a boy again instead of the solemn young man. He leaned across the railing to rub his nose against hers, then kissed both cheeks European style. "Love you, Mom."

"I love you too." She held him tight. "And Jesus loves you."

"I know."

He went to get the nurse.

The simple faith of a child. She was grateful. He had found something strong enough to get him through what was coming.

She panted for breath. They would clear her lungs again, and soon would have no choice but to put her on to the respirator. She feared she would never come off it. The doctor's reassuring words could not change what she knew in her spirit was coming. She gripped the roses and a thorn pierced her finger. Despite the fever she was shivering again.

She would be leaving Marcus with only his father. It was a heavy burden to place on an eight-year-old's faith. A single tear escaped to slide down her cheek. She had already cried for her husband and her son, for everything lost that could have been. Tears now would literally choke her. *Jesus, be my son's guardian. He needs You.*

Renee closed her eyes and focused on living one more day.

Marcus scuffed his tennis shoe against the tile floor and stared out the waiting room window, wiping furiously at the tears. He had to stop crying; they would see and they wouldn't let him visit anymore. The thought was a panic rising in his chest. He gulped back a sob and worked his jaw.

She wasn't getting better.

He had to pray harder.

One

U.S. Marshal Marcus O'Malley tucked the cellular phone tighter against his shoulder as he studied the latest photographs sent by the North Washington district office. Eighteen faxes. The picture quality grainy at best; the information about each individual sketchy. Each had made threats against judges attending this July conference at the Chicago Jefferson Renaissance Hotel. The pages crinkled as only cheap fax paper could as he thumbed through them, memorizing each one.

"Kate, what are you not telling me?" He was trying to have a telephone conversation with his sister while he worked and it was…interesting. He would have said aggravating, but he loved Kate too much to get annoyed with her easily.

His sister Kate O'Malley could be clear or ambiguous at will. As a hostage negotiator she knew how to choose her words, and she was being deliberately obtuse at the moment. It was 7:05 P.M. Friday night; Supreme Court Justice Philip Roosevelt would give the keynote speech at 8:00 P.M. before an audience of over twelve hundred, and Marcus did not have time to read between the lines.

Kate was trying to tell him something without breaking a confidence; that told him it was family related. And it was important enough she was willing to go to the edge of that confidence to let him know about it; that told him it was serious.

"She was supposed to tell you last night…"

Marcus flipped back to the ninth fax and frowned. Something about the picture was triggering a glimmer of a memory. Tom Libour: Caucasian, early forties, clean shaven. It was an old memory, and he could feel it flitting just beyond his recall. He didn't forget cases he had worked. Maybe something his partner had worked? He scrawled a note beside the photo, requesting the incident report be pulled. He passed the stack of faxes back to his deputy. "Who?" Jennifer, Lisa, or Rachel? In a family of seven, Kate had just cut the list in half.

The seven of them were related, but not by blood—by choice. At the orphanage—Trevor House—the decision to become their own family had made a lot of sense; two decades later it still did. As the oldest, thirty-eight, he accepted the guardianship of the group; as the next in line Kate protected it, kept her finger on the family pulse. He didn't mind the responsibility, but it often arrived at inconvenient times. What was going on?

"I've said too much already; forget I called."

"Kate—"

"Marcus." Her own frustration came back at him with the bite in her voice. "I didn't ask to be the one she chose to tell. I'm stuck. I'll push her to tell you; it's the best I can do."

The family was close, but Kate—she was the one he talked with in the middle of the night; they had shared the dark days. They were the oldest, the closest, and there was no one he trusted more than her. "How serious is it?"

He retrieved his black tuxedo jacket from the back of a folding chair. He would be standing behind the Supreme Court justice during the speech doing his best to look interested while he did his real job—decide who in the crowd might want to shoot the old man.

"I'm pacing the floors at night."

Marcus, reaching to straighten the lapel of his jacket, stopped. Kate had the nerve to walk into situations where a guy held a bomb; the last thing she did was overreact. Something that had her that worried—his eyes narrowed. "Who, Kate?" He couldn't take the weight off her shoulders if he didn't know. If Kate had given her word, she would never say, but he couldn't just leave it. He needed to know.

"Can you get free later tonight?"

Time was tight. This was the biggest judicial conference of the year, but he wasn't about to say no. Quinn would do him a favor…. "The banquet and its aftermath should be wrapped up by ten-thirty. I can meet you after that."

"We'll join you even if I have to drag her there," Kate replied grimly.

"Deal. And even if it's just you, come over."

"I'll be there. Besides, it's probably the only way I'll get to see Dave."

Marcus spotted FBI Special Agent Dave Richman on the other side of the room, deep in a discussion with the hotel security chief.

This conference had attracted explosive media attention. The Supreme Court was about to go conservative. With the announcement by the president of a nominee to replace retiring Justice Luke Blackwood, the landscape of the law across the nation would forever change. Most of the judges on the president's short list were in attendance. Dave had drawn the unenviable job of trying to figure out how to control and manage the media access.

"He's here. Do you want to talk to him?" Dave and Kate were dating. Dave having even gone so far as to formally ask all the guys in the family for permission. It was serious on her side too—Kate didn't let just anybody outside of the family get close to her heart.

"No, I know you're swamped. I just miss him."

She was in love. Everyone in the family knew that. Her face brightened when she saw Dave, and that impassive control she kept around her emotions, so necessary for her job, disappeared. Even her Southern accent intensified. Marcus kidded her about being love struck and she teased him back about hovering. That was okay; she needed a big brother watching out for her. "Then you definitely need to come over tonight. I'll tell Dave to expect you."

"Let me surprise him. Besides, knowing my job, I'll probably get yanked by a page on my way over there."

She sounded irked, and he enjoyed that. "Love can be so rough."

"Just wait; your turn is coming."

He wasn't seeing anyone now, and short of someone colliding with him, at the moment he didn't have time to notice anyone. His hands were full with his job and the O'Malley clan. But knowing Kate, she would probably try to set him up the first chance she got. She loved to meddle in his life, just like he did in hers.

And he knew if she did he'd have to grouse about it just for the principle of it, but he wouldn't really mind. There was never going to be time to date in his schedule; it would simply have to be found. "Good-bye, Kate. I'll see you later."

He closed the cellular phone and his amusement faded. What was wrong? Jennifer O'Malley had just gotten engaged; he didn't think it was her. That left Lisa or Rachel. Lisa was always getting into trouble with that curiosity of hers, but if he had to place a bet he would guess it was Rachel. She had been unusually quiet during the Fourth of July family gathering only days before.

Marcus had no choice but to set aside the problem for the moment. He joined his partner Quinn. "Are we ready?"

"I think so." Quinn looked like he hadn't slept in the last couple days, but then he normally looked that way so it was hard to tell. Quinn had general hotel security: 37 floors, 1,012 rooms, and 50 meeting rooms to cover—it was like trying to plug a leaking dam with cotton balls. Unlike a federal court building where they could screen who entered or left the building, what they carried, this hotel was wide open to the public.

"I got the hotel to agree to close delivery access to the kitchens for the evening; it freed up another three men for ballroom security," Quinn noted. "And I moved Deputy Ellis to Judge Blake. Ellis has covered the Fourth Circuit in the past, maybe he'll be able to talk the judge into following basic security guidelines."

"Thanks. Nelson was showing the strain."

"I can't blame him. Blake is by far the most difficult of the judges on the president's short list." Quinn closed the folder of assignments and tossed it on the cluttered desk. Neatness had disappeared under the churn of numerous problems. "Do you think any of them have a chance of getting the nomination?"

To the U.S. Marshals, who knew the judicial personnel across the country better than the president who appointed them and the congress who confirmed them, a Supreme Court nomination was a race they handicapped with the skill of veteran court watchers.

Marcus considered the names for a moment, then shook his head. "No." The names on the list so far were good judges, but not the great ones. They were the political appeasement candidates, on the list until the scrutiny of the press gave the president something he could use as cover for not nominating them. The real candidates would be in the next set of names that surfaced.

Marcus adjusted his jacket around the shoulder holster, checked the microphone at his cuff, then did a communication check on the security net. He tried to get himself mentally prepared for the long coming evening covering the justice. "I swear Deputy Nicholas Drake ate bad sushi for lunch on purpose. Tell me again how I got elected for this honor rather than you?" he asked while he scanned the room, reviewing where they were at with a check of the status boards. As usual, they were having a conversation but their attention was on anything but each other.

"You're better looking."

Marcus grunted. "Sure. That's why I get asked for *your* phone number." His partner Quinn Diamond attracted attention without trying. The man looked like he had just stepped off his Montana ranch. There was something untamed about him and women seemed to know it. His face was weathered by the sun and wind, he could see to the horizon, and his gaze made suspects fidget. He called women ma'am and wore cowboy boots whenever he could get away with it. Marcus enjoyed having him as a partner; life was never dull. They had tracked fugitives together, protected witnesses, and kept each other alive. Quinn didn't flinch when the pressure hit.

"Actually, Marcus—I'm afraid I kind of blew it the other night," Quinn admitted.

Surprised at the sheepish tone of voice, Marcus glanced over at him. "How?"

"Lisa." Quinn reached into his jacket pocket and took out a folded cloth. He flipped back the folded velvet to show a sealed petri dish. "She sent me a petrified squid."

It was so like his sister Lisa, Marcus had to laugh. "Sounds like a no to me," he remarked dryly. Was this what Kate had stumbled into? A tiff between Quinn and Lisa? It didn't fit Kate's reaction, but it was certainly an interesting development.

"Where did she get this thing?"

"A forensic pathologist—I imagine that was one of the more tame replies she considered sending you."

"All I did was ask her out."

"Quinn, it is painfully obvious you did not have sisters." Marcus took a moment to explain reality. "Two years ago you asked out Jennifer—she's now engaged. Last year you asked out Kate—she's now serious with an FBI agent. This year you asked out Lisa. You just told her she's your third choice. Rachel might forgive you; Lisa will never let you forget it."

"Can I help it if you've got an interesting family?"

Even a friend like Quinn wasn't going to be allowed to hurt his sister. "Flowers will not do; you'd better get creative with the apology."

"I'm still going to get her to say yes."

"I wish you luck; you're going to need it." Quinn would be good for Lisa. He was one of the few men Marcus thought would understand her and the trouble she got into because of her curiosity. Marcus was beginning to feel a bit like a matchmaker having just subtly pushed Kate and Dave together less than a month ago. "Tell you what. I need to free some time late tonight to meet with Kate. Swap the time with me and I'll talk to Lisa for you."

"And tell her what?"

"Only your good points."

"Why don't I believe you?"

Marcus grinned. "I've already told her the bad."

The security net gave the five-minute warning to the start of the evening program. Judge Carl Whitmore would speak first, and then it would be his Honor Justice Roosevelt. Marcus would be glad when the evening was over. "Come on, Quinn, we need to talk to Dave about press access to Justice Roosevelt after the keynote speech."

"Please—give me crowd control; anything but his Honor. I love the man, but he likes nothing better than to rile the media for the fun of it."

"He's appointed for life; his life is boring without controversy."

"You mean he's too old to care if someone decides they want to kill him."

"Exactly."

"You're going to owe me for this one. The last time his Honor held one of these media question and answer sessions, I had to expel a heckler and I ended up all over the evening news."

The Jefferson Hotel served chicken kiev, rice pilaf, and steamed asparagus for the main course at the banquet. Judge Carl Whitmore was too nervous to eat. He politely ate a few bites and moved food around on his plate before finally pushing his plate aside.

Soon after the dinner plates were cleared away, the man beside him rose, moved to the podium, and gave a warm welcome to the guests. He began an introduction that Carl knew would take at most two minutes to give. Carl reached for the folder he had forced himself not to open during dinner.

The introduction finished.

Carl took a deep breath and rose to his feet. He shook hands with the man who had introduced him. Polite applause filled the room.

He slipped off his watch and set it down on the edge of the podium, removed the pages of his speech from the folder and arranged them neatly to the left of center on the podium, and then took a final moment to slip on his reading glasses.

Shari had written a note at the top of the first page with a bright pink felt tip pen—*Remember to smile*—and she had dotted the i in her name with a small heart. That fact, as much as her note, made Carl smile as he lifted his head, faced the bright lights, and smoothly began his prepared remarks to the twelve hundred guests in attendance.

Bless her heart. What would he ever do without her?

Carl had been given such loyal friends. He had gone to law school with her father. Shari, her brother Joshua, and her parents William and Beth, had flown out from Virginia to be here for this speech. The hour of his greatest disappointment was also the hour he learned how rich his life really was.

The president's short list of judges had become known Tuesday, and his name had not been on the list. There had been early rumors that he was being considered, and those rumors had taken on substance when the FBI quietly began checking his background. Carl had begun to let himself hope. He was a bachelor, his life was the law, and to serve on the Supreme Court was his lifelong dream. His disappointment was intense. But in the audience were four people who understood, who shared his disappointment, and were determined to lift his spirits. He had been blessed in his friends. He had the important things in life.

He began the speech he had waited his lifetime to give—a perspective of conservative thought in judicial law.

The lights had partially dimmed as the speech began. Shari Hanford was grateful, for it helped hide the fact she had started to twirl her fork, reflecting her nervous energy.

Even though she had not written this speech, she had worked on minor refinements and knew it word for word. Fifteen years in politics, the last ten of them as a speechwriter, and she still couldn't get through listening to a speech without holding her breath. She knew how important this was to Carl. If something she had suggested didn't work…

She gave up trying to hide the obvious and reached for a roll left in the basket on the table and tore it in two. Maybe it would settle her stomach. She regretted eating the chicken kiev; she should have been smart like Carl and waited to order room service later.

She would much rather be the one giving the speech. When she was at the podium, the nerves gave way to the process of connecting with the audience, adjusting the presentation: the inflections, the timing, the emphasis necessary to persuade people to her point of view.

Her brother Joshua looked over at her and gave her a sympathetic smile. Normally he would be kidding her about her nerves, but not tonight.

Carl began page two of his prepared text. His presentation had been flawless so far. Shari rested her elbow on the table, her chin against the knuckles of her right hand, and ate the bread as she watched him, feeling his passion for the law come through in his words. She didn't understand why he was not on the Supreme Court short list. Someone at the Justice Department had really fumbled the ball in not recommending him.

Lord, I still don't understand why he was passed over. The quiet prayer was a running conversation that had been going on for days. *It's an enormous disappointment. Didn't the hours invested in prayer mean anything? It's not like I expect every prayer to be answered, but the big ones—*

This was the dream of Carl's life. Why build up hope with the FBI background check and then yank it away? Surely there could have been an easier cushion for delivering an answer of no. I have watched this man love and serve You all of my life. He could make a difference to this nation like no one else on the short list. He would be a great justice.

Her pager vibrated, Shari jerked, and her water glass rocked. It was her emergency pager; she had left her general pager upstairs. Her heart pounding, she pulled it from her pocket. Her job demanded the two pagers; prioritizing people clamoring for her attention was a necessary part of her life.

Only the VIPs in her life had this number, and most of them were sitting at the table with her. She read the return number. It was John Palmer, the governor of the Commonwealth of Virginia. Her boss and longtime friend, he was not one to page unless it was urgent. And for him to call, knowing Carl's speech was tonight—

She rubbed her thumb across the pager numbers, feeling torn, then reluctantly acknowledged she couldn't ignore it for twenty minutes. She reached for her handbag and retrieved her cellular phone. "I'll be back in a minute," she whispered to her mom, slipping away to call John back. Her movement attracted notice from the tables nearby and she cringed, hoping Carl hadn't noticed. The last thing she wanted to do was interrupt his speech.

Opening the side door, she slipped out of the ballroom. To her surprise she found herself in what appeared to be a back hallway—across from her was an open door to a utility room. The hallway was empty, narrow, even somewhat dark. She had obviously come out the wrong door. Shari hesitated, then shrugged off her mistake, glad not to have to worry about the press being around. She dialed John's number.

She had worked for him for over ten years. She added elegance to his communications, his message. She was working long hours as his deputy communications director to get him reelected. What was wrong?

Shari paced the hall toward the windows as she waited for the phone to be answered, then paused and closed her eyes as fatigue washed over her. The Fourth of July campaigning had been four days of nonstop travel, crisscrossing Virginia. She had been home a day to pack and then she had met her parents and brother to fly out here to Chicago for the three-day conference. It was supposed to be a rest break for her, but it wasn't happening. Her body clock was off, leaving her wide awake at 2 A.M. and fighting sleep at noon. She struggled to suppress her fatigue so it wouldn't show in her voice.

Her pager went off again. She scowled. There was apparently a crisis breaking in Virginia and she was halfway across the country in Chicago. She had known getting away in the middle of an election was a bad idea.

Normally she thrived on diving into the problems and being in the center of the storm. Joshua called it her hurricane mode: dealing with incomplete information, immediate deadlines, impending catastrophes—she found being in the center of the action a calm place to be when she was the one controlling the response. That wasn't the case tonight, she was too far away. She lifted the pager to look at the number and see who else was demanding her attention.

It was like getting physically battered.

Sam. He hadn't called her directly in almost five months, not since she'd slammed the phone down on him last time. She rarely lost it so elo-quently, and she had done it in style that evening.

Sam Black. The man she had let get deep into her soul and curl around her heart; he was like a black mark she couldn't erase. She had loved him so passionately and today just the sight of his number was enough to bring back a flood of emotions to paralyze her. It had not been a gentle breakup between them, for dreams had imploded and expectations had been crushed. It had been intense, painful, and a year later it still haunted her.

Sam was another prayer God had not answered.

She wanted to swear, did slap her hand against the wall and pace away from the windows. She was trying to solve her growing dilemma about prayer while stuck on a phone walking the halls of a hotel in Chicago.

She hated not having her prayers answered.

You're spoiled, she told herself with a wry smile. *And God still loves you anyway.*

She looked again at the pager. Sam had the ability to be cordial, even friendly when they spoke, and the best she could do was chilly politeness as the embarrassment of what could have been washed over her and the sound of his voice brought back all her hopes. She chose to ignore his page even as she wondered why he would feel the need to call.

The phone was finally answered. "Sorry about the delay, Shari. Thanks for calling back so quickly."

She briefly wondered how John had functioned before caller ID. "Not a problem. What's happening?"

"How would you like Christmas about six months early?"

She could hear the smile in his voice. "What?"

"Carl is going to make the short list. Your brief helped, Shari."

Her heart stopped momentarily. "You're serious." She had labored over that brief presenting Carl's qualifications for the court; she knew Carl's past cases better than his own law clerks; she knew the man. It was the best position paper of her life. John had passed it through to Washington—one voice in a sea of voices.

"I just got off the phone with the attorney general. They've recom-mended Carl to the president. The attorney general expects a positive deci-sion to happen tonight."

She closed her eyes, knowing she needed to apologize to God. "John, you couldn't have given me better news."

"Keep him near the phone tonight?"

"Of course! I'll make sure we're prepared to celebrate when the call comes." She rubbed her forehead, gave a soft laugh. "Talk about a reason for an ulcer—Carl makes the list and then we wait some more. The president makes his choice in ten days."

"At least you'll be pacing for a good reason."

It was a running joke between them, her habit of pacing when she thought, talked, waited. "Any other major issues?"

"Nothing that won't wait another day."

"I'll talk to you tomorrow then." She closed the phone after saying thanks once again.

Carl was going to make the short list. Her high heels sank into the carpet as she spun around, feeling like she would burst keeping such a secret for even a couple hours. *Lord, thank You! And I'm sorry for thinking it didn't matter to You.* She had to at least tell her brother Josh. They could order a special room service dinner for Carl—lobster, maybe. After the call came, they could invite a few of his friends to join them.

Lord, the anticipation is so strong I can taste it.

Carl might actually be sitting on the Supreme Court when it opens its next session. The image of that was incredible.

She pulled open the side door to the ballroom so she could slip back inside.

"Oh. I'm sorry!" Shari pulled up at the sight of men in suits carrying guns. They turned, the three nearest her, blocking her line of sight into the rest of the room. This was definitely not the ballroom.

None of the doors in the back corridor were marked. She had obviously gotten turned around as she paced and talked on the phone. She had walked in on men carrying guns. Her heart rate escalated, about the same instant the three men near her actually relaxed. Their assessment had been swift.

The man on the right removed his hand from inside his jacket. She wanted to give a nervous laugh as she realized he had instinctively put his hand on his gun. This was clearly not turning out to be her night. She had been introduced to foreign dignitaries and hosted senators for dinner and never fumbled as much as she had in this one evening.

"No problem," the man nearest her said as he smiled, disarming her panic with a charm that made her blink. His entire demeanor softened with that smile. Tall, edging over six feet, the seams of the tuxedo strained by muscles, a gaze that pierced. He would have been a threatening figure without that smile, but it changed everything. It was like getting hit with a warm punch when his attention focused on her.

She had come in the side door of what was obviously a security control center, and now stood behind two long tables where cables and power cords from PCs and faxes snaked down to the floor. The room was actually quite busy, at least twenty people present; most had paused what they were doing at her entrance and quiet had washed over the room.

"That door should have been locked; it wasn't entirely your mistake," the man commented, stepping around the tables and over the wires to join her. His black jacket hung open, his shoulder holster visible. She instinctively knew he was one of the men in charge. There was a confident directness to his look and words. His hand settled under her elbow and without being obtrusive about it, steered her back out of the room. She felt the power in that grip checked to be light. "You came two doors beyond the ballroom."

She was acutely embarrassed, but he was being nice about it. "I've always been directionally challenged. I didn't mean to go somewhere I didn't belong."

"No harm done."

She had never been able to shake that one fatal flaw in her makeup—her inability to keep her sense of bearings—and it was her own fault. Frankly, she didn't pay enough attention until it was too late to correct the mistake.

Every year she made a solemn New Year's resolution to try harder, and every year she managed to forget that promise and get herself back into situations like this with painful regularity. And to do it in front of three good-looking guys…there were times she really did want to be able to shrink into the woodwork.

She took a deep breath and let it go; the damage was done and it was time to recover as best she could. The realization touched her smile with humor. "I'm Shari, by the way."

"Shari Hanford. Yes, I know." He firmly closed the door behind him, then released her elbow and offered his hand. "Marcus O'Malley."

She blinked at the fact he knew her name, then realized a man in his position probably knew most everything; a fanciful notion but not one she would bet against. She had attended too many judicial events where men like him melted into the background not to have a healthy respect for what he did. Not that Marcus would ever melt into the background of any-thing—he'd be the one attracting the attention.

Up close, the reality of his presence was overwhelming, absorbing her senses. Weight lifter, runner, something…he was an athlete and it showed in his build. She looked because she couldn't help herself. Her gaze finally met his and she blushed slightly at the confident directness and quiet amusement she saw in his eyes.

"Marcus. It's nice to meet you." His hand was strong and callused, and when it closed around hers she felt the clasp of warmth through her fingers, palm, and fine bones of her wrist. She wanted to believe it was her imagination that had her hand trapped in his for a beat too long, but then he smiled, still holding her hand, and she realized it was not her imagina-tion. She wanted to blush again but found herself holding his gaze instead.

It had been a long time since someone not associated with work looked at her with that kind of frank appreciation. It did wonders for her sense of morale. She didn't have to worry that he was going to be hitting her in the next moment with a request for a quote from her boss. She knew she looked her best. She had pulled her hair up, chosen gold jewelry, and defined her eyelashes around her blue eyes. In her new white linen suit she looked not only professional but elegant. It was nice to have that fact noticed.

"It's a pleasure to meet you, Shari." He released her hand. "I've got a minute, I'll see you safely back to table six."

"Oh, that's how you knew my name," she remarked and instantly wanted to kick herself. That was a really elegant comment. What would she think of next? The weather? She wanted to impress him not leave a bigger impression of a scatterbrain.

His smile deepened. "Yes." He nodded to the phone and pager in her hand. "You got a page?"

"Yes. And I tend to pace as I talk, hence the total confusion when I fin-ished the call."

"Was it at least good news?"

"Very."

"From that smile, I would think so."

"Are you always this direct?" she asked, both amused and charmed.

"When I'm killing time with a pretty lady."

She would have preferred beautiful, but she could live with pretty.

What he had said registered. Someone was running a security check. She had wondered; they were ten feet from the door to the ballroom and they were standing still. *Josh, I managed to make the U.S. Marshal's security breach logbook.* It was going to be hard to live this one down.

Marcus had to be swamped tonight, and this was taking time from more important duties, but he was not making her feel stupid. The opposite actually. She deeply appreciated his ability to be kind. She grinned. "Should I tell you all my secrets now, or do we wait for someone to find my file and tell you all of them?"

His brown eyes deepened and warmed to gold. "Security precautions are part of a conference like this; it will only take a minute. But if you have some interesting ones...?"

"None that I'm willing to share unilaterally."

There was a beat in time and then he laughed, a delightful sound, warm and rich. "Well said."

She wished she met guys like this more often; politicians rarely had a good sense of humor. She leaned against the wall, letting her shoulder absorb her weight and take the strain off her sore right ankle that she had wrenched earlier in the day playing tennis with Joshua. Marcus looked comfortable in that tuxedo and at home with the authority he wore like a second skin.

"Have you been enjoying the conference?"

She risked showing her interest. "Yes, but it just got much nicer."

His slow grin...she wished she could bottle the warmth it gave so she could enjoy it again later. "I see I'm not the only one who knows how to be direct."

"I have a feeling I'm about out of time. They'll have me cleared soon," she replied easily while her heart thumped a patter she hadn't heard in a year. The guy didn't have a ring on, he was breathtakingly handsome, he could turn her to mush with his smile, and he didn't have a thing to do with politics. She was feeling unusually courageous. Tonight had already been such a roller coaster of emotions that she figured one more would fit right in.

"Why do you dot your i's with a heart?"

She blinked. "How did you know that?"

"They actually cleared you a few moments ago. Among other things, you signed for the table six tickets."

"Marcus."

He didn't look the slightest bit apologetic. "Saying good-bye wasn't at the top of my priorities. Listen, would you be interested in joining me for coffee tomorrow morning? I'm already having a late dinner with my sister tonight."

She didn't know quite what to say. Yes, she did; she just didn't know how to say it. She took a breath and let herself drop into the unknown. "I would love to join you for coffee."

Any question of whether that was a good move or not disappeared when she saw his expression. Knowing she had put that look of satisfaction on his face…it felt good. Very good.

"I'll call you." He gestured toward the ballroom. "Let me see you back."

Shari walked with him, bemused by the turns this evening was bringing.

They had almost reached the correct door when it opened and her brother stepped out. Shari paused, surprised, and Marcus actually drew her back a step behind him. She got the feeling he automatically assumed a threat and quietly put her hand on his forearm, felt his muscles flex under her hand, as she stepped forward and passed him to meet her brother. "Hi, Josh. Did you think I got lost?"

"You have been known to in the past," Josh agreed easily, putting his arm around her shoulders. "Just making sure the page wasn't bad news."

"Some of it was very good." She reached up and comfortably grasped her brother's wrist with her hand. He was assessing the man with her and not being too subtle about the fact. "Joshua, this is Marcus. Marcus, my brother."

His right arm around her shoulders, Josh didn't try to shake hands, he simply nodded politely. "Nice to meet you." The two men looked at each other for a moment, then Josh glanced back at her. "We'd better get back. Carl is just wrapping up his speech."

"Carl!" She had totally forgotten him for a moment. "How's he doing?"

Joshua laughed. "Excellent."

Marcus apparently heard something over his earpiece; his expression became distant as he lifted his hand and replied into the small microphone at his cuff, saying something too soft for her to hear. When he glanced back at her, his gaze was still warm, but it was obvious his attention had been diverted. "It was nice to meet you, Shari. Please excuse me?"

She nodded and watched him walk purposefully away, back the way they had come.

"Security?" Josh asked.

She nodded and didn't bother to explain how they had met or about the invitation to coffee. "Let's catch the end of Carl's speech. I've got some great news to tell you!"

"Pretty lady," Dave commented, his British accent conveying an extra weight to his choice of the word *lady*.

Marcus glanced at his friend as they crossed to the elevator that was reserved for security use this evening. "It took you long enough to confirm it was an honest mistake."

"I noticed you weren't complaining."

Dave was probing and Marcus knew it; he just smiled and ignored the comment. The family grapevine would love to hear news that he had met someone he liked. He didn't intend to feed it even unintentionally.

They wanted him to be happy, and every couple years his social life became a hot topic behind his back on the family grapevine. It would settle down when someone else in the family became more interesting.

Family. He had to love them. Dave was fitting right in.

Shari fit what he was looking for at the moment. She was someone he could relax with for a few minutes in the midst of a pressure-filled weekend. He had learned to seize those unexpected moments in life.

Over the security net came word Justice Roosevelt was ready to come down. Separating the conversation he was having with the security net conversation he was monitoring was habit after all these years. Marcus completed a sentence with Dave and made a request on the security net with barely a pause in between. He got back confirmation from the three agents securing the area into the ballroom that they were ready. Satisfied with his own inspection of the area, he gave the go-ahead. "Send his Honor down."

Dave watched the elevator numbers start down from the nineteenth floor. "Going to find an excuse to meet her again?"

There were some things that couldn't be kept a secret in this tight knit security community and in this instance Marcus didn't even try. "We're having coffee in the morning."

"Can I tell that to Kate?"

If Dave mentioned it tonight, Kate would likely find an excuse to drop by the hotel in the morning. "Save it for when you need to dig yourself out of the doghouse for something," Marcus replied, drawing a laugh from his friend.

Connor Gray sat at table twenty-two and twirled his fork as he listened to Judge Whitmore's speech. He listened and his hate grew; his target was now in sight.

His older brother was dead because of this judge. For twelve years the death penalty appeals had wound through the system and no one had stopped the sentence given by this man. It had been carried out.

Now he would return the favor.

He had thought about it, as he had promised his brother he would do. He had thought about it for nine months. He had almost decided to let it go as Daniel had asked, until rumors of the Supreme Court nomination had surfaced.

Connor had gotten hold of a copy of the brief floating around. It was good. Very good. It laid the road map for a senate confirmation of Judge Whitmore. The president was known to be heavily weighing that reality as he made his decision; it wasn't going to be easy to get a conservative justice confirmed. The brief tipped the ultimate decision strongly in favor of Judge Whitmore. There was no way Connor would allow this judge to sit on the Supreme Court.

He could get away with the murder. He knew what it would take to convict him, and they wouldn't have it. He had planned with a logic his brother would have been proud of. The mistakes others made had been eliminated. Witnesses. Evidence. He knew what it would take to create reasonable doubt. He had more than just alibis in place.

And he knew the value of the character card at trial. He had been forced to become the good son, to pay for the sins of his brother. As a result he was a man who didn't even have so much as a parking ticket to his name. He could claim the best schools; he had a Rolodex of the right friends, a distinguished career.

He was being forced to act sooner than he had planned. Judge Whitmore wasn't on the president's short list yet, but Justice Department sources said the judge's name would be added soon. Once he was on that list, reaching past security to get to him would be impossible.

As it turned out, even that change in timing had worked out to his benefit. He was here, within sight of his target, and no one suspected what he had planned.

Connor excused himself as Judge Whitmore's speech concluded.

Two

S hari was safely back at table six. Marcus saw her seated there as he scanned the room. He stood behind Justice Roosevelt: listening, watching, attuned to any movement in the crowd, staying relaxed, ready to react. An older couple, a second look confirmed they were her parents, sat to Shari's left. Joshua sat to her right. A nice guy, her brother; young but protective. Not many men would have made that direct a silent challenge to him.

As an older brother himself, he had accepted the silent challenge with more amusement than personal irritation. Shari was frankly too open with strangers; she needed a Joshua in her life watching out for her.

He was going to enjoy having coffee with her. He liked her willingness to admit with self-directed humor to being directionally challenged; he liked the confidence in her gaze when she met his. She carried herself with the ease of someone comfortable with who she was. He smiled just thinking about her comeback regarding sharing secrets unilaterally. Someone who could laugh at herself was rare and very appealing.

She was pretty; not classically beautiful, but pretty. When she'd walked into the Belmont room by mistake he'd captured details out of habit: brunette; blue eyes; five-feet-three; slender; midthirties; a small, white scar on the left corner of her top lip; teeth so straight she had probably worn braces as a child. A few minutes with her and she had his full attention. She reminded him of his sister Jennifer, someone who vibrated with life.

It was such a subtle sign, Shari reaching up to grasp her brother's wrist, but it shouted. In her world, family was close, special, and trusted. She had been given that gift by luck of birth; he had found it with the O'Malleys. They'd share at least one thing in common: love of family.

He wished he had bumped into her under different circumstances. This was bad timing. It wasn't like either one of them lived in Chicago; it wasn't like he would get a chance to see her after this weekend if he wanted to follow up coffee with a more substantive invitation to dinner. Unless…the back of Shari's photograph had given her name, listed her residence as Virginia.

He traveled constantly with work, was based out of Washington, but his apartment was in Arlington, Virginia, just across the Potomac River, north of Arlington National Cemetery. When he was in town, he took advantage of the hiking trails maintained on Roosevelt Island for his morning run. If Shari were interested, if she lived somewhere in his area of Virginia, maybe he wouldn't have to meet her once and then say good-bye…

"Movement on the right, yellow zone, subject unidentified."

Marcus turned his attention toward the threat without appearing to move. If someone unidentified broke the red zone, ten tables from the speakers' table, they would be forcibly stopped. The waiters were not all waiters.

Nothing had happened; it was the best kind of evening. Marcus stretched a cramp out of his right shoulder and rubbed his forearm. Ever since the O'Malley baseball game on the Fourth of July when he'd backhanded a throw to catch Dave out at first base, the muscles had been acting up. He smiled, remembering Kate's outrage when Dave had been called out. A sore arm was worth it.

Chairs fell with a clatter. Marcus turned to see two workers move to pick them up. The hotel crews were beginning to take down the decorations in the ballroom, rearrange the tables. In seven hours this room had to be reconfigured for a breakfast meeting for six hundred.

"Marcus, we've got a problem."

His partner Quinn was striding across the room toward him. "The evening was going so well. Justice Roosevelt?"

"Thank goodness, no. He's safely tucked back in his suite on the secure floor. Washington just called. The president added Judge Whitmore to his short list."

Marcus raised one eyebrow. "The president added him at this time of night?" He shook his head in answer to his own question. The decision had likely been made some time ago and they were only now hearing about it. His frustration showed in his scowl. "When are they going to realize they need to warn us first, *before* they take the names to the president for consideration?"

"Exactly. Be glad they didn't leak the name during his speech."

"Is there a room free on the secure floor?"

"The East Suite."

Marcus glanced at his watch. Kate would be here soon. "Let's go find the judge and get him moved to the nineteen floor. Did you pull his threat file?"

"It's being faxed over now. Apparently it's pretty clean."

"That will change as his name leaks out." They left the ballroom and moved through the lobby, skirting past guests to the private corridor. "Do we have a deputy we can assign?"

"I was thinking about Chuck Nance," Quinn replied. "He's covering the live television interviews in the Ontario Room; he'll be free within the hour."

"He's good; okay, get him assigned. How else is it going?"

"Besides a fender bender, a paparazzi trying to get a photo of Judge Frenston kissing the wife of Judge Burkhaven, and the hotel running out of imported caviar? It's just wonderful. You should have this job."

"Burkhaven's wife?"

"Don't worry. I was tactful when I suggested they might want to find some privacy."

"I wish I had been a fly on the wall."

"This keeps up, I'm going to ask for a reassignment. I hired on to chase bad guys, not be a diplomat."

"But you're so good at it," Marcus protested, chuckling at Quinn's scowl. Marcus saw Dave ahead of them, just stepping into an elevator. "Dave, hold the elevator."

Dave caught the door so they could join him. "What's up?"

"We've got a judge to move to the secure floor. Can you give us a hand?"

"Sure. Who?"

"Whitmore. Room 961," Quinn replied.

Dave pushed the button for the ninth floor of the hotel.

"Shari, you're pacing again." Joshua, stretched out on the couch, waved her out of his way so he could flip through the television channels looking for the late news.

"The phone is never going to ring."

"Would you quit worrying? The call will come. Carl is not even back yet. He was still talking to the conference host when we left to come up."

Shari knew he was right, but still... She walked over to the desk where she had temporarily set up shop for these three days, looking for something to do to keep herself occupied. Patience was a virtue she would one day have to work on. "How long before dinner arrives?" They had settled on ordering Italian, Carl's favorite.

"Fifteen, twenty minutes."

She rummaged to find a pen and pad of paper, deciding she might as well do some work. She was working on a major school reform speech. The same day the speech was given, a detailed position paper would be released. Getting the two to meld together with clarity was a challenge.

The suite she was sharing with her parents was like many hotel rooms she had stayed in over the years, and as usual her things had sprawled. Abandoning the desk since it did not have room for her, she settled in one of the plush wingback chairs, and set her glass of iced tea on the side table.

She had always found it easy to get lost in her work, but tonight it was a struggle. When she realized she'd scrawled the name Marcus in the margin of her note page, she forced herself to turn the page. Marcus was tomorrow morning's distraction, and if it was one thing she prided herself on, it was keeping her focus.

Not that she had heard a word of Supreme Court Justice Roosevelt's speech tonight, not with Marcus standing behind him on the stage. She was almost certain Marcus had looked her way more than necessary during the evening. She would like to imagine he had really winked at her, but she wasn't quite certain enough to risk asking him in the morning. Marcus got better looking the longer she had looked, and she'd sat there bemused for over an hour.

A cop. She was interested in a cop. She gave a silent chuckle. Given her profession, it was probably as good a choice as any. She'd love to have him at her side when the mud started to fly at one of the numerous social gatherings she attended as part of her job. She had a feeling politicians would temper their words around him.

Anne was going to enjoy hearing this news. John's deputy chief of staff, her longtime friend, had been encouraging her to get over Sam for months. Of course, it wasn't exactly going to be easy to find the right words... *Anne, I bumped into this guy with a gun.* She grinned. Yeah. That would work.

She glanced up when the sound of footsteps came her direction. Her dad had changed from his suit.

"Working on John's speech?"

Dad knew her well. "Trying to." He had read the first draft yesterday.

"You've got a challenge making the intricacies of bond refinancing clear."

"Tell me about it. I just keep reminding listeners it's money. Either pay now or pay more later. That always catches attention." A knock on the door interrupted them. Joshua got up to answer it. Room service had arrived with dinner. Shari set aside the work to help Josh clear the table so they could set it out.

"Is Carl back?" her dad asked.

Shari heard something from next door. "There he is now, right on time."

She walked across the suite to the connecting door with the adjoining hotel room, carrying one of the hot cheese-filled breadsticks Josh had ordered for an appetizer. The good news hadn't come yet, but this feast couldn't wait. She tapped on the door. "Carl, dinner's here." The connecting door had never been latched and it swung open under her hand. "Josh thinks your speech—"

The muted sound of a silenced gunshot echoed through Carl's room. Horror swelled inside Shari like a wave as she saw Carl crumble backwards to the floor, his face turning toward her. His eyes showed unspeakable fear, surprise, then a blank nothing. The breadstick dropped from her hand. The shooter stood to her left, less than six feet away. She had surprised him; that fact registered in the brief instant when she simply stood there.

He wore a dark suit, tailored, with a burgundy red tie, a white herringbone shirt, and black shoes polished to a high shine. His face showed angry determination, and his gray eyes as he turned to look at her were filled with intense hatred.

She tried to scream and when it came, it ripped from the back of her throat.

He was already firing as he swung toward her; the first bullet kicked up wood from the door frame inches from her face. Her hand flew up at the sharp sting.

Joshua hit her; it was a full tackle with no finesse, catching her low in the ribs and knocking her out of the doorway. She slammed into the side table, and the lamp crashed down with her as she tumbled over the couch. Her forearm hit hard wood, her right knee twisted, and her chin cracked against the floor, sending shooting pain through her face.

The shots went on and on, emptying into the room, and then it went deathly quiet. Shari could hear nothing but the pounding of her heartbeat. She lifted her head slowly from the carpet abrading her cheek, heard a door slam somewhere in the background, and turned her head, quivering.

"Josh!" He lay partially over her lower legs, crumpled to the floor with his arms outstretched. He wasn't moving. She tried to slip free without her high heels hitting his face.

As soon as she was clear, she turned and scrambled back toward him on her hands and knees, seeing a spreading pool of blood staining his white shirt around his right shoulder and his upper back. The sight terrified her. All her life she had watched him be the adventurous one, the athlete, and now he lay crumbled with his eyes closed as if all the strings had been cut. She turned him awkwardly so he wasn't lying on the wound.

She heard her mother moan and looked around, then froze as she watched her mom try to lift the limp body of her father into her arms. A streak of blood along the wall showed where her father had been flung back by the bullet's impact; he had crumpled there. He couldn't be dead. No! He couldn't be dead.

It registered and yet it didn't; disbelief was overriding what her eyes were telling her. Someone had killed Carl; tried to kill her; and shot her brother and her father.

It hit so hard she couldn't breathe. Couldn't think. Couldn't pray. Words weren't connecting.

Joshua's eyes flickered open: blue, dilated. Almost immediately they began to glaze over. He made no sound, but his eyes…

Her thoughts cleared. Her mind sharpened. The moment crystallized. An icy calmness settled across her.

"Mom, lay Dad flat. Get pressure on the bleeding," she said, hoping it wasn't too late for him.

She pressed her hands tight against Josh's shoulder, feeling them grow slick with his blood. "Hold on, Josh. Just hold on." She could see her hands shaking but couldn't feel it. "You're going to be all right."

He struggled to breathe. It was a frightening sound.

The table was on its side and she yanked the fallen phone toward her by the cord. She had to hang up the receiver to get a dial tone back. She hit zero, leaving a bloody fingerprint.

"There's been a shooting in suite 963. We need medical help." She was stunned at how clear her voice was. She was so tense her muscles were going to break bones, but her voice was calm. Joshua and her dad couldn't afford it if she panicked.

"Ma'am—"

"My name is Shari Hanford. Someone just shot Judge Whitmore. My dad and brother were also hit. I need help, now! Suite 963," she repeated.

"It's on the way." She had rattled the reception desk attendant. "Stay on the line—"

Shari dropped the phone to the carpet, not hanging up, but needing both hands for Joshua. "Mom, how's Dad?" She swiveled around on her heels and saw her mom's face. If she wasn't already having a second heart attack, she was on the verge of one. Her mom was one of the strongest ladies Shari knew, but not in her health. A heart infection after surgery ten years ago had made her vulnerable, and a mild heart attack two years ago had worsened that outlook. A shock like this could kill her. "Mom, where are your pills?" Shari asked urgently.

"I'm okay for now. Stay with Josh."

Shari looked at Josh, then back at her mom, a sense of panic taking hold. Help wasn't going to arrive in time. *Jesus, I need You more now than I've ever needed You before. Please, send help quickly!*

"Shots fired! Suite 963. Repeat, shots fired, suite 963!"

Marcus, Quinn, and Dave flattened against the side walls of the elevator, realizing with a startled and then grim glance between themselves that the elevator doors were opening on floor nine at that very instant. Marcus hit the emergency stop button, relieved they had silenced the alarms during the security preparations. Guns drawn, they moved out of the confined space, covering for each other.

The elevator opened into a small alcove. A gold plaque on the facing corridor wall showed rooms 930 to 949 and stairs to the left, rooms 950 to 969 and vending to the right.

A glance up showed none of the guest elevators were moving. The shooter hadn't gone out this way. "Freeze the southwest elevators," Marcus quietly ordered the control center. "Three officers now on the floor."

Dave slipped a small four-inch mirror from his pocket and used it to check both directions of the corridor. "Empty."

The only sound was the faint one of the ice machine down the hall. It didn't mean much. Marcus knew these hotel rooms were nearly sound-proof, having more than once opened the door to his suite to find that Quinn had the television blaring so he could listen to the news as he shaved.

Marcus touched Quinn's shoulder and pointed left toward the stairs.

Quinn nodded and moved that direction.

Marcus tapped Dave to help him investigate suite 963.

The vending area at the end of the hall worried him and he kept his attention on that danger point as they moved down the hall. A guest room door opened and they both pivoted, guns aimed, only to immediately check their movements. Dave waved the horrified guest back inside his room.

Marcus reached the closed door to suite 963, stopped, and Dave slid past him to the other side. Dave removed his master hotel card key and quietly tapped his knee, indicating he would go in low. Marcus nodded.

Dave silently inserted the card key, then pulled it out. The red light flashed green.

Marcus met Dave's gaze and in that intense moment knew Dave was thinking the same thing he was. Kate would kill them both if either one of them got hurt.

Dave pushed open the door.

It caught on the chain.

Marcus, his momentum already taking him forward, barely checked in time to avoid hitting the door. They had the right suite number. A false alarm? No. The smell of gunpowder lingered in the air and it was impossible to miss the smell of blood. Someone had slipped the chain in place out of fear? *Or had the shooter barricaded himself inside?* "Police! Open up!"

Dave prepared to kick the door open. Over the security net Marcus could hear the coordinated response of U.S. Marshals, FBI agents, and uniform cops rushing to close the area. Backup was coming, but they didn't have time to wait.

The door chain jangled as someone tried to open the door.

The door swung open. Marcus and Dave instantly elevated their weapons to the ceiling. It was a lady in her fifties. Her identity registered at first with disbelief. It was Shari's mom, Beth Hanford. Marcus reached out and caught her elbow to keep her from falling. Her face had a distinct pale grayness, and there was blood on her dress.

"I've got her." Dave wrapped his arms around her waist to lower her to the floor. Marcus heard the grimness in Dave's voice, the shared impact this was having on him. They had been talking about this family only a few moments ago.

A scan of the room showed carnage. Shari's father had been shot. Joshua had been shot. Shari turned from where she was kneeling beside Josh, desperation coupled with intense relief in her eyes.

Marcus hated the fact he had no choice but to ignore her. First he had to know the rooms were secure. Dave was moving to the left, checking the suite bedrooms. Marcus moved to the right and the open connecting door.

He drew a deep breath. Judge Carl Whitmore lay on his back, the empty look in his eyes confirming the worst. Marcus had never lost a witness or a judge on his watch and fury washed over him.

He forced himself to take a deep breath before he walked past the judge to check the bathroom, anywhere someone could hide. When he was sure he was alone, he knelt to confirm the judge was dead, careful where he stepped so as to minimize what he disturbed of the crime scene. "Judge Whitmore has been killed." His words over the security net quiet and cold.

Judge Whitmore had died facing into his room. Someone had been inside the room. Waiting. Marcus hadn't known the judge and the Hanfords were friends, but the open connecting door suggested they were. The lock had to be released on both sides. Were the Hanfords just unfortunately in the wrong place at the wrong time, or were they targets as well and the hit had gone bad? It was an ugly thought.

The dead could wait; there were survivors to attend to.

Dave was already working on Shari's father, William. Marcus skirted the overturned furniture to reach Shari and Josh. He closed his hand carefully around Shari's shoulder and looked her over swiftly, trying to tell if she had been hit as well. He had seen victims walking around so deep in shock they didn't even realize they were hit.

There was a nasty gash on her right cheekbone just below her eye and her face had been scuffed, but the blood staining her suit and her hands, some of it dark red, having dried, and other patches bright and wet, didn't appear to be hers.

"I can't get the bleeding to stop."

Her voice was steady but she was quivering under his hand. He wished he had time to wrap his arm around her and hug her, try to stop the shivers. That this should happen to her and her family the same night he had met her…it made him sick at heart. "It's okay, Shari," he said gently. He eased his hands under hers, wedging his fingers under her palm, keeping the pressure on Joshua's shoulder steady. "I've got him."

She was leaning forward over her brother and Marcus was crowding her space now they were so close together. Did she realize her eyes were wide and her breathing fast, that her heart was pounding? He counted five beats in the moment he realized the twitch showing at her throat was her heartbeat. Calm down, he wanted to urge and was helpless to help her do that. She'd just lived through a nightmare. She blinked. *Good girl. Come on, blink again.* She finally did. *Where are those paramedics? I need to get you out of here.*

He turned his attention to her brother. He had to rip Josh's shirt to get a look at the injury. The bullet had hit him in his right shoulder, deflected off his collarbone, and come out at an angle just below it. Nasty, and bleeding heavily. Joshua's pallor was sharp; his eyes were closed and his lips were beginning to turn slightly blue. The young man he had admired earlier that evening was dying Marcus realized with grim resolve, determined not to let that happen. One fatality was more than enough.

"I need to get Mom's heart pills."

Marcus looked toward Beth and saw what Shari had. "Go," he said urgently.

Shari nodded and got to her feet, almost falling, catching herself with a hand on his shoulder. Her hand tightened as she drew a deep breath, took the first step away. His eyes narrowed as he watched her walk toward the bedroom. It looked like she was in danger of folding, but she kept going.

The sound of gunfire and someone tumbling and striking concrete burst over the net. "Shooter on the stairs. He's heading up!"

Marcus jerked. Up toward the secure floor. "Quinn? Come back."

"He winged me. I'm okay," Quinn replied, his breathing ragged. "You guys coming down from nineteen be careful you don't shoot me by mistake and finish the job."

His partner was under fire. Marcus looked over at Dave, desperate to go. They had to be two places at once. Dave, his face taut, shook his head. Marcus hated it but accepted the fact Dave was right. They couldn't leave Joshua and William before help got here. "Where are those paramedics?"

"Coming up under escort. I told them to rush it and get medivac on the way."

"Mom, your pills," Shari said. "I grabbed Dad's prescription bottles too. The paramedics will need to know about the blood pressure medicine."

"I'll tell them. His medical alert tags, they'll need those too."

"Dad's wearing them," Shari said a moment later. "Mom, do you need to lie down? Are you okay?"

"I'm okay. Go, help with Josh. The man needs the extra hands."

He most certainly did. Marcus glanced over, ready to tell Shari to stay with her mom despite that fact, only to meet Beth's firm gaze. The lady might be having a hard time physically coping with the suddenness of the shock, but there was steel in those soft gray eyes looking across the room at him. Beth was a fighter; that boded well. He studied her face for a moment, then gave a slight nod to her and looked over at Shari. He really did need her hands.

Shari rejoined him. She had thought to grab a stack of towels while in the bathroom. "Will these help?"

He took one, grateful. "Absolutely; thanks." He glanced over to see she had already given Dave several.

"He just started shooting."

Marcus looked sharply at Shari. In the back of his mind he had been hoping she had been in the bedroom, somewhere else, at least been spared actually seeing her brother and dad shot. Given what she had just said, he was surprised she had any composure left. "One shooter?"

She nodded and her brow furrowed. "White, late-thirties. Not tall, maybe five-foot-eight—" she visibly struggled with her words as she remembered—"well dressed."

Over the security net he could hear each step of the hunt to pin the shooter down. Men were moving to seal the entire wing of the hotel. "What was he wearing?"

"A dark suit, navy, and a red tie."

He relayed the information as fast as she gave it. "Did you see his face?" When she flinched he momentarily hated himself.

"Gray eyes. They were so violent. And his hair was dark, almost black, really thick."

"Glasses, beard, mustache?"

"A thin mustache, wider than his mouth, no beard or glasses."

"Anything else about him? Did he say anything?"

She shook her head. "I remember thinking 'I surprised him,' then Josh hit me."

Marcus glanced again at the open connecting door, the overturned furniture, and this time he was the one who flinched. Shari must have been the one to open the connecting door. The splintered wood on the door frame was level with that gash on her face. The shooter had tried to kill her. Marcus felt his hands go cold at the realization.

Quinn swore over the security net. "He's out of the stairway. Repeat, the shooter got out of the stairwell. He's somewhere on floors eleven to fifteen!"

"Rule out floor fifteen, we've got the corridors covered," another deputy called.

Several moments later, another voice came across the secure channel. "I'm on fourteen. There's a merger meeting going on in the telecommunication conference center. The security guard says it's been quiet. The shooter's got to be somewhere on floors eleven to thirteen."

Three floors were still an eternity of space. There were service elevators, guest elevators, two sets of stairs, and that didn't even consider the hotel rooms. Marcus broke into the security net traffic. "We need a hostage negotiator located. Now," he ordered. "See if Kate O'Malley is in the hotel."

Dave turned to give him a frustrated glance. "Why does it always have to be Kate who's around when trouble breaks?"

"Tell me about it," Marcus replied, feeling a growing anxiety that this situation was so rapidly spiraling out of control. He knew the risk he had just potentially dropped into his sister's lap. "Nobody handles barricade situations better than Kate, we both know that. The shooter is pinned; he's not likely to give up without a fight when he's got rooms of hostages available to choose from."

"Someone shoot him before then, please," Dave replied tersely.

Marcus silently agreed, knowing if this became a barricade situation, they were facing high odds there would be another innocent victim. Kate had the nasty habit of putting herself between a gunman and a hostage. She was still getting over a hairline rib fracture from the last time she had done it. The Kevlar vest had stopped the bullet and she'd walked away from the situation annoyed with all the fuss he and Dave made. Marcus didn't think she had any idea how much gray hair she had given them in those twenty tense minutes.

He listened as men began to evacuate the hotel rooms one at a time. "How's William doing?"

"Not good," Dave replied. "Joshua?"

"Not much better," Marcus replied grimly. "Shari, keep pressure right here." He took her hands to show her what he wanted, felt the coldness in her long fingers as he placed them over the towel. "I need to get his feet elevated." Anything to stop Joshua from bleeding out. Over the security net came word the paramedics were passing the seventh floor. Finally.

The bleeding was slowing. "Just keep it steady there, okay?"

She nodded.

They had a shooter loose. Judge Whitmore had died facing into his room. Someone had been inside. And according to Shari, it hadn't been a lady. Marcus broke into the security net traffic again. "The shooter may have a room pass key. Maybe even a master."

"Any other good news?" Quinn asked.

"He likes to wait and take his victim by surprise."

"Wonderful. We'll try to avoid walking into one of his surprises," Quinn promised. "Clearing these rooms is going to be slow work. It would be nice if we could get a sketch of this guy. From the description, it could still be one of many guests. Mustaches are in favor this year."

"It's a priority," Marcus promised. He looked over at Shari. She was biting her bottom lip and her face was pasty white. He hoped she was a fighter like her mom. As soon as they got this situation stabilized, he was going to have to take her through the last twenty minutes in detail. There were times he hated what he had to do in his job. It was not how he had wanted to get to know her.

"Shari." She finally looked up. "The phone call to the desk, helping Josh, describing the shooter—you did good."

Tears flooded her eyes. "Thank you," she whispered.

Three

The paramedics arrived, and with them came enough help to secure the ninth floor. For Marcus the relief was palatable. The paramedic who joined him lifted the pressure pad from Josh's shoulder to get a quick look. He shook his head. "Jim, get the stretcher over here and get me an ETA on that medivac helicopter."

A paramedic was helping Shari's mom. Two paramedics had begun working on William, their words terse and their actions fast as they worked to get the bleeding stopped and his breathing stabilized. Shari had moved to join them and looked lost as she knelt near her dad and watched them. As soon as Marcus was sure Joshua was taken care of, he moved to her side.

He was finally free to wrap his arm around her and try to stop the shivers. "Hold still." He reached over to the open case the paramedic had brought up and tore open one of the gauze packages. He used it to wipe at the blood on her cheek. Her blue eyes were wet, the pupils very dilated. He changed his mind; she was beautiful. A guy could drown in those eyes. It was a nasty gash. She winced when he taped the bandage in place. "Sorry."

"It's okay."

"We need to get your mom out of here," he said, knowing it was the best way to get her out of here as well.

"I know. But I don't want to leave Josh and Dad."

"They are going to be medivaced to St. Luke's. We'll meet them there," he promised. She didn't protest when he lifted her back.

Marcus motioned Officer Young over. "Is there an empty hotel room nearby?" Marcus quietly asked the officer.

She checked on the security net, then nodded. "966."

"Shari, I want you to go with Tina and change clothes, wash up, then get together what you think your mom will need."

It wasn't much, but at least the blood on her hands and clothes could be dealt with. She looked down at her hands, turned them palm up, and flexed them as if they hurt. She seemed to be seeing it for the first time.

Tina encouraged her to turn toward the back bedroom to get her things. Using a different room was necessary, for this suite was now a crime scene. Marcus watched until they disappeared in the bedroom, and then he had to take a deep breath, letting it out slowly. He'd just watched Shari's life disintegrate. In a few days, his might be the last face in the world she would want to see as he became part of the memory of what had happened tonight.

The paramedic with Shari's mom motioned him over.

"Mrs. Hanford?" Marcus knelt down beside the stretcher to be at her level. The lady was beautiful, but the last half hour had aged her severely. She'd been lying when she told Shari she was okay; it was there in the strain on her face and the faint labor of her breathing. But when his gaze met hers, any suggestion of fragileness disappeared. There was anger there.

"Tell me how Josh is, they won't tell me anything."

"He's not as badly hurt as your husband." It wasn't much, but to a mother it would mean something.

She searched his face, then nodded, relieved. "Thank you." Her eyes closed. He would have moved back but she took a deep breath and opened her eyes, and what he saw in her gaze made him go still.

"Find the man who did this." It was an order.

"We will." It was the one thing he was certain of. They had a judge murdered; they would find the shooter. "Did you see him?"

She shook her head with regret. "I was in the bedroom. I heard Shari scream, and then I saw Bill.... I wish I did have something that could help you."

The paramedic, out of her sight, shook his head and indicated they had to get her out of here. Marcus eased back to disengage, only to stop when Beth's hand closed on his arm, gripping it with surprising strength. She was fighting to keep tears from weakening her voice. "Shari's going to need me tonight and I'm going to be worthless to help her once the doctors get hold of me. Promise me she won't be left on her own while Josh and Bill are in surgery. Promise me."

"Beth, you've got my word," Marcus reassured softly. Shari was a witness; there would be security with her around the clock. But even if that security hadn't been necessary, he would have still stepped in to make arrangements for her. The guilt already hung heavy. There should have been a way to prevent this from ever happening. Shari wasn't going to be left to pace a waiting room alone tonight.

Beth's hand on his arm loosened. She even gave a glimmer of a smile. "Don't let one of the political 'close friends of the family' sit with her either. They'll want to distract her by talking about the governor's race. That's the last thing my daughter needs. Her guy is losing, and she absolutely hates to lose. She'll end up in the hospital bed next to me."

Marcus couldn't help but return her smile. "No politicians, no press." He eased free, aware of how gray her face was even with the oxygen the paramedics now had her on. "They are going to take you to St. Luke's hospital; I'll be bringing Shari there in a few minutes."

Beth nodded, and Marcus rose to let the paramedics take her out. He liked Shari's mom. Stubborn grit, his sister Jennifer would have said, and said it with admiration.

Shari would be a few moments. Marcus moved across the suite to the connecting door, turning his attention back to the victim.

Within the hour, the national news would have the details and this investigation would become a coordination mess. The only way to survive the firestorm was to solve the case fast. When he found the shooter…

"What do you think?" Marcus asked Dave.

"The shooter had the nerve to walk into a place full of cops; the hit was well-planned. He got surprised and didn't finish off the witnesses, so he's not an ice-cold, paid professional. This was personal," Dave replied, thinking out loud.

Marcus began to string together what he saw. "The shooter waits for the judge to enter the room; kills him with three shots to the center of the chest. He's surprised when the connecting door opens. He hits the door frame instead of Shari, and the other shots fired into their suite appear to be scattered, so he's acting panicked. A little more control and all of them would be dead."

"His plan is blown. And for him, the plan was everything."

Marcus went back on the security net. "Quinn?"

"Go ahead."

"This shooter had a plan, a detailed one; it got blown by unexpected witnesses and his reaction shows a distinct lack of control. He's running now without his plan. Anything is possible."

"Permission to give this manhunt back to you?" Quinn asked dryly.

"I'll get you a sketch of the shooter. I've got witnesses to get out of here," Marcus replied. Anything was possible. Including the shooter doubling back to try and eliminate his mistake. Shari might be the only one who had seen his face, and that made Marcus very uneasy. "How bad are you hurt? I can send up a medic."

"The shot grazed my left arm, it can wait."

Marcus had no choice but to accept his word for it. Taking Quinn off the manhunt was the last thing he wanted to do. There were very few marshals with his expertise. "Make sure you get a firewall established below floor nineteen; moving Justice Roosevelt is more dangerous than it's worth. How's the evacuation going?"

"About a third done. We're moving the guests to the Paris conference room, doing interviews there to see if anyone saw or heard anything."

"Has Kate arrived on scene?"

"She's with me now."

"Hi, Marcus. Thanks for the business."

Her voice over the net was her working one: clear, calm, not yet bored. She only sounded bored when she had a gun pointed at her head. "Kate, quit chewing gum on the security net. It's annoying."

"Sorry. Are you under control down there? I could use a look at the scene. I need to know how this guy thinks."

"Emotionally," Marcus summed up in one word. "As soon as the paramedics get done, Dave's going to own the crime scene. He can arrange a walk-through."

"I appreciate it."

"Marcus, it's Quinn again. We're flushing these three floors. We've got this hotel wing secure, but this shooter was moving fast."

"You think he might have slipped through."

"We're coming up on fifteen minutes and I haven't been shot at again."

"Point well taken. Consider this situation no longer contained."

"Got it."

With that simple decision, the response had just leaped from the hotel to six blocks around the hotel and all the airports, train stations, and other means of exiting the city.

Marcus dropped off the security net.

Beth and Joshua were wheeled out. The paramedics moved to transfer William to a stretcher.

"William doesn't have much of a chance. He took two hits to the center of the chest," Dave said softly.

They had a witness to a murder who might lose members of her own family; it complicated matters enormously. If William died—it could either strengthen Shari's resolve to help or create enough fear that her memory would become vague. Marcus had been around witness protection long enough to know there was no way to predict how someone would react to such an event. Shari's world right now was her mother, father, and brother. Getting them somewhere safe was critical.

"I'll stay with them at the hospital, work with Shari," Marcus decided. "You've got this crime scene; tear it apart. And let's hope we've got another witness somewhere on this floor. I don't know how much more Shari will be able to give us."

The paramedics headed out with William. Marcus watched them leave, then turned back to Dave. "Talk to Mike down in the command center. We need the full file on Judge Whitmore: Get men digging into his past cases, and find out *everything* there is to know about who knew he was going to appear on that short list and when they knew it. Then get men working on a profile of William Hanford and his family. They were friends of Carl. The shooter got surprised. I want to rule out any possibility he had them further down on his master plan."

"You've got it, Marcus."

Marcus slapped him on the shoulder, more grateful than he knew how to say that Dave was here. Almost family counted. Six months, he figured, probably less, and Dave and Kate would be engaged.

He picked up one of the extra towels left in the living room to wipe the blood off his hands, pulled his signet ring off to drop it into his pocket until he could clean it. His watchband would need to be soaked to come clean, he recognized with some dispassion.

Officer Tina Young appeared in the suite doorway, and Marcus turned, expecting Shari. The expression on the officer's face had him abandoning his task to cross the room. "She washed up, changed, and then—" The officer stepped aside and pointed to room 966.

Marcus moved to the other hotel room.

Shari was standing by the sink in the bathroom, one hip resting against the marble countertop. She'd changed into jeans and a pink sweater but was still barefoot. She looked painfully young.

The tears were falling unchecked. She wasn't making a sound, but her shoulders were shaking. Her right thumb was rubbing at the remnants of dried blood on her other palm, trying to erase it from the crevices of her hand. She'd washed, but not all the blood had come off.

Even knowing this was inevitable, that the controlled calm during the crisis would give way to the shock, didn't ease the impact seeing it had. Words weren't going to help. Marcus bent and picked up the wet towel she had been using that had dropped to the floor. He slid his hand firmly over the back of her wrist, capturing the offending hand in his, feeling her fluttering pulse under his long fingers. The wet towel had grown cool. He turned on the water faucet, made sure it got no more than moderately warm, and picked up the soap.

It didn't take an expert to know what seeing her brother's blood on her hands was doing to her. He finally got her palm clean. He spread her fingers and washed the faint traces of blood from between them. He could do little about the blood under her nails. Very neat nails with light red polish, two now jaggedly broken.

"The water always stays pink."

"Shari, look at me." He had to repeat it twice before she raised her head. The tears were ending, but behind them was a heavier blackness. "You can't help your family if you fall apart."

He had to stay blunt. She needed a reason to focus and the best thing that could happen would be if this despair could be replaced with anger at the shooter. It would give her the ability to get through the coming hours.

She drew in a deep breath as if he'd slapped her. "I'll be okay."

He squeezed her hands, regretting that he couldn't step in and coddle her. He would love to wrap her in cotton right now and deny the world any chance to get close to her and cause her more pain. That wasn't possible. "I'm going to need your help in the next couple hours."

"I'm having trouble with my own name right now."

"The shock will fade," he calmly replied. Her hands were clean now, her fingertips had even begun to wrinkle. He reached for a dry towel and folded her hands in his, drying them. "Ready to leave?"

The first stark glimmer of a smile appeared. It was a painful reminder that the lady he had met and found so enjoyable earlier that evening was now gone; her smile was fractured. "Absolutely."

"Good." He held her gaze for several moments, wishing he knew how to read what she was thinking. She was looking at him as if she wanted to ask something but was mute. She turned toward the bedroom and the moment was broken.

Tina had found tennis shoes for her. Shari sat on the side of the bed and pulled them on.

"Joshua was airlifted to the hospital about a minute ago. Your father should be airborne in a couple minutes. Your mom is already on the way and I've got a car downstairs for you."

She nodded.

Tina handed Shari a shopping bag. "The clothes for your mom."

"Thanks."

"Come on," Marcus said gently, putting his hand on Shari's back to direct her. He didn't like the fact he was leaving while the hunt for the shooter was still in progress, but he had no choice. In the triad of witness, shooter, and crime scene, they were all critical. He trusted Quinn to handle the shooter, and Dave to handle the crime scene. He would rather have Shari and her family remain his responsibility.

He escorted Shari down the hall to the elevators, keeping his hand under her elbow. She was limping and it looked like she was favoring her knee, not her ankle. He would have to make sure a doctor checked her out when they got to the hospital.

The elevator controls had been overridden so that only the security center could activate them. He asked for the first floor. They were going out a secure entrance on the first floor rather than descend to the lobby where the press could see them. Shari leaned back against the elevator wall as it descended.

Marcus didn't break the ensuing silence. She needed time to collect herself, and he needed time to think. They had contingency plans in place for hospital security, but his first order of business would be to get them strengthened. This shooter had shown no qualms about acting in the midst of heavy security.

The media was going to be a problem as soon as they learned which hospital they should haunt for news. This was not going to be a one day story; he would have to plan security for the duration of the time Joshua and William were in the hospital. And Shari and her mom would eventually need other accommodations—he couldn't risk bringing them back to this hotel; they would need someplace close to the hospital.

"Carl's really dead."

He looked over at Shari, understanding the need to be told what she already knew. "Yes."

"Why did this happen? Why him?"

It was the hardest question to answer about any crime: why. If they caught the shooter and he confessed they would get a definitive answer. Short of that, it would take a long investigation to figure out the motive. "We'll find out."

She rubbed her eyes. "He never knew he was going to make the short list."

His gaze sharpened. "You knew?"

"That page during dinner was John passing on the news. Josh and I had ordered a special dinner to the room to celebrate. Carl hadn't eaten much at the banquet. I should have told Carl rather than wait for him to get the official call, but it was going to be a surprise. He needed some good news. And he died never knowing…"

Her voice drifted off. Marcus waited a moment to see if she would say anything else. "Who's John?"

She took a deep breath. "My boss, the governor of Virginia. I need to call him."

The governor of the Commonwealth of Virginia was her boss. This situation, already highly political, would have the extra dimension of the Hanford family being personal friends of Governor Palmer. "I'll get it arranged," he promised. "Shari, did you tell anyone about the page?"

"Joshua knew, and my parents, but we were waiting for Carl to get the official call before we invited his friends to the suite to help us celebrate. Do you think Carl was killed because he was going on the short list?"

There was no sense trying to keep the obvious from her. She would be in the middle of this investigation until its conclusion. "It's possible." The look of pain that crossed her expression was intense, as if that answer wounded her personally. Why? "Do you think you can help me put together a sketch of the shooter?"

"I'll try." She bit her lip. "I only saw him for a few seconds, Marcus. And after that first moment when I realized what I was seeing…it's scattered."

"Do you think your brother saw him?"

She shook her head. "He was off to my right when the connecting door opened. I was still screaming when that bullet hit the door frame, and Josh hit me in that instant. I don't think the shooter moved beyond the doorway." Her eyes closed, and she shivered. "Josh got shot because of me."

"Shari—" He waited until she looked over at him. "Trust me. Josh is glad he was able to reach you in time. As hard as it is for you to see him hurt, just remember, he would feel worse if you were the one hurt."

She gave a glimmer of a smile. "A guy thing."

"Yes."

"Are they going to be okay? Josh…and Dad?"

"Can you handle the truth?"

"No, but I would prefer it."

The job demanded he keep a professional, impersonal distance. There were times that kind of distance didn't fit the circumstances. He reached over and gripped her hand, having found long ago that bad news delivered with a touch sometimes helped lessen the sting. For both of them. "I think you'd better be prepared for the worst," he answered gently. "Josh is hurt, but he's young. I think he'll make it. But your father…it looks bad. He might not make it through surgery."

She had to know that, had to be prepared, and it would be wrong not to warn her. He felt her flinch, saw her jaw work, then she shuttered her expression. "He'll make it. He has to," she whispered fiercely. "I'll help you however I can with information about the shooter, what happened. But can you wait to talk to Mom until tomorrow? She's already had enough shock for one day."

"I think so. We're going to make this as easy on all of you as we can; that's a promise."

"Will you be staying with us at the hospital?"

She'd just been shot at and she sounded apologetic for asking if he would be around to help as all the churn hit. He knew his life was going to be chaotic in the next few days as he worked the case, but it was nothing compared to what had just hit hers. She was a witness; her family was hurt; within days any secrets she thought she had would be considered fair game for reporters across the country…she'd just lost her life as she knew it although he didn't think she fully realized that yet.

"I'll be watching out for you throughout this," he replied, determined to do what he could to throw a shield around her from the worst of it. "That's a promise, Shari."

He felt it, those words. It was an O'Malley promise. She wouldn't understand what that meant, didn't need to. It was enough for him to realize the line he had crossed. The shooter had made a fatal mistake. He had shot a judge with impunity. He had hurt a lady Marcus knew. He had made the case personal. Marcus would put the weight of the O'Malley family behind solving the case, and together they were a group it was unwise to cross.

She squeezed his hand. "Thank you."

Marcus looked at their linked hands. Her hand not only fit his but looked right there. He rubbed the back of her hand with his thumb. She was strong like her mom. She'd get through this. With a little help from him. He squeezed her hand before releasing it. The elevator doors opened. "Stay close."

Kate O'Malley positioned herself beside Quinn by the door of room 1124. It was one of eleven rooms on this floor where they hadn't been able to get an answer on the phone. They had used the registration information to try and track down the guests in the hotel and failed to do so. They had no choice but to assume the room was a threat situation.

They were using fiber optic cameras under the doors to make a first look, then opening and searching the rooms. Kate leaned her head back against the wall. She was at Quinn's elbow on the distinct probability they might open a door and have a gunman with a hostage waiting for them. Those first seconds would be critical and all hers to deal with.

"What do you think, Kate?"

They had to do these sweeps fast, eliminating rooms; every minute without the gunman found simply spread the threat area. They also had to move with caution. It was the adrenaline draining; the worst kind of search. It didn't help that her gum was getting old. "You're bleeding on the carpet."

Quinn looked and scowled. "A few drops; you would think I was bleeding out the way you keep hassling me. At the price they charge for rooms, the hotel can probably afford to shampoo the carpet."

"Lisa's not here; someone's got to hassle you." Kate rather liked Marcus's partner, and the fact he annoyed her sister Lisa only increased that conclusion. She took another glance at the fiber optic feed. This was a suite of rooms, one of the highest risk entries since they could see only a portion of the rooms. They were at fifty seconds and still no sign of movement. "Open the door."

Quinn popped the lock and they swept into the suite; four men from the SWAT team, Quinn, and Kate following them in.

"Clear."

"Clear."

"Clear!"

The cops were efficient and thorough; all rooms, closets, and other places where someone could conceal himself were methodically checked.

"This is getting old," Kate commented, feeling her heart rate slow down.

"Tell me about it," Quinn replied. "Any ideas?"

"Get a structural engineer up here. I'd love to know what other ways there are off these three floors. Air ducts and the like. We're running out of rooms to check."

Quinn nodded. "Worth trying. There should be an engineer in the Belmont room." He made the call down to the security center, requesting the man be found and brought upstairs.

The guest room door was sealed with police tape to show the room had been swept. They moved to the next room on their list and began the careful process of setting up the fiber optic feed.

"A dead judge; two wounded. Want to lay odds we're going to open a door and find our shooter has killed himself?" Quinn asked.

"Doubtful. He acted in the middle of a hotel full of cops. He had a plan to get away. The mere fact he went up instead of down is striking."

"This guy gets away, life is going to get very ugly until he's caught."

Kate nodded. She was already bracing for the worst. Marcus had always been there for her when she needed him; it looked like she was going to be returning the favor. A U.S. Marshal having a judge killed— someone was going to have to sit on Marcus and remind him to get some sleep occasionally.

She held up a hand, made a fist, and the officer moving the fiber optic lens held steady. Quinn took a look at the small display and agreed with her. Only two feet wearing blue socks were visible, but someone was lying on the bed. He motioned an officer to dial the room phone again; Kate saw no movement. He wasn't moving to answer the ringing phone.

"Room registration?" Quinn asked.

"Kevin McCurry. A judge from the seventh circuit," another officer replied.

Quinn looked at her. "Your call."

"Thanks a lot." Kate considered the situation for a moment. "We've either got another victim, a very heavy sleeping guest, a hostage, or a dead shooter. The room lights are off. We kill the hall lights, unlock the door, open it a fraction, and we slide the fiber optic camera in high, so we can see the room. In the worst case, we risk getting gunfire back at us."

Quinn nodded. "It will work."

Ten minutes later, they were dealing with an irate guest whose hearing aid had been turned off.

She had just gone to bed and her pager was going off. Lisa O'Malley rolled over and squashed it with a forceful hand. Bleary-eyed, she tried to find her shoes. They had been kicked off haphazardly when she collapsed on the bed. Her boss had promised her a weekend off call, but she didn't truly mind, even though it had already been a sixty-hour week. If she slept, she would dream, and thanks to Kevin they had become the kinds of nights she would prefer to forget.

The ER doctor had been a steady date up until six months ago when he'd taken a slap at her profession and she had been stunned to realize he meant it. She had come home, curled up on the couch, and cried, and no guy had done that easily since she was sixteen. She had promised herself to tell Kevin no in the future, but last week he'd caught her at a weak moment and she'd said yes to dinner. It had been a disaster. Would she never learn? He was still a rat.

A squeaking metal wheel broke the silence and she looked across the room at the metal cage with the spinning wheel. Her white mice were awake. "Sorry, guys. I didn't mean the insult."

A page at this time of night could only mean one thing: the lab was dealing with so many homicides they were shorthanded and were calling in other shifts. And since she was one of the few forensic pathologists in the office that enjoyed the on-site work, she would probably be spending the middle of the night in some city alley. She would rather go deal with the dead than with another living person. She turned on the bathroom light and winced. She looked like one of the dead.

She looked like Quinn. That realization didn't improve her mood. She was glad she had said no to Quinn's offer for dinner. Women liked him too much for her to want to compete for his attention. And while she knew she wasn't the most sparkling or witty lady in her family, being asked out third was humiliating. She was the O'Malley that couldn't stay out of trouble and couldn't seem to get her social life together. Quinn had been feeling sorry for her.

Enough. She was off men. They didn't make them as nice as her brothers and there was no use having her heart hurt again. She had been crying on Jennifer's shoulder last night, feeling like a wimp, and she hated that.

Lisa picked up the pager and went to work wondering who had died.

Four

"Shari." Marcus held out the Styrofoam cup. It was hot tea, very sweet. She took it from him with a murmured thanks. She was still too shaky on her feet for his comfort. If this didn't get some color back in her face, he was going to insist she accept a sedative. "Are you sure you don't want a doctor to look at that knee? You keep rubbing it." They were the only ones in the hospital waiting room. Security had this section of the hospital floor closed.

She glanced at him. "I'll be okay. I just aggravated an old injury. Josh talked me into skydiving once and I landed hard."

It said a lot about Shari that she would allow her brother to talk her into trying something like skydiving. She was either fearless or brave enough to face a petrifying fear. Stepping out of an airplane took a lot of nerve. "Adventurous."

"A sucker when it comes to family." She leaned her head back against the wall.

"Your mom is settled?"

"In room 841 down the hall. They gave her something to help her sleep. With her history of heart problems, the specialists didn't want to take chances. She was…annoyed at their insistence, but she took it."

"She struck me as strong willed."

"She's never been one to accept without a fight the fact her health is not good."

"The surgeon said it's going to be another hour before there is any news on Joshua and William," he commented, glad now that he had intercepted the doctor coming to see Shari. He left unsaid the grim assessment the doctor had made about her dad. She had enough to deal with at the moment, and nothing the doctor had said would change the outcome.

"Until they are out of surgery, and that will be hours, no news is good news." She sighed. "I should probably get on the phone, begin making some calls."

Her voice was steady; her color was coming back, but he could hear the reluctance. "No reason to rush it." He drank his coffee and waited.

"Has anyone ever told you you're good at being tactful?"

"I'm a cop, Shari, but I've also been in your seat waiting for news about family. I can give you a moment; not much more than that, but at least a moment."

"I appreciate it." She finished her tea. "Open your notebook. I'll give you what answers I can."

Marcus glanced at his watch and noted the time on his notepad. "Walk me through what happened tonight."

"Where do I start?"

"Anywhere safe," Marcus suggested quietly. "How about early this evening when you went down to the banquet?"

"We went down together, Carl and my family, about 5:45 P.M."

Marcus started filling pages as she talked. She thought her family had gotten back to the suite about 9:45. Room service had been delivered. Carl had been shot minutes later. Marcus wrote a note to himself to make sure they immediately interviewed the hotel employee who had delivered that room service. The security net had put out the alert of shots fired at 10:20, so Shari's time estimates sounded accurate.

"When you knocked on the connecting door, it swung open on its own?"

"The latch hadn't caught."

"Where was Carl when you saw him?"

"In front of me, about five feet inside the room." Her voice choked. "He was falling backwards and I knew his head was going to hit the wall. I heard the echo of the shots."

"Where was the gunman?"

"To my—" she looked momentarily confused.

Directionally challenged. "You're facing into the room. Where's he standing?"

She held out her hand, her look grateful. "Here. By the foot of the bed."

"Was there much distance between them?"

"Four feet? Five? Not much more."

The gunman must have stepped out from the bathroom to the end of the bed and fired. "Did you hear Carl say anything? Cry out in alarm?"

"He seemed surprised, startled."

Surprised to find someone in the room, or surprised because he knew the shooter?

"What happened after that?"

She stumbled over the words when she tried to describe the minutes in the suite before he and Dave had arrived. Marcus paused her. "Relax. Take it slow." He had to ask. He needed to know if she had noticed anything else about the shooter after that first shot.

"I'm sorry, Marcus. After Josh hit me..." She shook her head.

"It's okay. Let's change subjects." He picked up the larger pad of paper he'd borrowed from another officer, then removed a second, more expensive fine-lead pencil from his pocket. "Let's try to get a sketch."

"You're an artist?"

"I'm decent at the basics." The importance of faces to his job had given him years of practice. "Close your eyes, think about his face, and just tell me what you see."

Her eyelashes fluttered closed, and she drew and released a deep breath. "Think tough. Intense. He's got wide cheekbones and broad eyebrows. Everything about his appearance is well groomed, except it looks like he has run his hand through his hair."

As he sketched, Marcus paid attention to how she remembered details, listening for when she hesitated. He had worked with a lot of witnesses over the years. Shari had an unusually sharp memory for details; very little of what she said was vague. "What do you do for the governor?" he asked idly.

"I write speeches; I'm working on his reelection campaign."

"You use memory tricks to remember the name and face of everyone you meet." It was more a statement than a question; the answer was pretty obvious. He sketched in the jawline of the suspect.

"Yes. It's instinctive now."

There was something about watching a quarry appear under his pencil that always made an impact on Marcus. It became personal, the attachment of a face to the crime. The face would stay with him for years, would remain vivid until the case was solved. Since most of his cases were tracking down fugitives, he often spent his time traveling modifying sketches of suspects to age them, change their appearance, until he knew their face as well as he knew his own.

"How would you adjust this?" He turned the sketch to her.

"Hey, it's not bad."

He smiled at her surprise.

She took it from him, studied it. He watched her close her eyes, then open them for a brief instant and close them again—it was a memory trick, a way to give her a good comparison. She handed the sketch back and indicated the cheekbones. "Lower the cheekbones just a little, and broaden his eyebrows."

Marcus refined it.

"Better."

Over the next twenty minutes, he changed it until Shari could think of no further adjustments. "That's him."

Marcus studied the face, memorizing it. He added all the specifics Shari had told him about the shooter to the bottom of the page—age, height, weight, clothing. "Let me get people working on this. And I am going to get someone to look at that knee," he warned. "You need an ice pack on that and probably a dozen other bruises."

"Josh hits like a linebacker. And I am starting to feel the effects. My ribs ache."

Shari was just like his four sisters. Downplaying what hurt unless he called them on it. "Then it's definitely time for you to see a doctor."

He glanced at his watch, found it was coming up on midnight. "I won't be long. And I'll have Craig stay with you while I'm gone."

"I'm okay, Marcus."

"I know you are, but humor me." He reached in his pocket. "Until we can get your things cleared at the scene, I got you another phone."

He hesitated, then pulled a blank page from the back of the notebook and wrote down two numbers. "Memorize them," he said quietly. "If you ever need me, for any reason, a problem, a question, just to chat about the weather—" he smiled—"or to share one of those secrets of yours, page me and put in the second number. It's unique. I'll call, no matter where I am."

She looked at it, puzzled.

"You don't need to understand. Just use it if you need it."

"Some kind of secret code."

He smiled faintly. "Something like that. A family one." He picked up his notebook. "I'll try to bring your address book back with me. Should I bring your pager, or would you like me to conveniently lose it?"

"What a tempting thought. But you'd better bring it."

"Will do."

"Marcus, how much can I tell people?"

He hesitated and became serious. "Don't tell people you saw him."

"Do you think that information can be suppressed?"

"The longer it can be kept quiet the better."

He squeezed her shoulder lightly as he rose, reassuring her again that he would be back. He didn't want her feeling abandoned in the middle of the commotion, something that could happen without it being intended as investigators working the case focused on the dead at the expense of the living. "Listen to what the doctors tell you. And if you do need to leave this secure wing for some reason, take Craig for company."

"I've got a baby-sitter."

"Something like that," he replied. "Like I said. Humor me."

"Right. Okay. It's a guy thing."

He chuckled. "A U.S. Marshal one at least. I'll be back."

Shari watched the door close behind him and found it took a few moments for her smile to fade. She really liked that man; he was definitely the right person to have around during a crisis. He was right about her habit of memorizing a face and name, and she had the habit of also remembering first impressions. For Marcus it was an interesting combination of words: tough, strong, kind.

She looked at the numbers on the slip of paper, memorizing them. She had worn her emergency pager far too long not to understand the significance of what he had given her. She was frankly surprised at the scope of what he had just offered.

His hand when he had squeezed her shoulder had been warm and comforting, if impersonal. He thought she could get through this; it came through in his steady gaze and touch. Shari wished she shared his confidence.

She rubbed the back of her neck. She more than just ached; the headache was becoming vicious. The muscles in her back had tightened to the point they would break; her bones refused to unlock. She got to her feet to walk the length of the room, willing to accept the pain from her aching knee to try and get her muscles to relax.

What she needed to do next… Where did she start? There were relatives to call, distant ones, but a lot of them. Shari felt ashamed to realize at that moment she was actually glad her family was in Virginia and wouldn't be able to descend for a few hours. She simply didn't have the means to cope with a crowd right now, and they would want to talk about the details. Aunt Margaret, Mom's sister, would be a great help to have here, but she lived in London. It would take a day for her to make the trip.

Carl's friends. How was she going to break the word Carl was dead? Shari shuddered just at the thought. He'd been in her life since her earliest memories, a friend of the family, the uncle she had never had. How was she supposed to tell his friends he had been murdered?

A heart attack she could have handled, but shot to death—maybe John could make those calls for her. Someone would have to call before they found out from the media.

She knew Dad was executor of Carl's will, and he was in no position to deal with that responsibility. Neither was Josh. That meant Carl's funeral arrangements would fall to her. And she would have to get plans underway quickly or Mom would try to step in. That was the last kind of stress Mom needed right now.

She had never planned a funeral before.

"I need that pad of paper," she murmured. She was starting to think, and she wished she could shut it off for a moment, the assault of things that needed to be done. She didn't want to be the one to handle them, but by default she was elected.

She was thirty-four, and until this point in her life the toughest challenge she had been asked to face was the defeat of legislation she had poured months of effort into, the defeat of a candidate she believed in, and the heartbreak of a relationship gone bad.

The terror she had struggled to push down and contain while Marcus was here broke through, and she leaned her head against the window, her breath fogging the glass.

Jesus, why?

She felt tears sliding down her cheeks as she remembered Carl lying dead, Josh shot, Dad shot.

I've never seen so much blood before. This is my family and it stands on a precipice of being shattered in one night. Carl is dead. Mom is at risk. Josh and Dad are both in surgery. I feel like Job tonight who lost his family in a single day.

She needed her dad and brother to recover; she didn't even want to think about God giving a different answer to her prayer. How was she supposed to pray? She had no eloquence, and not many words, only emotions. *I am so scared, Lord. Did my brief cause this? I prayed so stubbornly for Carl to reach the court and I poured all my skills into writing that brief. Did I walk Carl into getting killed?*

Jesus, I am so scared that I did just that. And now Josh is hurt, and Dad might die too!

It had been unintentional, but the guilt swamped over her like a wave.

It took time for the words memorized long ago to come through the turmoil. When they came, from Psalm 68, they settled over her with softness.

"Blessed be the Lord, who daily bears us up; God is our salvation. Our God is a God of salvation; and to God, the Lord, belongs escape from death."

Jesus had already proven His power over death. *Bear me up, Lord. Hold me tight. And get all of us through this night. Please…*

They should have found the shooter by now; Marcus knew it. He strode into the hotel past the security, past the growing crowd of reporters, his jaw tight. At least with a solid sketch they could turn the tide back in their favor and force the shooter to hole up and thus stay in the area.

The emotions from being with Shari were finally beginning to bleed off. There was no such thing as impassively being around grief; it always rubbed off and had to be dispelled somehow. Some cops dispelled it in morbid humor; others absorbed it and it tore apart their personal lives. Marcus tended to direct the emotions he felt back in intensity toward the case.

He couldn't undo what had happened to her, to her family, but he could help bring her justice. Swift, complete justice. He had never lost a judge before and it stung, viciously.

The security center activity appeared chaotic on the surface, but only until it became apparent how the groups had appropriated space. Mike had overall coordination of the room at the moment, and he was pacing as he talked on a phone.

Marcus held up the sketch and waved Mike toward the east side of the room where Luke was working; he got a nod in reply.

He joined his deputy, Luke. "Shari was able to give us a sketch of the shooter. Put priority on getting copies to Quinn and to hospital security. Then put a rush on getting it run through our databases. I want an ID on this guy."

"Do you want it given out to the media?"

"I want to hear Dave, Quinn, and Mike's opinions first, but probably. I would like to get a name to go with the face first. The media's all over this?"

Luke nodded. "News got out about twenty-five minutes ago. We've made all the networks. The phone lines have been jammed with the volume of TV crews and print reporters. We've implemented our contingency bank of isolated numbers. So far they know it was Judge Whitmore killed; they know there were others hurt. It hasn't leaked yet that there's a witness and so far we've been able to suppress the Hanford name, but I don't expect that to hold."

"Neither do I. Grant is coordinating all press information?"

"Yes."

"Get a copy of the sketch to him as well. And tell him to do what he can to kill the witness information somehow. The shooter knows Shari saw him, but I'd rather not keep reminding him of that fact."

Luke handed over two manila folders. "Carl's threat file and what there is so far on the Hanford family."

Marcus flipped open the file on the Hanfords. They had pulled together a lot in a short time: pictures, bio sketches, newspaper clippings. He focused on Shari's personal friends. She needed someone with her tonight. If he could get it arranged, all the better. "Luke, track down Governor Palmer of Virginia for me. He'll have heard by now, I'm sure. Tell him I want to speak with him about Shari."

"I'll get him for you and forward the call."

The number of newspaper clippings on Shari was thick and this was only a brief set compared to what would come with time. A good rule of thumb: Anyone in the news this often had enemies. "We need someone focused solely on building Shari's file. She's our only known witness and I don't like the look of this file. She is way too public a figure—these are news articles not social page clips. That means trouble. Tell them to pull everything for the last three years and get it to me fast."

"News footage as well as print?"

"Yes."

Marcus opened Judge Whitmore's file. Carl's threat file was indeed slim—twelve threats in five years. Marcus skimmed the codes on the index page. Three death threats, but none of them in the last couple years. He frowned. There wasn't much here to work with. "Anything at all on Whitmore's personal life? Relatives, background, finances, anything?"

"They are digging."

"Have someone track me down as soon as it comes in."

"Will do. There's a growing list of calls coming in for Shari and her family. The hospital knows not to give out information, and the hotel has been instructed to simply take messages. Any change to that?"

"No, keep that blackout in place. I'll ask Shari if there is a family friend she wants to have return calls on their behalf. They are going to need a family spokesperson to deal with the press. Quinn is upstairs?"

"Yes. Nothing turned up in the floor sweeps."

"The shooter's gone." The clock was a harsh master.

"We'll plaster the city with the sketch. You know the local cops will do a full-court press to be the ones to bring him in."

"There is that," Marcus agreed, just wanting the guy found. "I'm going to touch base with Dave and Quinn, then head back to the hospital. Page me if we get anything."

He stepped out of the Belmont Room and literally bumped into his sister Jennifer. He automatically reached out a hand to steady her. "Jen, what are you doing here?" He was surprised, not only that she was here, but that she was inside the security zone.

"I patched up Quinn while he growled at me. Your partner doesn't like doctors. He's as bad as some of my pediatric patients."

"How bad was he hit?"

"Sixteen stitches, but he bled for a good hour and a half before he paused to let me fix him up. And he would have refused the local if I hadn't told him to shut up."

"It sounds just like Quinn."

"He's stubborn as a mule," Jennifer agreed. She took a deep breath.

"Actually, Marcus, I'm glad I bumped into you. I've got a 9:00 P.M. flight, and I need to talk to you sometime before then."

He went still. "You came over with Kate for dinner."

"Yes."

"What's wrong?" Kate, who knew what was going on, was very worried. He brushed back her hair, tipped up her chin, and tried to read her expression.

"Nothing that won't keep until later today."

"Jennifer—"

Her hand settled firmly on his forearm. "It will keep; I'm serious." She gave him that tolerant smile he had come to know only too well as she talked people into what they didn't want. "I promise we'll talk before I have to leave."

Trivial things did not have Kate pacing the floor. Marcus was not about to let this be pushed aside. Unfortunately, at the moment Jennifer was right, there were competing demands on his time he couldn't ignore. "You're sure?"

"Yes. Do you need any help at the hospital?"

Given the circumstances, he had to accept the change of subject. "Yes, I think I will. Can I page you? Will you be around the hotel?"

"Yes, I'll be here. Go to work."

Marcus had no choice. "I'll page." He headed to the elevator.

The crime scene had extended to encompass the entire ninth floor. An officer assigned to serve as case scribe recorded Marcus's badge number, name, and time of arrival to the floor. With the guests evacuated, the floor now effectively sealed off, only necessary officers remained.

Two crime scene technicians were taking a powerful light down the hallway, looking for evidence that might have been missed on the first pass.

Dave came to meet him. "How are Josh and William doing?"

"Still in surgery, but holding on. How's it going here?" Two men from the medical examiners office were waiting with a stretcher and a folded body bag; Judge Whitmore hadn't been moved yet.

"It's under control."

Marcus followed him into the Hanfords' suite. The crime scene technician videotaping the scene paused to change cassettes, mark the first one into evidence. It was necessary to walk with care; yellow numbered evi-

dence tags marked items slated to be collected once they were pho-
tographed.

He stopped at the connecting door. His sister Lisa was kneeling beside
Judge Whitmore's body, studying his left hand. Marcus was surprised to
see her, then realized it made sense. This was as high a profile case as you
could get. The medical examiner and the state crime lab commissioner
would have talked, assigned one of the central staff to coordinate the
scene. "Lisa."

She glanced back. "Hi, Marcus."

"What do you see?"

She rocked back on her heels. "Very light powder burns. He tried to
block the first shot."

She wore latex gloves but was spinning a gold pen. Marcus had
learned to leave her pens alone. She liked gold because the blood would
wipe off. On the clipboard tucked under her arm, he could see part of her
preliminary scene sketch.

"We've just started to actually process the scene. It will be another
hour before we can move his body, probably five or six hours on evidence.
Dave said you were the one who entered this room in the initial minutes
after the shooting."

"Yes."

"I need your shoes."

His shoes. Of course. "My room is downstairs. Can I get another pair,
then bring these back?"

She frowned back at him. "I suppose, seeing as how you've been over
to the hospital and back in them."

"There's a hole in my sock."

"Is there?" She was amused at that. She looked back at the area of carpet in front of her. "Thanks for sealing the scene as early as you did. This
place is a treasure trove."

"What have you found?"

"Your shooter made a mistake." She gestured with her pen, indicating
an oval area to her left. "There's a gun powder residue pattern here, and he
walked through it when he crossed over to the connecting door to shoot
the Hanfords. And over there—" she pointed to the right—"he put his
right foot down on a blood splatter arc. Inside the door he's left the edge
of a shoe print with blood on it. We've got blood traces in the hall coming

from the sole of his right shoe."

"Can you tell me anything about him?"

"Sure. He's not a very good shot." She indicated the shots that had killed Judge Whitmore. "Look at the spread of these three hits."

Marcus had never figured out how things that made even cops queasy Lisa could work around without a qualm. Death didn't bother her.

"Other than that, not much. Ask me again after I get the autopsy finished and start putting together the forensic data. I'll have to put some geometry into the entry and exit wounds, the blood splatters. Give me enough time and I'll probably be able to give you the shooter's height, weight, and what he ate for dinner."

She wasn't being facetious. In a case last year she had figured out the killer liked clams from a toothpick found at the scene. In a town with one seafood restaurant, it had been useful information. "Shari said his shoes were highly polished," Marcus told her.

"Really? Useful. I may be able to get you a brand name on the shoes. Think she might be able to remember details?"

"I'll ask."

"This is a nice, tight, dense weave carpet. We should be able to get some good images with a high contrast photograph." While she spoke, Lisa collected several samples of Carl's blood, sealing it into vials. It was a harsh reality, but by the time the body reached the morgue to be autopsied, most shooting victims had bled almost totally out.

She got to her feet, careful to step back on the black tape. "If you have to enter the room, stay by the tape," she warned. "We've done a fiber lift from there so we can move around, but the rest of the room is still unprocessed."

She closed the vials in a biohazardous evidence bag, sealed it with a bar code, initialed the tag, and passed the sack to a technician to document. "We should be done with the photographs within the hour, then the real work will begin. Between the fiber evidence and the fingerprints, we'll be here well into the day."

There were shell casings numbered. Holes in the plaster circled with black marker. Mistlike blood splatters typical of gunshot wounds. Marcus saw evidence marker number 74 set beside the overturned phone. "The bloody fingerprint on the phone is likely Shari's. She was the one who called the desk."

"A lady that can keep her cool."

"Yes."

"Whenever you can make the unobtrusive request, I'll need her fingerprints and those of her family."

"I'll arrange it."

"Dave, I'll need fingerprints of everyone who entered the room, including the paramedics."

"I'll get them."

"What's this?" Marcus asked. A black circle had been drawn on the carpet.

"We've got one bullet that ended up in the hotel room one floor below," Dave replied.

"How did that happen?"

"A fluke of bad construction. We were lucky; the room was unoccupied."

"Am I the only one already beginning to think this case is going to be bad luck around every corner?"

"Quinn would agree with you. He's growling."

"He hates getting shot at, not to mention not being able to track his quarry."

The hotel lounge off the sixth floor atrium was abuzz with word that there had been a shooting. Connor sat at a window table, sipping his drink, ignoring the commotion.

The judge was dead. *Retribution* was a beautiful word.

"Did we negotiate a great deal or what? They folded, just like you predicted, more concerned with the size of their own golden parachutes than the final terms of the sale." His partner in the merger talks was in festive spirits. When the formalities concluded tomorrow on the 43 million dollar merger of the two law firms, the man would personally walk away with almost 4 million. "Having the talks under the cover of this conference was a stroke of brilliance. There won't be anyone cutting in to steal this deal away."

Connor turned the glass in his hand, only half listening. The merger could have gone in the trash for all he cared. The discussions had already accomplished what he hoped for—they had given him an alibi that would be very hard to penetrate. He watched the officers down below on the street look for him: a well-dressed man with thick black hair and thin mustache.

His premature gray and receding hair, lack of mustache, dark glasses, and rumpled shirt showing the effects of working marathon sessions for the last three days had not merited him more than a passing glance by the cops moving through the hotel. Even with the sketch he envisioned they would eventually have, they were in for a rude surprise. Tomorrow he would stroll out of the hotel, just another guest. The gun was locked in his room safe. What better way to protect the evidence than to let the hotel do it for him?

Did they realize he was still sitting in their hotel? Personally, he thought that was the most brilliant portion of his plan.

There should not have been a witness to the actual shooting and he scowled again at that memory. Their presence had cut severely into his escape time and had nearly gotten him caught. Now the excitement was over. He had always assumed someone would see him near the judge's room and had used that to his advantage. It was the best principle of deception. They were looking for him, without realizing they were looking for someone who looked only vaguely like him. And a lot like someone else.

And all they needed to do was bring in one suspect, conduct one eyewitness lineup based on that misleading information and he would be able to discredit any eyewitness testimony they tried to use later. Reasonable doubt allowed for so much useful maneuvering.

Only one person had really seen him, and he had seen her. He had tonight to figure out how to deal with that. And he would…he most certainly would. Daniel had warned him it took only one mistake.

His father would be horrified. His good son had just gone irreversibly bad. Connor smiled at his drink. He'd never wanted to be the good son. By the time Titus realized what he had done, all the loose ends would be wrapped up. Even Titus would not be able to deny him his rightful place in the business then. Connor had earned his place.

He raised his drink and silently drank a toast to his dead brother Daniel. May he now rest in peace.

Five

S hari leaned against the wall beside her mom's hospital room window and watched traffic flow on the street below, red taillights breaking the darkness marking outbound traffic. Two A.M., and still the city did not sleep. She had been down in traffic like that before, rushing home only to turn around and come back to work while it was not yet dawn. In the intense last few months of campaigns, life ran at a seven day a week, twenty-four hour a day pace. She wished her life was that simple again, when being rushed for time was the biggest stress in her day.

Someone murdered Carl.

Who? Why?

Her dad and brother being shot were incidental to him. He destroyed her family and it was incidental to him. She wanted this guy. Desperately. And while she knew the marshals would be all over this case because Carl had been killed, she couldn't leave it there.

There was no one who knew Carl better than herself and her dad. She had personally read all of Carl's cases and writings in the last few weeks. Somewhere in her memory, or in her father's, was the person with a motive to kill Carl.

She drank the hot coffee the nurse had gotten for her, pushing back fatigue. Waiting for news was hard. There was no word from the doctors on Joshua or Dad. At least her mom was stable for the moment.

Shari prayed again for her dad and Josh, feeling the heavy weight of guilt knowing they had been hurt because of her. If only she had never written that brief. *Lord, give me strength*. The emotion had run its course and now there was only deep weariness. She prayed for the long night to be over.

Shari turned when the door opened slowly with a soft whoosh of air. In the dim light of the room she recognized Marcus. She didn't envy the man the job he had to do. He paused in the doorway and looked over at her mom, then nodded to the hall.

With a final look to confirm her mom was soundly sleeping, she crossed the room to join him in the hallway.

Marcus weathered better under pressure than she did. His gaze was steady and calm. She knew every bit of the stress from the last hours reflected in her face, and he wasn't missing much of that as he studied her. She hadn't been under this kind of intense scrutiny in a while. He was judging how well she was holding up, gauging what she could handle hearing.

"They've looked at your cheek?"

His question surprised her. She touched the bandage. "Yes, it will heal. Thanks for asking." The doctor had warned there might be a scar, but she didn't care. It was only the outward scar of a much bigger inward wound she would carry forever. "You've got news?"

"They're bringing Joshua down from surgery to the recovery room. He'll be there about an hour before they move him to the ICU, but the surgeon okayed a brief visit now."

Shari hesitated.

His look gentled. "The unknown is always worse than the truth."

"Even when the truth is going to be pretty bad?"

"Even then. Let's go talk to the surgeon."

The surgeon met them outside the recovery room still wearing his scrubs. Shari listened but didn't really hear much of what he was saying, her focus on the marked doors behind him. "Thank you, doctor."

"He came through surgery well, Miss Hanford. Please remember that when you see him." He held the recovery room doors open for her.

Shari followed a nurse, aware of Marcus immediately behind her, glad she wasn't entering this sterile, white place alone. The faint hum of machines was as much a part of the backdrop of sound as the quiet movement of the nurses.

"Joshua." She swallowed hard when she saw him, for most of the right side of his chest and all of his right shoulder were swallowed in bandages.

He was breathing on his own and his color was pretty good, but the amount of damage was worse than she had expected.

A warm, firm hand curled over her shoulder and squeezed gently. "It looks worse than it is," Marcus whispered. "Remember what the surgeon said."

Pins in his collarbone. Torn muscles. Ninety percent recoverable. That was all supposed to be positive news. It just didn't change the fact Josh had been shot. She hated hospitals, was afraid of what she saw; it reminded her too much of those long weeks when they had almost lost mom.

Push it away. That's the past. And family needs you now—strong, together. She leaned over and gripped Josh's hand. "Hey, Josh. There's a pretty nurse here you haven't even noticed yet." He didn't stir, wouldn't for hours yet. "You always did like to sleep through the big adventures." She wanted to cry rather then razz him, but she refused to let the tears fall.

"Sit down, Shari," Marcus offered, having retrieved a chair. "You're the best medicine there is for him right now."

She took the seat, grateful, and continued talking to Josh, letting the conversation wander, just wanting him to hear her voice.

Josh was going to have a nasty six months of recovery. There would be months of physical therapy to be able to lift his arm, rotate his shoulder, carry a briefcase. Even writing was going to be a problem in the next few weeks. He had paid that price for her. How was she ever going to repay him?

Marcus pulled over a seat for himself, sat down, and stretched out his legs, steepling his hands. Shari appreciated his quietness. He was a man with stillness inside, not someone in perpetual motion. She wished she could borrow that trait. She burned through energy like a hot candle. At the moment she felt like she was burning down to the end of the wick. "You need to change your shirt." There was dried blood on the white cuff.

"I'm sorry. I didn't notice—"

She stopped him with a hand on his arm. "I didn't mean it that way. You paid a price for tonight as well. I'm sorry about that."

"I would have preferred being able to stop him."

At the disgusted sound in his voice she turned toward Marcus. He really meant it. He would have preferred to be in the middle of an unavoidable shoot-out with the man than to have arrived too late to do anything about it. His job took a courage she would never understand.

As calm and still as he was, she suspected he was actually very much on a hair trigger to react if necessary. He wasn't sitting beside her with his jacket open and a sidearm visible because he had free time. He was beside her because there had been a realistic judgment among the marshals that she needed that kind of protection.

He was responding like a cop. She wished she knew how to tell him thanks. "The shooter nearly destroyed my family and it was entirely incidental to him."

"Trust me, it's not incidental to those of us working the case."

"I wish I had been able to help you more with what happened."

"On the contrary, you gave us a great deal. Focus on your family; we'll find the man responsible."

"I want to help."

"Shari—"

"I know I fell apart on you earlier, but I won't again. You need a motive and there is no one who knows Carl better than myself and Dad."

He didn't say anything for several moments. "Deal."

He attached no strings, but she knew they were there. To get access to the investigation, she would put up with a lot of strings. She hadn't grown up around three lawyers without understanding how a criminal case was built. They would find the shooter, and she would insure they had a conviction. Not to do everything she could would be to let down Carl and the price he had paid.

Jesus, You say not to hate, but the hatred is getting me through this crisis. I can feel it building toward the shooter as I look at Josh and think about Carl, about Dad. I cry like David did—destroy my enemy! Make him pay. Whoever did this, I pray with an intensity that wells from my soul that You will lead the marshals to him. Answer this prayer. Please.

Marcus looked over at her, concerned, and she realized her emotions must have been showing on her face. She forced herself to relax. Josh stirred and she tightened her hand on his. *Get better, Josh. I need you. I don't want to be the strong one in this family.*

After they left the recovery room, Marcus walked Shari back to the waiting room. He watched with concern as she sank down on the couch. "You need to get some sleep." It was coming up on 3 A.M., and her voice was beginning to drift when she spoke.

"I close my eyes and I see it happen," she admitted quietly. "I'll wait a bit longer before I face the dreams."

Marcus took a seat in the chair near the couch and braced his elbows on his knees as he studied her. He felt for her and the reality of what she would go through in the next few weeks. The trauma would show in so many ways: being spooked by sudden sounds, hesitation before walking into a room, fear of the dark, headaches, mood swings—her system would purge the emotions of that memory trapped in a slice of time in numerous ways.

He wasn't a trauma counselor like his sister Rachel, but he knew where the healing had to begin. "When you close your eyes, where does it start?"

"With my hand reaching up to knock on the door. If only I hadn't froze—"

He wasn't surprised at what troubled her the most. "Because you froze in the doorway, it was your fault?"

"It feels like it."

"How long did you freeze? Two seconds? Three? How long before it registered and you got voice to scream?"

"A few seconds."

"If you had been able to scream and distract the gunman, would his shots have missed Carl? Would he still be alive?"

She blinked. "When the door swung open, Carl was already beginning to fall; I heard the echo of the shots."

"So you couldn't have saved Carl," Marcus said quietly. "If you'd been able to scream sooner, would you have been able to save your father?"

"I don't know."

"Shari, your screams saved your family. They flustered the shooter." He had to make her understand the importance of that. "Don't let your emotions believe a lie. They will never heal if you do. You did the only thing you could."

"I'm never going to be able to forget."

"No, but you'll remember the reality, not a distortion. You're dealing with it remarkably well."

"I'm shaking like a leaf."

"But you're not folding. Give yourself credit for that." He wished he could convey to her just how impressed he was with that fact. The strength inside her was showing. "Are you sure you don't want me to get someone to wait with you? There are a number of people who have asked if they can come up. Friends of your family, of Carl."

She shook her head. "No. I'm hiding; I know it. But at the moment it's easier. The family will be arriving later today, there will be plenty of people then." She looked over at him and there was some ruefulness to her look. "In the meantime, I'll just dump it on you."

"I've got broad shoulders," he replied, willing to take whatever pressure he could off her. She had put up a wall between herself and the rest of the world as a way to deal with the crisis, and he had no desire to push her out of that safe security. "You really do need to get some rest though, at least catnap for a while. I'll wake you the instant there is news."

Since she was yawning, she didn't protest again. She stretched out on the couch, tucked her arm under her head. "Would you pray for my family?"

Her request surprised him, and put him in a hard position. He had believed, a long time ago, but now...

She noticed his hesitation. "You're not a believer."

It was more complex than that, but—"No, I'm not."

"I won't apologize for embarrassing you. You should be."

No apology, no backpedaling. A woman not afraid to keep to her position and believe she was right. He found that frankness refreshing. Even if he knew she was wrong. "I'll be glad to ask those I know who do believe to pray."

"Thank you. I would appreciate it."

He heard the warmth in her reply, she meant that, and he added another nugget to what he knew about her. It didn't bother her when someone didn't agree with her. That was rare.

Lisa was like that. Confident of her positions, willing to swim upstream to defend them. Kate staked a position and frankly didn't care if anyone agreed with her as long as she knew she was right. Jennifer wanted everyone to agree with her but would stand alone if she could convince no one else to stand with her. He smiled. The family never let that happen.

He watched Shari drift to sleep.

The only sound in the room was the muted passing of people in the hall outside. He needed to go talk to Quinn. It was after 3:00 A.M. and the manhunt should have seen some results with the sketch, but he found himself reluctant to move.

He had noticed that when Shari spoke about the terror, she had not mentioned the fact the shooter had tried to kill her. What she had mentioned was that she hadn't done enough to help her family. While he understood that, he would do anything for the O'Malleys, he also knew the silence spoke volumes, for it was signaling that was the one fact she couldn't cope with and so hadn't yet processed.

The harshest night of her life and the only thing he could really do was make sure no one tried to kill her again. It was a bleak assessment to live with.

He hoped she would sleep until morning but knew that was doubtful.

He reached for his phone and punched in the numbers to page Jennifer. It was one thing he could offer Shari. He had seen her reaction to entering the recovery room. He didn't want her facing the maze of medical questions and doctors without someone there to interpret what was said. And no one had a better bedside manner than Jennifer. Having spent a short time with Shari and knowing Jennifer, he suspected the two would strike it off as friends.

"Show me where you lost him, Quinn."

Marcus followed Lisa and Quinn into the stairway. Listening to them when he was functioning almost totally on caffeine was not a smart move. Lisa was peppering Quinn with questions that had no answers.

Marcus had worked cases with Lisa before; he knew how good she was. Not only did she approach cases differently, her mind simply didn't work like most people's. She saw connections others missed. Her curiosity only got her in trouble when someone let her get out into the field without a chaperone. He didn't think Quinn would be letting that happen in this case.

Lisa paused and rubbed her thumb across the scar in the concrete where the bullet had been removed. "You fell down the stairs."

"Guilty," Quinn replied. "I was looking down the stairs thinking he had gone that way when he shot at me from above. I wasn't worried about saving my pride, just getting out of the way."

"I wasn't implying it was funny. I'm glad you didn't break an ankle."

"The last I saw him was…there." Quinn pointed. "After I stopped tumbling and worked my way back up the stairs, he was gone. So where did he go? The agents coming down from above had him pinned below the fourteenth floor."

Lisa walked up the stairs and disappeared from sight. "For him to have gotten a shot off at you—" her face reappeared—"he had to be here. Then he turns…" She hit the wall with her hand. "As soon as I reach for the stairway door, I drop out of your line of sight. He could have gone out of the stairway as soon as he fired."

"Do it. Exit the stairway at the tenth floor and let's see if we can hear you," Marcus asked.

He looked at Quinn as they both heard the metal door close. "I don't know, Marcus. By the time I stopped falling and could hear again, the door could have already clicked closed."

"Could you hear it?" Lisa called down.

"Yes. Go up to eleven and try it there. And run up the stairs."

They could hear her on the stairs. "I'm sure I heard him on the stairs, Marcus. I remember it sounded like a clatter; Lisa is wearing tennis shoes and it was more distinct than that. I don't think he got off on ten," Quinn said.

The sound of a stairway door closing was audible but much fainter. "It could have been eleven," Marcus realized.

"Yes."

They walked up the stairs to join Lisa at the eleventh floor landing. "What do you think?"

"Eleven, twelve, or thirteen," Quinn confirmed.

"You said you heard his shoes?" Lisa asked.

Marcus recognized that vaguely unfocused look on her face. "What?"

She shook her head and looked at the stairs going up. "Start back at ten and look hard at the steps for anything that looks like a print, a scuff. The technicians were through here once but came up blank, and that was a surprise." She started walking up.

Marcus and Quinn shared a look. They had just been dismissed to doing tech work. "You can almost see the idea percolating," Quinn remarked.

"She's a bulldog." They started down the stairs. "Where are we at with the sketch?"

"We're getting decent coverage: the hotel guests and staff; officers throughout the area—the airports, trains, and buses—they're also running it by taxi drivers, giving it to tollbooth attendants. We've got officers canvassing the surrounding six blocks showing it around; we'll repeat that at dawn.

"All flights going out of O'Hare, Midway, Meigs, or Milwaukee before 8 A.M. are being checked. We're also tracking down every vehicle we can place in this area: the parking garage and area parking lots, pulling the drivers licenses.

"The database guys promised to work a few miracles. By morning, several variations of this sketch will be on every law enforcement officer's desk in the nation. I don't think this is his first criminal act. Someone has to have dealt with this guy before."

Quinn's experience showed. All it would take was a nibble somewhere along the line and this manhunt would spring forward. Quinn could be ruthless when he was hunting. "When do you want to release it to the media?"

"Top of the hour. We should be ready to absorb the false leads by then."

"Have there been many claims of responsibility?"

"At last count—nine. The two that seemed credible have already been eliminated. They are working to clear the rest."

"You have enough men?"

"I'm getting whatever I ask for," Quinn assured. "Washington was clear on that. What I need now is some luck."

"You'll get it."

"Or Lisa will create it."

Marcus looked at his partner and smiled. "That she will." He sighed and looked down at the stairs. "You know, it is a lot easier tracking someone outdoors."

"Give me a case that has open air, dirt, and mud any day," Quinn agreed. They spread out to see what they could find.

"Does this look recent to you?" Marcus asked several minutes later. There was a chip in the paint on the wall in the turn to the eleventh floor, about waist high. The gouge was angled, about half an inch long, and deep at one end. Loose plaster fragments were still in the crevices.

"Yes, it does. His gun clipped the wall," Quinn speculated.

"That would be my guess."

"At least we found something. Which is more than Lisa can say."

"I heard that," she called down. "When you get tired talking about a paint chip, you want to get Walter? And tell him to bring his full kit."

Walter was the best crime technician at the scene. Marcus glanced at Quinn, and the two of them moved up the stairs. "What have you found?"

She was sitting on the thirteenth floor landing, in her stockinged feet, having sacrificed one of her tennis shoes to use as a doorstop. She had on latex gloves. She was studying the bottom edge of the door. "Does that look like shoe polish and specks of blood to you? It sure does to me." She glanced up at them, a self-satisfied smile on her face. "Your shooter was in a hurry to open the door. He pulled it open right into his highly polished and bloody shoe. At least I think so. The lab will be able to prove it."

"Very nice."

She narrowed her eyes at Quinn. "You call me ma'am, I'm going to push you down the stairs."

"I wouldn't dare; ma'am."

Marcus put his hand on Lisa's shoulder to keep her seated. Quinn still hadn't learned. Lisa never made an idle threat. "Think you can track where he went once he got out on this floor?" he asked to distract her.

"We'll do a luminol test down the hallway carpet, see if we can pick up any more traces. I'll need you to get the hotel to momentarily shut off the hall lights."

"I'll get it arranged," Marcus agreed. "Okay, half his escape route has been found. Quinn, let's talk about the interviews being done. We need to talk to everyone on this floor. And I want to start a detailed look at those attending this conference or working in this hotel. Whoever did this was comfortable being here. Lisa, what about Carl's hotel room door? Carl had his room key in his hand. So what did the shooter use? Was it a master passkey? A copy? Is there any way we can find out?"

"I'll take a look at the logs and the mechanism."

"I'd appreciate it. Find him for us, Sherlock."

"A guy did this. How hard can it be?"

Marcus laughed.

Quinn held out a hand to help her to her feet. "You solve it, I'll buy you dinner."

"I solve it, I might even accept."

The ICU was silent at 4:00 A.M. Shari leaned back against the wall, watching her brother. She had been able to get an hour of sleep before the dreams came; she supposed she should be grateful. "Jennifer, Marcus mentioned when I first met him that he was planning to have a late dinner with his sister. Was that with you?"

It was nice having Marcus's sister here. Jennifer was comfortable around the ICU; the medical equipment didn't intimidate her. And Shari found it very helpful to just have someone listen.

"Kate and I," Jennifer replied. "You had met Marcus before this happened?"

"Earlier this evening. I got lost in the hotel," Shari replied, feeling like it had been a year ago. A decade ago.

"That was an interesting comment for him to have made."

"We were going to have coffee later this morning," she said quietly.

"Really? I'm sorry events overtook that."

Shari looked over, hearing the interest in Jennifer's voice. "It was just coffee."

"Still, an unusual request on his part."

Beneath the fatigue, Shari felt a glimmer of curiosity. "Marcus doesn't date?"

"No. And Kate, Lisa, Rachel, and I have been trying to change that."

Four sisters? Shari smiled at that, wondering if Marcus felt it was a blessing or a curse. Probably a blessing. "You've got a big family."

"There are seven of us, but it's not exactly a traditional family. We're all orphans. We sort of adopted each other, became our own family. Legally changed our last names."

Shari had heard of many families breaking up but rarely of one so intentionally forming. That must have been a powerful pact. "Seven?"

"It's a great group. We are constantly stepping in and out of each other's lives. Marcus is the oldest."

"A nice older brother to have. He's protective."

"The guardian of the group," Jennifer agreed.

"Which are you?"

"The youngest of the family—" Jennifer smiled—"everyone's favorite."

"An older sister doesn't get the same respect," she replied lightly, amused, thinking about her close relationship with Josh.

Shari crossed back over to a chair. Her body hurt and she eased herself down. Her spirit hurt worse. She could feel the dark depression creeping over her. In the middle of the night it was hard to hold on to optimistic thoughts. "From what you have said, Jennifer, I'm guessing—are you a Christian?"

"Yes. Kate and I are both recent believers."

"I think I embarrassed Marcus when I asked him to pray for my family."

"Don't worry about it. He needs someone to remind him he should reconsider his position. It's hard, after losing parents, to hear Jesus say I love you and know He means it."

Shari could only imagine how hard that must have been, losing the security of loving parents. She also heard the reality—Jennifer hoped to someday change his mind. "Carl was a Christian. Joshua and Dad believe. I'm grateful for that, but it doesn't take away the pain."

"The grief must be huge right now. Carl being in heaven doesn't change the fact he was killed."

"It's never felt this dark," Shari admitted softly.

"Jesus can find you in the darkness."

Those sounded like words from personal experience.

Life had shattered, and none of this made sense anymore. Shari looked at Josh. She let her hand touch the bandage on her cheek. A few more inches and she would be the one in the hospital bed...or dead. *Marcus, please find the shooter. I'm afraid of him.*

Six

Joshua, do you remember Carl meeting or calling anyone?" Marcus asked. The sky had begun to lighten outside the ICU window. He had confirmed what he feared, Joshua hadn't seen the shooter. Shari remained the only eyewitness.

"Not that I recall. We had a quiet Thursday and Friday. He was working on his speech with Shari, playing backgammon with Dad." Josh worked his good hand, pain etching his face at the simple movement. "How's Shari?"

"Hopefully still sleeping. She saw you in the recovery room about 3 A.M. You were out of it."

"Not entirely. She's right. The nurses are pretty." He gave a glimmer of a smile, then grimaced. "They told me Dad was in the recovery room. Is there any more news?"

"They'll be bringing him down to ICU soon." Marcus hesitated, but accepted it would be better if the news came from him rather than Shari. "It's not good."

Josh stilled. "What are the surgeons saying?"

"His blood pressure isn't stabilizing."

He was silent for a long time. "He's a fighter, like Mom." He looked over and held Marcus's gaze. "Where are you at in finding the shooter?"

"Shari was able to give us a good sketch."

"I almost wish you hadn't said that. Security is with her?"

"Tight. She doesn't realize she's got a permanent shadow."

Josh nodded. "Thanks. Keep it there, and if she raises a fuss, let me know."

Marcus recognized the worry of not only a brother but an assistant DA. "Will do."

"Has my extended family arrived yet?"

"They should be arriving shortly after 10 A.M. I suggest you get what rest you can before then."

Josh gave a reluctant laugh, then groaned. "The understatement of the year. I love them all, but there are a lot of them."

Josh's expression firmed, and Marcus recognized the burning anger in the man. "I can't protect Shari right now; I can't help her. And she has a nasty habit of assuming she can handle a stressful situation on her own without leaning against someone. Be careful with her. She's had a hard few months and she'll shatter if she gets pushed too hard." He gave an irritated grimace. "And whatever you do, don't let her get near the press. She'll consider it her professional obligation to get out there and answer their questions."

"You can relax a bit, Josh," Marcus replied. "You haven't told me anything I haven't already suspected. And I've read the press clippings on her from the last few years. She's stubborn, but I'm more so. I'm not letting her get in the midst of this press swarm; they would eat her alive. I like her too much for one thing, and second, she happens to be our only witness at the moment. If she gets annoyed with me, it won't change things. I don't plan to budge."

"Good. Let her hit a brick wall. I owe you."

"And I'll collect if I need it," Marcus warned.

"Fair enough."

Shari twisted her wrist, moving the cellular phone receiver away from her mouth so she could sip at the hot coffee. "No, Chris," she interrupted, pulling the phone back down. "There won't be press coverage at Carl's visitation. I want something private and by invitation only."

John's press secretary was a good friend, but she wasn't letting him sway her on this decision. She understood his point of view, but solving the press pressure wasn't her problem. "John is giving the eulogy at the funeral, but there is not going to be press coverage there either. That's assuming we bury Carl at the church next to his parents—we're still talk-ing about Arlington National Cemetery with the military honors he's due as a decorated veteran. It's been offered."

She drank another sip of coffee, feeling much steadier after a second catnap. She had woken up, found a pad of paper, and got to work. She didn't want to grieve yet, and the only way to handle the emotions was to ruthlessly deny them any room to emerge. There would be time to cry later, when she had some privacy. She had the nasty suspicion once she started to cry, she would cry for a long time.

Carl had been a friend, and she was going to make certain what hap-pened in the next days and weeks honored his memory and didn't make a spectacle of the crime.

Dad was in recovery. Get him into ICU, firmly back on the road to recovery, deal with a thousand details from family to press, and after it was all past, then she would stop and let the emotions take over.

"We're going to make the final decision after the family gets here. Call me back about 1 P.M. and I'll let you know details. You can release them then," she offered, giving him at least something to work with.

"In the meantime, could you send me out copies of all the area news-papers? I want to see how this is playing and correct any inaccuracies I can before they spread. And before you release John's itinerary, give me a heads up so I know reporters have it."

"I'll do that. How's your father?" Chris asked.

"Still in recovery. We're not releasing information yet. Anne volun-teered to serve as our family spokesperson. I'll let her release a statement once she gets here."

Shari spotted Marcus coming from the ICU and cut Chris off. "I have to go. Call me at one."

The phone closed and tucked in her back pocket, she walked across the hospital hallway to meet Marcus, bringing with her a second cup of coffee she had poured when the nurse told her Marcus was in with Joshua.

He smiled as she drew near. "Your idea of a double hit of caffeine?"

"Double latte this is not," she agreed, longing for a stop at Starbucks for her normal start to the day. "But in this case, I thought you might need it," she offered, holding out the cup. "Black. And strong enough to drop an elephant."

"I'll risk it," Marcus said, accepting the Styrofoam cup.

"You haven't had any sleep yet," she observed, reaching out to touch his forearm.

"Too much to do. I'll get around to it later."

"In that case, I hesitate to ask, but do you have a minute?"

He sipped the coffee, smiled. "Absolutely. What's happening?"

"I've been thinking about who might have had motive to kill Carl."

The humor disappeared from his gaze. "Go on."

"There's a document in my briefcase back at the hotel that I think you should read. It's a brief, recommending Carl for the court."

"You wrote it?"

She nodded. "There's a section that addressed his controversial cases. Some of them sound obscure, but I've read the transcripts. I'd like to sit down and go through them with someone."

"Shari."

"You said I could help."

"We are already looking at his past cases."

"Please. I know them better than his own law clerks. And it would help feeling like I'm doing something. He was a good friend, Marcus."

He rubbed the back of his neck, then finally nodded. "Later today, after your family is here and settled?"

"Thanks."

He nodded toward the officer who had been with her all morning. "Is Craig working out okay?"

"He's been a doll." And never more than a few feet away even on this well-secured hospital wing. Shari found that…interesting. She didn't want to hear why Marcus considered it necessary.

Marcus winced. "Don't tell him that."

She laughed. "I didn't plan to."

The floor nurse came to get her. "Shari, your father is being brought down from the recovery room."

She took a deep breath. The light moment had just been swallowed by reality. She knew seeing her dad was going to be a shock. The surgeon had been down twice to talk with her since Dad had been moved to the recovery room. "Let me get Mom."

"Shari."

She looked back at Marcus.

"He's a fighter. Remember that."

It helped, just hearing Marcus say those words. Dad would get through this. She had to believe that. She nodded her thanks and went to join her family.

The hospital chapel was a small room. Shari came seeking relief from the exhausting pressure. The chapel had padded pews and rich red carpet; a simple layout designed for all faiths. The room lights were muted. Shari walked to the front and slipped halfway into the second pew.

Her hands reached for the back of the pew in front of her and she rested her chin on the wood, looking not at the muted watercolor on the wall before her but back in time at memories, at the days before the shooting had occurred.

She pressed her forehead against the mahogany wood of the pew. Would her dad ever wake up? *Jesus, I can't take much more of this.* The day was creeping by without change and it was killing her slowly. *Please let him wake up and get stronger. I can't lose him. I can't.*

Tears ran down her cheeks and she wiped them away. She couldn't fall apart. Her family was here, and they had enfolded her in warmth, but they also required her to be strong. She didn't have any strength left.

She just wanted God to answer her prayer. She was trying not to let fear get the upper hand. God was in control. But as the day progressed with little change, it became harder and harder to pray without sounding desperate.

Her mom was at peace even in the midst of this uncertainty. Shari knew it came from her mom's own two brushes with death: the heart infection and the mild heart attack. Beth had accepted her life was in God's direct hands. And facing this crisis was her way to say Bill was in God's hands and rest at peace.

Try as she might, Shari couldn't find that same quiet trust and peace. She wanted to wrestle with God like Jacob had done to get the answer she wanted—her father to stabilize. Which was better? The passive, simple trust her mother had, or the intense, this-matters-to-me persistence she felt?

She wished she understood prayer. Two decades as a Christian and she still struggled with it.

Her pager went off. It was her emergency pager; she had shut off her regular one. It was Sam. She waited for the reaction to arrive, the intense emotion at realizing it was him and felt…nothing. The upheaval their relationship represented no longer was the emotional swamp it had been before. It was trivial compared to the reality she now had to deal with.

He had called several times during the night and the course of the morning; she had the message slips but had not returned his calls. She would take this page, she finally decided, knowing she needed to talk to him. But not here. She got to her feet. Craig was standing by the door at the back of the chapel.

"Would it be possible for me to just walk around this hospital floor?"

"Sure. Just give me a minute." He went on the security net and a minute later nodded. "We can circle this concourse, come back around to the waiting room where your family is staying."

"Thanks." She placed the call as they walked. "Sam."

"Shari. Thanks for taking the page."

It was awkward. "You've heard?" She knew he had, but she wanted an excuse not to have to talk about the specifics.

"I'm with John now. How's your dad?"

"Holding his own."

"Josh?"

It brought a tired smile. "Already proving to be a bad patient."

Sam hesitated. "And you?"

Jesus, what do I say? The pain of the past had lost its grip and dropped away. The friendship was still there, under the hurt feelings of the relationship that had failed. And right now she really needed what they had once shared. "It's been a bad weekend, Sam." She wished he were here so she could get a hug. He had always been good for a hug.

Windows overlooked a central courtyard. Shari stopped there, rested her forearms against the oak railings, studied the play of sunlight across the grounds.

"How can I help?"

She had known those would be his next words. He had always been a practical man, never more so than when someone was fighting tears. "I'll need someone at Dad's law office on Monday to help me with his court calendar, let me know what can be postponed and what has to be transferred."

"I'll handle it. What about Josh at the DA's office?"

"Josh spoke to his boss this morning."

Sam knew her; he didn't ask the emotional questions of what had happened. He asked about her family, about things that needed to be done, focusing on the immediate future. They talked for twenty minutes, and it helped more than Sam could ever know.

"It was good to talk to you," she finally said, relieved to have the past finally feel closed.

"The same. I really would like to come out if you'll let me."

"No, it's okay. Family is here. And it's more of a relief to know you have things handled back there."

"If you change your mind, just ask. I'll call later when I've got these details for you. Please tell your family I'm praying for them."

"I'll do that."

After they said good-bye and she hung up, Shari didn't immediately move.

The sadness was intense. It had gone so wrong with Sam. They should have meshed so well, but it had instead come apart in ragged fashion.

He was one of the best state legislators around, and she had liked him from the first moment John had introduced them. When Sam had asked her out, she had felt so special. And the year going out with him had made her life sweep by.

Sam had been supportive of her work, had listened to her dreams. She wanted with a passion to someday be in politics herself, not just working behind the scenes for someone else. And then the day had come that still haunted her.

Sam had proposed marriage with the assumption that she would stay as the person behind his own political career. Maybe it wouldn't have been so hard to accept if he hadn't also said he wanted to postpone having children.

She had looked at being the wife of a politician and she had loved him enough she had almost said yes. But in the end she had turned him down. And over the painful months that followed had come to resent what he had done. There wasn't a place for her dreams in his vision of the future, not for a family, not for a career of her own. She had been honest from the beginning and he had heard what he wanted to hear.

She had pushed to have a relationship and what she had gotten was burned. *Jesus, I don't understand what went wrong. I know I made a mistake in that relationship with Sam. Was this again a case of wanting something so badly I didn't see the problems; I saw only my dreams?*

"What's wrong?"

Marcus had replaced Craig sometime during her reverie. Shari closed her eyes, frustrated. Marcus was seeing her fighting tears again. This was getting embarrassing. She wiped her eyes with her sleeve, then turned. "Ever have something you wish you could go back and undo?"

He rested his arms against the railing beside her, kindly ignoring her tears. "Shall I count them?"

"Mind naming one?"

"I told my sister Kate I liked her broccoli casserole."

Caught off guard by his rueful tone, she had to laugh. "You lied."

"I felt sorry for her. Now I just feel sorry for me. She makes it nearly every time I go over for dinner."

She needed that. A lighthearted moment in the midst of this mess. "Why don't you tell her?"

"I'd hate to hurt her feelings."

"She probably suspects."

"Knowing Kate, that is more than just probable. But as the years pass, there are some secrets that take on a life of their own."

"True."

Shari grew serious and looked at the phone in her hand. "I wish I could change two years ago. Make a yes to a dinner invitation a no. It would have saved so much heartache."

"You were just talking to him?"

Trust him to assume the truth. She nodded. "It's hard, picking up the friendship after the relationship falls apart."

"I know. It can take a lot of apologies on both sides. But it is worth that effort." He held out his hand. "Want some ice cream? I've heard chocolate fixes most problems in life."

He surprised her again. "You brought ice cream." He had arranged lunch to be catered in earlier for her family, as there was a large press presence in the cafeteria.

"Guilty. I promised your young cousins Heather and Tracy."

She took the hand he offered and let him turn her away from the railing and the memories. She would have liked to keep hold of his hand, an embarrassing realization; when he released her hand, she pushed hers into her pocket. "Was this before or after you answered their dozens of questions about being a marshal?"

"I like kids."

"I noticed." She tilted her head to one side and glanced up at him. "I don't suppose you brought cherries to make a sundae." She was craving a sugar fix right now.

"And whipped topping. The good stuff is in the details."

"That's a great line. Could I borrow it and use it someday?"

"Use it? In a speech you mean?"

"Absolutely. Speechwriters love the perfect phrase. Evil empire. Where's the beef? Nixon's checkers speech. Every speechwriter dreams of having something they wrote become part of the national lexicon."

"Anything of yours reach that stature?"

"I'm working on it. I want something funny to be my legacy."

"Not something profound?"

"There are too many boring politicians. Trust me, I listen to the speeches." Her mouth quirked in a grin. "Besides, profound isn't very likely to happen. So I'd rather be remembered for something funny."

"It's good to have a dream in life. Someday you'll figure out that perfect line."

"You seem certain of that."

"Trust me, Shari. You'll think of it." He paused to let a nurse pass in the crowded hallway. "Is there anything else I can do for your extended family here? Anything else you need?"

"Could you get me the national newspapers? I don't want the TV on because they are only able to speculate right now and keep repeating what happened."

"All of the national papers?"

"I'm news starved. I admit it. It's an election year."

"And it's a good distraction for you to have right now."

She appreciated the fact he understood that. She forced herself to turn back to serious matters. "We've got Carl's funeral arrangements decided."

"I spoke with your mom before I came to find you. Don't worry about transportation back to Virginia. There will be assistance for all those kind of details."

"I appreciate that." They turned the corner back to the secure wing of the hospital. He reached around her to open the waiting room door for her. She wanted to keep talking with him—she was enjoying the conversation—but the kids came to join her, reaching for her hands.

"I'll be around, Shari," Marcus reassured. "And if something comes up, just page."

She nodded her thanks and had to leave it with a smile as her good-bye.

Seven

"Jennifer."

It was 5:45 P.M. Saturday night, and Marcus had walked out of an update meeting before it concluded, leaving Quinn, Dave, and Mike to handle the last details with Washington. He had to talk to Jennifer before her flight. It was too important a conversation to let this case push it into something done over the phone.

Jennifer turned from where she stood looking at the window display of one of the shops in the hotel main corridor. He could see the fatigue. She had been at the hospital visiting with Shari's family. He had paged her to come over to the hotel but now wished he had arranged to meet her there instead. His tentative idea that they could get a quiet corner of the restaurant and talk changed to something more practical. Room service would do fine. Kate would be joining them soon.

"Do you mind if we talk upstairs? It will be a lot more private than anywhere else. I promised Kate dinner when the meeting she's in finally gets done, and room service sounds like the best option."

"I'd prefer that," Jennifer agreed.

Marcus dug out his room key for the suite on the eighth floor he shared with Quinn and gestured Jennifer to the nearest elevator. "How are things at the hospital? Any change with William?"

"His blood pressure is still fluctuating. That's not a good sign. But he's held on this long."

"Still unconscious?"

Jennifer nodded. "Shari and Beth have been taking turns sitting with him. It's hard on them, the waiting. But at least Joshua appears to be firmly out of the woods. The doctors are talking about moving him from the ICU sometime tomorrow afternoon."

"Good—for more reasons than one. He strikes me as a man able to keep Shari from carrying the weight of the world on her shoulders."

"You don't have to listen to her for long before you realize how close the two of them are. But if you think Josh can keep her in line—"

"Okay, she'll humor him, but she'll listen to him."

"That I buy."

Marcus unlocked the door to room 812 and held it open for Jennifer.

"I can see Quinn is being his normal meticulous housekeeper." Jennifer picked up two shirts tossed across the living room chair and added them to the stack on top of Quinn's open suitcase that was dumped by the door of the suite rather than put away in the bedroom.

"Neatness is a virtue I have yet to instill in him," Marcus replied dryly. With four sisters, he had learned early. "Cut him some slack, his mind has been on other things."

Marcus flipped closed the stack of files on the couch and put them back in his briefcase so he could sit down. He vaguely remembered reading them Friday afternoon before all this had begun.

"Does Quinn travel anywhere without this hat?" Jennifer picked up the cowboy hat tossed onto the side table and tried it on for size, laughing. "This thing needs to be given a decent burial somewhere. It's been beaten. And it smells like a horse."

"Now that I think about it—no. It's his part of home that always comes along."

Jennifer set it back down. She gathered up drinking glasses, disposed of fast food sacks, tossed shoes into the bedroom. Marcus knew better than to suggest she leave it. If he let her deal with clutter for five minutes, she would be able to sit and talk. Make her sit with the room still a mess and she would fidget the entire time.

"Is it the fact Quinn is less than neat about minor things the reason Lisa says no to his dinner invitations?"

Jennifer glanced over at him. "Has Quinn been walking around with a puppy dog face after being turned down?"

"Sadder than a hound dog. What's Lisa's problem?"

"Kevin."

"I thought that was over months ago."

"That's what we all thought. He must have caught her at a weak moment. She said yes to another date and came home with her jaw all rigid and her back up. I spent Thursday night with her and she was positively morose about the entire species of things male."

"I knew I should have paid that guy a visit after last time. I would have if Lisa hadn't insisted I leave it alone."

"Don't worry. Jack was going to say a few words on all the O'Malley's behalf; I told Stephen to go along as Jack was a little hot under the collar. And I told him not to tell Lisa until after the fact."

"Good. Thank you. Lisa doesn't deserve the jerks she gets in her life." Marcus snapped his briefcase shut and moved it to the floor. "She needs Quinn. He will not laugh at or belittle her profession, and he won't hurt her heart. He's a little old for her, but he's a guy with deep roots. She needs that kind of stability behind her. He won't budge when she gets herself in trouble."

"She doesn't want to live in the middle of nowhere."

"That's it? That's honestly why she's been saying no?"

"There's that, and the fact he typically looks good enough to eat and most every woman in the room notices him."

"Minor problems." Marcus understood Lisa. She was the only one in the family who had been cast away at birth, had spent her entire life in foster care. She was the most independent of the group; used to going her own way. She had never locked onto feeling like she belonged, so he and the rest of the O'Malleys had simply swallowed her up and made her a place.

Frankly, if they wanted an adventure, they all knew the best one would be had by joining Lisa for a weekend. She was the fun in the family, and they all loved her. Marcus hated to learn she was hurting. "Think she'll kill me if I send her some flowers?"

"Marcus, haven't you seen her scrapbook? She's got a flower pressed from each bouquet you've ever sent her."

"You're kidding."

Jennifer laughed. "She's sentimental, although she will kill me for saying it. Send her flowers, or better yet, why don't you send her something for her ferret? Lisa had me in stitches Thursday evening laughing at the antics of her latest pet. She's doting on that animal."

"Empty paper towel tubes still his favorite?"

"Yes."

Marcus sank back into the sofa seat, feeling the tension drain away. "Jennifer, what's going on with you? It's been too long since we've really talked. I've missed you with you being all the way down in Texas."

She sank into the plush chair she had cleared and looked at him, her smile fading to be replaced by...sadness; an expression so unusual for her he didn't know what to think. "I've been thinking of how to tell you this and now I don't have words."

"Just tell me, Jennifer," he said gently. Two decades of watching out for this family had taken him through the high and lows of each of their lives. He didn't know what was wrong, but he would fix it, somehow. It was the one thing he could offer the family that was uniquely his to give. "I think I'm prepared to hear about anything."

She looked across the six feet of the room separating them, and suddenly there was moisture in her eyes. "Marcus, I've got cancer."

He wasn't prepared for that. It stung hard, like a knife in his ribs when his guard was down. He visibly flinched and forced himself to take a breath. "Cancer." She looked fine, but her eyes never wavered from his, and this wasn't something anyone in the family would joke about. A dragon from the past roared toward him and the image of his mom flashed by. No. This couldn't be happening. Not someone else he loved getting sick.

She came over to sit on the couch beside him and he had to force himself to hear her words through the rushing memories. "I'm sorry. I know how hard it is to hear. It's around my spine, has touched my liver. I start radiation Monday morning at Johns Hopkins."

The cold was like a grave opening up. "You told Kate."

"She's the only one that knows," Jennifer said softly.

His hand settled on top of hers and his thumb rubbed the side of her wrist finding the reassurance of her steady pulse. Anger surged over the pain. Anger of a man mixing with anger of a boy—all of it pouring toward God. *Not again. Please, not again.*

"When did you find out?"

"I got the first suspicious test results a month ago. That trip to the Mayo Clinic? It wasn't a consult on a case; I was the patient."

How had the family not clued in to the evidence? A month. The family grapevine normally knew the moment anything of significance happened, and she had been dealing with this for a month without saying anything. Alone in a hospital, without family to visit and keep her company…it broke his heart. "Jen, I wish I had known."

"Kate needed you, Marcus. I couldn't help her in the midst of the toughest month of her life working that airline explosion investigation. What I could do was insure she had your undivided attention. Kate needed you, and I didn't want to distract from that."

"You needed me too."

She squeezed his shoulder. "I knew you were only a phone call away," she reassured. "That was such a comfort to know. They were doing the tests and poking and prodding me; it was still an undefined enemy at that point. I kept hoping that when they gave an answer it would be better news than it turned out to be. This is going to be a terrible, long battle, Marcus. Rest assured, I'm going to lean hard against all of the O'Malleys."

"The engagement."

"Tom didn't want to wait. We're going to postpone the wedding until the immediate course of treatment is past. Hopefully I'll get a period of remission."

She wasn't talking about a cure. "The prognosis is that bad?" he whispered.

"People don't live with this kind of cancer, Marcus."

He'd find a way to help her beat this; it would get every breath of energy he had. "You will." He was the guardian of the O'Malleys—he had to find a way.

She looked at him, and there was compassion there, for him, for what this meant. *She was dying and she was worrying about me.* He forgot sometimes just how stubborn and intense every member of this family was.

He closed his eyes for a moment and forced himself to look forward, to what she was going to need. He wanted to give her a hug and realized he was scared to death he would hurt her. If it was low around her spine, he couldn't even hug her without thinking about it first. His hand settled on her shoulder. "Is Kate going with you to Baltimore?"

"It's not necessary. Tom is flying out to stay with me."

He looked at her and she grimaced. "Sorry."

"The family will be there. I'll declare the emergency if you won't."

"Marcus, I want the family there. I'm going to be leaning on all of you like crazy, but the next few weeks are going to be long days, boring even, and I'm going to be sick for most of them."

"Do you honestly think any one of us would care?"

"I will."

"Tough," Marcus replied, for the first time feeling a glimmer of hope touch his voice. "Are you going to tell them or do you want me to?"

"I've made rather a mess of it I'm afraid. I didn't want to cast a shadow over the Fourth of July festivities and everyone's first chance to meet Tom. And I was going to tell Lisa Thursday night, but she didn't need this kind of news on top of the week she was having. Then when I left her place, it seemed more crucial to tell Jack about what was going on with Lisa than to hit him with my news. I've run out of calendar days."

"Kate and I will solve it. Don't worry about it. Your flight tonight is at nine o'clock?"

"Yes."

"What happens tomorrow?"

"I get admitted at Johns Hopkins, they repeat the blood work, take more X rays. If everything is still a go, they start the radiation treatments Monday morning."

"Family will be there."

"Marcus—Shari really needs you right now. The others have jobs and commitments to keep. I really will be okay. Radiation and chemotherapy are a normal part of life for a cancer patient."

"I hear you, Jennifer. Now hear me—we need you. We're going to be there for every inning, not just the peaks and valleys." He saw her eyes glisten, saw her blink back moisture.

"I knew you would respond this way."

He wiped her eyes dry with the sleeve of his shirt. "You're our favorite. An O'Malley has never lost a fight yet; we're not going to start now. Tell me the details, all of them, everything the tests have shown, what you've read, what the cancer doctors have said."

They talked for half an hour and then Kate came to join them. Marcus understood in one brief look at Kate how relieved she was now that he knew. This secret must have been killing her. He'd seen the strain on occasion and written it off as her adjusting to dating Dave. He could not have been more off target.

The three of them talked until Jennifer said she needed to get to the airport. They walked with her down to the lobby. Marcus was reluctant to see her go. "Is it safe for a hug?"

"Yes. And I'll be bummed if you don't."

He folded her carefully into his arms and buried his head against her hair. "Can I send you flowers?" he whispered, and felt relief as her laughter bubbled from her chest.

"I hope you'll fill the entire hospital room by the time I get released."

"Just the hospital room?" Marcus asked, pulling forth humor he didn't feel. "I'll call you every day and be there as soon as I can."

"I know, Marcus. Please don't worry; I promise no more surprises. You'll know everything going on."

"I'll keep you to that." He reluctantly let her go.

Jennifer hugged Kate.

"Call me when you get in," Kate said.

"I will," Jennifer promised.

Marcus looked over at Kate after Jennifer left and felt a heavy weight settle across his chest. "Kate, I'm so sorry you had to carry this secret alone. I knew you were stressed, but I thought it was everything going on in your own life, never something like this."

"I didn't like keeping the secret from you but didn't feel like I could push Jennifer any harder to tell you. She's still struggling with this, a lot deeper than her words are reflecting."

Marcus wrapped his arm around her shoulders. "Come on, I'll order us room service. We've got to talk."

"Deal."

They returned back to the suite and Marcus glanced at the room service menu but had no interest in eating.

"You have to eat," Kate said, reading his expression. "Order two cheeseburgers. If I'm going to eat, so are you."

She was right. Marcus ordered the two cheeseburgers.

Sharing a dark day and doing it with Kate, there was no one he would prefer to be with. "How many crises have we weathered through the years?"

"Too many. And this one is going to be the toughest." He could hear the tension in her voice, the fear, for her Southern accent she used as a shield shifted to stretch the vowels. It was subtle, not many people would notice, but he could hear the change. The accent was like a cloak she pulled around her when the emotions were high. Language and the tone of words were both her profession and her way of expressing what she felt. And when she dropped that accent and reverted to the Chicago clipped speech she had grown up with…he'd only seen it happen a few times, right before her anger exploded.

"We're not going to lose her," Marcus assured softly, going to the heart of her fear.

"It's going to rip the fabric of this family if we do. I'm so glad she's a fighter."

"Does Dave know?"

"Yes." Kate hesitated. "Did Jennifer tell you she was baptized last month?"

Marcus was startled at the news. "No."

"Tom introduced her to Jesus."

"She's praying to be healed." He said it with dread, knowing how badly she was setting herself up to be hurt.

"Yes."

She'd believe, pray, and when they weren't answered, it would cut like a dagger. Prayers were answered as much by chance as by a caring God. "She's grasping at straws. I don't want her to feel that disappointment if things get as bad as she described it could, if her prayers are not answered."

"Marcus, she's not the only one who made that decision to believe. I did too."

Kate. This couldn't be happening—it was his job to protect his family and they were walking down a road that would hurt them. How had he lost touch so quickly with what was happening in their lives? It had been an extraordinary few weeks with the airline bombing and the discovery Kate had a younger brother, but still, he should have seen what was going on. "Why—"

"I don't think it's false hope. I think Jesus really does care, really is God, and He's powerfully involved in our lives." She stopped him when he would have interrupted. "I know what happened with your mom. You and I both know what it feels like to be abandoned. But I think you're wrong to let that close the door on Jesus. The Bible says He was forsaken too— the day He died on the cross. He understands; He definitely knows what that pain feels like. And if He hadn't been willing to accept the pain of the cross, Jennifer and I wouldn't have the hope we do today."

Her words were calm and sure, and Marcus felt a degree of envy slip in alongside his deep doubts. She was logical, certain, and she had done the one thing he had thought was not possible: find a way to be comfortable with God.

It wasn't a subject he wanted to tackle with her, not when it would mean opening the door of his past with all its pain and disappointment. It was so much more than just God not answering his prayers. It was God abandoning his mom, not answering her prayers. There had been no one more committed and faithful to God than his mom, and she had died in that hospital because she could no longer breathe. He'd traveled this road already and did not want to see Kate and Jennifer hurt.

It wasn't the right time to have the discussion. He shifted the conversation back to Jennifer. "We have to call a family emergency."

It meant tossing Rachel on a plane in the middle of the night to get here, having Stephen and Jack pull in favors to get their shifts covered at the firehouse, have Lisa somehow get her pager reassigned. But if ever this family had had an emergency, they had one now. They had to talk face to face. "I want an O'Malley there with Jennifer on Monday."

"Agreed. I've already been working my schedule so I could go," Kate replied. "I'm worried about how Rachel will take the news. It will hit her the hardest, I think."

"She empathizes when a moth hits the car window; she feels everyone's pain as her own. It makes her a wonderful trauma psychologist, but when it's family—"

"She'll never be able to find that internal distance. She'll be absorbing the implications of this as deeply as Jennifer."

"She'll want to go out east immediately; that's a given. Do you and Rachel want to go out east first?"

Kate nodded. "We stay through the week, then Stephen and Jack shift their vacation time around and come out next—we can cover the next month without a problem."

"I'll talk to Washington about getting Craig assigned to be primary for Shari and her family."

Kate shook her head. "Don't do that. I understand why you want to, but I don't think you should. Jennifer will accept us being there when we are using vacation time; sliding in visits between assignments. If you step out of an active job it will make her feel guilty, and that is the last thing she needs adding to the pressure she already feels. If Quinn can cover for you briefly, Dave can fly you out and back so you can visit."

"Kate, I need to be there for me; it's not just for Jennifer's benefit."

Jennifer was dying. It suddenly struck him what Shari must be feeling. How was she still able to walk around and function? He felt like someone had just slammed him and ripped apart his world. He faced losing Jennifer and he felt like the walking wounded. For Shari to have lost Carl, now to be watching her dad struggle to hang on...

"We fight, Marcus. I've already got a four-inch binder of information for you to read. We're about to become cancer specialists."

"I never dreamed this would happen. I worry about Stephen and Jack getting disoriented in a fire, of you encountering the one hostage situation that can't be resolved, of Lisa stumbling into someone with a real skeleton in his closet; but when I worried, it was never about Jennifer. She's a pediatrician; she's the safe one."

"You can't protect this family from life."

"It's my job to try."

Kate gave him a look that fell somewhere between pity and loyal admiration. "Page the others. We'll meet as soon as Rachel can get a flight back."

The hotel directly across from the hospital was vintage versus modern, Old World elegance adding to its peaceful charm. Marcus checked one last time with the three men on the security detail watching the floor where Shari and her mom were now staying, then let himself into the adjoining suite to theirs. Her family had been given other rooms on the floor. It was coming up on midnight. They were short staffed everywhere, and Marcus had decided in the end it was best to be near the hospital tonight.

Craig looked up from the paper he was reading.

"All quiet?" Marcus asked it softly, for the connecting door between the suites was open.

"Yes." Craig folded the newspaper. "Do you want me back here in the morning or should I meet you at the hospital?"

Marcus shrugged off his jacket and loosened his tie. "Why don't you report to the hospital about nine; I'll make sure they are covered to there."

"Will do. You've got several messages."

Quinn would have paged with news on the shooter; that was the one message Marcus was waiting for. "I'll get to them. Thanks."

Craig rose with a nod, said good night. Marcus locked the door behind him. He walked through the dark rooms lit only by the moonlight, too restless to settle even though he was exhausted.

Jennifer. He needed to be there at Johns Hopkins, and soon. He had bought coffee for an oncologist at the hospital after talking with Kate, and the medical information swirling around in his head all felt black. Jennifer hadn't been kidding when she said it was going to be a tough fight.

All the O'Malleys had been paged. Rachel was able to grab a cancellation on a late flight and should be halfway back to Chicago by now from her current Red Cross assignment in Florida. She had returned the emergency page and asked only one question. "Where?" It had been the typical response of all the O'Malleys. The number of family emergencies called in over two decades could be counted on one hand. They would meet first thing in the morning, and by then he had to decide how he would break the news.

Faint sounds echoed from the adjoining suite. Marcus walked over to lean against the door frame. "Couldn't sleep?"

His quiet words startled Shari, and she stopped halfway across the living room. "I didn't realize you were here."

"We're trading off shifts for the evening."

She waved her hand toward the minikitchen in their suite. "I was just going for something to drink."

"Want some company?"

"Sure."

He walked toward the minikitchen. "Anything in particular you would like?"

"A glass of milk."

He smiled at her tone. "Don't apologize. It's good for you." He found a glass and opened the refrigerator, knowing from past stays in this hotel that the suites came complete with all the makings for breakfast. "Want something to eat to go with that?"

She declined.

He poured her a glass of milk, then retrieved a piece of cold pizza for himself from the box one of his guys must have ordered. He had, in the end, only pushed around the cheeseburger while watching Kate eat.

"I've eaten a lot of cold pizza in my life, but rarely by choice."

Marcus felt the tension uncoil at finally having something on which the world would not rise or fall to talk about. "Cold pizza is great. It's the best way to eat leftovers. Now Chinese, that is not good cold."

"You live on carryout."

"Travel enough, it's a requirement of life." She settled on the couch and he took the chair by the window. "How's your father?"

"No change. There has been little this entire day."

"I'm sorry about that, Shari. Truly sorry."

"He'll pull through."

He didn't bother to try and temper her hope. He now knew all about hope at any cost, against any odds.

It was late, and he didn't hurry to start a conversation, content to simply share her company. She curled up with her feet against the cushions, her back braced against the side arm of the couch, her hands holding the glass linked across her knees. Her hair was still tousled from restless sleep, and the black college sweatshirt she wore looked beaten up and faded, matching the jeans. It was a far cry from the elegance of the first time he had met her, but Marcus decided he liked this Shari better. She had vibrated with life and energy before; this version was a look inside when the comfortable circumstances were stripped away.

He tucked away another nugget of information about her; she was not troubled by silence, didn't feel a need to fill it with sound. The quietness after the turmoil of the day felt good, and it was nice to share it.

She eventually stirred. "I would like to go to church in the morning. Would that be possible?"

"Would the chapel service at the hospital be okay?"

"Yes."

"I'll be glad to make the arrangements."

"Thank you. I know you don't believe, but it's important to me."

"Shari—trust me, it's not a problem." He should have been more careful in what he said. As many doubts as he personally had, he had a heritage from his mom that respected religion, and Shari didn't need any more sources of turmoil in her life. He changed the subject. "I read your brief recommending Carl for the court."

"Did you?"

"You're good. You certainly convinced me."

"Communication is what I do for a living."

She said it quietly, and it took a moment for the significance of what she had said to register. He'd lived in Virginia for a long time; she worked for the governor, was working now on his reelection campaign. "Modesty doesn't suit you. You're very good at what you do." He smiled. "And despite your protests to the contrary, you can write profound and elegant sound bites. I actually haven't minded listening to the campaign speeches."

She returned his smile. "You're being generous, but thank you. I can write the speech, the brief, just don't ask me to sit through its delivery by someone else. I would much rather be the one giving it."

"So you do have an Achilles heel."

"I've got a couple to go along with those secrets I don't plan to share."

Her dry humor in this moment was deeply appreciated. "Good secrets, are they?"

"I bet you've got a few."

"More than a few," he agreed easily.

"Care to trade one?"

"There's a grapevine in my family, so you'd have to promise to keep it quiet."

His words got her interest, and her curiosity; she sat up straighter. "Okay."

"I know who swiped Rugsby the raccoon, our family mascot. There is about to be a ransom demand made for him."

"Please tell me that's a stuffed animal."

"Jack won him for Kate at a carnival when we were in our teens."

"Who took it?"

"Rachel and Jennifer. They decided to give the others a real puzzle to solve."

She chuckled softly. "Let me guess, you put them up to it."

"Every good plan needs a mastermind. Besides, no one in the family would ever suspect it could have been Rachel and Jen."

"That's good."

"Very. I think I'll stump them. Your turn. Give."

"Josh has been using a marked deck of cards for when we play rummy, and he doesn't realize it."

Marcus choked on his soda.

"One of the kids left the deck of cards at the house, and it got put away on the shelf of games."

"And you feel guilty winning as a result."

"Worse, I'm having to count cards to make sure I lose half the games."

"An honest cheat. You could just tell him."

"Remember when you said there were some secrets that take on a life of their own? This one has."

"You're a card player?"

"Josh is. That and dominoes. I personally prefer Scrabble, but he refuses to play because I wipe the board with him most games. Are you a game player?"

"Within the family, it's Monopoly. There have been a few games that have gone on for days. Personally, my partner Quinn and I play a lot of chess."

"Any good?"

"I haven't beaten him yet."

"How long have you been trying?"

"Oh…" Marcus thought about it, "about five years."

"Years?"

"I'm a slow learner. And the guy is brutal at the game."

"It's the victory you dream about."

"Yes."

The clock chimed another quarter hour gone. Shari got up and carried her glass to the counter. "Thank you, Marcus."

He leaned his head back so he could see her. "For what?"

"Just being here. For providing a distraction and a laugh. I'll see you in the morning." She moved back through the rooms to return to bed.

Marcus watched the door she had left through and smiled. The more time he spent around Shari, the more he liked her. Her habit of falling back on humor in the midst of the crisis told him more about her than she probably realized. She had learned to cope with ongoing crisis and stress from somewhere. Since her family appeared close, it had to be her political job.

Marcus finished his drink, speculating on what was an unusual discovery. He knew what it took to cope with ongoing pressure. She had developed a skill that would not only calm down her own reaction, but also those around her. John had made a good choice when he put her to work on his campaign.

He sighed. This situation was out of her league. They had to find the shooter, and quickly. Asking Shari to cope with this crisis for more than a few days would be asking her to endure a weight that would break her. The intensity of it came back as he thought about how little progress they had made during the course of the day.

Shari needed him. Jennifer needed him. In a few hours all the O'Malleys were going to need him. He had never been one to shy away from responsibility, but this burden he wished he could give to someone else. He got to his feet, weary. A day couldn't get worse than this one.

Marcus woke to the sound of his pager, reached over to check the number, and then picked up the phone. "It's Marcus." He rubbed his eyes at the news he was given. "Five minutes. Have the car brought around to the underground garage." He went to wake up Shari and her mom. William Hanford had just taken a turn for the worse.

William Hanford coded at 3:07 A.M. Sunday morning.

Marcus pulled Shari out of the way as nurses and doctors worked to bring him back from cardiac arrest. They stood on the other side of the glass watching as CPR was done and repeated attempts were made to get his heart started. Beth, her sister Margaret, and a nurse with her stood off to one side inside the room. Marcus had never realized how long doctors would continue the fight. Ten minutes passed, fifteen.

Shari watched it all…silent, still.

He could almost feel the intensity of her prayers.

As a child he had tried so hard to believe enough to have his prayers answered, but one by one they had failed. His mom had died. His dad had continued to drink. And eventually he had been abandoned. It wasn't just family that abandoned him, it was God. For the first time in years, he wished he could pray and know it would be answered. *Shari believes. Please answer her prayers. Please don't abandon her.*

The doctors worked another five minutes. And then the activity slowly ceased.

"No." It was a quiet wail.

Marcus turned Shari into his chest and away from the reality before them. "I am so sorry."

He could feel the pain flow off her in a wave. He tightened his arms, enclosing her in a firm grip, afraid she would fall. And then with a deep gulp of air she turned back into the room. "Mom." She pulled away to join her mom at her father's side.

Marcus had to look away from the grief. Anger flared hot and intense inside: at the shooter, at fate, at a God who didn't care. He was sick and tired of religion that offered false hope.

Shari didn't have the reserves for this kind of emotional hit. God got all the praise and thanks for fortunate coincidences attributed to prayer, while men like himself had to deal with the disappointment, disbelief, and grief when those prayers were not answered. It wasn't right to raise hope and disappoint, and that was what religion did.

And as he watched, fear wrapped itself hard around his heart. This was the face of the pain he would feel if he ever lost Jennifer; this was the pain that would rip apart the O'Malleys, and he didn't know how to brace himself for the possibility the unthinkable would one day happen.

The waiting room had become Shari's private place to grieve. Joshua was awake now, had been told. As she had expected, his reaction had been intense. He'd tried to throw the vase on the bedside table through the wall. And he'd gotten mad at himself for not stopping the shooter, for not yanking the door closed and throwing the lock when he knocked her out of the doorway.

Mom and Aunt Margaret were sitting with him. She had slipped away from the other family. Shari couldn't handle Joshua's grief, her mom's, on top of her own. *If only she hadn't opened that door!* Tears ran down her cheeks and the Kleenex clenched in her fist was worthlessly sodden. She wiped her face with the back of the sleeve.

She was more than just hurt, she was angry, and it was bottled up like an explosion inside. She paced to the window. She, too, felt like throwing the coffee mug she held against the wall, watching it shatter. She could almost taste the fury.

God how could You do this? Mom grieves but says this was Your will. Well it wasn't mine! I want my father back. I want my prayers over something critical to matter to You!

The sobs were wrenching her chest so hard she couldn't breathe. It wasn't the best way to handle this; it wasn't the mature Christian thing to do, but she couldn't stand the stoic acceptance others in her extended family were determined to showcase. If God didn't like her getting angry it was His problem, frankly she didn't care. There wasn't much left in life He could strip away from her.

The anger eventually burned out into exhaustion.

She sank down on the couch and leaned her head back against the fabric, looking up at the ceiling. *I don't like You anymore, God.*

The silence felt sad.

What was this family going to do without Dad?

Shari contemplated the impossible and tried to find a way to accept it.

Someone sat down beside her. She didn't bother to look over. Marcus. She was becoming used to his stillness. She wanted to bury her head against his shoulder and cry until there were no more tears, to take him up on the friendship he offered and pass to him this weight collapsing down on her. But there was only sadness now, too deep for any more tears. She lowered her head and sighed. "Marcus, I want this all to be a bad dream."

He brushed back her hair caught on the bandage on her cheek. "I know."

There was rain hitting the window. A soft rain, leaving drops on the windowpane that eventually joined together and slid down the glass. "The sky is crying," she commented, fatigue making the observation significant.

Marcus's hand closed firmly on her shoulder. "Shari, you're going to get some sleep. You'll deal better with this after you've slept twelve hours."

"It won't change the fact Dad is dead."

"No, it won't."

She wanted time to stop, but life was going on without Carl and her father. "I'm tired."

His other hand hovered and then settled against her back. "Come on, Shari."

Shock best described the O'Malley family reaction as they gathered at the hotel late Sunday morning and heard the news about Jennifer. Stephen and Jack looked grim. Lisa stunned. Rachel wrestling with disbelief. Kate, who already knew, had reached to grip Dave's hand. Marcus looked around the hotel room and felt like his heart was breaking.

"She's already in Baltimore?" Jack asked.

"Her flight was late last night."

Rachel took a deep breath. "What's the plan? We need to be there."

"If we juggle schedules, I think we can cover the full time she is in the hospital."

Every one of them wanted to fly out first. Marcus smiled, for it was the first moment of relief since Jennifer had given him the news. He wasn't carrying this alone. He kept forgetting at times just how powerful this family was when it came to rallying around one of their own. "Get your calendars. Let's figure it out."

Shari woke up late Sunday morning, not certain at first where she was at, vague memories of ugly dreams clouding her thoughts. There was movement in the suite outside her closed door.

It hit her again, the heavy weight of what she had to carry now because of what one man had done. Her eyes were too dry to cry anymore. Dad was dead. So many things pressed against her that had to be done. His funeral arrangements. His law practice.

The door cracked open. She turned her head on the pillow, looked over, expecting her mom, saw it was Marcus.

"Awake?"

"Of sorts." She swung her legs to the side of the bed. The sweats she had worn to the hospital, collapsed in bed wearing, were rumpled but at least warm; her bones were still chilled. "Come on in." The grief was so heavy that she couldn't remember what it had felt like to once smile. "Any news on the shooter?"

"No."

She eased to her feet and crossed over to the chair, sat down to take the weight off her aching knee. She wearily looked at the window and the sunlight streaming in. "I slept a lot longer than I intended."

"Your mom wanted you to sleep."

"Is she here?"

"I just took her back over to the hospital. She's with Joshua."

She should probably join them. She frowned at her shoes, then awkwardly pulled them on. She got to her feet. Her thoughts drifted.

"Are you okay?" He had crossed the room to join her.

She heard the concern in his voice and wanted more than anything to find her composure and not appear like she was going to fall apart on him. "I'm fine." She gave him a polite smile and was totally disconcerted when he lifted his hand to push back the hair on her forehead. Her eyes closed as the pressure of his palm eased her aching headache.

"You've got a slight fever."

An aching headache, a strained voice…she should have known. Add a fever and it was her common pattern for when she got a cold. "Stress reaction. A couple aspirins will knock it down." He looked skeptical but she had weathered this reaction too many times to be worried about it. And at the moment a cold didn't seem like something of much significance.

She ran her hand through her hair. "Let me get my hair brushed. I'll join you in a few minutes."

"I'll find you those aspirins."

"I appreciate it."

In the bathroom she washed her face in cold water, looking in the mirror at eyes that were weary and dull. There was no life left inside. She forced herself to get ready, to brush her teeth, then picked up her hairbrush and ruthlessly tamed the matted hair. She went to join Marcus.

He would have had a great deal less sleep than she had, and yet he looked alert and focused as he stood by the window scanning the street below. Again his stillness struck her. She had met only a few men able to function under stress with that kind of focus.

He turned when she entered the room, and she didn't miss the fact the suit jacket he wore concealed his gun. It was odd, how rarely she thought of him as a cop. It was the memory of their first meeting that prevailed.

He handed her two aspirins. "See if these help." She took them, grateful. He held out a coffee mug. "I promised you coffee. I'm sorry it's under these circumstances."

"So am I. I was rather looking forward to that date."

Her words caused his impersonal, assessing look to disappear momentarily, and she was enveloped once again in the warmth of his smile. "So was I."

Marcus. How I would have preferred this weekend to be different. I would have more than just enjoyed sharing coffee with you; I would have been hoping for your phone number. I don't want to lose this potential friendship to the crisis this has become.

She returned his smile with a brief one of her own, wishing she had more emotion left she could put behind it. She settled down on the couch. The coffee was strong and hot and it helped give her something to focus on.

"I've got something for you." Marcus reached into his pocket. He handed over what looked like a pager, but it had no LED display.

"What is it?"

"A pager with a special frequency. Depress the button and it sounds on our security net. It's a precaution. Get in the habit of wearing it clipped on your jeans. If you get in a situation that makes you uncomfortable for any reason, and I mean any reason, and one of us is not already at your side, press it. Don't think twice about it."

She turned it over in her hand and nodded. It was an indication of what might happen. She was a witness. It was settling in what that meant. It wasn't just testifying one day in the future; it was getting her safely from now to the time the shooter was caught and she could testify.

Just looking at the device strengthened her resolve. "How can I help with the case? This guy killed my father. I need something concrete I can do. I hate feeling this helpless." She could see from his expression that he didn't want to pursue it right now. "Please."

He settled into the chair he had sat in last night, his expression guarded. "You knew Carl well."

She knew how he liked his eggs for breakfast, what his favorite comic strip was, what musicals he enjoyed, what authors he favored... Somehow she doubted that was what Marcus needed to know. "He and Dad went to law school together. I've known him all my life," she replied softly.

"Then help me figure out motive."

I've been thinking about nothing else and I don't know. He was a good man. "What can I answer?"

"Tell me about Carl's family."

"His only family is an aunt on his mother's side. She's eighty-nine, has Alzheimer's, and doesn't recognize anyone. Carl has been her legal guardian for years."

"No one else?"

"Carl was an only child and he never married."

"His estate is large?"

"He was conservative with his money. He didn't travel. Other than upkeep on his estate, books were probably his largest expense. Maybe 8 million?"

Marcus's eyes narrowed at that estimate. "Who benefits?"

"Charities. The house is slated to be sold with the proceeds going into trust to care for his aunt."

"Any business ventures? Active investments that might be having problems?"

She shook her head. "Stock index funds, bond funds, and cash. He didn't want to have to worry about it."

"Anyone in his life? Was he seeing someone?"

"The law was his life. He had a lot of friends, but no one in particular he was seeing."

"That leaves his work."

"The obvious connection, given where he was killed."

"Tell me about his career."

"Going back to the beginning—he was a district attorney, a state judge, a federal judge, then Court of Appeals for his last seven years. In one word, his record is conservative."

"Your brief listed several cases. Which do you think merit attention?"

"Last year on the appeals court, there was a bank fraud case that cost a lot of people their retirement savings. Carl wrote the opinion that upheld the lower courts' finding dismissing the central charge. It was the right legal decision, but not necessarily the right moral one if you wanted justice."

"A judge and jury can't convict if the evidence isn't there."

"I know, but that didn't stop the hate."

"What about your family, Shari? Any enemies?"

His question threw her, and then what he was asking settled in. She felt cold suddenly, very cold. "You think it relates to us? I surprised the shooter."

"Yes. But why didn't he lock the door? I can't dismiss that you might have somehow been a target as well."

"Dad has been in corporate law and estates; there has been no personal threats that I know of. Joshua—he works for the DA, some of his cases are intense." Shari thought about that in detail. "But no, I don't think so. I've been in politics for years. Behind the scenes but definitely in the center of things. I'd be the one with enemies. But they would be political enemies. No one likes to lose, and these races and policy issues can consume a lot of cash."

"Any names keep you up at night?"

"No."

"Think about it."

"You're just trying to scare me."

"Trying to open your eyes," Marcus said soberly.

Connor dropped the newspaper on the park bench, the sketch on the front page below the fold. "We've got a problem."

His cousin Frank didn't look up from the crossword puzzle he was working. "So I saw."

"It's got to be dealt with before Titus gets back from Europe."

"It's going to take some planning. I already checked. She's under tight security."

"And we're only going to get one chance. Contract it out?"

"I can handle it," Frank replied. He turned over the newspaper and tapped the article. "That's where we act."

Eight

"Lisa, what do we have?"

Marcus found his sister seated at the round work table in her office, one hand wrapped around a carryout Chinese carton showing two protruding chopsticks, the other around a small cassette recorder being used to record observations as she studied eight-by-ten photos from the crime scene. How she was managing to eat was a mystery.

The lab he had walked through was pristine, her office another matter as she chased every idea that occurred to her. He cleared the spare chair of files to have a place to sit.

"You look horrible," Lisa observed.

"Thanks. Tell me you have something." It had been six days of frustration and he would really like to end this week with some good news. They were chasing leads in four states with nothing substantial to go on.

"Fibers," she replied.

She handed him the Chinese carton. "Eat. You look like you've been skipping meals." Spinning her chair around, she reached for the pale blue folder balanced on top of her phone.

"In your interview with Shari, she said the shooter was well dressed, wearing a navy suit."

Marcus nodded. The chow mein was lukewarm. Lisa must have been holding the carton for the good part of the last hour.

"It's blue-gray actually. European wool, European dye. I doubt it's a suit that comes off the rack. I'm working on getting a manufacturer. That's a freebie. I've got something better." She shifted the photographs on the table to one side and laid out large perspective shots. "Look at where the shell casings fell."

Seven of them were shown in one photograph of the room, four in the other. "Okay. What am I supposed to be seeing?"

"Where was the shooter standing when he shot Carl?"

"Somewhere about here, at the end of the bed," Marcus indicated.

She nodded. "I used Carl's exact height, the entry and exit wounds, and the blood traces and projected those back. The shooter was standing right here." She pointed with a pen. "He shot Carl. That gives us these three shell casings." She indicated the three in a close grouping. "What did he do next?"

"Turned to shoot Shari."

"And hit the door frame kicking up wood. He was firing as he turned." She held out her right hand and swiveled. "Like this?"

It hit him then, what she was showing him. "The bullet should have been buried in the door frame or the wall as his hand came around, not splintered the door frame."

"He's left handed."

Marcus reached over, wrapped his hand behind her neck, tugged her over, and planted a kiss on her forehead. "You angel. Can you prove it?"

She giggled. "What do you think?"

"Show me."

She pointed to the picture. "Okay. That fourth shot, the shell casing is up here; it struck and nicked the side of the dresser. The only way to get it angled in there is if he was firing with the gun in his left hand as he swiveled left to right."

She laid down a close up of the door frame. "See the angle of entry? The way the wood chip was kicked up? Here's the line." She laid down a ruler on the master grid she was using. "Same thing. The only way to generate the chip and throw it out like this is to be at this angle. Either the shooter stepped back before he turned and fired, or the gun was in his left hand."

She pushed aside the photos to lay down one that was a contrast photo. "And look at this. The bright white is the gunpowder residue luminescing. We're looking straight down at the carpet in this photo; this is the edge of the bed. Look at the bright line of the arc."

"It goes left to right relative to the bed."

"And if the gun was in his right hand, the gunpowder residue would have fallen more on the top of the bedspread and it wouldn't have hit the draped portion. Instead it's bright on the falling edge of the bedspread."

"You've convinced me."

Lisa leaned back in her chair. "Good, because that's the most useful news I've got. The rest you're not necessarily going to like."

"What is it?"

She had to search her office to find it. She retrieved a red folder from the floor by the whiteboard. She opened it and handed it to him. He recognized a photo taken from a microscope; the bottom index showing it was taken at 120 times magnification. It was a blowup of a dark, curved fiber.

"See the change in color at the base of the curl?"

Marcus nodded.

"Your shooter doesn't have thick, dark hair. He has a very good hairpiece."

"Our sketch is wrong."

"Distorted. A hairpiece suggests he might actually be bald. This was found lying on a blood splatter, so it's not a historical fiber to the room."

Marcus rubbed his eyes. He did *not* want to have to tell Shari this news. They had begun to suspect something like this as the hours and then days went by without the sketch producing the leads they expected. "Anything else?"

"The shell casings don't match anything in the national databases. But the firing pin impressions on the shell casings do show a unique off-center flaw. We'll be able to get a definite match if we ever get the gun, even if they try to destroy the barrel riflings."

"What about the shoes?"

"He's a size nine and a half. We don't have enough to generate a brand. We do have a wear pattern that we might be able to match if we get the shoes."

"No fingerprints?"

"Actually, forty-three distinct prints, but they are all tracing to people who work in the hotel or who stayed in that room in the past. Dave has the list."

Marcus knew how hard she had been working to get them this much inside of a week. He needed more. The threat to Shari, rather than lessening with time, had only intensified. The shooter was out there, thinking, planning, knowing he had made only one real mistake. Shari. Marcus could feel the danger, and Quinn was coiled tight with the frustration of having nothing but one dead end after another to chase. "What next, Lisa?"

"The scuff mark on the thirteenth floor stairwell door. I want permission to take crime technicians through all those hotel rooms. We never found a trace of where he went once he reached that floor. Maybe he never left it."

Marcus absorbed that observation. "He had one of those hotel rooms."

"He had to dump the disguise somewhere, and if he had yanked it off in the hallway, the search should have found fibers similar to this one. We didn't."

"Thirty-seven rooms? It will take some significant crime technician work and time."

"I'm more worried about the hotel having a fit."

"I can take care of that," Dave said from the doorway.

Marcus swiveled around.

Dave smiled. "Hotels rent rooms. We'll just rent the entire floor. That should keep them happy."

"Your own pocketbook?"

"Consider it a cheap solution to the fact I would like to see Kate this month. A few more weeks of these kind of hours, and she'll forget why she's dating me."

Dave didn't make a big deal about his family's wealth, but he did use it on occasion to move obstacles out of the way. That family wealth had led to the kidnapping and death of Dave's sister Kim. What other people saw as only good, Dave knew for both its good and bad. And having grown up in Britain, he had a cool practicality to his sense of the family fortune. It wasn't something he owned as much as something his family for generations would have. Marcus knew Kate was still struggling to get used to the idea she was going out with a guy who could spend whatever he liked whenever he chose to. Marcus thought about Dave's offer for a moment, accepted the practicality of it, and nodded. "Thanks. Arrange it."

"What are you hoping for, Lisa?" Dave asked.

"That he used a room to change his suit. There should be gunpowder residue on that suit, and very probably blood splatters. If he set it down on the bed, dropped it on the floor, we'll find traces. And we can match fibers. Find the room he used, and maybe we get the grand jewel—that he took off his gloves and left us a few prints."

Marcus trusted her hunches. "Sweep the rooms, Lisa."

It was after 11:00 P.M. Monday; the hospital floor was quiet. Shari took a handful of jellybeans from the dish at the nurses' station and ate them as she walked back to meet Marcus. Over the last nine days, life had fallen into a routine, if it could be called that.

Waiting for leads on the shooter; waiting for Joshua to get back his strength. Adjusting to having security with her at all times…she would be so relieved when this was over. All the family but mom's sister Margaret had returned to Virginia. The funerals were scheduled tentatively for Friday depending on Josh's ability to travel.

She found the extra time on her hands hard to cope with. The two deaths had ripped a void in her life. The hole in her heart regarding God ached. She no longer tried to pray. She was simply too tired to want to risk getting hurt again.

Left unspoken was the fear of what would happen if the shooter was not found soon. Life couldn't go on like this indefinitely. And she didn't want to leave the protection of having Marcus around. He was a strong shelter against the danger.

He was sitting in what she had come to think of as his seat, one of the cushioned chairs in the open area just across from the elevators where he noticed everyone who came and went on the floor. The television was off. She had noticed he preferred not to watch the news, while she was feeling the withdrawal from its absence.

Craig normally had the day shift, but at about 10 P.M. Marcus took over after having spent his day working the case. Shari had to admit she looked forward to the evenings. They talked about the investigation, but they also talked about family, both his and hers. Marcus had been intentionally drawing her out about her dad, Carl, and that helped. He was being the one thing she most needed right now. A friend.

He was reading a book while he waited for her, taking a moment to relax. It was a different one than last night she realized when she saw the spine. She'd read it last month. She was restless. She glanced at the page he was on: 69. "Do you know who did it yet?"

"Davidson, the brother-in-law."

She settled on the arm of the chair near him, hearing the certainty. "You're sure?"

"Yes." He looked over at her, settled the open book on his chest. "Read it?"

She nodded.

"I'm right, aren't I?"

His slow smile caught her attention and she wished she could say no. "Yes, you are."

"The only author I've found that consistently stumps me is H. Q. Victor, but since she's soon to be extended family, that's okay."

The thick crime novels by the British writer were some of her favorite reads. They were so real: stories about children who disappeared, were found murdered, and the hunt to find those responsible. "H. Q. Victor is a lady? You're kidding me, right?"

"Dave's sister, Sara."

She had met Dave a couple days ago, found the man Marcus called a friend charming. He'd kissed her hand while Marcus glared and she'd laughed at that. Shari couldn't decide now if Marcus was serious or not. But H. Q. Victor was British, and the first thing she had noticed about Dave was his delightful accent. "You're joking."

"It's a small world."

"I can't believe you know her. I love reading her mysteries."

"I'll mention she's got another fan when I see her. Ready to go?"

"Yes."

She gathered together her bag and briefcase. He escorted her through corridors the hospital security staff had established as safe corridors, taking her eventually out through the basement to the parking garage, where a car was brought around to meet them.

The press presence around the hospital was intense. So far Shari had chosen not to speak directly with the reporters, encouraged in that action by Joshua and Marcus. Anne released statements on her behalf and handled the press inquiries. Marcus wanted to keep the reporters and cameras a far distance away and Shari had to agree. He did it for security reasons; she did it for privacy reasons. She didn't have much privacy left. What she did have she wanted to protect.

The formal press briefings were held at 2 P.M. at the FBI regional office, and she had been watching them on television, knowing in advance from Marcus what would be discussed but always hoping against hope there would be breaking news to report. This had become an intense, slow, grinding investigation that would eventually find the man who killed Carl and her father, of that she was certain.

She had been in fights like this before in a political sense, when moving legislation required tenacity and hours of hard work in the face of no apparent movement. Then it would suddenly break free and everything would happen swiftly. It took a husbanding of energy to endure events like this. She was slowly accepting that.

They crossed the street to the hotel, using the private underground entrance. The day she could walk across the street was over, Shari realized with grim humor. She wished she could have a moment of normalcy back. She hadn't appreciated it nearly enough until it was stripped away.

She paused with Marcus as he stopped to talk with Luke, confirming security arrangements for the night. Shari had gotten to know most of the security detail by first name, and she was impressed with their focus. They were professionals, but she had also picked up on the fact this particular case was also personal. No one wanted to let Marcus down.

Her mom had come back to the hotel with Aunt Margaret earlier in the evening. Shari unlocked the door to the suite, found a solitary light on and the rooms quiet. They had apparently already turned in for the night.

Marcus crossed over and closed the drapes against the night. "What would you like from room service?"

Shari was getting accustomed to Marcus and his late night snacks. Ever since she had blown off dinner one evening, he had been unobtrusively ensuring she would have to be rude not to eat something. "How about some supreme nachos?"

"Sounds good." He picked up the phone and placed the order. "Ten minutes," he commented, replacing the phone.

She settled on the couch, pushed off her tennis shoes and flexed her stiff knee, relieved to be back at the hotel. "Josh managed to do reps lifting the five-pound dumbbell with his good hand."

"Excellent."

"Yeah. Only then he dropped it on his foot. I laughed and he tossed me out of the room," she added ruefully.

"I would say he's about ready to travel."

"What time is our flight back to Virginia Wednesday?"

"We'll be taking a private flight, so it's at our discretion. We'll probably leave the hotel around 9 A.M."

"It will be good to be home. Being executor of Dad's estate is a lot more complex than I realized. I thought I knew what to expect until I started wading through all the logistics. And since Dad was executor of Carl's estate, both have fallen to me like a tidal wave."

"Take your time. You'll do fine. I'm sure your dad chose you because he knew you would do an excellent job."

She looked over, surprised at the comment. It was nice to hear that confidence expressed.

The food arrived, and Marcus positioned the plate between them.

Shari tugged one tortilla chip free. "I like this quiet time of night. I always used to be a morning lark, but I'm becoming a night owl."

"I figured it was the bad dreams causing you to avoid bed until sleep forced you there," Marcus countered.

He'd noticed, but his response had been to simply adjust his own schedule to spend late evenings with her until she was willing to turn in. She should have realized it. "Some of that is happening too."

"Try reading at night. It will distract you."

"Can I borrow a book?"

"Sure. As long as you don't choose a mystery or suspense."

"You've got something else?"

"I think there's a biography in my briefcase."

His pager went off. Accustomed to the interruptions that were a frequent part of his life, she was surprised at his reaction when he saw the number. Pages related to work often resulted in a look of distance, occasionally she could pick up subtle tenseness, but this—before he even took the call he looked worried. "Excuse me, Shari."

He retrieved his phone and dialed, crossing the room to the windows. Shari tried not to eavesdrop, but since he hadn't left the room she couldn't help but hear. His words startled her.

"Kate, what's happening? What did the doctors say? How is Jennifer doing?" He had been expecting the call hours ago. Kate had been good about calling after each scheduled treatment.

"I walked in on Jennifer crying today, not that soft it-hurts kind, but the bone-wrenching crying that makes you ache because there is nothing you can do. Between the pain of the spreading cancer pressing against her spine and the effects of the radiation that makes her so sick she can't eat— she is being pushed to the literal breaking point."

Marcus closed his eyes, feeling his heart wrench. Jennifer had been lying to him, keeping her voice steady and confident when they talked when she had to be so scared. The distress and tension in Kate's voice was obvious. He needed to be in Baltimore, needed to see them. He was letting them down. His family needed him and he wasn't there.

Just as soon as Shari and her family were back in Virginia and security had been figured out there, he was going to get to Baltimore. "Please tell her I'm thinking about her. I'll call her again in the morning. How's Rachel holding up?"

"Much better than I am," Kate admitted. "She's good in these situations, Marcus. I never realized how good. When Jennifer is resting, I've often found Rachel down one flight on the pediatrics ward, lending her special touch there, bringing smiles to children with not much to smile about. Then she comes back and joins Jennifer and tells her about each one. Rachel knew without being asked the best distraction she could offer was the pediatric patients Jennifer loves."

"I'm glad to hear that."

"Your latest gift of pink roses arrived this afternoon. Jen wouldn't let me read the card, but whatever you wrote, it made her day."

"I intended it to," Marcus replied. "And no, I am not going to tell you what was in the card," he told Kate with a smile. He and Jen were making arrangements for Rugsby to reappear. It was at least one laughter-filled distraction he could offer Jennifer. "I talked to Stephen last night. He said he was flying out in the morning with Jack."

"They get in at ten. Tom is going to meet them at the airport."

"You haven't said how he's doing."

"He's a guy I would have fallen in love with had Jennifer not found him first. You can see it in his eyes, Marcus, the knowledge he has as a doctor of just how grim things are, but he's never beside Jennifer with anything less than optimism."

"He sticks, no matter what the cost. We both knew that the day we met him."

"He loves her so much you can feel it when you see the two of them together. When they are quiet and simply holding hands…I've left the room a few times rather than intrude."

"I'm glad you are there. I'll be out as soon as I can get it arranged."

"Jennifer knows that."

"Please, call me if there is any change."

"Day or night, I'll page."

"Thanks, Kate."

He slowly closed the phone. Jen. He felt tears moisten his eyes. Life wasn't fair. It wasn't fair at all.

"Jennifer is sick?" Shari didn't want to interrupt his thoughts, but she did desperately want to take that look of hopelessness from his face.

Marcus turned, pulled from his thoughts. "Cancer," he replied heavily.

Shari felt shocked. Jennifer had been so nice to her the evening of the shooting; there had been no indication anything was wrong. "She never said anything."

"She just told the family. And it hit like a bombshell. She's at Johns Hopkins, undergoing radiation and chemotherapy."

"It's bad."

"Very."

She ached for him. She thought about commenting on Jennifer's faith, but it would sound like a religious Band-Aid. She had faith and she still felt angry at the platitudes people said as they made their condolences. She missed her dad and Carl so bad it ached. And Marcus was in a harder position, being asked to accept months of knowing the worst might happen. "Marcus, I am so sorry. Please, come sit down. Can you go see her?"

"Once you and your family are back in Virginia and the security is tight, I'll cut away for a day and fly up to see her."

"Is there anything I can do?"

"Pray."

She heard the skepticism, the faint trace of irony…and the agony. He needed hope. She wanted to comfort, not debate, but she simply didn't know what to say. She wrapped her arms around her knees, leaned her chin against the fabric of her jeans.

It's not like I've got a great track record, Lord. You and I are barely talk-ing right now. I prayed intensely for Carl to make the short list, and he ended up dead because that prayer got answered. I prayed with every bit of emotion in my body for Dad to make it, and he died. What am I supposed to tell Marcus?

"Why don't you believe?" she finally asked, not sure if he would answer her.

He sat down heavily. "I did once, as a child, before the orphanage. My mother believed. But her prayers didn't seem to make a difference, and after a while it became easier simply not to hope."

"Hope deferred makes the heart sick," she murmured. "The Bible says that in Proverbs."

"There's truth to that."

"What happened to your mom?"

"She died. Pneumonia."

A terse reply; he would have been young, and she could hear the hurt that still lingered. He had lost his mom just like she had lost her dad. Had prayed, and watched her die. And he had decided as a result not to believe. It hurt, how much she could empathize with him. If she didn't have two decades of faith anchoring her down and causing inertia, she might have broken under this pressure and stopped believing too.

She hugged her knees tighter against her. "What was it like, when you lost your mom?"

He didn't answer her right away. "Like I was the one being put in the grave. The thing I feared most had happened. She was the only light in my world, and it was gone." He looked at her. "Like it must feel with your dad being gone."

She knew exactly what he meant. "I've spent my life with Dad always there as a compass, believing in me, convinced I could succeed, backing my dreams; and now he's gone. It's a horrible void. I find myself going through days waiting, hoping, for something to come along and take away that ache."

"Time fills it. And the good memories return."

"I don't think anything in life is going to be harder than attending the funerals."

"Shari, you'll get through them."

"Because I've got no choice."

"Because you're a survivor," Marcus corrected.

Shari blinked, his assessment catching her off guard. She had only spent a little over a week with him, but he had managed to understand her in a more profound way than Sam ever had. On the surface her life might appear easy, she had the family wealth, the close family, but her professional life was defined by her stubborn ability to fight on against the odds. And in prayer... She wasn't ducking her head and accepting what had happened; she had practically picked a fight. "Yes, I am. And so are you, Marcus."

He gave a rueful smile. "Yet one more thing we have in common."

"I think this one is more important than a love for chocolate ice cream and a habit of keeping humorous secrets."

"Oh, I don't know. It depends on what kind of day it's been."

She laughed. "You're good for me."

"Of course I am." He leaned over to his briefcase and pulled out a biography of Roosevelt. "Take a book and go curl up in bed. You need some sleep."

"Political history. Nice choice."

"Guilty. I thought of you when I picked it up." He quirked an eyebrow. "Don't stay up reading all night."

"Yes, sir."

"Good night, brat."

She tweaked his collar as she passed behind him and said good night.

Nine

Shari didn't think she was going to make it through the eulogy at her dad's funeral. She fought the tears, struggled to keep her voice steady. It was the toughest speech she had ever written, ever tried to give. She had labored for hours to find the right words.

The church was filled to capacity. It was a private service by invitation only, because of security, because so many wanted to attend and the church could only seat three hundred. Her dad had been loved.

Joshua had come up to the stage with her. Her voice broke and she felt his hand come to rest against her back. She couldn't look at the crowd. She raised her eyes desperately to the back of the church instead. Marcus stood at the back of the sanctuary and her gaze caught his.

Marcus, this is so hard.

His gaze was steady as he looked back at her. He believed she could do this. He'd sat up with her for over an hour last night just listening when she hadn't been able to face turning in. He was one of the few men she had met that didn't cringe when someone cried. He'd just pushed over a Kleenex box and stayed, not trying to solve the pain, just sharing it. She took a deep breath, looked down at her notes, and when she resumed, her voice steadied.

Joshua had given his remarks before hers, and when she finished he led her from the stage back to her seat beside their mom. "You did a good job," he whispered, leaning down to hug her. She wanted desperately to give him a full hug in return, but with his arm strapped to his chest she had to accept simply wrapping one arm around his waist. "Thanks," she whispered. "So did you."

The final song began. The service was nearly over and with it part of her life.

Beth took her hand. Her mom was bearing up under this burden so much better than she was. For Shari, it was facing all over again the reality of what had happened two weeks ago. "Honey, this is a day to celebrate, despite the sadness."

Dad was in heaven. Shari forced herself to smile. She wished that fact would take away the pain, but it only made her aware of how long it would be before she saw him again. She focused on the flowers adorning the front of the stage, picking out the beautiful bouquet from the O'Malley family. She wondered if Marcus had any idea how much that gesture had meant to her mother as well as herself.

And what he had done for Josh... She didn't know how to say thanks to Marcus for what she had only now begun to notice. The one-on-one conversations between the two men, the coordination going on—Marcus had put Josh firmly in the middle of every decision being made.

Marcus's actions had passed on the mantel of head of the family, made it real and concrete. She wasn't surprised by Joshua's maturity and steadiness; under his carefree approach to life he had always been a decisive man like their father. But Marcus had given him the gift of acting on that reality. And it had helped Josh cope with his grief.

The funeral concluded. The organ music resumed as ushers came to escort them from the front pews of the church down the center aisle. The graveside service was being held at the adjacent cemetery. Shari was dreading it. There was a hole dug out there, the dirt turned up, and even the false green carpet of grass laid across that dirt and around the stark evidence would not hide the truth. She was afraid her composure would break.

Carl had been buried early that morning at Arlington National Cemetery. It had been easier to maintain her composure with that very formal ceremony. The honor guard, the folded flag, it represented the tribute of a nation to a good man.

This was the tribute of a family to a husband and father.

Marcus appeared at her elbow as the family prepared to go outside.

"There is a canopy set up to provide shelter from the wind, and they have set out chairs for the family. Please stay under the canopy after the short service until Quinn and I join you."

Shari nodded. She was very aware of the fact they were physically keeping her surrounded as she moved around outside. For the first time since the shooting almost two weeks ago, she was not in a protected environment. It had been well advertised in the media where she would be today and when. It would scare her, that realization, if she didn't have so many other emotions absorbing her.

She trusted Marcus to keep her safe.

She was the only witness to the shooting, and the burden of that sat heavily with her. Two men were being laid to rest today and justice for them now rested with her. She knew that, Marcus knew that, and somewhere out there the shooter knew that.

She walked out to the graveside with her mom and Joshua, accompanying the rest of her extended family.

Remarks at the graveside were simple. Their pastor read from Psalm 34, Dad's favorite. A prayer was said. And then two ladies from the choir closed by softly singing *Amazing Grace*. The words rang through the glowing sunset of evening with a sweetness that finally brought peace.

Shari placed the rose she held on the smooth casket. *I'm going to miss you, Dad. Until we meet again in heaven...* Her hand rested one last time on the polished wood and then she stepped away.

A chapter of her life was over.

It was a good night for a sniper, Marcus realized as he checked with the men securing the perimeter of the church property. They were running behind schedule and Marcus could feel the danger of that. Twilight was descending. In the dusk settling in the open areas around the church, around the clusters of towering oak trees, the shadows themselves spoke of hidden dangers.

The perimeter was tight, but there was a lot of open ground around this building. Marcus scanned the area as he headed to the side entrance leading into the sanctuary. With the lights on in the building and dusk turning to darkness outside, Shari was rapidly becoming a clear target. The building had too many glass windows and doors to keep her away from all of them as she mingled with the guests.

It was time to move.

Judging from the cars in the parking lot, there were still about thirty guests present. The governor and his wife had left not quite half an hour ago, and with them most of the remaining VIPs, reducing the security at the church to its lowest point for the day.

The press was being held at a distance at the entrance to the church grounds, but several were still there with their long camera lenses, hoping to get a picture or even a few words from those who had attended the private funeral.

Marcus raised Luke on the security net. "I'm changing the travel plans. We're going to take the family out the back entrance. Cue us up to leave in five minutes."

"Roger."

Shari, her mom, and Joshua were all near the front of the sanctuary talking with the minister and his wife. Marcus had been too occupied during the last hour to really look at Shari, an unfortunate reality that went with the job, it was everyone else who was the threat. He looked now and what he saw concerned him. She was folding. He could see it in the glazed fatigue, the lack of color in her face, the betraying fact Josh had noticed and now had his hand under her arm.

Definitely time to leave.

Marcus moved to join them and relieve Craig.

Shari saw him coming and broke off her conversation to join him. "Marcus, could—"

The window behind her exploded.

Shari heard someone gasp in pain and the next second Marcus swept out his right arm, caught her across the front of her chest at her collarbone, and took her feet right out from under her.

She felt herself falling backwards and it was a petrifying sensation. She couldn't get her hands back in time to break her fall and she hit hard, slamming against the floor, her back and neck taking the brunt of the impact. His arm was pressed tight across her collarbone, his hand gripping her shoulder. He wasn't letting her move even if she could.

"Shari—"

She couldn't respond her head was ringing so badly.

That had been a bullet.

She wheezed at that realization; her lungs feeling like they would explode. Around her people were screaming.

Another window shattered.

Oh, God, I don't want to die. I'm sorry for getting angry with You. Help me!

Marcus yanked her across the floor with him out of the way. "South. Shooter to the south!"

She could hear him hollering on the security net, and it was like listening down a tunnel. Who was bleeding? Someone was bleeding, she could see it on his hand.

He swore. A firm hand settled on her face. She gasped.

His elbow had nearly broken her nose.

It was coming home to her now, very much home. Someone was trying to kill her...again.

"Cover us! We're going out the back."

Shari felt herself being lifted, sandwiched between Quinn on one side, Marcus on the other. "Mom!"

"Craig's got her. Go!"

Quinn grabbed her hand to propel her forward. She knew this church, and as they moved left past the music room she got her bearings well enough to realize where they were going and managed to take the stairs with good speed.

In the back of the church they exited into darkness, surprising Shari because there should be building lights on. A van was waiting. Shari found herself literally lifted inside, after her mom. She was dazed with the speed it was happening. Joshua was helped into the front seat. She hurriedly moved over on the bench as Marcus slid in beside her and the door slammed shut. Quinn stood outside the van and slapped the side door to let the driver know he was clear, and they immediately started to move.

As they turned the corner of the building the streetlight shown through the van windows and Shari saw the bright red blood. It was a brutal flashback. The shakes hit hard. She looked toward Marcus. And she panicked.

———∞∞∞———

"You're hit!"

"It grazed me," Marcus replied forcefully, trying to get a look at her face. His left arm burned with fire as painful as getting hit directly, but he wasn't worried about himself. Shari was bleeding profusely.

She was nearly frantic. "I'm okay, Shari." He wrapped his arm around her and pulled her tight, absorbing the shakes. "I'm okay," he said deliberately. She'd seen enough people bleed.

"Lean her head back," Beth urged. "And get pressure on that bleeding." She passed up what Kleenex she had left. Marcus looked back at Shari's mom, was relieved to see her color was still good.

He turned back to Shari. "Lower your hands, let me see." His own hands were shaking as he worked to stop the bleeding. Thank goodness it didn't look like her nose was broken.

"Was anyone else hurt?" she struggled to ask.

Great question. "Craig?"

Craig was already on the closed circuit radio. It took a minute to get an answer. "No one else was hit. Tactical is moving. They are getting the last guests safely out of the building."

"What about the shooter?" Joshua asked.

"Quinn's working it," Marcus replied, knowing it was too early to get an answer to that. He had seen the cold fury on his partner's face. The shooter would likely be caught; he had to have known that, and still he had made the choice to try and kill Shari. Marcus felt a fear that went deep. They had to stop him tonight. The next time it might have a very different outcome.

They had already worked out contingencies for this; they were heading toward the Hanfords' house. They had established good security there before allowing the Hanfords to land in Virginia, and they didn't need another variable tonight. Marcus looked forward to the driver. "Luke, call ahead and get us a doctor at the house."

"Already done."

"Josh, how's that shoulder?"

"Fine."

Marcus glanced back toward the front of the van again. *Not fine.* If Josh had ripped those stitches…one problem at a time. "The press is going to be heavy at the house. News of what occurred will be out, and I wouldn't be surprised to see a television helicopter show up. So even after we stop, stay put until I clear you to move," he instructed.

It was a brief drive, for the Hanfords lived only a few miles from the church. When the van arrived at the house, Luke pulled through the security perimeter and around to the back of the house.

Marcus pushed open the van door. He counted nine men in the security detail that had assembled to meet them. "Jim?"

"We're secure."

Marcus opened the door for Josh, helped him ease out. "Keep your mom and Shari in the kitchen for a minute," he asked Josh in a low tone. "And next time lie better. You're pale as a ghost. You nailed that shoulder hard."

"Yeah. But Mom will forgive me, and what Shari doesn't know she won't worry about," Josh replied grimly. "Besides, you don't look too good yourself."

Marcus knew again why he admired this man. "Go."

He slid open the van door. "Beth." He extended his hand and helped her out. Her face was tense, but it was worry for her daughter not for herself. Marcus had come to love this lady, for she reminded him of his own mom. He gave her a brief hug and passed her to Jim. "Into the house." He turned back to the van. "Okay, Shari."

She didn't want to take his hand because of the blood staining hers. He reached in and grasped her forearms, sympathetic to the problem. She was showing definite tremors as adrenaline faded.

He didn't expect her balance to be good, and he didn't intend to risk letting her stumble. He lifted her down, ignoring the pain that tore through his arm. She started to say something, but he shook his head. "Inside." He tucked her close and hurried her toward the house.

When they entered the house the doctor who had been called was waiting and Marcus didn't give Shari a chance to turn her focus on him or her brother. He eased her into a kitchen chair and let the doctor take over. "I'm so sorry about the nose."

She leaned her head back, closed her eyes, and relaxed. "Josh has done worse. He nearly broke it one time. But if you could find a couple aspirins, I would dearly love you."

Dearly love you... In the emotions of the moment, the words first hit his heart and made him blink before his mind sorted out the figure of speech. If she ever said it and meant it...he shook his head as he inwardly smiled at his reaction, part of him still caught off guard. "Not a problem."

He got them for her, then wordlessly handed the bottle to Joshua. Finally admitting to himself how seriously he also was hurting, he swallowed four.

"Marcus, let the doctor take a look at that arm," Beth insisted.

Shari struggled to lean around the doctor to see him. The last thing he needed was Shari seeing the reality of someone else who had been shot. "In a moment," he assured Beth. He stepped out of the kitchen. "Jim, what are you hearing?"

"They got plates on a black SUV. An APB just went out. They're looking. So far—" Jim shook his head.

The shooter had gotten away. It physically hurt. "Are we in a position we can hold here for tonight?"

"Yes."

"Okay. The detail is yours while I get this gash bandaged. After the doctor looks at Joshua's shoulder, send him back to the spare bedroom."

Marcus had not yet unpacked; he wrestled his suitcase open with one hand, found a clean short sleeve shirt. He walked into the adjoining bathroom.

The bullet had scored through his suit jacket and shirt. Marcus sucked in his breath as he eased off the material. The O'Malley clan was going to be all over his case when they heard about this.

The gash wasn't deep, but it was long with very ragged edges, and it burned like fire. Marcus was grateful it hadn't cut deeper into the muscle. Another two inches over and it would have shattered bone and possibly ruined his career. *And if a fluke of glass hadn't deflected the shot, Shari would be dead.*

That was the source of the real fury he felt. He should have overruled them on the funerals and refused to let Shari attend. He should have gotten her out of the area immediately after the graveside service. Regrets didn't change reality.

He hated being shot. He was trying to wipe off the blood when the doctor joined him. "How's Joshua?"

"Bruised, but the stitches held."

The doctor was good, efficient, but did not have the bedside manner of Jennifer. "I can try and butterfly it closed or just stitch it."

Marcus did not like needles any more than Kate did. "Butterfly it."

He let out a deep breath when the doctor finally wrapped gauze around his upper arm.

"Change it tomorrow morning. If the bleeding seeps, we'll have to stitch it."

He nodded and slipped on the clean shirt. "Let Jim get you past the press out there."

"Will do."

Marcus headed back to the kitchen.

Beth had put on coffee. "Let me," she gestured to the collar he was trying to straighten one handed. "Shari went up to change, and Josh is handling the onslaught of phone calls."

"I'm sorry that William's funeral was touched this way. I'm more sorry than I can say."

She looked at the bandage on his arm, then back up at him. "We knew this risk existed, Marcus. We took a gamble and we lost, and it looks to me like you paid the price for our decision."

"It's just a graze."

"Sure it is. I'm grateful for what you did. Thank you for keeping my daughter safe." She reached up and kissed his cheek.

Marcus blushed slightly. "You're welcome." His mom had been like this, always calm despite the circumstances. And those were the best memories he had, of an innocent time before his own life had gone wrong. "I need to head back to the church. Jim will keep security tight here."

"Please be careful."

He gave a rueful smile. "You've got my word, for what it's worth at the moment."

"It is worth a lot. Godspeed, Marcus."

"Let's go back on videotape, Ben," Lisa requested. She broke the seal and entered hotel room 1319, pulling on a fresh set of latex gloves. They were looking for blood, for gunpowder residue, for fibers. With thirty-seven rooms to cover, the process was painfully slow. They had been at it for a week, working late into the evenings. This was the third room she had looked at today, and she was only doing the quick tests, a complete team was coming behind her.

She broke open the tape on a rolled up plastic guard used to give a safe footpath until fiber collection could be done. Every precaution that could be taken to preserve evidence was being made. She just hoped the effort would only be wasted in thirty-six of the thirty-seven rooms.

"Lisa."

She paused and came back to the doorway. "Yes, Walter?"

"You're going to want to see this."

She pulled off her gloves, made sure Ben had her on tape as closing, sealing, and initialing the tag for the room. She was determined to make it hard for a defense attorney to challenge the evidence collection.

She moved to join Walter at the door of room 1323.

Two technicians were working with him, and they had both stepped out into the hallway, leaving the room empty. She scanned the room. It was orderly, the bed made, but she noticed the less than straight way the bed-spread draped. Someone had disturbed it since housekeeping had last made up the room. A light gray dust used to raise fingerprints coated the furniture showing the progress the technicians had made.

There were no fingerprints. It hit her like a shock, how even the gray dust was. Not a single tape lift had been made of a print. And that made this room shout like it had been painted red. "No prints at all?" she asked, incredulous.

"Not even on the wooden coat hangers," Walter replied.

It couldn't be this obvious. "Where's the room paperwork?" Walter handed her the clipboard. She flipped through the stack of notes. "This room was not done by housekeeping since the last guest checked out on Saturday?" she asked, one eyebrow raised.

"Maintenance had been pushed off until the conference was over. This was one of a block of rooms marked unavailable so that they could upgrade fixtures in the bathroom, replace the closet doors. They were planning to also replace the shower caulking and the bathroom tile grit. The work order is here; they just hadn't gotten to this room yet. Housekeeping wasn't scheduled until after that work was done."

Lisa looked at Walter, and her friend who rarely reacted to what evidence suggested until the last lab tests were run actually smiled. "We've got the room exactly as he left it."

She looked back at the paperwork. Henry James. He had used a credit card for payment. "Fingerprints, what else?"

"We were just getting ready to luminol for blood."

"Ben, I want both you and Tom videotaping. Mark, go to the highest contrast film you have. We're going to do this room a foot at a time. Expect the traces to be faint."

Fifteen minutes later, with preparations complete, the room lights were shut off. They worked clockwise around the room.

Lisa shifted back on her heels to avoid brushing against the bedspread. Faint places began to glow as Walter sprayed the carpet. "Hold it there," Lisa asked as a streak appeared.

Against the tight weave of the carpet it appeared at first as a quarter inch wide straight line and then the smudge appeared. It rolled to the right. She frowned, studying the surprising pattern. She was expecting something from his shoes or his clothes… "He sat down, took off his shoes, and one rolled on its side."

"Shoe polish?" Walter asked, indicating with his pen dark spots in the pattern.

"I certainly hope so."

She waited until Mark had photos taken, then moved to collect several samples, using a penlight clamped between her teeth for light, sealing the swabs in vials. "I may want to cut out this piece of carpet. Grid it off."

"The hotel will love you."

"And I'm just getting started."

She completed the evidence tags on the vials.

They moved to the bedspread and found nothing. "Give us the room lights," Lisa requested. She blinked as her eyes adjusted. "Fold up the spread, we'll take it to the lab. The same with the sheets. Walter, I'm going to start working fibers on the carpet. See what you can raise in the bathroom. If he washed up—"

"I'll find it."

She used what had once been a lint brush, tape sticky side out to collect the fibers, rolling it on the carpet, then rolling the tape onto evidence strips of paper, documenting where each lift was made. It was slow work, hard on the knees, as the carpet was gone over with care to insure nothing was missed.

This evidence analysis would take hours of microscope work back at the lab. Lisa found the first visually promising fiber an hour into the work. Against the white of the paper strip, the fiber trapped by the tape was dark.

She made a side note to put this fiber strip at the front of the queue to be analyzed.

Having covered the carpet by the bed, she began working toward the wall.

"Lisa, we're negative for blood traces in the bathroom."

With the entire room wiped of fingerprints, the news was disappointing but not surprising. "I don't suppose he left the obvious? Something in the trash can?"

"Not even a gum wrapper."

"I would have preferred he left the gum," Lisa replied with a smile as she carefully lifted another tape. It was rough as she smoothed the tape against the paper. A closer look tilting it to the light showed it glittered. Glass fragments?

She looked with curiosity back at the carpet. A foot from the wall and the carpet was smooth. The shards weren't crushed deep into the fabric as if they had been vacuumed over. It was an odd place to find glass.

"Is there a glass missing from the set on the bathroom counter?"

Walter checked. "All four are here, still wrapped. What do you have?"

"I'm not sure. Do you still carry that jewelers eyepiece?"

"Sure." He passed it to her.

The light refracted through the shards captured under the tape. She looked up at the wall, saw a faint stain on the wallpaper. "Someone got mad and shattered a glass against the wall?" It would take some force to break one of the thick hotel drinking glasses.

"Walter, the housekeeping records for this room—they've got a missing and restocked items checklist on the back of the forms. Did they replace a glass recently? And have we done an inventory of the room? Towels, soaps, those plastic dry cleaning bags, the contents of the minirefrigerator—I'd like to know if anything is missing."

She worked twenty minutes lifting glass, finding nothing larger than slivers. Someone had spent time trying to clean this up. "Let's kill the room lights; I want to look again at this area."

Nothing showed when they sprayed the surface of the carpet. Lisa used a straight ruler edge to rifle the carpet fibers. A few faint glimmers appeared down in the carpet. She nodded, pleased. He'd cut himself picking up the shattered glass, probably no more than a paper cut, but it was there.

"Think there will be enough to test?" Walter asked.

"Doubtful. And it's odd that there isn't a glass missing from the room. This may be old. Mark, give us room lights."

She eased back to her feet. "Check the trash bag for any hint. And swab that stain on the wallpaper. It looks like a liquid splash the way it trails down."

She took a step back trying to get perspective on what she knew from what she suspected. No fingerprints. Everything else maybe. If she made the wrong call…"Walter, I'm going to go give Dave a heads-up. I want the room sealed when we're done and an officer assigned to sit outside the door and make sure it stays that way. Get a forensic team working on the paper trail—the guest signature card that was filled out, anything with room service."

"Will do."

She clipped on the security badge needed to get her past the security one flight up. The command center had moved to the telecommunication conference room on the fourteenth floor, freeing up the Belmont Room for the hotel and letting Dave coordinate easier an investigation now active in four states.

As soon as she entered the room, Lisa knew something was going on. The tension was palatable.

"Any word from Marcus and Quinn?" Dave asked, pacing.

"Not yet," Mike replied. "The situation is still fluid." The large screen at the far end of the room was shifting satellite feeds. "The local television station has a cameraman at the scene; we're tapping into their uplink to get a firsthand look."

It emerged out of the snow on the screen, the picture zooming in on the building, recognizable as a church even in the fading light. The audio was that of the reporter and cameraman talking to the station manager; this feed was not going out to a live audience. When the camera panned left to right, the back of the building appeared dark.

"Tactical is there," Mike observed. "There's Quinn."

"Dave."

"Not now, Lisa. Someone took a shot at Shari."

"We found the room."

"I'll be done—" He spun around. "What did you say?"

⁓

Marcus found Quinn walking across the church parking lot. "He got away."

"Left the sandbag he used to brace the rifle and walked away," Quinn replied. There was a touch of admiration in his voice; even the hunter could appreciate when an adversary made a smart move. "Come on, I'll show you."

Quinn led the way from the church grounds across a footpath that ran to the nearby ball diamond into a grove of elm trees. Marcus could hear the faint sound of water in the quiet night. There was a drainage tile forming a narrow ravine. Quinn stepped over it and up a slight rise. Large spotlights had been set up with bright yellow crime scene tape wrapped around a section of tree trunks.

The rifle lay on the ground in the underbrush, the barrel resting on a twelve-inch wide, rough fabric sandbag. Someone would have noticed a guy carrying a rifle, but leaving it and just walking away—it showed cool nerves. And the fact the shooter wasn't worried about it being traceable.

"The clear weather worked in his favor, the sun behind him, the elevation giving line of sight into the sanctuary. It appears he walked out after the shooting by circling around the shed used to hold the groundskeeping equipment for the ball diamonds. The SUV was sighted there."

"Our patrols?"

Quinn tipped his powerful flashlight to the right and luminated a crushed path through the tall grass going through the grove. "Our two man patrol. The guy was fifteen feet away and wasn't seen. He probably had his blind in place before dawn."

Marcus swore.

"We've got an APB out on the black SUV, it had local plates but we don't have the tag numbers. No one apparently saw him but we're canvassing for a mile. And I've got men getting copies of all the video shot by both the news media on the ground and the helicopters flying over this area."

"Is it the same man?"

Quinn handed him a .308 shell casing. "Someone that gets flustered enough to miss at close range and someone skilled enough to miss by an inch at two hundred yards on a windy day through thick glass?"

"Two shooters."

"Two shooters."

Marcus crumpled the soda can in his fist.

"Make them disappear," Quinn advised.

"You have a preference?"

"Both shooters have shown they can blend with the city. Let's get them on our turf."

"Agreed."

"How bad were you hit?"

"It hurts," Marcus replied tersely. "Quinn, I'm tired of being on the receiving end."

"Tell me about it." Quinn rubbed his own arm. "They're two for two, and next time it's not going to be one of us."

"Have we ever had a case where we *both* got winged?"

"No. And it's beginning to make me mad," Quinn replied. "Did you hear the news from Dave? Lisa thinks she found the room."

It was the first good news of the evening. "I knew she would come through."

"Stubborn lady. I'm going to owe her dinner."

"If you're lucky, she'll collect on the debt."

Quinn smiled. "True. Listen, head back to the house and get the Hanfords ready to move at first light. There's not much else to do here. We're going to stay and canvas again at daybreak, but this scene looks contained. We'll start tracing what we've got down to the type of sand used in the bag. The rifle, the bag, even the way he set up to make the shot—something is going to register with an existing MO. This wasn't his first time; it's too high profile an attempt."

"Agreed. Find him, Quinn."

"Between Lisa and me, these two shooters are going to wish they had never thought of reaching out to kill a judge, let alone threaten a lady you like."

Marcus shared a look with his partner, then simply slapped Quinn's shoulder and turned to head back to the van. Quinn knew him. This case had long ago become very personal. He'd like to wring the neck of the man who had gone after Shari. He'd settle for putting him behind bars for life.

Shari carefully lowered herself to the edge of her bed, her back muscles aching. The headache had grown in intensity.

God, I'm sorry. You've got a generous, merciful heart. Forgive me for being a jerk. I'm sorry I turned a cold shoulder to You. Not talking to You only hurt me.

She wrapped her arms around her waist. The man who had killed Carl and her dad had tried again to kill her. That fear made it hard to think. She wished Marcus were here. Even though he had been injured, she knew he wouldn't let that danger push him away. He would know what she needed to do.

She was worried about him, out there tracking the man who had done this. She was only now beginning to appreciate the fury she had sensed in Marcus this evening as events had unfolded. She hoped he wouldn't take any undue risks. She didn't want anyone else hurt because of her.

She couldn't stay here with her family. She was putting Josh and Mom in danger. She didn't know how to deal with that fear.

It was so confusing, everything that had happened. All the way back to Sam. Her life was in tatters. *God, I need time to figure this out and deal with all these emotions. And I need You to keep me safe. I've been hurt and angry, but now I'm scared and I'm rushing back to You because I know You are the One who is my refuge.*

There was a tap on the door. She looked up and smiled slightly. "You look like you feel worse than I do."

Josh crossed the room to join her. "I sometimes think the doctor's help is worse than the injury. And it takes forever for the muscle relaxants to kick in. How are you doing?"

She knew her face was bruised and swollen. And her jarred back and spine made movement come at a high price. "I'll be okay." She looked at her brother as he sat down. "What are we going to do, Josh?"

"First, get that tone of defeat out of your voice. We're okay." He brushed back her hair. "He won't get another chance at you. We'll make certain of that."

"Josh, he almost shot Mom. Another few inches to the left—"

"He didn't."

"I can't take the chance he'll try again." She wanted to run and didn't know how or where.

"We'll let Marcus make the recommendation on what we do next."

Her brother was handling this so much better than she was. He hadn't once complained about the fact he had been shot, and his recovery had been far from easy. She sighed. "Tomorrow, I want you to update my will."

"Shari!"

She shook her head. "It's not morose thinking. I want to know everything is in order. Because Dad's is so out of date it's making dealing with the estate a problem. And he is listed as my executor." Somewhere in the house a phone rang. "You should probably forward the phone to the answering service again." Their phone number was unlisted, but that hadn't mattered. The press had found it. They had hired a firm to take messages.

"Mom is waiting on a call from Margaret."

"Josh, it's for you," Beth called from downstairs.

He got to his feet. "Come downstairs. It's not good to brood."

She smiled when he ruffled her hair. "In a minute. Thanks, Josh."

"Sure."

Shari was still up. Marcus had been expecting that, even though it was close to midnight. She wouldn't find sleep this evening easy.

"Can I get you some coffee?" she offered, getting up from the kitchen table where she had been sitting, reading a book.

"Please."

Shari poured him a cup.

He hadn't seen her before he left to return to the church; what he saw now made him wince. He had really done a number on her face. "Let me see." He crossed over to her and tipped up her chin. "You need some ice on that cheek." He rubbed his thumb very lightly across the darkening bruise, absorbing the pain of what had happened. He'd hurt her. It left a deep ache inside. If only he had been able to react faster...

"Marcus, don't worry about it. It's like walking away from a car wreck with only a bruise—you definitely don't mind the bruise. You saved my life."

"I think the wind and a thick plate glass window did that. I just helped."

She smiled, reached up, and kissed his cheek. "I'll take helped. And I will let you get me that ice. It's starting to ache again."

He hesitated for a moment, feeling an unexpected warmth roll through his chest. *Shari, you have the habit of slipping under my guard. I don't mind, but I wish I deserved it. I let you and your family down.*

He had been afraid she would come out of this crisis quivering in shock, but she was rolling with it. When it was her family in danger it was one thing, herself another. He felt the same kind of admiration coupled with unease he felt with Kate. His sister never let the danger she was in bother her, and Shari was mirroring that by trying to keep a strong front in place.

He shook off the distracted thoughts and moved to the freezer. He improvised an ice pack with a clean towel. "Try this."

She winced when she touched the cold to the soreness. "It will help." She sat back down at the table and watched him. "This is proving to be a very rough day."

"A terrible, horrible, no good, very bad day," Marcus replied, borrowing a line from the children's story. It was that or apologize again, and he was starting to sound like a broken record.

"No luck with the shooter?"

He shook his head, debating with himself how much to tell her. He wasn't ready yet to tell her they suspected there were two shooters. Not until he had spoken with Josh. "There is a lead on his vehicle. We're looking." He sat down with his coffee. "In the morning we're going to be moving you from this house to a place that is more secure."

"All of us?"

"Yes."

"I would prefer not to be near Josh and Mom."

"I can understand why you feel that way, but I think it's best if you stay together. Once you're tucked somewhere that hasn't been broadcast by the media to the world at large, the situation will be much easier to manage. Your mom needs the rest, and she won't get it if you're someplace else and she's staying here amid the security we would have to bring in. Josh needs to focus on regaining his strength, and being battered by the press isn't going to help him out. Think of it as a much needed family vacation."

He watched her rub her forehead with her hand before she looked up at him. "I don't mean to make this difficult, but how long do we plan for? Days? Weeks? I've got two estates to deal with. My job. The campaign. It's not like I can walk away from all of this and come back later. In an election, every day is critical. I need to give John and Anne some idea of what I can do, what has to be transferred to others."

"When you are out on the campaign trail, you're working by phone, e-mail, and fax. Pack up what you will need and plan to work that way for the next few weeks. You can still work behind the scenes, just not from here."

"I'm going to have to go through all the paperwork here just to know what I need for Dad's estate, the same at Carl's home office."

"Ask your secretary to box it up and we'll arrange to transport it; you and Josh can go through it together."

"Can I at least sleep in tomorrow morning before I have to pack?"

He smiled at that. "Sure, as long as you're packed by seven. This is for the best, Shari. I wouldn't ask it if it wasn't."

"I know. I don't have to like it, but I do believe you."

"You killed a judge! Just like that...*poof*. I will kill a federal judge!"

Connor had walked into the family estate prepared for this explosion from his father. The demand that Connor come had arrived with blunt intensity within minutes of Titus's return from Europe. For ten minutes he had taken it...but no more. "He sent my brother to his death. *Your eldest son.* But you ignore that. You let it pass without reply. Someone has to look at what that means for the family name. You make it weak!"

His father turned at that, swift as a cobra, his voice cold. "Because you are my son I will forget that you said that. But do not push me again. We are not too weak to act...we are too powerful! This family cannot afford the ire of the government, and you have brought it to our front door. This is no longer a business where passion rules but pragmatic power. You learned nothing from what I have spent fifteen years teaching!"

Connor was aware of Anthony, his father's first lieutenant, pacing outside the room, and for the first time he felt the touch of fear cross his spine as he faced his father's anger. For the first time he felt the irreversibility of what he had done. He braced his feet.

He had been in this study since his childhood answering to his father. Anthony would understand why he had acted and killed, Anthony was the old school. But he was left cooling his heels outside, which said his father had already overruled Anthony's suggestion for what should be done.

"Who helped you?"

Connor thought about lying but knew it would be useless. "Frank."

"I'm glad you admit it."

His father tossed the newspaper onto the desk, the hated sketch on the front page below the fold. "You were careless."

"There is no evidence connecting me to the shooting. There is only one witness. The others didn't see me," he replied, willing to placate. "She can be eliminated."

"So I see," Titus replied with great irony. "You did a great job with that too."

"Frank missed. He won't next time."

"Frank has been taken care of."

Connor blinked. Titus had killed his cousin? A chill crossed his spine at the dismissive way his father had said it.

"Did you really think you could set me up, Connor?"

Still feeling the cold of the previous comment, this one caught Connor off guard. "What? I didn't—"

"Because I didn't know what was happening in my own family, I am now liable for conspiracy for the murder of a federal judge. It was my eldest son sentenced to death by Judge Whitmore. Frank worked for me. I paid him while he went on those errands for you. Whether I ordered it or not, as the saying goes, 'the buck stops here.' I can't prove I didn't know what you and Frank were planning. The jury will assume I not only sanctioned it but set it in motion."

"That wasn't—"

Titus waved him to silence. "My interests happen to coincide with yours—for the moment. I solved your problem. I hired Lucas Saracelli. Your witness is as good as dead. But now I ask you. Who's going to solve my problem? You!"

Connor knew he was in trouble as that cold fury hit him. "I have no interest—"

"Shut up. You will go back to your law office, back to your good job, and you will keep your mouth shut. You will toe the line so hard that it squeaks. And to help you out, Joseph is joining your firm tomorrow. He is at your side until I say otherwise. And Connor…I mean it. Keep your mouth shut. Now get out."

Connor wisely left.

Ten

It was a former hunting lodge, now someone's expensive vacation home, with two wings of bedrooms around a central kitchen, den, and living room. It sat a few hundred feet from a sprawling lake. Shari wondered who had owed the marshals a favor; it must have been a big one.

"The town is two miles to the east," Marcus commented, pausing beside her on the spacious porch. "We know all the residents of these homes by sight."

"Would it be too much to ask where we are?"

"The middle of nowhere."

"You are obstinate. How about the state?"

"Area code 502, given you'll find that out when we set up a mirrored e-mail account."

"The western part of Kentucky."

He laughed. "Nice to know you remember the important things in life." The laughter faded and the seriousness returned. "There are ground rules."

Having had them drilled into her by both Marcus and Joshua, she felt like rolling her eyes. "No one is told this location; all phone calls are made on the special cellular phone you got me; all mail is routed through my office."

"And you go nowhere without a shadow."

"I was hoping you had forgotten that one."

"Not likely. Choose your room, I'll bring in your bags. East if you want a sunrise, west if you want to sleep in."

"West," she said decisively. It felt good to make a firm decision for her-self. She took one step toward the front door but then paused and came back. She hesitated, then rested her hand on his arm. "We're safe here, Marcus?" *You're safe?* She didn't want anyone else getting shot because of her.

His hand covered hers, linked with her fingers, offering a reassuring grip. "Only two people know where we were heading: Quinn and Dave. I didn't even tell the pilot until we were in the air, and he's got a memory that is notoriously forgetful."

She felt the intensity in his gaze, the strength in this man. She wanted to cling and did tighten her hand in his. "Thank you for this."

He reached up and brushed back her hair, blown by the wind across her face, his gaze holding hers. "I'll do everything I can to keep you and your family safe; that's a promise."

Did he understand what that meant to her, to have a man care that much? He had already demonstrated he'd take a bullet for her. She was growing attached to him in ways that went deep into her heart. She released his hand, placed hers on his chest for a moment and with a quiet nod, turned and wisely went inside.

It was a beautiful home, a place to retreat and let time heal some deep wounds, a place to get her perspective back together. Marcus was sliding into the void left by Sam, and as powerfully beautiful as it was to be cheri-shed by such a man, she knew their futures would eventually diverge. She was sold out to God, and he was still struggling with a difficult past. To face another heartache so soon after Sam... *Jesus, I didn't choose any of this. Don't let me get hurt again. And please, don't let me hurt Marcus. It's the last thing in the world I ever want to happen.*

Marcus dropped his bag by the side of the bed, wearily unfastened his shoulder holster and secured the 9-millimeter Glock and placed it beside the bed. He sank into the pillows face down, let the mattress absorb his weight, felt the sunlight streaming in the west window warm his back. They were safely here; it had been his one focused goal and it had been accomplished. Craig had security for the next few hours. Unpacking could come later.

Marcus fell deeply asleep and didn't waste energy dreaming.

He was pulled awake by a noise he couldn't ignore.

His pager was going off.

He had no idea how much time had passed, five minutes, several hours. All he was certain of was that he had been deeply asleep. His eyes blurred as he read the numbers, and he had to squint. Baltimore. Jennifer.

His hand groped across the bedside table for his cellular phone and he dialed from memory. "Hi, precious. How are you doing?" he asked sleepily.

"Much better for hearing that endearment."

"Tom might be your guy now, but I'm not giving up that title easily. You've been my precious since I chaperoned your first date." He shoved a pillow under his shoulder to make himself more comfortable. "You sound better than you did yesterday."

"I got a reprieve, treatment was moved to this afternoon."

"Did your latest company arrive?"

Jennifer giggled. "No, but I know they are on their way. Stephen has sent a dozen pages tracking their progress across the country. And he's been calling from the plane to tell me these stupid jokes. I keep telling him to stop, and Jack just keeps telling Stephen new ones to pass along. The last call was from the airport here, they were just getting ready to land."

"No wonder you're giggling. Jack's jokes can make your ribs hurt from laughing so hard."

"Exactly, and laughter's good medicine." Her tone became more serious. "I just wanted to call and tell you the Rugsby trail is ready."

The conspiracy had begun. "What did you and Rachel decide on?"

"The Rugsby ransom requires each O'Malley to do something specific. Seven letters are ready to be sent."

"Am I going to groan when I open mine?"

"Yours is the best of all of them."

"Jennifer—"

She laughed. "This is so much fun. Rachel is going to mail them tomorrow."

"I knew I was starting something I would live to regret."

"The only way out of paying the ransom is to figure out who took Rugsby. He's well hidden?"

"Definitely." He'd just arranged for the animal to be shipped back to

Rachel; she didn't know it was coming. It would give her a bit of a jolt when the mail arrived. "Lisa might figure it out if you give her enough time to work on it."

"The ransom is payable in a month. We should be okay." Her tone changed; she laughed. "I just got invaded, and Stephen's carrying one of the ugliest wrapped packages I have ever seen."

"Since I know what he's bringing you, you don't know the half of it," Marcus replied with a smile. "Talk to you later, Jen."

"Bye, Marcus."

He hung up the phone, awake now, but not in a hurry to get up. He was glad he had set the entire Rugsby silliness into motion. Jennifer's laughter helped ease at least one source of concern. She was a fighter, his sister, even if she was the soft, gentle one in his family. And he wanted—needed—to see her soon just to share a hug.

Stephen had found Jennifer a truly ugly shirt. It was loud, obnoxious, startling, and just the kind of thing to make her laugh. Knowing Jennifer, she'd wear it too.

Marcus linked his hands behind his head, found his thoughts drifting sharply back to Shari and what had happened.

Two shooters. What did that tell him about the man who had killed Carl? It reaffirmed what shooting Carl had told him—the man would take big risks. Two people involved meant he would risk having someone else who would be able to turn and testify against him. His frustration would be high after this failure. And he would likely try again. Marcus sighed, glad he had been able to get all the Hanfords relocated.

It was going to be a long day.

He picked up the phone. "Dave, where are we at? Do we have anything on the rifle?"

He arrived on a midmorning Tuesday flight into O'Hare from Saudi Arabia and took his leisure checking through customs. His jeans were worn, his blue casual shirt bore the small logo of an oil drilling company, and his boots were scuffed. A man accustomed to working anywhere at short notice, a veteran of worldwide travel, he was relaxed as his one bag was scanned, his passport checked. His passport gave his name as Larry Sanders but his real name was Lucas Saracelli.

His only luggage was the one carry-on bag. Once through customs he stopped at the first shop with newspapers and bought the *Chicago Tribune* and the *Chicago Sun Times*. He was behind on the sports news. At a pay phone he called a private taxi service that came in limousines rather than yellow cabs, then walked down the concourse. He'd get a good steak and fries for dinner he decided and find a bar with a baseball game. It was good to be back in the States.

His ride was pulling up as he exited the terminal. Lucas handed his bag to the driver to stash in the trunk, took a seat in the back of the limousine, and reached for the complimentary soda sitting in ice. "Take me to the Jefferson Renaissance Hotel please." He had long ago learned the easiest place to begin a search was at the beginning.

Shari Hanford.

He thought about the picture he had been sent as he drank the soda, scanned the first newspaper, and occasionally glanced up to watch the towering city skyline grow ever closer.

A witness.

He sighed. He hated going after witnesses.

At least there would be security around her and he wouldn't have to take down someone totally defenseless. He hoped the men on her side were good at their jobs. If this hit turned out to be easy, it would leave a bitter taste for months.

He had to find her first.

It was the part of a contract he enjoyed the most.

Arriving in the middle of the day had shortened the commute time. The driver pulled up to the entryway of the Jefferson Renaissance Hotel before Lucas finished reading the first newspaper. He folded the two papers and tucked them under one arm, gave the driver a generous tip, and entered the foyer of the hotel looking around with interest at the press and the security present.

At the desk he flirted with the receptionist, signed the register, and accepted a room key. He was given a room on the seventh floor and after dropping his bag at the end of the bed, opening the drapes, turning down the air-conditioning to cold, and placing the do not disturb tag on the door, he wandered back down to the bar. "What's all the excitement about?" Within five minutes he had found a reporter eager to be a fountain of knowledge.

Eleven

I t had rained during the night. Shari sipped her coffee and watched the wind stir the lake waters. The sky was just beginning to lighten as the sun came up, the blue very pale, the one cloud in sight tinged pink. She sat watching from the window seat in the den, the spot she had chosen over the last four days as her favorite in this spacious home. For wanting to sleep in, she had been awake way too early. The bad dreams had been there again, just beyond memory, and the anxious feeling as she awoke was just beginning to fade.

The nearby trees in her line of sight had shed some of their leaves and their trunk and branches were black silhouettes against the lightening sky behind them. Black and stark could be quite beautiful. It was an unexpected observation. There were times when black and stark could be turned into something of great beauty.

Thanks for that reminder, Lord.

She saw Marcus and Quinn reappear from around the boathouse. She braced her chin on her drawn up knee and watched the two men. She had been surprised when she first saw them down at the lake. When did those two sleep? She wondered at times if they did.

Steam was rising off the lake waters behind them. She was beginning to think this was one of the most peaceful, beautiful places she had ever stayed.

It was quiet here. She had been up almost an hour and the phone had not rung. She had her time to think. And over the last few days she had spent a lot of time doing just that.

Having life stop had shown her a pattern to her life that she didn't necessarily like to see. To distract herself from the pain of her breakup with Sam she had turned her focus to work. To distract herself from grieving for Carl and Dad she had been using the long list of funeral and estate details. She had been using anything to push away the confusion over prayer. She had been hiding, and that was for a coward.

Her life wasn't going as she had planned, and she had let anger flare toward God rather than step back and reconsider what was propelling her.

She wanted a life in public service, wanted it with a passion that went back to her teens. It was the noble cause her father had inspired. And she wanted a family. She had defined what those two things looked like, had defined the timetable for them, and for someone who prided herself on her ability to be flexible and compromise to get things done, she had been rigid when they came apart.

She didn't want to rethink her life, but she was getting a chance, tucked away here, stripped of the time demands that drove her schedule when she was working at home.

She wanted another distraction. She *needed* a distraction. And he was walking back to the house right now. Marcus.

What would have happened if they had simply been able to have coffee that Saturday morning? If none of this had happened? She'd never know.

He had gotten shot protecting her. And he was here with her family when she knew he would rather be with his sister. She wished she knew what made him tick. He was a fascinating man, hard to get to know because he was a man with so many deep layers, but a true friend.

If only he hadn't pushed away God…. She sighed and avoided following the thought.

She picked up the pad of paper she had carried downstairs with her. It was time to work out what her priorities had to be for the day. She missed her newspapers. She always started the day with coffee and a stack of newspapers to peruse.

Priorities for today. She wrote down one word with a grimace. *Estate.* The boxes of information had arrived last night. Today she would sort and try to get a handle on what was there to deal with.

"You're up early."

She started. Marcus was going to give her a heart attack with his habit of sneaking up on her. She hadn't heard him enter the house.

"I couldn't sleep." She looked hopefully at him. "I don't suppose the newspapers have come?"

"Sorry. It will be another day before they are being forwarded."

"This is worse than taking the batteries out of my phone."

"Had breakfast yet?"

"The least you could do is sympathize."

He grinned. "That you don't have your dozen newspapers? You need to get a life for a few days."

"It appears I've got no choice. Breakfast—you're not on duty? I saw you walking with Quinn."

"Craig has the detail until noon." He held out his hand.

Shari set aside the pad of paper and let him pull her to her feet.

"So what do you have on your agenda for the day?"

She groaned. "Paperwork."

Shari reached into the cardboard bankers box for another thick file folder. She had always thought of her dad as organized until she sat down to go through all the paperwork. Arrayed around her on the table and floor were various stacks of information—insurance, stocks, car titles, bank statements, tax return information. Her laptop was open and she was trying to complete a spreadsheet of everything the estate would need to have appraised.

"Josh, have you found the paperwork on Grandfather's farmland?"

"Somewhere." Her brother searched through the stacks on the coffee table. "Here it is."

She added it to physical assets.

The folder she had picked up was past brokerage statements. She began putting them into date order. In the back of the folder she stumbled on a set of pictures that must have fallen into the box when it was packed.

The top image brought an instinctive laugh. She must have been about twelve in the picture, Joshua nine. They were both draped around a dog that had earned the name Mutt. She flipped through the others from the camping trip they had taken to the Rockies. "Oh my. Mom, you'll like these."

Beth had the photo albums open around her. Shari handed the pictures over. "We had such fun on this trip. I remember standing on the Great Divide in the snow while Dad took our picture. And the striped chipmunks that would eat peanuts. Oh, and that lake that turned pale pink when the sun set."

"Don't forget the trout," Joshua added.

Shari glanced out the window at the lake. "Do you suppose this lake has good fishing?"

"It's a great lake for bass fishing," Marcus replied from the doorway.

Shari swiveled around. "Really? Could we go fishing sometime?"

"You would have to be willing to get up at dawn."

"I could do that."

"We might be able to some time," Marcus agreed. "Beth, could I speak with you for a moment?"

"Of course. I was just about to get some iced tea. Come join me."

Shari watched her mom take Marcus's arm as they left the room. "What do you suppose those two are up to now?" she asked Josh, slightly envious of her mom for the close relationship she had formed with Marcus.

"They were talking about the nearby town this morning over breakfast. I know Mom would like to visit the local shops," Josh replied, not looking up from the paper he was reading. "What do you want to do about the contents of the safe deposit box? There's a note that the original of this document is there."

Shari turned her attention back to the task that had to be done. "Do you think Dad's secretary can access it for us?"

"I'll write up a limited power of attorney from the estate."

"I can arrange a birthday cake from the local bakery," Marcus suggested once he and Beth were in the kitchen away from Shari's hearing. Finding out Shari's birthday was a week from Saturday had thrown him. It was bad enough she would have to deal with her father and Carl not being present, but to also have to spend her birthday here, away from her friends—it left a bad taste.

Beth poured herself a glass of iced tea. "I've got plenty of time to do some baking. I'd just need you to get my recipe file sent from the house. How about a chocolate cake with a layer of pudding inside?"

"Is chocolate her favorite cake?"

"She's a cupcake person. Don't worry; I'll make her several. She likes lots of icing and those colorful sprinkles on top."

"Does she?" Marcus smiled. "Well, I personally love the idea of a chocolate cake."

"Will we be able to go shopping for gifts?"

"The trip will have to be planned, but it won't be a problem. I'll get you a list of shops that are in town. Getting Shari occupied elsewhere will be the real problem."

"Nonsense. You can take her out to lunch or a movie while Josh and I shop."

"Subtle, Beth."

"I like you. Shari could do far worse."

He looked at her, at this lady he had come to admire, and had to smile. "She's a witness. Please remember that."

"You won't be protecting her forever. You're good for my daughter."

It didn't do any good to point out the problems. The stark difference in backgrounds. The fact he couldn't say he believed. Beth had already heard them and waved them aside. Shari could adjust; he could change. And Marcus was amused to realize he knew better than to assume Beth wouldn't get her way. "And you're the nicest mom I've ever protected."

"The only one."

"Still the nicest." Marcus accepted a glass of iced tea. "You remind me of my own mom."

"One of the highest compliments I think you could give me."

His pager went off. "Excuse me, Beth."

He walked down the hall to get some privacy. "Yes, Dave."

"Washington called. The president has made a choice for the Supreme Court nomination. He's going with Judge Paul Nelcort."

Marcus frowned. "When will it be announced?"

"There will be a White House Rose Garden announcement at 2 P.M."

He moved to where he could see Shari. "The timing could be better."

"I thought you could use a heads-up before they find out the news."

"I appreciate that." This moment had been inevitable, but it was going to cut sharp. When he hung up, Marcus found himself torn over whether to tell them now or wait.

Beth touched his arm. "There's news?" she asked, concerned.

He nodded. Best to do it now rather than wait. "Let's join the others."

He walked back into the room with Beth at his side. Shari was laughing with Josh, and it was a sound Marcus had rarely heard. He didn't want to rob that laughter from her.

Shari's smile slowly faded when his serious expression registered. "Something has happened."

There was no way to cushion this but to simply say it. "The president has decided to nominate Judge Paul Nelcort to the Supreme Court."

It was a shock; there was no other way to describe how she took the news. It brought back that night, that image of seeing Carl die. Marcus saw it happen and willed her to push through that pain. There was nothing he could say that would make that easier to deal with. She just had to accept it.

"He's a good man," she finally said. She got up from her seat, crossed toward Mom, then shook her head. Her fist struck the door frame as she turned toward the stairs. "Excuse me."

"Let her go, Marcus," Beth said, stopping him with a hand on his arm.

"She's feeling this was her fault. That she wrote that brief."

"I know. But telling her it's not true won't change what she's feeling."

Shari pushed the clothes she had tossed on her bed that morning to the floor and sprawled face down on the comforter. The emotions roiled and she grabbed a pillow to silently bury her head against it. She wasn't going to let herself cry. She wasn't!

Jesus, the only thing I can do is pray that the shooter will be found. Please. I lift that prayer to You again. I've been doing my best to quietly trust You like Mom does, but this…my heart fractures. I need there to be justice for Carl. I need the shooter found. It feels like You don't care. I know that isn't true, but the days pass without news. And I'm afraid of him! I need him found.

She rolled over and reached for her Bible on the end table. She turned to the bookmark she had left at Psalm 4 that morning. The first verse had caught her attention.

"Answer me when I call, O God of my right! Thou hast given me room when I was in distress. Be gracious to me, and hear my prayer."

She had hung onto that verse when she found it, for it not only expressed David's own moments of turmoil with God, his distress, but also his similar need to have a prayer answered. She read the words again and clung to them.

Lord, You're a God who loves justice. Bring justice. Swift, complete justice.

She rolled back over and looked up at the ceiling. *And Lord, maybe it's time to also say one other quiet, private prayer. Please let Marcus reconsider believing in You.*

She needed a future, and she wanted him in it. And she needed someone to talk to. It couldn't be family, for they would only be hurt by the questions she'd ask. Marcus could help.

Marcus closed the phone, frustrated. Someone took a shot at Shari and they had no leads. All the evidence they had and right now it led exactly *nowhere.*

"Someone will see him, someone will talk," Quinn observed from his seat at the other end of the front porch. "It will happen. Just because the rifle has led nowhere doesn't mean someone didn't know what was planned. Two people are involved. That's one too many. Somewhere the nibble is going to appear."

"Care to take a trip back to Chicago and help shake that tree?"

Quinn tipped back his hat and glanced over. "If you like."

"I think so. We're secure here." Marcus leaned against the porch railing, studying the trees. There were men watching the road, and three patrols covering the grounds. They knew flights that came in to the small local airport, and guests that checked into the local hotels. This location was secure, but someone determined… They had to find the man who shot Carl soon or he was eventually going to find them and make another attempt.

"Lisa will come up with something from the room."

"Maybe."

"What's with the pessimism? You're normally the optimistic one of the two of us."

Marcus swung his arms in front of him, restless. "This case is different."

"I've noticed," Quinn replied dryly.

"I don't mean Shari, well, not entirely."

"I know, Marcus. Someone killed a judge this time. It's different,"

Quinn agreed. "At least the Hanfords seem to have settled in here. It's not a bad place to stay if we need it for a few weeks."

"Shari's not sleeping," Marcus said heavily. A glance back at the house showed the den lights were still on. She had settled there after dinner with a pad of paper, working on a speech for John, and she was still there now, long after Beth and Josh had turned in.

"Did you really think it wouldn't be a problem, having been shot at twice?"

"It would help if she would talk about it."

"She will when she's ready."

As the days passed, Marcus wondered if she would ever get to that point. "She needs to blow off some stress."

"See if she likes to play basketball."

"What?"

"She's not the only one who needs to blow off some stress. You're pacing. And you don't pace. If you're not going to open a Bible and start resolving the questions you've been avoiding for years, then at least admit what avoiding them is doing to you. Ever since news of Jennifer's illness broke, you've been building to the point you're going to blow."

"I know you're a Christian, Quinn, but I really don't want to talk about it."

Quinn swung his feet down from the railing. "Good enough. I'll be around when you do. When Josh goes into town for physical therapy, take Shari over to the gym near the hospital. I'm sure it would be possible to reserve some private court time."

Shari playing basketball. It was an interesting idea. And goodness knows he would love to run the court for a while. "I'll think about it."

Quinn scanned the dark night. "When do you want to relieve me?"

"6:00 A.M.?"

"Sounds good. I'll schedule a flight back to Chicago, sleep on the plane."

Marcus straightened from the porch railing. "Say hello to Lisa for me."

"That sounded like a subtle push to me."

"Do you need one?"

"Nope."

"I didn't think so. I'll see you in the morning, Quinn."

His partner nodded.

Marcus opened the door and walked by memory through the dark house to the kitchen. The fatigue was heavy, and normally he would have taken advantage of going off duty to get some sleep. Instead he found himself retrieving two tall glasses, opening the freezer, and finding ice cream. He got out two sodas and set about making two floats.

He walked through to the den.

Shari was curled up in the big leather chair, several pages of a yellow pad of paper turned back. She was spinning a pen between her fingers, lost in thought. Marcus paused in the doorway for a moment just to enjoy the sight.

There were deep stapled stacks of research materials, read and underlined, dropped on the floor around her. He could see her early frustration in the wadded up pages tossed toward the wastebasket. She was struggling to find the words. She started writing, ran out of room at the bottom of the page, and rather than turn to a new page, turned the pad and wrote in the margins.

He waited until she finished writing. "Making progress?"

She glanced over. "Finally. You can't believe how hard it is to make the environmental issues surrounding water resource management something interesting to listen to. John's got a great legislative initiative drafted, but writing a speech that can convince people why it matters to their lives just like taxes and education—even I'm having a problem staying awake."

She accepted the float. "I'm going to get spoiled if you keep this up."

"Sure you are." He settled on the couch across from her. He enjoyed the picture she made, curled up, comfortable.

She set aside the pad of paper to sample the float. "Very nice."

"Drink slow, you'll get an ice cream headache."

"Warning noted."

He reached down, picked up one of the wadded pages, and lofted it toward the basket.

She winced when it went cleanly in. "Ouch."

"I'm a better shot than you."

"True. But I wasn't trying very hard."

"Your competitive streak is showing."

"Good. I would like to think Josh taught me something."

"I saw you working weights with him this afternoon. How's he doing?"

"His good arm is just about back to full strength. He's ready to see the physical therapist."

"It's all arranged. He starts tomorrow afternoon."

She nodded and went quiet.

He settled back, enjoying his float, waiting, wondering what her topic for tonight would be. She always had one. Ever since those early days at the hotel when late night room service had become habit, they had talked late at night after the others had turned in. Marcus enjoyed the time.

"Tell me about your sister."

They had talked a lot about family in the recent weeks. He had been drawing her out about her dad, pulling out the good memories. She in turn was fascinated with his large family, had seen the photos in his wallet and laughed at the humorous stories he told. "Which one?"

"Kate."

Marcus sank down against the back of the couch, feeling the taut fabric give slightly. "My middle of the night phone buddy," he said easily, in simple words encapsulating the heart of his relationship with Kate. She had always been there no matter what the time or reason for the call, and it had been the same going the other direction. Those hours in the middle of the night were priceless to him.

Kate had been kidding him recently about the unusually late hour of his calls. Marcus had not told her they were getting delayed because he was first chatting with Shari. He knew Kate wouldn't mind, but she would find that fact too fascinating for comfort.

To describe Kate…he didn't want to brush off the question with a simplistic answer. It was sometimes hard for people to see the real Kate behind the impassive negotiator wall she presented: polite, nice, but very hard to know what was going on behind her watchful gaze.

"As a negotiator, she's without compare. The higher the pressure, the more bored she appears. Kate is…it's hard to put into words. She's the heart and soul of the O'Malley family. I may be the leader of the group, but Kate is the fighter, the courage, the well of fire that cements us together. She's the passion behind all that we are. When trouble strikes, she jumps in with both feet, plants herself, and takes the battlefield with her elbows out. When she's beside you, it doesn't matter what the odds are, you can relax; she's like a big rock, immovable. She defends the family. I love her for that."

"And you defend Kate."

"When she needs it. I would trust her with my life and have on occasions. Kate's the one who knows my secrets."

"All of them?"

She doesn't know I'm enchanted with you, but she's a very perceptive lady. She's probably already figured that out. Your name has a habit of coming up a lot.

"Almost all of them. She doesn't have to know that I did kind of push her toward Dave, or that I punched the boy harassing her in sixth grade, or once had Jack swipe her car keys so she couldn't go after a fellow cop that blew a negotiation—minor stuff like that."

"For the good of the family kind of secrets."

"Something like that. You still owe me another one of yours. I'm ahead."

"You need to check your tally."

"Scout's honor."

"Were you ever a scout?"

"No."

She wrinkled her nose at him. "I'll give you the benefit of the doubt." She settled more comfortably against the leather chair. "Let's see, another secret…" She smiled suddenly. "I voted for my opponent when I was running for high school senior class president."

"You threw a political race?" He found that idea amusing.

"Just one vote. We had this debate on the small wattage radio station that the high school guys ran. I found my opponent's arguments very persuasive."

"Who won the race?"

"I did. By a landslide," she admitted. "But then I understood the need for a turn-out-the-vote drive the day of the election."

"It sounds to me like you wanted to make sure he got at least one vote."

"Well…maybe that too."

"Was that your first taste of politics?"

"It was running for office. I'd been stuffing envelopes, passing out campaign literature as a volunteer since I was twelve. I fell in love with the idea of campaigns and the intricacies of issues and getting your guy to win."

It was new to him, meeting someone with politics as her passion. He found he enjoyed it. There was depth to her knowledge of issues that he admired, and more than once he had gotten her to debate with equal fervor both sides of the same issue. She worked very hard to understand the point and counterpoints to an issue. It was a work ethic he really admired. "When did you start writing speeches?"

"I'd see campaign flyers, and think they didn't get the message across. So I'd rewrite them. I'd listen to John give speeches; he would ask what I thought, so I'd tell him. I would quote back what worked and what didn't. Anne finally hired me. I fell in love with the job."

"A self-starter."

"Or at least able to indulge a passion."

"You're fortunate. Your passion became your career."

"Yes." Shari agreed, but her eyes shifted away as she said it. Marcus noted the unspoken qualification she made. Something to figure out here, he noted, and tucked it away to think about.

"Do you still enjoy it?"

"Most of the time." She grimaced. "Except when I'm under deadline and the speech isn't working." She held up the pages. "Like this one."

"Keep working on it, you'll get it."

"Or rip it up trying." She held up her float. "Thanks for this."

"You're welcome. Do you have an extra pad of paper? I'll do some work while you finish that speech."

"You've got more confidence than I do." She passed over a blank pad of paper.

Marcus pulled the sketch from his pocket, the one they knew was misleading.

"I'm sorry I got that sketch wrong."

He wasn't letting her take the guilt for that, and it was ground they had been over several times in the last week. "Don't be. It was just one of many ways he arranged to misdirect us." He started modifying the sketch, creating yet another permutation to the dozens he had made in the last few days.

The room became quiet as they both worked. Marcus turned the page to make another sketch. And instead found himself sketching Shari.

She was focused on the speech, lost again in thought. He'd been studying her over the last weeks with more care than he realized. The sketch came together with great detail. He would never be able to capture the quality that most fascinated him, the joy that lit her face when she smiled, but he tried.

Her posture when she worked was atrocious. He smiled as he saw her wiggle down in the leather chair to get more comfortable. She sprawled. Just like her stuff. Between the books, the newspapers, the pages she had printed from Web sites and stapled together, the crumpled pages of rejected words, someone would have to want to invade her domain to get near her.

He wished she wasn't a witness. It made this situation difficult, because one of these days he wouldn't mind invading her space to kiss her good night. She had, after all, spent the last weeks doing a very effective job of invading his heart.

Twelve

H aven't you ever heard of the word *sleep?*"
Lisa looked up from the microscope, startled to find someone in the lab at 4:15 A.M., even more surprised to see Quinn. He was supposed to be somewhere in Kentucky with Marcus. He wasn't exactly the person she would have chosen to stop by.

"Don't frown. I come in peace."

He held out a small white sack and she was curious enough to glance inside. "Food is not allowed in the lab."

He shook it slightly, making the M&Ms rattle. "I asked for extra red ones."

She glanced at him, saw the twinkle in his gaze, and took a handful.

He tucked the sack in his jacket pocket. "Tell me what you've got so far."

She sighed. "Not enough." She had been back over the hotel room with a fine tooth comb and it was frustrating her to no end.

"What's the carpet?"

She had cut out two sections of carpet from room 1323, one with the blood and shoe polish trace and the other where the glass fragments had been found. "I found shattered glass fragments on the carpet. Some tested positive for traces of blood so I'm trying to recover enough to get a DNA test."

"Think you'll be able to?"

She held up the thin vial she had worked most of the day to collect. "I'm having to take the carpet weave apart thread by thread to find them. We'll see. It's a long shot."

"I owe you dinner, but would you be willing to change that to breakfast? I'll be glad to feed you while you tell me the details."

Lisa looked at the work left to do.

"It will still be there in a few hours."

"Make it somewhere still serving a cheeseburger and fries at this time of morning and you've got a deal."

"I think I can oblige."

Lisa put the evidence back under lock and key.

"Do you want to walk or take a cab?" Quinn asked as Lisa signed out of the building, and they cleared security.

"Walk," Lisa replied. She found the walk with Quinn helped revive her energy. She had been practically living at the lab since this case began. "I found—"

Quinn cut her off. "Give yourself five minutes off work."

She was surprised at the stringent tone of the order but nodded. It got very quiet. She didn't know what to say to him if it wasn't about work.

Quinn led the way to a restaurant six blocks away, a hole in the wall that she had heard about but never visited. It catered to taxi drivers and construction workers. It was busy even at a quarter to five in the morning. Quinn steered her to a booth rather than a barstool. The menus were thick, with everything available at all hours.

"Cheeseburger and fries?" Quinn confirmed, Lisa nodded, and he placed an order for both of them. The food arrived within minutes. The fries were thick wedges and the cheeseburger more than a handful, thick and stacked with onion, lettuce, and tomato.

"When was the last time you ate?" he asked as she dug into the fries.

"I don't remember. I think it was a candy bar lunch."

"I'm flush enough to be able to afford a second cheeseburger."

She was finding the food too enjoyable to mind the remark. "I'll accept."

He waited until half the cheeseburger was gone and the sharp edge of her hunger had been satisfied. "Okay, now you can tell me what you have found."

She picked up a fry, grateful to be free to talk about something she was comfortable with. "It's Carl's blood and shoe polish on the carpet. We've got more fibers from the hairpiece the shooter wore. And a few more fibers that match his suit. There was a trace of gun residue in the safe. It's certain now that the shooter used the room. He had the arrogance to store the murder weapon in the room safe. But we've got no fingerprints."

"What about the registration of the room itself? Someone was there."

"It's a block of rooms reserved by the conference. Show up with a conference ticket and they hand you a room key. The credit card that was used for extra charges turned out to be stolen. The name Henry James leads us nowhere. The signature card has only the prints of the hotel reservation clerk. Whoever was in that room used the express checkout and carried the weapon, his disguise, out with him on Saturday."

"Keep looking. He made another mistake."

Lisa wished she had his confidence. "I hope so." She changed the subject. "How's Marcus?"

"His arm is fine. His heart—" Quinn smiled—"that's a different matter."

Lisa paused, intrigued. "Shari?"

"That would be my guess."

She set down her drink and leaned back against the bench. Marcus was getting serious. Well, it was about time. "Shari." Her smile widened. She had met Shari briefly, and Kate and Jennifer had both mentioned her in their calls. There had been speculation, but nothing firm.

"Don't put it on the family grapevine until I am away from here so it won't be obvious I'm the one who passed on the news."

"Quinn, there are times I like how you think." She was feeling very generous at the moment and the normal reserve to her smile dropped away as she beamed at him. "Going to finish your fries?"

He blinked, then smiled back. He slid his plate toward her and handed her the catsup bottle. "Enjoy."

Marcus leaned over Beth's shoulder to watch her ice another cupcake. "Are we ready for tomorrow?" A week had passed since Quinn had left for Chicago to try and move the investigation along. Marcus had turned his impatience with the delay into going overboard with the birthday planning.

"All set. I'll just need you to keep Shari busy for about two hours while I get the decorations put up."

He sneaked a taste of the icing from the mixing bowl. "Not a problem. I'll make sure she comes with me when Josh goes to see the physical therapist."

"You can have a cupcake if you like."

"Better yet, can I have one for tomorrow to soften the blow when I tell Shari she's about to be had?" Shari was so absorbed in work; they had managed to plan what amounted to a small-scale bash without her noticing.

Beth laughed. "Sure."

Marcus squeezed her shoulder. "The gift you asked to have delivered arrived. I put it in your closet upstairs."

"Think she'll like it?"

The dress Beth had bought Shari was gorgeous. Marcus leaned against the counter beside Beth and gave her a knowing smile. "I do."

She didn't bother to hide her humor. "Good."

"Craig has the rounds this evening. I'm going to go find your daughter and convince her to take a walk. Would you like to come along?"

"Thanks, but I'm planning to watch that Columbo movie with Josh at the top of the hour."

"Making popcorn?" he asked, hopeful.

"I'll make extra."

"Thanks. Shari promised me a Scrabble rematch tonight."

"She'll tromp you again."

Marcus chuckled. "Probably. But she feels so bad when she wins it's funny."

"She likes you."

"Think so?"

"Marcus, you're as bad as Shari. Don't you two ever talk?"

"We talk all the time."

She snorted. "Then why are you both asking me the important questions?"

"Good point." He leaned over and kissed her cheek. "Like I said, I'm going to go find your daughter."

As the days passed, security had fallen into a pattern. Marcus was comfortable they had the situation here contained. It didn't lessen his guard, but it did help the coil of fear in his gut relax. Shari was safe here. That was the important fact in life. As restless as he was to be back in Chicago where the action was, to be in Baltimore with Jennifer, here was where he needed to be. Since that was reality, he had let himself seize the moment and enjoy it.

He found Shari in the den. He was becoming accustomed to her work schedule. She worked hard. Too hard, he sometimes wondered, for the motivation to solely be the work that needed to get done. She had something to prove and he was beginning to think it was with herself. She was a lady in a tough profession, very good at what she did, and she didn't cut herself much slack.

She was still in the midst of a phone marathon, working on a speech on fiscal policy. She needed someone to remind her to slow down. When she hung up the phone and before she could dial again, he leaned over the back of the couch and set his hands down on her shoulders. "Slip away and come watch the sunset."

She leaned her head back to look at him. "There are more calls to finish."

"Those will wait. The sunset won't."

She considered for a moment, then set aside the notepad. "Sure, why not. It's not like I'm making much progress. I'm back to negotiating my original language from this morning."

"That just means you were right this morning."

"Well, I'm lousy at convincing people of that."

He came around the couch, offered his hands, and pulled her to her feet.

"I knew John was dumping a hornet's nest in my lap."

"So why did you say yes?"

"Because I like a challenge. But I hate writing a speech by committee."

They stepped outside. The wind had picked up, and Shari reached up, pushing her hair back.

"I found a great place down the beach."

She fell into step beside him. "It's good to get outside."

"You need to take more breaks."

"True. Another good intention I haven't followed through on."

Marcus pointed out a fallen log. Shari sat down, bracing her arms on her knees. A low front had brought in a band of white wispy clouds. The reflections of the clouds glittered on the water. "You're right. This is a great view."

They sat together in silence watching the colors change as the sun set. Marcus felt no need to break the silence.

The colors drifted into darker hues. "Which do you like better, a sunset or a sunrise?" she asked idly.

Marcus glanced at her, considering. "Sunset."

"Why?"

"Because you're never awake to share a sunrise with me."

He watched the startled faint blush spread across her face. "Marcus—"

"You asked."

"Are you flirting?"

"What do you think?"

"I think you are being very nice."

Nice. Marcus buried a sigh. *And I'm trying to get your attention. Nice wasn't the word I was hoping for. So much for making the point subtly.*

She leaned her weight back against her hands and turned her attention back to the sunset. "I used to date a guy named Sam."

Marcus went still. He had not been expecting her to come back with an offer for a serious discussion. He turned so he could look at her. Sam. He knew that name from the file developed on her, had seen a couple newspaper clippings, and remembered the conversation she had referred to at the hospital. "What happened?"

"We had different visions of where we would go as a couple."

"Do you regret it now?"

"No. It hurt like crazy, still does at times, but it was the right decision."

Shari looked over and considered him for a moment. "Marcus, are we going to be friends when all this is over? Or is this one of those special friendships that exists for the moment and is one you remember with gratitude when the event is passed?"

"Which do you want?"

"I like you."

He smiled. *Finally.* "It's mutual."

"And you're a complicated man."

She had looked further than the surface. "I'm an O'Malley." He wished he could explain everything that meant, about what it meant to be part of the family he had chosen to lead. He went back to her original question. "As far as I'm concerned, these last couple weeks are an interruption to what will be a very long friendship."

"An interruption? Why?"

"Because I'm working. That changes the situation."

"Constrains it, you mean."

Trust her to be direct. He had always admired that. "If you like."

She was silent for a long time. He would have said something, but her expression had become serious. "I need a friend right now, Marcus." She sighed. "I wish you believed. I really need someone to talk to."

"What about?"

She shrugged her shoulder, didn't answer.

"I may struggle with it and have my doubts, but I've got two sisters convinced the Bible is true. Trust me. I'll do my best to understand."

She gave him a small smile. "I still think you'll eventually come around."

"Don't get your hopes up."

"Jennifer and Kate strike me as being persuasive."

"They can be. Talk to me. What are you wrestling with?"

"Why Dad died."

"Because you prayed for a different outcome?"

She nodded.

"Jennifer is praying to be healed."

"And you're wondering if she has a chance at getting a positive answer."

"I've wondered," he said simply.

"A twenty-year Christian and an unbeliever wrestling over the same question. If you find an answer, I'd appreciate hearing it." She shook her head slightly. "Change of subject. How is Jennifer? You haven't said much in the last few days."

"She says she's fine. She's lying," he replied, weary. It was impossible to imagine what it was going to mean, the radiation and chemotherapy not working.

"Fine can be a matter of perspective. Someone broken of spirit can be worse off than someone physically ill. When do you go see her?"

"If things work out I'll take a predawn flight Tuesday, spend the day, and take a late night flight back."

"I wish you had been able to go last week."

"It couldn't be helped. Jack and Stephen are there. And I've been talking to her every day."

The shadows were beginning to lengthen. Marcus got to his feet and held out his hand. "The sunset is fading; it's time we were inside." Since the church incident, he wasn't taking chances. She slipped her hand into his. "Want to go into town with me tomorrow? I thought I might go play some basketball while Josh is at physical therapy."

"I can get out of the house?"

"Just to the gym. No shopping I'm afraid."

"I'll still take it."

He led the way back down the beach, skirting driftwood.

"Would you teach me how to play?" she asked.

"What?"

"Basketball."

He looked over and caught her half smile. "Now you tell me."

"I'm kind of athletically challenged too."

"You're smart. You can learn."

"Tell me that after you've spent an hour chasing the basketball. What time do we need to leave?"

"Nine o'clock will be early enough."

Time alone with Marcus was worth this. Shari shut off her alarm and crawled out of bed, trying to remind herself of that. It was not yet 7 A.M. She vaguely remembered seeing 2 A.M. This was horrible. And it was her birthday. She considered crawling back in bed and burying her head under a pillow. She would prefer to sleep through this day rather than be up at dawn. No. If she ducked back into bed, she would never hear the end of it.

She staggered downstairs after a hot shower, barefoot, carrying her socks, in desperate need of coffee.

The radio was on in the kitchen. She wasn't surprised to find Marcus working at the counter. He was in jeans, a black T-shirt, and tennis shoes. The casual attire didn't eliminate the obvious signs of his job—the badge, gun, and radio on his belt, the small earpiece he wore to keep him in touch with the other officers.

He set down the spoon he was using to mix muffin batter, wiped his hands on a towel, and gave her a smile, wide and welcoming. "Sit down. I'll fix you breakfast."

He was cheerful at this time of morning. She wanted to groan. If she had to talk coherently, she was in trouble. She took the coffee he offered, retreated to the table, and found the first newspaper, searching through it for the comics page.

He tugged down the newspaper. "Happy birthday."

"Please, don't remind me."

"How old are you today anyway?"

She wrinkled her nose at him.

"That's okay. I already know," he remarked smugly.

"If I have to endure this day, please feed me."

He laughed and returned to the stove. "Do you want hash browns with your omelet?"

"Please."

He was a very good short-order cook and she had long since stopped trying to suggest she should help. Breakfast was his domain. If she wanted to fix and bring him lunch to wherever he was working, that was another matter.

There was quiet for the next several minutes. Shari read the comics, turned to the national news, then moved to the political page.

Marcus set down a plate with a western omelet, toast, hash browns. He set a glass of orange juice beside the plate.

She looked at the orange juice with distaste.

"Eat. And orange juice is good for you."

"I'd rather be told to drink milk. Orange juice is nearly as bad as grapefruit juice."

"Since it's your birthday…" The glass was removed and was replaced with one of milk. "Better?"

"Much. Sorry, I don't mean to be so cranky."

"Sure you do. It's your birthday. It's already started off as a bad day."

"Please don't be cheerful. It's bad for my digestion."

He laughed.

She bit into her toast. "Aren't you going to eat?"

"Already did. I fixed the guys breakfast."

"Well, I hope you're still hungry. If I eat all of this I won't be able to move."

"It's a competitive advantage to have my opponent slow on her feet."

"Well, I think—"

He cut her off with a raised hand. "Yes, Craig."

Shari recognized that distant look as his attention shifted in an instant to work. He was pushing back his chair and heading to the door moments later. "Shari, stay here in the kitchen. Luke will be joining you."

She felt an intense wave of panic. Something was wrong. Her attention immediately swung to windows and she shoved back her chair and moved to the other end of the kitchen away from them. Marcus had said to stay in the kitchen. She wished he would have said for her to go upstairs.

Was someone out here? The shooter?

Josh came into the kitchen carrying his tennis shoes. "Shari, can you—" He saw her face. "What's wrong?"

"I don't know. Marcus just got called; he left in a hurry."

There was a heavy pause as they both considered the implications. Josh reached for a chair, swung it around. He pulled on his shoes with his good hand. "Can you tie my shoelaces?"

"Sure."

"Not knots like you did last time."

He was trying to distract her as well as get ready in case they had to move. She forced herself to smile back. "Me?"

"Yes, you."

She hurriedly tied neat bows.

"Thanks. I'll go see—"

She caught his arm. "No. Stay here."

They heard the front door open. "Miss Hanford?"

"In the kitchen, Luke."

He joined them and held up his hand to stop the questions. "There was a traffic accident up the road. You'll be hearing the police sirens soon."

"Marcus didn't react to an accident."

"Accidents make a good diversion. We're sweeping the grounds as a precaution. Go ahead and get ready to head into town. We're comfortable this was simply a minor traffic accident."

"You're sure?"

"Mrs. Garrett clipped her cousin Joe's truck. We've known both of them for years. This is nothing more serious than a failure-to-stop-in-time fender bender."

But it was a reminder of why she was here. The last time she had gone out in public she had put her family at risk, and Marcus had been shot. "Maybe I shouldn't go—"

Josh settled his hands on her shoulders. "It will do you good to get out of the house for a while. Go finish getting ready. You're not staying behind because of this."

She knew that tone. She wouldn't be winning this discussion.

He turned her toward the door. "It's your birthday. You're getting out of the house."

Shari went upstairs to finish getting dressed. She was looking forward to the day. Her mom was just finishing her makeup. "Good morning, honey. Happy birthday."

Shari stopped to give her a hug. "Thanks, Mom."

Her mom gave her a knowing smile. "Have a good time today."

Shari couldn't help the small blush. "I will."

When she went downstairs half an hour later carrying her gym bag, Marcus stood by the front door talking with Josh. He held out his hand when he saw her. "Ready?"

"Yes."

He stopped her at the door after Josh had stepped out on the porch. "If something doesn't feel right, what do you do?"

"Press the panic button."

"*Before* you try and figure out what it is that bothers you."

"I remember."

"Good. You can leave the rest of the worrying to me. Luke and I have it covered. Deal?"

She squeezed his hand. "Deal."

"Then let's get out of here."

She followed him around the house to the driveway.

"You're in front with me," Marcus directed. "Josh and Luke are in the back."

It felt strange being back in a car. Marcus noticed her tension as they drove along the winding roads toward town. "We're fine. That's Craig in the truck in front of us."

The trip took only ten minutes. Marcus took Josh and Luke to the hospital first, then drove on to the gym. He waited until Craig parked, got out and scanned the area, then signaled it was clear before he shut off the engine. "We'll go in the back entrance. Stay close."

Shari nodded. He circled the car and opened her door.

Marcus paused on the basketball court when Shari joined him from the women's locker room. She had dressed in black shorts and a burgundy T-shirt. Her tennis shoes were so white they had to be brand new. She had pulled her hair back in a ponytail and it bounced as she walked.

"We've got the court to ourselves?"

"For the next hour and an half."

"I wondered." She set her bag down on the bleachers next to his and crossed the gym floor to join him.

"This is a basketball." He bounced it to make his point.

She bit back a quick grin. "I think I remember that part."

"Remember free throws?"

"Just give me the ball."

He tossed it to her and she caught it with a clean slap.

She dribbled twice, then sent it in a clean arc toward the hoop. It was short, coming off the front of the rim, but her shot was good form. Marcus scooped the ball up and with one hand tossed it back to her. "You've played before."

"Ages ago."

She set herself, dribbled twice, and sent up another free throw that hit the backboard and went slightly right.

By the time he had fed her back the ball a dozen times, she had found the basket. "You're a bit too much of a perfectionist. You wince every time you miss."

"I bet you rarely miss free throws."

"Not often," Marcus agreed, "but then I rarely get to shoot them. The family doesn't often call fouls."

"Enough shooting. I want to burn some energy. Let's actually play."

"One-on-one?"

"You don't play girls?"

"Just making sure your ego can handle getting beat." He tossed her the ball.

He was between her and the basket and she came right at him, cutting right as soon as he committed himself to come toward her. No one would mistake the determination on her face. He moved to cut her off and she spun back out to the top of the key. It was a good percentage shot, and she took it, sending up an arc to the basket.

He blocked her shot.

"I see you don't give freebies." She had chased down the ball first, stood dribbling just outside the three-point line.

"Do you want one?"

"Not particularly."

She came in on the baseline, her shot missed, and Marcus recovered it. The basketball was warm, rough in his hand. His first shot hit nothing but net. "What do you want to play to?"

"Twenty-one."

He tried to purposely miss often enough to give her a chance.

"You could at least cheat without making it obvious," she remarked without heat, having chased down one of his misses.

Her shirt was damp with sweat, her breathing rapid. "Want to take a break?"

"Not till the game is over."

He was three baskets away from putting the game away; there was no use leaving her in misery. He put up the next three shots as soon as he touched the ball, made sure they were flawless, hitting nothing but net.

She stood back with her hands on her hips and watched the last one go in. "Ouch."

"I've been playing a long time," he commiserated.

"I would have never guessed," she replied dryly. She sat down on the bench, picked up a towel, and offered him one.

He took a seat beside her, watching her mop her face. "Thanks for playing. You're a good sport."

"I enjoyed it." She tipped her head to glance at him. "Even if you are a poor winner."

"A what?" he asked, laughing.

"You should be celebrating the victory. You finally beat me at something."

"Since it's your birthday, I'm being kind. I'll wait to gloat until later."

"Thanks."

He glanced at the clock on the wall. "We've got another half hour before we pick up Josh."

"Good, I can take a shower."

He nudged her white shoes. "Those need breaking in."

She raised one foot. "I bought them because I had this great New Year's resolution to start running. You can tell how far that idea got."

"You need a running partner to get you in the habit. I go most days I'm home to jog the hiking trails on Roosevelt Island."

"Really?"

"I could probably be talked into buying the coffee if you'd like to join me."

"Run? Early in the morning?"

He buried a grin. "Yes."

"That's brutal."

"You might enjoy it."

"Or I can decide I won't and not bother to try."

"Somehow that doesn't sound like you."

"That's exactly how Josh got me to try skydiving. You'll have to try another tactic."

"Don't worry, I'll come up with one."

"Why do I get the feeling you're going to keep asking until I agree?"

"Who? Me?"

She got up with a laugh and tossed her towel at him. "I'm going to take that shower."

Shari came out of the locker room, shuffling her gym bag, towel, and tennis shoes and trying to get everything to fit inside the bag. She collided with Marcus, saw the gun in his hand, and froze.

"What happened?" He was propelling her back down the hall and toward the alcove.

"I'm fine." She stammered the words because it was obvious something was wrong. Marcus was tense, terse, and hustling her out of the hallway.

"Then why—" His eyes closed and he took a deep breath, then he shook his head and reached around the gym bag to the pager clipped on her belt. He shut off the panic button. "You nearly gave me a heart attack."

"I'm sorry! I didn't mean—"

He kissed her hard, stopping the apology.

Shari went from being panic stricken to being unable to think bliss in the blink of an eye. This was absolutely heaven. She felt her heart leap in delight and recognized joy. Her hands came up to curl around his forearms and she leaned in against him.

He pulled back half an inch to breathe again. "I do not mind false alarms. Don't get the wrong idea. I was just too far away."

She blinked, still rolling with the shock of that delightful, unexpected kiss. He had such alive brown eyes; she found them absolutely fascinating.

She could feel him breathing. She should be feeling embarrassed, but being held in the shelter of his arms was absolutely wonderful. She looked ruefully at the fact but for the gym bag squashed between them, there was no space separating them. She could feel the blush starting. "You're not anymore."

He looked at her for a moment, then dropped the gym bag to the floor. "Come here," he said softly. He gave her a moment to decide and then pulled her close.

This kiss lasted long enough for her to close her eyes and get lost in the wonder of it.

Marcus ended the kiss and rested his forehead against hers. She felt his silent chuckle. "Should I apologize, or just say happy birthday?"

"It is my birthday."

They stood that way, silent, sharing the moment. Shari had no desire at all to come back to reality and deal with what had just happened.

He finally eased back half a step. "I've been wanting to do that for a long time, but I apologize for the timing, and the circumstances."

He was apologizing. She wanted to slap him for that, but he sounded so chagrined she decided to be magnanimous and not take it like the insult it felt like. She glanced around at the potted plants and empty chairs in the alcove. "A public place. You could have chosen worse. And Marcus...I don't kiss and tell."

"Get that look off your face. I enjoyed kissing you tremendously, and if you keeping scowling at me I'm going to do it again." He wrapped his arm around her shoulders, gave her a brief hug, and tugged her ponytail. "And I'm grateful you'll keep this quiet. I'm the one with the active family grapevine."

She relaxed. "Come on—I top that. I've got Mom. Your family is still learning compared to her."

"I'll grant you that one." He turned her toward the hallway. "We need to go meet Josh or he is going to be worried."

She didn't want this moment to end. "Can we talk tonight?"

"Are you going to pretend not to be tired at midnight?"

"I haven't been hiding the yawns," she said, chagrined.

He gave a small smile as he brushed back her bangs. "Not very well."

"Then I'll take a nap."

He laughed. "If you're up, we'll talk," he promised, to her delight.

Thirteen

They picked up Josh and Luke at the hospital. Shari was grateful when Marcus engaged Josh in a conversation about how the physical therapy had gone, what the schedule was for the next week. She wasn't sure she could hold a coherent conversation at the moment.

She thought about the kiss, absently touched her lip. Just thinking about it made her heart warm. What had it meant to Marcus? He had been reacting to the emotions of the moment; she had felt that in the kiss. But it went a lot deeper as a possibility of what might come. The ride back to the house was too short; she needed time to think before she accidentally said the wrong thing. Would he feel she was ducking him if she retreated upstairs for a while? At least she had a powerful distraction to get her through her first birthday without her father and Carl.

Marcus pulled around the house and parked.

Josh and Luke got out of the car.

"Shari." Marcus paused her as she would have opened the car door. "Hold on a second."

She looked over at him and was puzzled as he reached around to the backseat, and retrieved a small white bakery box.

"For you." He said simply, holding it out. He quirked a smile. "Happy birthday."

She opened it and grinned when she saw it. He had gotten her a cupcake. "How did you know?" She shook her head. "Mom."

"Yes."

She lifted it from the box, peeling back the wrapper. "Like a bite?"

"This one's yours. I sampled as she baked."

She laughed as she got icing on her fingers. "This is great."

He waited until she finished, then reached over and wiped away a spot of icing she had missed at the corner of her mouth with his thumb. "I know you would have preferred to skip recognition of this day. I know how you miss your dad and Carl, but you need to let those around you celebrate. It helps them have something positive to do."

"What did you guys do?"

He came around and opened her car door, offered his hand.

"Marcus?"

"I figured you should have at least a small warning."

He walked with her to the house, took her gym bag when they reached the porch, and reached around her to open the door for her.

"Surprise!"

Marcus had given her about a minute to adjust and prepare, but it would have been hard to prepare for this no matter how much time she had—the streamers, the balloons, the hand drawn signs done in colorful markers. The dining room table had been set out with a buffet of finger foods. The guys from the security details, those off duty, had joined her family. It was like being fifteen again and finding herself the focus of the extended family. "How did you—" She just shook her head and laughed. "Never mind. I don't think I want to know."

Josh wrapped his good arm around her shoulders. "We had fun."

Shari let herself be tugged into the room. She grinned as she recognized where all the cartoons from her newspapers had been going. They were intermixed among the streamers. "Cute, Josh."

"Get yourself a plate. We'll let you eat while we drown you in presents."

"Impossible. I can never have too many presents."

She hugged her mom. "Thank you," she whispered.

"Your dad would have been proud of you today. Enjoy it."

They had insured it would be impossible not to.

She picked up the first plate and officially opened the party.

Shari was very aware of Marcus through the afternoon, as he slipped in and out of the room, talking on the security net. He had made this possible. She deeply appreciated it.

When Josh insisted, she settled on the couch in the den to open presents. There were videos, and locally made taffy, an engraved watch, and a large puzzle. Small gifts that reflected the circumstances.

Mom had bought her a dress. It was absolutely beautiful. Her gaze caught Marcus's across the room. She looked down with a blush when she saw his smile.

Josh had gotten her a hand-tooled leather briefcase. It was the gift her dad had been threatening to get her for years. She looked at it for several moments, then reached over and wrapped her arm around Josh's neck, hugging him. "Thanks."

"You're welcome."

With a laugh she let him go. The wrapping paper had bunched beside her on the couch. She reached for the trash bag.

"One more."

She leaned her head back at Marcus's words. He was holding out a thick package. It was wrapped in heavy brown shipping paper. She accepted it, curious. "From you?"

"Something to keep you occupied."

It was heavy, and she would have thought it was a book except the package gave and she had to grasp it with both hands to steady it. She set it in her lap and opened the package. "What's this?"

Marcus just looked at her, a slight smile edging up the corners of his mouth. "What's it look like?"

It was well over a ream of loose pages. The top page simply said *Paula*—centered, on the middle of the page. It took her a moment to realize she was holding an H. Q. Victor manuscript. It was…she checked… 728 pages.

"Her next book. I asked Quinn to bring it back with him. It should keep you busy for a few days," he said, satisfied.

She caught his hand when he would have stepped back. "Marcus. Thank you," she whispered.

"My pleasure."

Most of the party banners and streamers had been cleaned up, the party was over. Marcus made his final rounds for the night, then passed off security to Craig. The lights were still on in the den. He had wondered if Shari would turn in early, given how long her day had been. He leaned against the doorpost, delighted to find she had waited up for him.

She was reading the manuscript. She was slouched in the seat with the manuscript in her lap, turning pages with one hand and eating a carrot with the other. He was willing to bet she had been seated just like that for the last several hours. The bag of vegetables left over from this afternoon's tray was almost gone, and about a hundred pages of the manuscript had been set down in a semineat pile on the floor. There was an absorbed expression on her face as she read.

"Is it any good?"

"What?"

He moved into the room. "The story. Is it good?"

She stretched her arms back over her head, arched her back, and smiled. "One of her best."

"Am I going to interrupt if I join you?"

"No, but I'm tossing you out if you yawn so I can keep reading," she replied with a small laugh. She set the manuscript down beside the chair.

He settled down on the couch. "Thanks for being a good sport today. I'm afraid once the planning started, it got out of hand."

"Mom told me you instigated the food."

"Guilty. I enjoy the leftovers."

"Thank you for arranging it. I didn't want to celebrate without Dad, and that would have made the day drag by. With the celebration, the day flew by and it was much easier to handle."

"It's hard to feel sad when Josh is tossing peanut shells at you for flubbing a joke."

"Yeah."

He saw a look of private amusement cross her face. One he had seen in his own family. "What?"

"I short-sheeted his bed."

"You know if you start going tit for tat, it's going to escalate on you fast. There's plenty of time while you are stuck here to dream up the practical jokes."

"I know. And I'm going to enjoy it." Her amusement changed to seriousness. "What do you want to talk about tonight?"

He had thought about that a great deal throughout the afternoon, and he chose to offer a serious, difficult topic, one he knew they needed to talk about. He had made the decision he wanted a lot more with her than just a friendship, and it was going to mean facing some topics that were going to be difficult for both of them. He was a cautious man when it came to introducing something that would hurt a friend, and he knew the risks. He brought up the subject of religion as an indirect observation. "Jennifer is going to want to talk about what she believes."

"Very likely."

"Shari, she's praying to be healed, and instead she's having to face growing worse. I don't understand, and I don't want to say the wrong thing."

Her posture straightened, and her focus narrowed. "Do you really want to know what I've discovered about prayer?"

There was a frank challenge to her words. She didn't think he was going to like her answer. "Yes, Shari, I do."

"To be passive and throw up your hands and say, 'I don't care, whatever You want, Lord,' is as much a cop-out as pushing for only what you want and not being able or willing to accept something different. To deny Him being Lord." She looked across at him moodily. "It hurts to have prayers not answered. The difference is I still believe in the One to whom I pray, whereas you simply stopped praying."

Her warning had been with cause. It was the first time she had shown him the emotion behind what she thought of his disbelief. She didn't temper it, and he had to admit, hearing it stung. It pricked where he was vulnerable, being called a coward.

"We put everything we are into our prayers. What we think about Jesus. What's happening in the world around us. What our dreams are about how life should be. Our sense of hope. Prayer is the ultimate struggle. It can be exquisite joy, and it can also be painful tears.

"I don't want to belittle the pain you felt over what happened to your mom. But you decided through the eyes of a child what the world was like, what God was like. If adults struggle to understand Him and sometimes get it wrong, don't you think a child might too? Jennifer will get through this moment because she knows Jesus. However He decides to answer her prayer, she'll be the strong one. It's you I worry about."

Her words ran out and she flushed, dropped her gaze.

He didn't know what to say. "Ouch."

"You asked. But I didn't mean to say it exactly that way."

"Shari." He waited until she looked back up. "You're direct. I've always

admired that. And you are right in one thing. You kept trying to understand, and I gave up." He gave a faint smile. "And you just told me in more
eloquent terms than Jennifer ever will what she will be thinking."

He had offered an olive branch to diffuse the tension and he was grateful when she accepted it. "You're forgetting Kate."

He groaned. "Tenacious gets a new definition with Kate."

Her expression became serious. "Marcus, you can trust Jesus with
Jennifer. He loves her. I know that."

"I'll think about it."

"Thank you. I know you can't make a decision just to please me, or
Jennifer. You're kind enough you would probably try on most subjects to do
just that. But this is different. You have to make a decision you can live with."

"No, Shari. I have to make a decision I can live with and one I can
defend," he corrected. "I've got O'Malleys to deal with."

"I'd commiserate with you, but I'm secretly delighted they are there
pushing you out of your comfort zone. I like your family."

"I've noticed," Marcus replied dryly. "Kate calls me and promptly asks
for you."

She gave a small smile. "Like I said, I like your family."

"What do you talk about anyway?"

She laughed, and there was no mistaking that blush. "You."

That blush did it. He got up and invaded her space, resting his hands
on the arms of her chair. He leaned down, until he was inches away, then
went still, searching her gaze, finding the anticipation waiting there. He
had been thinking about the kiss from this morning throughout the day,
wondering. Apparently, so had she. He leaned forward and ended the lin-
gering questions.

This kiss was warm and touched with an intriguing sense of mystery.
The softness and sweetness pulled him to explore. He angled his head to
deepen the kiss as she reached one hand up and slipped it behind his
neck.

He forced himself to ease back. He was tangling with her emotions,
her heart, and he wasn't going to do that to her, not until he could promise
he was going to be a forever part of her life. She'd had enough tears; he
wasn't going to be the cause of any more. Her bemused expression made
him feel so good. "Finish your book," he whispered. "This is too explosive
for tonight."

"Probably." Her hand at the back of his neck tightened gently and then she grinned. "Sweet dreams, Marcus."

"Shari—" He swooped to steal one last kiss. "Good night, minx."

Fourteen

Marcus flew to Baltimore on Tuesday, taking a predawn flight. It was going to be a long, hard day, seeing Jennifer, then flying back very late that night. His sleep had been intermittent at best. Shari had accomplished more than she realized with that good night of hers. He had spent most of the night dreaming about what might be. He was almost glad to get the day away. A week ago he had thought it would be a chance to get back his perspective; instead it had become a chance to decide how best to proceed.

He lifted his briefcase to the empty seat beside him and opened it, intending to do some work. There was a small white envelope resting on his planner with his name on it. Surprised, he picked it up. He recognized Shari's handwriting. Under it was one addressed to Jennifer. Curious, he opened the envelope addressed to him and slipped out a piece of stationery.

Marcus, I wanted to say thank you for a wonderful birthday. You helped ease my way through a painful day. That was not only thoughtful, that was very kind. And I loved the gift.

I wish there was something I could do to repay that and help you get through the tough day you now face. I hope that seeing Jennifer will clarify how you can help her and your family.

I am so sorry I was abrupt last night when you asked about prayer. Please let me apologize again. You have become such a good friend, and at times I find the chasm of faith between us so frustrating, but that doesn't excuse "directness" that lacked tact. Forgive me. Hug

Jennifer. Because you love her, help her laugh. Because I believe, I'll pray for her. We will both be good medicine.

I'll be thinking about you today, and if you just want to talk, call me. You know my number.

She had dotted the *i* in her name with a small heart.

Shari. The very presence of the note touched his heart.

She cared about his family. He leaned his head back against the seat, his thumb rubbing the edge of the note. He felt a deep sense of relief. He was falling in love with her. And the idea no longer felt like bad timing. He had planned to get the O'Malleys settled first, but Shari was showing him she had room for his family without even realizing she was doing it. She was moving toward his family, inviting him to share them, and showing she wouldn't feel uncomfortable in their circle.

This case could not be resolved soon enough.

He closed his briefcase, putting aside the work, and leaned his head back, closing his eyes. How did he proceed? He had not only Shari and her family to think about, but the O'Malleys. To change the family dynamics in such a fundamental way—this wasn't going to be easy, and the last thing he wanted to do was hurt any of them.

The flight was landing in Baltimore before he had figured out a plan.

Kate met him at the airport. He saw her leaning against a concrete pillar watching the passengers as he entered the concourse from the departure gate. She was in jeans and a blue shirt, arms crossed, and even from this distance he could tell she was letting the post support her. His eyes narrowed at the sight, for to show that exhaustion wasn't like her. Hospitals and doctors had always been a strain for her, and the stress of the situation was now plain to see.

Kate saw him, straightened, and came to meet him. As soon as they were free of the crowds, Marcus wrapped her in a hug. He was going to have to get Dave out here to be with her somehow. Kate wasn't one to let many people support her, but Dave was one person who could get under her guard and take care of her.

"You look tired."

So do you, he thought but didn't say. "A little. Thanks for coming to meet me."

"My pleasure. How's Shari and her family?"

"Recovering. It's been quiet. How's Jennifer?"

"Delighted that you could come."

Marcus left his arm around Kate's shoulder as they walked the concourse. "Have I told you lately how much I appreciate you? You're a trouper to be carrying this for the family."

"I'll take the compliment, but nonsense," Kate replied, lightly slapping his chest. "You need to quit feeling sorry for yourself. No one in the family thinks less of you for not being able to be here. And we'd be kicking you back to work if you tried to come. You've got a case to deal with."

"I'm hoping we can get a break in the case soon. Something has to give."

Kate smiled. "With Dave, Lisa, and Quinn on the job, you've got good help. Tell me about Shari. How did the birthday go?"

"She's a good sport. And she got through it fine."

"I'm glad. Did she like the book?"

"Loved it."

"What else did she love?"

He tweaked her nose and she laughed at him.

He had brought only the one carry-on bag. They headed out to the parking lot. Kate indicated her car.

The trip to the hospital was too short for Marcus to feel mentally prepared to see Jennifer. He was nervous suddenly, that he would say the wrong thing, react the wrong way.

Kate walked with him into the hospital. "Marcus—go up by yourself. She's in room 1310."

He squeezed Kate's hand and moved to the elevator.

Marcus took a deep breath before pushing the partially open door back to Jennifer's private room. Bouquets of flowers lined the window ledge, and there were so many get-well cards, they had been clipped like streamers to a string so they would be visible from the bed. In the chair by the bed sat a big panda bear and a smaller green dragon. Marcus slipped into the room quietly, for Jennifer looked to be asleep.

She had lost most of her hair. A bright rainbow scarf had been tucked around her head to cover the baldness. It was such a visible assault it made him want to cry.

He took the seat beside her bed, hoping not to disturb her, but she stirred.

"Marcus…hi." Her voice was much softer than before, and she looked like a waif for she had lost so much weight, but her smile touched her eyes.

He clasped her hand and leaned over to kiss her cheek. "Hi, precious."

He kept her hand folded in his as he pulled the chair over. She shifted on the bed and couldn't cover the wince. He helped adjust the pillows she used to brace her back. "Better?"

"Much." Her fingers interlaced with his. "It is good to see you. What were you thinking, going and getting yourself shot?"

Marcus closed his eyes, laughed, and leaned forward to rest his chin on the side rail of the bed so their faces were close. Trust Jennifer to get right to the point. "Someone wanted to shoot Shari."

"So you stepped in front of a bullet."

"I would have if I had known it was coming. He missed."

"I'm glad he did."

"So am I."

"You like her?"

He nodded.

Jennifer searched his face, then reached up and brushed back his hair, smiling. "Try—you're falling in love with her."

"Just between you and me—yes, I think I am."

"That scares you."

He nodded again.

"Why?"

"She's a witness, Jen. And I'm afraid I'm going to get my heart broken when this is over and life gets back to normal."

"Nonsense. She's too smart to let go of a good thing."

Family loyalty was such an admirable thing. "Can I show you something?"

"Sure."

He reached for his billfold and withdrew the sketch he had made a few nights before while Shari was working. He unfolded it and smiled as he looked at it. He handed it to his sister. "A pretty typical pose for Shari."

Jen studied it, then laughed. "Oh, this is priceless. Did you show her?"

He shook his head. "She gets so absorbed in her work. She's good at it, Jen. Start her talking about policy and you had better have done your homework. And I'm starting not to wince when she tells whoever answers the phone to tell the governor she'll call him back later."

"An interesting circle of influence."

"Hmm."

"Marcus, we need her in this family," Jennifer said gently. "Someone has to be able to articulate with clarity what makes us unique. Shari would be perfect. We all like her."

"You do?" They had been talking about him on the family grapevine. He shouldn't be surprised, but he was.

"We do. She'd be good for you." Jennifer squeezed his hand. "She's got a good sense of humor. You need that. And she's already proving she can handle the pressures of your job. She's accustomed to traveling at a moment's notice. And she tells these really great stories on the phone that can leave you in absolute stitches. When you're away you can always call home and be cheered up."

"And here I was afraid you would be disappointed in my choice."

"Because her background is so different? Marcus, she likes you, and she really wants to fit in. I think she envies what you have with all of us. Kate likes her, and you know how careful a read of someone's character she is. We're thrilled with Shari."

He was bemused by her answer. "I wish it was as simple as waiting for the day this crisis is past, but it's more than that. Even if you are right, there are obstacles."

"I know. Shari and I have talked."

"It's hard, Jen, not to be skeptical. Shari's prayers for her father were not answered, yours to get well don't appear to be. I don't want to hurt any of you, but it doesn't fit."

Jen looked at him, thoughtful. "She's already felt the hurt that comes from having a relationship unravel over different expectations for the future. She isn't going to walk herself into a similar chasm on something as vital as religion."

"Sam."

Jennifer nodded. She thought for a moment. "I can't answer all your questions, but maybe I can answer one. About me. Try reading John chapter 11 again. When Jesus' good friend Lazarus was ill and dying, Jesus heard the news and He said something very surprising. He said 'This illness is not unto death; it is for the glory of God…' It makes me wonder what He said when cancer struck me.

"Jesus loved Lazarus. Jesus could have said the word and healed him;

He had done that with the sick in other situations. But in this instance He chose not to. He wasn't acting callously; it wasn't the fact He didn't care.

"When Jesus went on to say 'Lazarus is dead; and for your sake I am glad that I was not there, so that you may believe,' He was making a profound choice. He loved the men He was with to the point He was willing to let His friend die so that they might be convinced to believe. Then Jesus went and raised Lazarus from the dead."

"Your cancer is to get us to believe?"

"No. My cancer is because sin messed up this world and my body is dying. But the delay in answering my prayer for healing—that might have a silver lining. It got Kate thinking about God. It's thrown you back in turmoil." She squeezed his hand. "You've rejected God for years because of the hurt. Do you think I mind being used to tug you back? Marcus, I want you to have to face the past and deal with it."

She stopped him when he would have spoken. "Just think about it, okay? Shari and I are not going to convince you. You have to convince yourself." She pointed to the stack of magazines on the side table. "Change of subject. I need your opinion on something."

Because she was suddenly trying to sit up, Marcus hurriedly moved to help her. She was visibly weak and she collapsed back on the pillows he put behind her with a grateful smile. She picked up the top magazine and opened it to a turned down page. "So, what do you think about this wedding dress?"

"Jennifer."

She grinned and patted his arm. "A guy's opinion. That's all I want. I've marked five that I really like."

"Lisa, the lab results you were waiting on are in."

Lisa looked up from the arson investigation reference book she was scanning to find the burn point for latex to see Paula coming through the doorway of the lab. Her friend had been working on doing the DNA extraction from the glass fragments. It was after 9 P.M., the labs were quiet, most of the staff gone; they had both stayed late to see the tests finished.

"What's the verdict?" With only enough DNA recovered to do one test, they had rolled the dice on which test to do.

Paula smiled and held out the file. "See for yourself."

Lisa accepted the file, feeling butterflies in her stomach. If they had guessed wrong...

She scanned the printout and the transparency and felt relief deep inside. It wasn't a full panel of markers, but what she was seeing was going to be enough. They had the major markers. "Enough to index."

Paula nodded. "If he's in any of the databases, this should be sufficient to generate a match."

"Thanks, Paula. I owe you one."

"Good. Is your brother Jack seeing anyone these days?"

Amused, Lisa shook her head. "Not since Beth moved to New Hampshire with her new job."

"That's too bad about Beth."

Lisa laughed, knowing where Paula was heading. "I suppose he's on the rebound."

"Next time he stops by, convince him to take you to lunch and then remember you already had arrangements to have lunch with me so he'll do the polite thing and make it a threesome." Paula grinned. "You can get paged or something."

"You know, I could just tell him you're interested in going to lunch with him."

"Better if he thinks it was his idea."

Lisa thought about it for a moment, then decided it would be good for Jack. It was about time he was dating again, and the idea of it being with her friend was...intriguing. "I'll see what I can do."

"Great. I knew I could count on you. I'll catch you later." Her friend headed back upstairs.

It was time to find out if all the painstaking hours of work were going to pay off. Lisa flipped on lights as she walked through the lab carrying the test results. She headed to the secure terminal, where she sat down and began entering logins and passwords, working her way through the layers of security until she finally was able to log into the national crime reference database.

Working slowly to make sure she didn't make an error, she worked down the DNA panel, identifying and entering the marker values used by the national database. She started the search.

The system was slow tonight, hers was one of several indexes being run, and she pushed away from the terminal rather than sit and watch the screen. She went to brew a pot of coffee. What if this didn't pan out? What did she try next? She was tired enough she didn't know. She always tried to have a game plan in mind, an idea of what she would try next if this led nowhere, but this case was running thin on leads to chase.

She took her time fixing the coffee, making it strong, needing the caffeine.

Quit stalling. If nothing matches, waiting here isn't going to change that.

She walked back to the desk. On the terminal an index number had appeared, was blinking red.

She spun around the chair and took a seat, on the verge of having not only an answer for Marcus but the solution of the case. She wrote down the index number, switched databases, and pulled up the details.

Daniel Gray. Age 31. Armed Robbery. Aggravated Assault. Murder in the First Degree.

She scrolled down the screen.

"What the…"

She just looked at it for several moments, stunned.

Deceased. October 27, last year. Lethal injection by the Commonwealth of Virginia.

What in the world did she do with this?

She considered the probability the DNA tests were flawed and finally rejected it. She was not above a mistake, but she knew the care that had been taken with this sample, the safeguards at each step. It was solid.

Could blood on glass fragments survive over nine months in a hotel room? No. She also rejected that. The glass shards had not been scattered over and worn into the carpet, the sharp edges dulled from friction. The glass was recent.

The database used only a subset of the markers in its search. The DNA of the shooter was similar enough to match with a dead man? She had got a mitocondrial match. It could only happen with a close family relative.

She went back to the original database, pulled the full index panel, printed it, and grabbed a red pen. She clicked on the light box and set down the DNA panel she had developed for the shooter next to the one from the national database.

Forty minutes later she knew she was looking at the answer to the case. "Hello, Daniel Gray," she whispered, easing back from the light box. "Let me guess, Judge Whitmore sentenced you to death. So who in your family decided to get revenge? Your father, your brother? Someone did. And I don't have enough DNA markers from the partial test results to tell, so we've got ourselves a nice mystery here."

She reached for the phone…and hesitated. Quinn…if he understood the importance of her telling him before Marcus, then maybe she would start giving him the benefit of the doubt on other things too. She punched in Quinn's pager number and marked it urgent.

Ten minutes later when he still had not returned her page her frustration was intense. Forget it. She picked up the phone to call Marcus. As she punched in the third number, Quinn walked through the door.

"Your page was marked urgent." His cowboy hat and his jacket were wet. It must be raining outside.

"Sit down." She was still annoyed enough at the way her heart had leaped when she saw him that she wasn't feeling particularly friendly. He raised one eyebrow at her brisk tone and pulled over a stool.

She handed over the page. "The DNA test results on the glass shards are back."

He read it, then looked at her. "You're sure?"

"Yes. There's your motive. The shooter is someone in his family."

Quinn checked his watch, then reached for his phone and dialed. "Marcus, we need you in Chicago. Lisa has something you should see." He listened. "See you then," Quinn agreed and closed the phone. Lisa wasn't surprised that Marcus asked no questions. On her word alone, he would come without question.

"He'll divert to O'Hare. Who else do we need?"

"Dave," she decided. "And someone who can get us details of the Daniel Gray case."

Marcus got Quinn's page on the way to the airport. With luck of timing he was able to grab a seat on a United flight bound for Chicago just ready to pull away from the gate.

He walked into Lisa's lab very early Wednesday morning, coming straight from the airport. Her assistant pointed him down to the research library conference center. Dave was there, Quinn, and eight others from the investigative team. They squeezed in another chair for him. He set down his briefcase, accepted the coffee he was handed, and looked across the table at Lisa. "What have you found?"

The sunlight was streaming into the room from the big windows behind her. She was tipped back in her seat with her hands cradling a cup of coffee, and she had the unfocused look of someone who had not yet been to bed. She gave a rueful smile. "The shooter is dead."

He didn't even blink. "So are we looking for a body, a zombie, or a ghost?"

"Trust you to be literal." She leaned forward and handed him a sheet of paper, crumpled from having been passed around. "The DNA I was able to pick up from the shattered glass generated this hit."

"Daniel Gray." Marcus read further down, then looked up abruptly. "Executed?"

"The death sentence was given by Judge Whitmore. The DNA matches to the Gray family. There are subtle differences in the panels when you go beyond the tags used in the database index. The shooter is a close relative of Daniel Gray. A father, brother, cousin, son. But I didn't have enough DNA markers to work with to get it tighter than that."

Marcus felt intense relief. They had the motive. Someone had gone after Judge Whitmore because of the decision he had made in this death penalty case. "Okay, you've been working this all night. How far have you gotten in identifying who in the Gray family is the shooter?"

Dave sorted files in front of him and handed over two. "Daniel Gray's father is one Titus Gray. You'll need a week to read the full file. This is the Cliffs Notes. He's into every racket on the East Coast from drugs to gambling. The FBI has been focusing on his family for years.

"I would make Titus a natural for the shooter except for one thing," Dave continued. "Titus apparently disowned Daniel after he was sent to prison and has had absolutely nothing to do with him since. A search of the prison records has yet to turn up so much as one phone call or one letter, let alone a visit during the twelve years Daniel was incarcerated."

Marcus read again the printout for the executed man. Sentenced to death for the murder of an undercover cop. "Why disown him? I somehow doubt Titus would consider killing a cop offensive."

"As best we can conclude there was a power struggle in the family. The hit wasn't sanctioned."

Marcus nodded. "That I can believe. Okay. Who else?"

"There is one brother. Connor Gray. He was fifteen when Daniel was sentenced. Shortly thereafter, Titus sent Connor to a private school in Europe. From there it was Harvard Law School. Then private law practice. If Connor is involved in the family business, no one can find a trace of it. He's got a clean record, not even a misdemeanor. And he doesn't get along with his father."

"Was he close to his brother?"

"There are records of occasional visits to see Daniel, fourteen over the twelve years. He was not there when his brother was executed."

Dave picked up the last file. "We ran the alias Henry James, used to rent room 1323, through the databases again looking for some link to the Daniel Gray. The alias has been used by a man named Frank Keaton—he's a first cousin, has worked for Titus for fifteen years. He's suspected of two murders and about four assaults."

"A father, a brother, and a cousin."

Dave nodded. "And motive with all of them."

"There's more," Quinn added from where he leaned against the wall by the door. "Connor was at the Renaissance Hotel that weekend."

"You're kidding."

"Room 1317. He was involved in merger discussions being held under cover of the conference."

Three people in the family could have done the shooting; all had reasonable motive. "What about the sketch?"

Lisa silently handed him a file. Marcus opened it and groaned. It took only a glance to know they had a problem with their most powerful evidence. "So Shari saw either Frank or Connor. With the disguise that was used it could easily be either man."

Quinn nodded. "We've shown both Frank's and Connor's pictures at the hotel. The security guard for the fourteenth floor telecommunication center is positive on Connor. And we've got three who have identified Frank as being here the week before the shooting."

Marcus looked across the table at his sister, tapping the file in his hand. "Who's left-handed?" he asked quietly.

She gave a small smile. "Connor," she answered simply. "The one without so much as a parking ticket."

Connor and Frank had to be involved, but the father—had it been a family conspiracy to kill the judge? "The father, Titus. Is there any way he was not involved?" Marcus asked the room at large, looking for their perspective.

"His eldest son was sentenced to death by Judge Whitmore. Frank works for him. The church shooting sounds like Frank," Quinn added. "He's known to brag about his marksmanship."

"Missed at six feet, missed at two hundred feet by a hair. Two shooters. Connor and Frank."

Quinn nodded. "I think so."

"And Titus ordered them both to act," Marcus concluded.

"I don't think Frank would act without Titus's approval," Dave confirmed.

"Is there anything concrete on Titus?"

Dave shook his head. "He was in Europe when the two shootings occurred. Wiretaps that the FBI had in place for other reasons didn't overhear anything. We'll have to get either Connor or Frank to supply that connection. Frank is used to a hard life and jail time. Connor is more likely to turn on Titus if the pressure hits, but he's also his son. I think we'll need to have both Connor and Frank to get leverage to reach Titus."

Marcus ran the three names over again in his mind—father, brother, cousin. "Is there any way Titus and Frank acted alone? Without Connor?"

Lisa shook her head. "Connor probably hoped it would appear to be the case, but he made a fatal mistake. He's the only one who is left-handed. Connor is the shooter."

Marcus would trust that opinion. Connor had shot the judge at the hotel, Frank had shot at Shari at the church, and Titus had set them both in motion. "Where do we find them today?"

Fifteen

Marcus shifted in the plane seat to reach up and shut off his reading light. It was late, he was tired, and they were still over an hour from the lake house. Dave and Quinn were flying back with him.

With the reading light off, he was able to see again the view out the small plane window. The blinking light at the end of the plane wing lit the scattered thin clouds around the plane, bathing them in whiteness. Cruising at twenty thousand feet, they were in broken cloud cover with some clouds drifting by below them. When he could see the ground there were clusters of lights marking cities and towns and then black landscape broken only by the occasional line of lights from cars.

Marcus stretched out his legs and considered trying to get some sleep, only to discard the idea. He had never been comfortable sleeping with the low drone of engines as the background.

The plan was in place after a long day of conference calls with Washington.

If Shari could pick out Connor in a lineup of photos, they would move against Connor and Frank. Arresting Titus would have to wait for more evidence. No one wanted him to slip through when they had a chance to send him away on conspiracy to murder a federal judge.

Marcus felt an ache in his heart, knowing the gamble they were taking. The evidence was all circumstantial. But the risk of flight was simply too great to wait—Connor and Frank could disappear anywhere in the world at a moment's notice.

The warrants had to find the direct evidence. The gun used to kill

Judge Whitmore, the blood-splattered suit, the gloves, the shoes, the disguise. It was hard to accept the reality that Lisa, by being so thorough with the evidence, had done the defense attorney's job for him.

The evidence pointed to either Frank or to Connor—the partial DNA markers obtained from the shattered glass said it could be either one of them; the sketch Shari had given suggested both; witnesses placed both men at the hotel. The defense attorney would have a credible argument for reasonable doubt regardless of which man they attempted to convict.

They would never get a conviction on Connor if all they had unique to him was the fact he was left-handed. Frank had the criminal record; Connor didn't. And if they tried to convict Frank, his attorney could reasonably argue the shooter had been Connor.

They had to find direct physical evidence. Or they had to get either Connor or Frank to cut a deal and talk because the option was unacceptable. A conviction would rise or fall on Shari's eyewitness testimony. And that would place Shari's life in grave danger.

Marcus pulled out the sketch he had done from her description of the shooter and turned the reading light back on. A few subtle changes and it matched Frank. A few others, and it was Connor.

What if Shari couldn't pick out the shooter from the photo lineup?

For the sake of the case he hoped she could.

For the sake of her safety, he hoped she couldn't. He wanted her removed as a factor in this case.

He was concerned about how she would react when she heard the news they had a suspect, learned the crushing news they might not have the evidence to convict. If the worst happened—an acquittal, a hung jury—it would destroy her. And he didn't want to see the glimmer of fear in her eyes when she looked at the photo of the man who had tried to kill her.

Put it aside. There is nothing you can do but deal with it as it comes.

He wanted to protect Shari from what was coming and could only ensure he was there when she had to deal with it.

He hesitated for a moment, and reached over to his suit jacket. From the inside pocket he removed the slim book—a New Testament plus Psalms and Proverbs—that Jennifer had given him. He'd read the passage she had marked in Luke on the flight to Chicago, gone on to thumb through the text and read words that were familiar to him from his childhood.

He could remember his mother reading him the stories from Luke.

This was the last moment of quiet he would have for several chaotic days. He owed Shari a decision; he owed himself a decision about Jesus, about prayer. The turmoil he felt didn't set well. And while this issue remained between them, he and Shari would remain at best cautious friends.

He couldn't afford to make the wrong decision. He knew how profound his life would change no matter what he decided. If he chose to again believe, to lay aside the doubts, it might give him a future with Shari, but it would create a sense of turmoil within the family. It would make it very hard for Rachel, Lisa, Jack, and Stephen not to feel a sense of discomfort over the fact they didn't believe.

He had been the leader of the O'Malleys for over two decades. He knew what it meant to look out for the family—be there to comfort, provide for them, support, solve problems, see trouble coming and head it off, bail them out after a mistake, keep the peace, love them. He couldn't afford to make the wrong decision. He couldn't walk them down a road to being hurt. He wouldn't shake that sense of family unity without being absolutely certain it was the right decision to make.

Jesus said He wanted to be Lord. He said, 'Follow Me.' Marcus could feel the clarion call of that order and its absoluteness. It was one of the unfortunate realities with religion, there was no middle ground. He believed and followed or he didn't.

Marcus had no practice with prayer since he was a child, and it felt awkward.

Jesus, You're asking a lot of me. It would mean trusting the O'Malleys to You. Not to mention Shari.

He could admit to himself he was worried. Who would look out for the O'Malleys if something happened to him? He had no illusions about the coming danger. When Connor knew they were after him, when Titus did—arrests would not be made without risk.

If something happened to him, who would keep Lisa out of trouble?

Who would give Rachel a hug?

Who would talk to Kate in the middle of the night when she carried the weight of the world on her shoulders?

Who would ensure Jennifer got everything possible to help her get well?

Who would be the older brother Stephen and Jack needed behind them?

Jesus, I need You to value what I value. Is it wrong to want that? This family needs a good strong leader. Trusting You for me is one thing, for them is something larger and deeper.

From his childhood came the memories of intense tears, and the unexpected rush of emotions had him clenching his jaw. The pain crashed back with a furor.

Jesus, I've got only one question really. How do You reconcile a child being abandoned by a loving God? I believed in You once, and I got crushed when Mom died. That's the pain You have to deal with if I am to accept again Your statement that You love me. If I'm to trust You.

He wanted to be optimistic. But he wasn't walking into a land mine of disappointment again. The last words his mom had told him from her hospital bed as she held his hand in hers, in a grip so soft his hold on hers had been the stronger one, her last words had been the whispered ones: "Jesus loves you." His mom had died that night. Shari said a child couldn't have the same perspective as an adult. Maybe not. But a child was not as easily fooled by words. They saw actions.

He closed the New Testament and slipped it back into his pocket.

He wasn't sure what he expected, what he wanted to know or see happen to settle his questions. There was an honest willingness to consider believing in God again. But he didn't know what he sought, what the reassurance was he needed to have.

Circumstances demanded that the issue slide to the background for the next several days. He was almost grateful.

The plane touched down in the darkness.

It was a silent drive to the lake house. Marcus saw lights on in the den as the car curved around the drive. Had Shari waited up for them to arrive? It wouldn't surprise him. Marcus retrieved his suit jacket and briefcase but left the one piece of carry-on luggage in the trunk. They would not be here for long, regardless of the outcome of the photograph lineup; the only question was their destination. He didn't want to be away, but Luke could manage security here.

Marcus followed Dave and Quinn around the driveway to the porch and walked into the house as Shari came from the den. It was so good to see her, and her smile…it was like coming home. She didn't hide the fact she was glad to see him, and in another situation, he would have reached out his arm to gather her into a hug. He wished he wasn't going to be erasing that smile with his words.

"I didn't think you would be back tonight. Dave, Quinn—it's great to see you." She looked back at him. "How's Jennifer?"

Her words threw him back a day to the reason he had originally left. It didn't feel like it had been only a day since he had seen Jennifer. "She's doing pretty good, all things considered. She's picked out her wedding dress," he offered with a smile, then turned serious. "Shari, would you wake up your brother?"

She looked from Marcus to the others, her expression growing still. "What is it?"

"After your brother is here."

She hesitated, then nodded and moved upstairs to wake Joshua.

Her brother and mom joined them in the den five minutes later. Shari didn't sit down, stopping instead just inside the door.

"What is it?" Her voice was steady, but she was twisting her fingers together.

"We've got a photo spread for you to look at," Marcus replied, watching her accept the news. He nodded to Dave, who opened the folder he carried and set down the prepared photograph spread on the desk. There were eight pictures in it, all chosen to look similar. Two of them were Frank and Connor.

Shari stepped toward the desk.

Marcus watched her face for a reaction as she looked down; he saw the shock hit. "That's him." She looked up at him, her gaze startled. "How did you—"

"Who, Shari?" Dave prompted.

Without hesitation she put her finger down on Connor. "He lost the hair and mustache."

Quinn looked over at Marcus.

"Call the pilot and tell him we're flying out tonight," Marcus told Quinn. "I want to be in New York by dawn."

Shari turned toward him, and he could see the fire in her eyes. "Who is he?"

"He's just a suspect at this point. It's best you don't know until we investigate further."

"Marcus, I know this is him. Why did he kill Carl? Why did he kill my father?"

Marcus looked at Joshua, at Beth, and then told Shari the basics. "It may have something to do with the Daniel Gray case."

That news rocked her. "The death penalty case. Over a decade ago."

"Yes."

"Not the Supreme Court short list. Not my brief."

He should have realized the relief that would be. He crossed to her side, reached for her hands. "No."

"You're going after him."

She wasn't saying she was afraid for him, but it was written all over her face. "Yes, we are. I don't know how long we will be gone."

Her hands came up to grasp his. "Marcus, be careful."

There were moments where caution didn't fit. He leaned down and kissed her. "I'll be careful. That's a promise."

She leaned against him, hugging him tight, and then she stepped back and looked over at Quinn. "Make him keep his word."

Quinn laughed. "Yes, ma'am."

"We need ideas; that place is a fortress," Marcus observed. Connor's home had full security, roving guards, and driveways leaving from three different sides of the grounds. By the time they served the search warrant, got access, and secured the grounds, Connor could destroy a lot of evidence and possibly even slip the grounds. And that was assuming they were not met with violence. They couldn't predict how the man would react when confronted. He had killed a judge; he didn't have anything to lose.

"We can serve him at his office."

"Walking into a law firm and arresting one of their partners will be like waving a red flag at their profession."

Dave pushed back his chair from the table where Connor's estate blue-prints were spread out. "We need to arrest Connor and serve warrants on his home, business, and vehicle at the same time."

"Agreed." Marcus looked at the marshal from the local office. "Gage, any ideas?"

"What about a street stop? Catch him between home and work. He drives himself; we should be able to establish surprise. And we can act with a small enough team we could limit any chance of a leak getting back to him once the warrant has been issued."

Marcus thought about it and nodded. "Have teams ready to move into his office and home as soon as he's been stopped?"

Gage nodded. "We should be able to prevent him from getting word out to anyone."

"Get it set up. Rick, is your team ready to serve on Frank's home?"

In five days they still had not been able to locate Frank. The decision had been made to arrest Connor, serve the search warrants, and hope to pressure Frank out of hiding.

"We're ready," Rick confirmed. "Those watching his house have seen three men present. We'll go in with four teams. There's an officer ready to shut down the security system when we move."

Marcus looked at his watch. "Let's get all the teams in place. We'll act when Connor leaves work."

The group separated to implement the details.

The waiting was over, and Marcus felt the change in focus inside. Five hours, and it would be over one way or another.

He considered calling Shari but didn't want to add to the stress she was carrying. Better to tell her after it was over.

At 4 P.M., Marcus walked with Dave and Quinn to the waiting vehicles, having gone through the plans in detail with Gage.

A street stop was a three vehicle maneuver. They were using an SUV, a blue sedan, and a white delivery van; nothing about them suggesting they were law enforcement vehicles. The nine officers assembled to assist them wore street clothes over the bulletproof vests. They would act somewhere on the drive between Connor's office and home, choosing the location that was most advantageous based on traffic.

They assembled across from Connor's office building where they could see his vehicle. When Connor left the office driving his Lexus, they slipped into traffic behind him.

The SUV, serving as the lead vehicle, eventually passed Connor's car and moved up in front of him. The delivery van and the sedan trailed Connor through town, eventually moving to be the vehicles immediately behind him. Connor's car turned east on Thirty-second street.

Marcus saw the streetlight changing to yellow up ahead. He keyed his radio. "We'll act here. Get ready."

The light turned red. Greg in the lead SUV came to a stop. Connor's Lexus stopped behind him.

"Do it," Marcus ordered.

The SUV suddenly backed up right to Connor's bumper. Connor saw it happening and went to this car horn. Gage whipped the sedan around the van and crowded Connor's driver's door at the same time Bill pulled the delivery van forward to touch the back bumper of the Lexus.

Officers were out with guns drawn at all sides of his car before Connor realized it was more than just someone backing into him. "Keep your hands on the wheel."

Surprise had him obeying.

Marcus let Gage take him from the car, formally making the arrest.

"I'm surprised at the timing of your arrest." Connor smiled as his hands were handcuffed. "You would have been welcome to walk into my office and serve your warrants." He looked around at the slowing traffic, then back at Marcus. "All this street stop buys you is some bad press that you have to explain when I'm eventually released. You don't have enough to hold me. You've got what? That I was in the hotel? It took you long enough to figure that out."

Connor shouldn't be talking, but there was truth to the saying a lawyer who has himself as a client was a fool.

"We've got Frank and an eyewitness," Marcus replied, making a deliberate move to shake the man up.

Connor blinked. His smile disappeared. And then he smiled again. A cold smile, thin, but a smile. "You don't have Frank, and your eyewitness will never testify."

It was a soft, distinct threat.

Marcus slammed Connor back against the car. "Who did you hire?"

Quinn and Dave leaped forward to pull him back. Marcus ignored them. He was looking into the eyes of the man who had killed Carl and Shari's father. Any doubt of that had disappeared.

"*I* didn't hire anyone."

Marcus heard the emphasis. Titus had made the hire.

"And if he doesn't get paid until a year and a day after your witness is dead, you are going to have a hard time linking the two."

Even Quinn paled.

"Dave, get him out of here." Marcus shoved Connor toward the waiting car.

"Marcus."

"I know, Quinn."

Only one man had that unique signature of payment. Lucas Saracelli. He didn't miss at two hundred yards. He didn't miss at four hundred yards. Dark. Wet. City. Country. It didn't matter. He had been on the international law enforcement agencies most wanted lists for the last twelve years.

"We've got to get her out of there. Fast. It's a cover that will never hold. And he's got a big head start."

Marcus could feel the fear; three teams on the ground would never hold. "Agreed. But where?"

"My ranch," Quinn recommended. "We want to avoid a fight with this guy, but if it happens, we had better have every advantage."

Lucas was sharing a beer with a flight attendant from Jamaica when the phone call came. The Washington, D.C., bar was noisy and packed, but he chose to take the call where he was. "They just picked up Connor in New York. The team was led by U.S. Marshal Marcus O'Malley. They flew in on a private jet."

Lucas smiled at the flight attendant. "Fine. Thank you for the call." He hung up and reached for another pretzel. Shari was somewhere in Kentucky, and her escort was now in New York. Interesting.

"Business?"

"Maybe. When's your return flight?"

"Seven."

"Then business can definitely wait until 7:15 P.M. I promised you an escort back to the airport."

She giggled. He liked the giggle. He set down the beer. "Come on. Let's dance."

Sixteen

Marcus took the call on the plane. They were on a private flight back to the house by the lake, having pulled together as many men as they could within an hour. "Yes, Dave."

"The search warrants have been served on Connor's office and home. We got some interference from the staff on duty at his home but it's been dealt with. We managed to get the surprise we hoped for, but I'm afraid that is all we've got going in our favor. The crime lab technicians are taking the place apart but so far there is nothing that can be directly linked to the crime. The two house safes are empty; the three weapons registered to him are accounted for and don't match."

"We need something, *anything*."

"We're working it. Just focus on Shari. I promise you, now that we've got Connor, we are going to turn his life inside out. If there is evidence here we will find it."

"Frank?"

"No sign of him. I've got a bad feeling about him, Marcus."

The reality that he might have already skipped town was very real. "Put the warrant out on the wires so if he is traveling in the U.S. we'll have a chance of learning about it."

"It will be out within the hour," Dave assured. "Stay in touch and let me know when you get in."

"I'll call as soon as we land," Marcus confirmed, and said good-bye. He closed the phone and looked back at Quinn. The lack of evidence was a serious problem he would wrestle with later, they had an even more serious one to deal with. "How do we stop someone who has no stop button? Once a hit is accepted, it can't be withdrawn with this man."

"Do you think Connor could have hired him?"

"No, he doesn't have that kind of money. It had to be his father, Titus."

"Can we crimp Titus to the point he won't be able to pay so the guy will make the decision on his own to back off?"

"We'd have to seize the entire operation. To do that we need inside information. If convicted of the murder of Judge Whitmore, the only way Connor could avoid the death penalty, avoid dying like his brother, would be to cut a deal and talk about his father's business. But he won't talk unless he thinks he will be found guilty, and he's confident Shari will never testify."

"A vicious circle."

"We've got no choice. We'll have to stop Lucas."

Marcus rarely felt fear such as he did now. Lucas could have been in the States looking for Shari for as long as a month. The lake house wasn't safe; nowhere truly would be until Connor, Frank, and Titus were convicted and sentenced. The escalation this represented was horrific.

In all his years as a marshal protecting witnesses he had never faced a challenge like this. That it was affecting the woman he loved...he forced aside the emotion lest it paralyze him. "He could have entered the country anytime since July 8."

"Titus had to get in touch with Lucas somehow in order to establish the terms of the contract. Maybe we can get a lead on him through that."

"If Titus went through his contacts in Europe to make the arrangements we may never find it. We might have a better chance locating Lucas from the sniper rifle he's going to need to acquire once he is here in the States. The one thing we can be certain of is that it will be custom made."

Marcus pulled out a pad of paper. "Walk me through the security arrangements we can make immediately and over the next few weeks at the ranch."

"Assume he learns Shari is at the Montana ranch: He then has to get to the ranch—by air, by car, across country by horse, or walk in by foot. So that's our first line of defense. We'll start with arranging for the county sheriff to close the bridge over the Ledds River. They've been discussing the need for repairs for the last four months, so local residents will not be surprised. That will make any traffic approaching the ranch from the south stand out and give us a chance to track it."

"How do we deploy the security detail?"

By the time the plane touched down at the airport near the lake house, they had worked out a security plan for the next several days. It wasn't sufficient, nothing really would be, but it was a workable plan.

On the drive to the house, Marcus tried to work out what he would say, and how Shari might react to the news. How was he supposed to break the news there was a paid contract out on her?

They arrived back at the lake house at 9:20 P.M. Marcus left the others fanning out behind him to cover the grounds and strode toward the house.

"Marcus!" Shari scrambled from the couch in the den to come and meet him. "He was arrested? You got him?"

"We arrested Connor." The relief that crossed her face was obvious, intense, and complete—and he was going to destroy it. He grasped her hands, cushioned them tight between his own. "Shari, get your things. We need to leave."

Her relief changed to confusion as his expression registered. "What's wrong?"

He stopped her words with fingers across her lips. "I'll explain later. Go. Pack what you can fit in one bag." He had decided the best way to handle it for now was to simply duck the question. Josh came from the kitchen and Marcus took advantage of it. "Josh, we need to talk." He nodded toward the den.

Beth was in the doorway of the den, a book in her hand, listening. Marcus crossed to her side, leaned down, and kissed her cheek. "It's good to see you. Help Shari pack? I'll explain in a few minutes."

She nodded, worried. "Of course, Marcus."

"It will be all right," he reassured her.

He strode through to the privacy of the den, Quinn joining him.

Josh closed the door behind them. "What's going on?"

"There's been a contract put out on your sister."

Josh absorbed that hit, his eyes widened and then hardened. "Can you keep her safe?"

"I won't let someone get to her." Marcus paced the room, anxious to get moving. "We need to get her out of here though. She's been stationary too long and we need someplace more isolated than this."

"You've got to tell her."

"Tell me what?"

Marcus turned, frustrated. Shari had ignored his request. He wanted her packing. And definitely not hearing the details now.

"Marcus, tell me."

He looked at Quinn and realized he had no choice. "Shari, sit down."

She complied only to the extent she perched on the arm of the couch. "What is it?"

He hoped she didn't panic. "Connor's family wants you dead. They've put a contract out on you."

She looked confused. "He's already tried to kill me twice. This is a surprise?"

"This time someone was hired to do it. We need to get you out of here."

"You're afraid."

"I'm...concerned. The man they hired is good."

"You're better," she replied bluntly, catching him by surprise. She surged to her feet. "We split up. I don't want Mom near me."

Josh looked over at him. Marcus had to agree with Shari on this one. They were going to need to move fast, and he was very concerned about Beth's health if things got serious. He couldn't guarantee medical help would be nearby.

It was clear Josh didn't want to leave Shari's side, but he reluctantly nodded. "Aunt Margaret's in London. Can I take Mom there?" Josh offered.

Marcus looked at Quinn. "Safer than staying in the States," Quinn agreed. "By the time their flight lands, we can have security ready."

"Josh, it would probably be best." Marcus paced over to stand beside Shari. "I'm sorry."

She shivered. "He's arrested, and I'm in even more danger."

"He's getting desperate." He wrapped his arm around her shoulders. "Trust me, this is almost over. Now go pack. We've got to go."

"Tell me about the man who was hired."

Marcus looked up from the very old photo of Lucas he was doing his best to absorb and update. The private jet was cruising at thirty thousand feet. Shari had moved back to join him. Her voice was pitched low, for around them the security teams of men were working. It was after midnight. He nodded to the seat beside him. "Have a seat."

He waited until she was seated and strapped in, then slid over the sketch he was working on. "His name is Lucas Saracelli. We don't have anything recent."

"You said he was good. Why? What makes him good?"

"He's a patient man. He doesn't leave a trail behind him. And he doesn't need to shoot twice."

"Then I'm not really safe."

"Not if he can find you, get close. We're going to make sure that doesn't happen." He reached over and squeezed her hand. "We don't want a fight with this guy. We simply want to lay low until the grand jury can be impaneled and you can testify."

"And the trial? It's going to be months away."

"We'll cross one milestone at a time."

"I'm afraid, Marcus."

"I know. It's justified." He ran his fingers through her hair. The fear he felt was intense for her, but he wasn't going to let it show. "I won't let anything happen to you. That's an O'Malley promise. My promise."

She leaned over to rest against him. "Thank you, Marcus." She snuggled her head down against his shoulder. "And to show how much I trust you, I'm going to catch a catnap. Wake me when we get close to wherever we're going."

And I wonder why I love you. He leaned over and kissed her forehead softly. "Sleep well."

He watched her drift to sleep.

Jesus, I wish I could trust You with her safety. She's now as important as any O'Malley to me. She's got a lot of courage, and she's trusting me not to let anything happen to her. Quinn and I know how good Lucas is. I'm going to need help.

That's my reality, Jesus. Are You as invested in my family and Shari as I am? That's my line. It's not one particular prayer, any one answer; it's a settled, absolute bedrock confidence that I can trust You with the people I love.

Show me the way back.

Shari looked down on the ranch as they descended to the private airstrip at dawn. She hadn't asked where they were going; had been surprised when twenty minutes ago Quinn had moved to the seat beside her, pointed out the river below, and indicated it was the start of his ranch land.

"Quinn, how do you ever leave here? It's beautiful." The ranch below was rolling hills, large stretches of timber, and a lot of pastureland. She could see the cattle from the air.

"Someone has to stick with Marcus to keep him out of trouble."

She heard the humor but also a lot not getting said. She liked Marcus's partner, but even after spending weeks with him, she had learned very little about him. Marcus trusted him absolutely and that was enough for her to do the same.

The plane set down on the airstrip and taxied toward an open door hangar with a Cessna inside. They were about a half mile from the ranch house she had seen from the air. When the plane came to a stop, Shari unbuckled her seat belt and gathered up the one bag she had with her and her briefcase.

"Stay inside for a moment," Marcus cautioned.

She waited for them to secure the area.

"Okay, Shari." Quinn offered her a hand down the steps as she left the plane. "Welcome to my home."

She looked around, curious. "Thank you for offering such a wonderful hiding place."

"It's my pleasure. Let's get you under wraps."

The security detail with them had already fanned out.

A truck pulled up. Shari dropped her bag in the back and got into the passenger seat as Marcus traded places with the driver. He turned the truck toward the house. "I need to explain a few things if you're up to it."

She looked over at him, seeing the intensity, and nodded. "Of course."

"Quinn has a number of ranch hands who will be patrolling the boundaries of the ranch, but it's open land. So what we're going to do is establish a very tight perimeter around the house, out at about five hundred yards. Inside of that will be constant patrols. I'm afraid it's going to mean you see a lot of the ranch house and not much of the ranch."

"I'll cope. Just tell me what you need me to do. I don't want any of you getting hurt."

"Trust me. We'll be fine."

They passed several large barns and a stable on the way to the house. She would love it here had she been able to visit under other circumstances. There were horses in the pasture near a barn.

Marcus parked in front of the house and came around to help her down from the truck. Shari walked beside him to the house. The one-story ranch house sprawled, breezeways and vistas connecting together what appeared to be three different wings. Flowers lined the walkway, and hanging plants, spaced between white columns, decorated the porch.

Marcus held the door for her; she stepped inside and stopped. She found herself standing on the threshhold of a great room—open, spacious, gleaming with hardwood floors. It was as modern as any she had ever seen—Western, masculine in tone and furniture, but filled with art, both sculpture and oil paintings, the open room adding an enormous sense of calm coolness, as if the house had seen generations and stood unaffected.

"This is Quinn's home?"

"He can surprise you," Marcus replied. "I'll introduce you to Susan and her husband, Greg, later. They maintain the house and grounds when Quinn is away." He smiled. "Susan's responsible for the order you see. You'll like them, I'm certain."

Marcus gestured to the hallway to the left leading into a wing of the house. "It's best if you take the first guest bedroom. It doesn't have the best view, but in this case that will be an advantage."

Shari nodded and walked through to the room he indicated. There was a Spanish flavor to the decor in its bold color bedspread and the rugs on the hardwood floor; the furniture was heavy mahogany. "It's beautiful, Marcus. I'll be comfortable here."

"Good. Unpack. I'll check with Quinn, then I'll give you a tour."

She nodded and lifted her bag to the bed, opened it, and began putting items away. She was grateful that they had chosen a private home such as this for the next few weeks. The house was beautiful. It conveyed a calm and restful tone—if she had to be housebound, at least it would be restful versus stuck in the impersonal quarters of a hotel somewhere.

Marcus and Quinn hadn't chosen this place at random. They wanted to be on familiar ground they controlled. They were setting up for a siege. She pushed the disquiet of that thought away, stored her empty bag in the closet, and went to find Marcus. She found him in the kitchen, talking on the phone as he poured himself a cup of coffee.

"Shari." Marcus held out the phone. He smiled at her puzzlement. "Your mom."

She whispered a thank-you as she accepted it. It was wonderful to hear her voice. "I'm fine, Mom. It's beautiful here."

She settled into a chair at the table and spent fifteen minutes reassuring herself that Josh and Mom were safe, reassuring her mom of the same with her. When Shari was done, she smiled and held out the phone to Marcus. "Thank you. That was nice, for both of us."

"You're welcome." He hung up the phone. "Are you fine?" he asked quietly.

She took a deep breath and let it out, accepting for the first time since she had been told the news just what was being asked of her. "I'm not letting the man who killed Carl and my father off. I'll testify. Your job is to get me safely there. I'll do whatever you say is necessary. Courage I don't lack. Common sense, yes. Courage, no."

He looked over at her, not saying anything for several moments. "You've got backbone. I admire that. This isn't going to be easy."

She understood that. She knew she didn't understand the risks and danger as he and Quinn did, that he would never reveal most of them, but she understood the fact she would have the best security that could be offered. "No, it's not going to be easy. But it's the right thing to do. I'm stubborn that way."

"We had to rush you away from the lake house. I'm sorry you were not able to have more time with your mom. And Josh is already frustrated with the distance."

"We're a strong family; Josh will get over it, and Mom has every confidence in you, in God. She'll worry about my safety, but she'll cope."

He held out his hand. "Come on. Let me show you your new home."

Shari followed him through the house, taking her time to linger on the art and the books and the photos. "I would never have imagined this to be Quinn's."

"He finds items he likes and sends them back here. Some of the pieces are works of his mom's. She was a gifted sculptor. This house is a memory to her and the love of art she passed to Quinn. He doesn't take enough time off to enjoy this place as he should."

"Why is he a marshal when he has this ranch? Surely it's a profitable enterprise."

"It's one of the best in the state," Marcus replied. "Quinn has good reasons for the choice he made. And the ranch will still be here thriving when he wants to come back to it full time. His ranch manager is an excellent man, dedicated to this land."

Shari was surprised that Marcus chose not to answer her question, then realized Quinn had also made the same evasion earlier. A mystery there. She tucked it away to think about over the next few weeks. Spending time here would probably give her the answer.

"Come on, let me introduce you to Susan."

They found Susan in the kitchen starting breakfast. Marcus introduced her and Shari knew immediately from the warm welcome that she had found another friend. She asked if she could help fix breakfast, and Marcus left her there while he went to touch base with Quinn.

Shari was fighting fatigue by the time Quinn and Marcus came back to the house and breakfast was served. The sleep on the plane had been short and broken. She forced herself to eat something, then listened to Marcus and Quinn as they discussed the plans for the next few days.

She carried her plate back to the kitchen.

"Shari, go ahead and turn in." Marcus paused at her side, his hand rubbing the back of her neck. "I know you're exhausted."

She wanted to lean against him and just accept the strength he offered. She accepted reality. "Yes. But don't let me sleep the entire day away."

"Four hours. Six, if you're deeply asleep," he reassured.

She walked through the house to the guest room. She was surprised to see a large vase of red roses now on the nightstand. Shari crossed over to them and withdrew the card.

You are the best: courageous, brave, and funny. Remember that. Marcus.

She blinked back tears. The tenderness was overwhelming. She pulled one bloom from the vase. He was a wonderful man. Special. And she was in love with him.

She curled up on the bed, holding the rose, and letting the tears she had denied for so long fall, too tired to fight the sadness that welled up inside along with joy. Optimism was breaking against reality and shattering. She was going to get her heart broken again. His doubts would pull her away from her faith if she let her heart become fully attached to him.

Jesus, why does life just keep getting harder? I love Marcus. I want a future with him. She wiped away her tears. She was tired of being afraid. *Protect me. Protect Marcus.*

Was it possible to resurrect her dreams? For a marriage, a future? *Lord, You've instilled them in my heart. Let them come true. I want these tears to turn to joy.*

Seventeen

D ave, consider something," Marcus directed his request toward the speakerphone on Quinn's desk. "Connor waited nine months after the execution of his brother to kill Judge Whitmore. Why wait? Why wait nine months and then take the risk of shooting him in a place full of potential witnesses and cops?"

"The murder was planned only after Judge Whitmore emerged as a contender for the short list," Dave speculated. "Connor didn't want the judge who sentenced his brother making it to the Supreme Court."

"Exactly. But I think it's even tighter than that. Whitmore's name was floated months before as a potential candidate. Why didn't Connor act then? It makes sense now, knowing that Whitmore didn't make the original short list of names, but how did Connor know he wasn't going to make that list? It wasn't until Shari's brief appeared that the odds became good that Whitmore would be added to the list and have a good chance of being nominated." Marcus tapped his knuckles on the polished wood of the desk. "Connor is a lawyer."

Dave's voice hardened. "He somehow saw a copy of the brief."

Marcus had a sinking feeling that this case was going to link back to Shari's brief after all. "Find out. His law firm has a Washington office so it's not implausible that someone at the firm has a contact inside the Justice Department. Something put this man in motion; I want to know if he saw a copy of the brief or if we can establish someone told him about its existence."

"I'll put a high priority on finding out," Dave agreed.

"That's my one new observation since yesterday. What do you have?"

"Regarding the timeline, we've got a few more pieces filled in. We know Connor took a flight to Chicago the evening of July 5; he booked those tickets on July 1."

Marcus flipped open his notebook on the desk and added the details to the calendar clipped inside. "One day after we know Frank was seen at the hotel."

"It plays. Frank was the advance man; he determined a hit at the hotel would be possible, and Connor booked to come out."

"Connor is going to argue it was the merger discussions suddenly getting serious that caused the abrupt decision to be in Chicago," Marcus replied, thinking as the defense attorney.

"If we can show Connor saw the brief and then sent Frank out to look at the hotel, we can at least establish a pattern of conduct leading up to the hit."

"We've got motive—we have to nail down means. How are we doing at establishing Connor's movements at the hotel the night of the murder?"

"I just talked to Mike. They've found three people who can confirm he was in the banquet room when Judge Whitmore gave his speech, and two that will testify they saw him leave as the speech concluded. That's obviously significant. After that—the security guard confirms Connor was at the merger discussions late that evening. So there's an open three-hour window to nail down."

"What do Connor's hotel room door logs show?"

"They muddy the waters. The door to his hotel room opened and closed with a card key five times during those three hours. He claims to have been discussing merger details on the phone with a partner in New York, that he went to the vending machine, stopped to buy a paper, then set out a room service order for the next day. For all we can tell, it could've been Frank using Connor's hotel room and providing an alibi of activity."

Marcus sighed. "No surprise there; we knew they planned this in detail. He's going to have reasonable doubt alibis in place. Where are we at on locating Frank Keaton? Anything?"

"The last confirmation we have on his location is from an FBI surveillance tape taken at the Potomac Shipping Company. He was seen there on Wednesday, July 19, accompanied by another man who works for Titus."

"Two days before the shooting at the funeral."

"We haven't been able to turn up anything suggesting Frank's where-abouts after that. Assuming we are right and he did make the attempt on Shari at the church, he appears to have fled immediately afterwards."

"Or something happened to him."

"How Titus reacted to the failure is hard to predict. Word is out on the street to see if we can get a clue."

"What was Frank driving?" Marcus asked.

"I checked. It was a light blue sedan, not the SUV we've been looking for."

There was a tap on the door and it opened. Marcus waved Quinn in to join him. "Anything at Frank's home?"

"We could charge him on a few weapons violations; he has a small arsenal that is unregistered—ballistics is checking them against prior unsolved cases—but other than that nothing useful."

"Dave, we know who did it, we know why, there just has to be a way to conclusively prove it. I gather Connor is no longer talking?"

"Titus had a lawyer here shortly after Connor was brought in. Now that guy is someone who is scary. A check of his past cases gives a Rolodex of names for people you do not want to know. Connor has been strikingly silent since having a conversation with his new lawyer."

"Find Frank," Marcus decided. "It's our best hope of breaking this case open. And focus on linking Connor to that brief."

"Will do."

"Have they convened the grand jury?"

"It's set for Saturday, September 2."

Another nine days. Marcus was relieved it wasn't any longer. "We'll arrange to fly out the night before the grand jury testimony. I don't want to leave this secure site before I have to. Could you arrange to come out with Kate and Lisa? I want to review this case from top to bottom one last time. I could use the additional manpower for the flight east."

"Good idea. I'll see what I can arrange and call you back."

Marcus concluded the update call and leaned back against the desk. He was weary to the soul with the twists and turns this case was taking. He looked over at his partner. "It is not supposed to be this way. Someone murders a judge; we're supposed to be able to do something about it. They take out Shari, he gets away with having murdered a judge."

"She'll testify."

"If we can get her there safely," Marcus replied. "What else can we be doing to find Lucas Saracelli? There has to be something."

Quinn tossed his hat on the table. "Good question, Marcus. I wish I had an answer. We have at best an old picture; at worst one that will no longer be close if he's had surgery done. We know the unique signatures of his MO. But the rest is a bunch of maybes—possibly American born and military trained because of the type of rifle and ammunition he favors; a probable residence in Europe as most of his contracts have been there. The few clues from the scenes of his hits show he is a man who plans in great detail, studies the area before each hit, and takes as long as he deems necessary to fulfill a contract."

"I hate this."

"Do you want to move her again before the grand jury convenes?"

Marcus thought about it, then finally shook his head. "No, you're right about this being the safest place to defend. Moving her will only leave another trail that's fresh. I would rather have our trail go very cold on him."

Going over the problem again wouldn't get a different answer. Marcus pushed away from the desk. "It's late. You missed dinner. I'll let you get to it."

"Shari's in the library. You might want to stop by."

Marcus raised an eyebrow. There was an unexpected note of concern in Quinn's voice. "Thanks, I'll do that."

Shari was curled on the couch in the library. Without the lights on. That was a bad sign. Marcus leaned against the door frame, trying to decide what was best. She had become noticeably quiet over the last week and it hadn't been easy to draw her out. "You want company?"

His question startled her. She turned to look back, then reached over to click on the table light. "Sorry. Come on in, Marcus. I was just thinking."

He had misinterpreted the situation. He had been afraid she was fighting tears, but her voice was steady.

"What are you thinking about?"

"How much can change in a short time. A month and a half ago I didn't know you, there wasn't someone trying to kill me, I had a family intact."

Her tone of voice bothered him; it had a bitterness he had never heard before. But he understood her emotions so well, was glad in a way that she was finally letting heaviness bleed off rather than try to accept it. The stress of what had happened was still coming, was going to break her or refine her before it was over. And the fact she was letting him see the emotion was itself a sign of trust that was a gift to him.

"This was a day Carl always celebrated—the anniversary of his first day on the bench."

The memories—he understood so well how they would appear unexpectedly from the past and bring back the pain. "Shari—I'm sorry."

She sighed, rubbing the back of her neck. "Sit down, I could use that company." She tossed the unopened pad of paper and pen she held onto the couch beside her. "You choose the topic tonight. I'm pretty morose."

He chose instead to simply take a seat and share the silence.

"You want to know something funny?" Her voice didn't sound amused.

"Sure," he quietly replied.

"I'm really getting tired of chocolate ice cream."

It took a moment for it to sink in, and then he leaned his head back and burst out laughing. "Oh, Shari."

"What are the odds that you can get some pralines and cream ice cream out here in the middle of nowhere?"

"Are you sure you don't want something easy, like maybe fresh lobster?"

"If that was an offer, I won't turn it down." She turned her head, shared a smile, and then gave a sigh. "I miss my family."

"I know. I miss mine too."

"Did you hear from Jennifer?"

"She sounds very tired. They were doing another round of bone scans today." He reached in his front pocket for a folded envelope. "Here. I think you ought to see this."

She reached over and accepted it. "What is it?"

"Rugsby's ransom demand. My part of it anyway." She unfolded the note, bit back a grin, but not before he saw it. His suspicions had been right. Either Jennifer or Rachel had recruited her. "Now I wonder who gave them that idea?"

"It's just a sketch," she replied.

Marcus folded his hands across his chest and watched her. "Sure it is," he said softly.

"I have to admit, I'm not sure I'm up on my Snow White and the seven dwarfs, but which one does this make you?" She looked at the sketch of the character, then back over at him. "Sleepy?"

"Try Grumpy," he replied with a gentle threat.

She giggled. "So if all the O'Malleys got tagged with a seven dwarf character as their clue, how does this get back Rugsby?"

"Turn it over."

"'*Deliver Snow White to me or Rugsby dies. Signed, The Wicked Witch.*' Ohh, this is good. Who's Snow White?"

"Guess."

She looked at him, then looked back at the note, startled. And then she started laughing as she held up her hands. "No way. I'm not getting in the middle of this. Your family makes jokes an art form."

"You started it. Grumpy indeed."

She passed back the note. "If I'm stuck here, you can hardly be expected to deliver me on the date specified. Who's the Wicked Witch?"

He folded the note and slid it back into his pocket. "At the moment I could label just about any of the O'Malleys with that title," he replied dryly.

She had a hard time stopping the laughter. "Marcus, I needed that."

"We both did."

He relaxed on the couch and simply watched her. "This will eventually be over."

"Not soon enough." Her expression turned sad again, tired. "I've been praying for patience. So far it hasn't worked. Or maybe it has and I'm just having to learn to appreciate the answer."

"Just take it a day at a time, Shari. That's all you can do."

She picked up a document from the stack beside her. He recognized her now dog-eared copy of the brief she had written recommending Carl for the court. "I can understand the hatred that drove Connor to kill. But I don't understand why he followed through with it when he did, where he did."

"Shari, trying to understand Connor's rationale—it will never really make sense."

"Was my family part of his plan?"

"No."

She looked over at him, moodily. "Did he want to make a public statement? Is that why he killed at the conference and not back in Virginia?"

"We don't know," he said quietly.

"Carl was killed because he was going to make the short list. Daniel had been dead nine months. The timing had to be significant."

He wouldn't lie to her, but he wouldn't support a conclusion that was only a speculation, not when it would hurt her. "If he chose the conference for any specific reason, it may simply have been for the confusion and the time it gave him to escape. We have no reason to believe he ever saw your brief, that he had any way to know Carl had made the short list."

"But you're looking for that link."

"We're looking."

Marcus watched with concern as she set aside the brief and leaned her head back to look up at the ceiling. How he wished he could strip away the pressure and give her some peace.

"Marcus, how do you cope with the sense of incompleteness? The sense that their lives were cut short? Both Carl and Dad? Time keeps running across events. It's not just the holidays and birthdays, it's the baseball games we had tickets to go see, weekend vacations we had planned."

"You loved them, Shari. There is no way to remove that void."

"I know God wasn't surprised. But it doesn't feel like there was much preparation beforehand for the shock that hit. I know it wasn't an accident that had you and Dave and Quinn close by to help, but it's so hard to accept I will never see Dad or Carl again. I still wake up of a morning and for a moment think everything's fine, then remember."

"It would worry me most if you didn't have this grief coming through. Do you still dream about that night?"

She grimaced. "I've been shot in my dreams so many times I think it's like a repeating tape."

"I wondered."

"The dreams no longer make me panic. Maybe that's progress."

"It is. Good progress."

"How long will it last?"

"Months, maybe years. I think your prayer for patience is the right one. You need time for the grief to heal, time for the memories to fade in sharpness, time to adjust your expectation for the future. Be gentle with yourself; you'll make it."

She gave a slight smile. "At least here there is plenty of time to pray."

"I envy you your ability to believe," he said abruptly, reopening a subject he had avoided talking about for the last week. He was searching for his way back, but it was hard. He had been rereading Luke. It was so hard to set aside the doubts. He just wanted some peace back in his life.

She looked over at him, curious. "Marcus, why do the O'Malleys trust you?" She let him think about it for a moment, then answered her own rhetorical question. "They chose to trust you. You can lead them into harm's way and they'll charge behind you without question. You know that, which is why you carry your responsibility so seriously. That's all I'm doing, choosing to trust Jesus even if I don't understand what or why something is happening. Jesus wants you to choose to trust Him again. He won't take that trust you place in Him lightly."

"Have you settled your turmoil about prayer?"

"Part of it. I've at least settled my confusion on how to pray. Mom quietly trusts and accepts what God does; I want a specific answer and I pray with passion for that. I always thought my problem was that I had to be like Mom, and I'm not made that way. An issue that matters to me inevitably becomes something I am passionate about."

"What did you learn?"

"Jesus was both. A simple answer, I know, but realizing it was a profound change. Jesus was both trusting and passionate. He brought His petitions with loud groans and tears. He acted like Elijah. 'The prayer of a righteous man has great power in its effects.' Wrestling powerful prayer. And conversely, there was the contentment of knowing He was speaking with the Father who loved Him. *Father, I thank thee that thou hast heard me. I know that thou hearest me always, but I have said this on account of the people standing by, that they may believe that thou didst send me.*

"I still don't have contentment over unanswered prayer, but I no longer wonder whether God loves me or if He hears me. If it's a prayer where I speak with passion, God's okay with that, and if it's the quiet trust of a child with a problem, that's good too."

"I'm glad you found some of your answers."

"You'll find your answers too."

"Trust isn't easy."

"Marcus, who's Jesus? What's His character like? Answer that, it will help." She rested her chin on the couch pillow she had picked up. "Can I ask you a personal question?"

Surprised at the change in subject, he nodded. "Sure."

"What do you dream about for your future? The reason I ask—I've had nothing but a lot of time to think in the last few weeks, about what is important, about what I want to do when this is over. Do you ever do that too, when you're stuck on assignments like this?"

What he said was important to her, he could tell from the way she was studying him as she waited for the answer. He hadn't talked about it much outside of the family, occasionally with Quinn. "I want to be director of the marshals one day. Move it forward as an agency, bring more mavericks like Quinn and Lisa in to help rein in the bureaucracy and keep the focus on the nuts and bolts of the investigations."

"You sound very sure of that dream."

"I know where I'm heading."

She glanced away. "What about personally? What about kids? I already know you like them. Do you want a family someday?"

He smiled at the way she tried to make her direct question indirect. *Yes, Shari, I would love to have a family with you.* They weren't at a place where he could say those words. "Absolutely. And I've thought a lot about someday adopting too. The O'Malleys would spoil them rotten."

"Six aunts and uncles. I can see what you mean."

"What about you?"

"I would love kids someday."

He heard the wistfulness. "You'd make a wonderful mom."

"Mom would love to be a grandmother."

She'd walked herself into thinking about her dad. He saw it when it happened. Quietness washed over her. He didn't try to break it. There would be no grandfather for her children.

He finally spoke. "Let it go."

"Yes." She looked across at him and changed the subject again. "I hope you don't lose Jennifer."

He didn't want to think about such a possibility, but he had to. He had to be prepared for it in order to be prepared to help his family. The sadness was overwhelming. And Shari understood it. He looked at her and felt the enormous emotions ease, just for being able to share them. "If the unspeakable ever happens, will you come to the funeral with me?"

She nodded.

"Thank you, friend." He wished he had the right to wrap her in his arms right now. And if he wasn't careful, he was going to say the wrong thing. "Come on, it's time you turned in," he wisely decided. She was not always going to be a witness. And that day was not going to come soon enough.

He walked Shari to her bedroom door and forced himself to simply say good night there. Rather than rejoin Quinn, he walked further down the hall to the guest room he was using. Out of habit he picked up the book on the nightstand, planning to read for a while, then sighed and set it back down.

He reached again for the Bible. Take one step forward, feel out if it was safe, then take another step. He felt like he was crawling back, walking on thin ice.

He was finally beginning to understand part of it. Those who believed, believed completely and trusted with abandon. His mom's happiness that he had basked in as a child had come from God. She had flourished in her faith despite circumstances—her spirit had been trusting, her smile always there. Decades later he was still grieving the loss of his mom. That was the most profound fact he had realized. It wasn't faith as much as it was grief. He had lost so much.

Who was Jesus? What is His character? Shari asked very good questions. He settled on the side of the bed and started reading where he had left off.

There would be a future with Shari, if everything worked out just right—he had to cling to that hope. His emotions were so involved that seeing that sadness in her tonight was overwhelming. He wished he could give her something to make the stay here easier. Missing family was something he understood only too well.

When he said Jennifer was doing as well as could be expected, he had been stretching the truth. Jennifer was in the fight of her life and she was at best only holding her own. It was the unsaid reality in Kate's voice, in Rachel's.

At least this ranch was like an island, an isolated spot.

But were their tracks covered deeply enough?

Eighteen

Marcus let the roan he was riding pick the way down the steep slope to the streambed. Only a thin stream of water snaked down the center of the cracked ground. This tributary to the Ledds River showed the effects of the unusually dry summer.

The sun was hot, and after two hours of riding his body felt the heat down to his bones. Quinn had already crossed the gully. Marcus sent the horse up the far bank, trying to ignore the crumbling dirt making the task difficult. He liked to ride, but he didn't do enough of it to be relaxed like Quinn and was still working out a relationship with this particular mount. Quinn's definition of broke for riding was not necessarily his.

The rolling pastures for most of the ride had given way to steeper hills, and ahead were the bluffs that cut through the south edge of Quinn's land. Bluffs that Marcus had walked with Quinn numerous times in the past.

Bluffs and a grave.

Quinn reined in to wait for him, scanning ahead with binoculars and reaching for the rifle. Marcus drew up beside him.

"There." Quinn pointed.

Marcus took the offered binoculars and followed the indicated direction. There was a faint curl of white smoke lifting on the still air from a small grove of trees in the distance. The daily air surveillance had seen it that morning.

"We'll follow the riverbank to that outcrop of rocks and then approach the grove on foot from the east," Quinn decided.

Marcus nodded and slid out the rifle he carried. Sending one of the ranch hands to check this out hadn't even been considered. The odds that Lucas would give away his position with smoke were slim to none, but an ambush to get information, shake them up—that was possible.

They left the horses and worked slowly to the grove.

Marcus looked over at Quinn, he nodded, and they moved in, rifles ready.

The site was deserted.

It had been a campsite, the crushed grass and holes in the ground showing where a small tent had been pitched, a worn path going west showing the campsite had been active for at least a few days, a crude fire ring of stones held bits of charred wood. A coffee can near the fire ring was the source of the thin, waffling white smoke and it stunk. Marcus approached it cautiously, watching his feet for any trip wire around it. A handmade wick was burning down into something that was a muddy white.

"Someone's homemade bug repellent," Quinn concluded, looking at it.

Quinn walked over the log that must have been used as a bench and spread out a pile of sharp-edged stones beside the log with his foot. "He was cave spelunking. These are the discards he gathered but didn't want to carry out."

"Not Lucas."

"Not unless he was amusing himself by killing time."

Marcus walked around the site. "He didn't want to carry out the smoke pot."

"Not exactly the sweetest smelling thing to carry with him."

"He was here at least two, three days. How did we miss seeing him?"

Quinn snuffed out the bug repellent pot. "You can't see this campsite from the air without the smoke, and someone walking in, we're only going to see him by luck or if he crosses into one of our tightly patrolled areas."

Marcus turned back on his pager and opened his phone, called back to the house, and alerted Luke to what they had found.

"Let's ride back along the bluffs and make sure he's left, not just moved on to a new site," Quinn suggested. Marcus nodded his agreement. He would like to know who this guy was.

They walked back to the horses.

Quinn became grim the closer they came to the bluffs. Marcus didn't break the silence; he knew what this place represented. Quinn's father had been murdered at these bluffs—why, who had done it, those questions had never been answered. They rode for an hour along the bluffs in silence and saw no signs of anyone.

They turned back toward the house.

Marcus finished his third water bottle and tucked it back in the saddlebag. When the situation was different, he would like a chance to bring Shari out riding for a day. He knew she loved to ride, and so far they had been forced to limit her to the immediate area around the ranch house. And now it looked like he had better limit it even more just to be safe.

His pager went off. Marcus reached for it and looked at the number. Dave. Marcus opened the phone, called a secure number, and then called Dave. "Dave, it's Marcus. What do you have?"

"We've found Frank Keaton. He's dead. Two shots to the head, execution style. His body turned up in a landfill this morning, which means he was dropped in a dumpster and hauled out here. Based on location in the landfill and the condition of his body, it's likely he was killed shortly after the shooting at the church."

Marcus drew in the reins of his horse; his attention focused on the news he had already begun to suspect would be the case. "Connor knew Frank was dead when we arrested him."

"That would be my guess as well."

"With Frank dead, splitting Connor and Titus is going to be next to impossible. Do you think there's any hope the ballistics are going to match with the gun that killed Judge Whitmore?"

"Gut feel? No. They look like they are different calibers. I'll know for sure in a day when ballistics is done."

"Pull any resources you need to investigate Frank's death. If the murder case against Connor and Titus for Judge Whitmore's death ends in a hung jury, I want to at least be able to nail them for Frank's death."

"Already working on it," Dave replied. "I'll call with an update this evening."

"Thanks."

"Frank?" Quinn asked when Marcus hung up.

Marcus passed on the grim news. The importance of Shari's testimony had escalated. The remaining week to the grand jury testimony felt like an eternity. Where was Lucas Saracelli?

Marcus nudged his horse forward. "Let's get back to the house."

She had to talk to him. Shari stacked the cookies she had baked and moved them to the glass tray. She was doing her best to fill time and stay busy. Susan had been gracious about turning over the kitchen to her this afternoon.

Her attention was still on the phone call she had had earlier that morning with Jennifer. Tired wasn't adequate to describe the weakness Shari heard in Jennifer's voice. The chemotherapy was taking so much out of her.

The results were in from the bone scans and they weren't good. They showed the radiation had only limited the speed of the cancer growth but had not been able to stop it. Jennifer was in unusually low spirits. Her hope that the hospital stay was coming to an end had been crushed with the latest news.

Shari had to convince Marcus to go back to Baltimore. She knew he wanted to be there, knew as well that he would not easily leave here given the threat Lucas represented. She had to find a way to insist that he go. If she could only think of something in Virginia that would demand his attention—if he was traveling east for the case, he would swing north to see Jennifer.

She wished she could see Jennifer, share more than just a phone call. They had become good friends over the last few weeks. Jennifer was using what energy she had for the best things in her life: time with her fiancé, planning her wedding, her family. Shari hoped she had that same grace should she ever face such an illness.

Shari frowned as she slid another tray of cookies into the oven. Marcus would take this latest news hard. Jennifer had been trying to prepare him for the worse, but Shari knew he was nowhere near being able to accept that he might lose his sister. And if time was measured in months, not years, this time mattered intensely.

She heard Quinn's voice in the hall, talking with Susan.

Shari wiped off her hands, relieved that the guys were back. She didn't know what had called them out early that morning, but she had seen them mount the horses and arrange security so they could be gone for several hours.

"Marcus will be in soon," Quinn reassured her when she joined him. "Everything is fine?"

"Absolutely. You've been baking?"

She gave a small smile. "Trying to."

"The guys will love you."

Marcus stepped inside the house. Shari could see the fatigue and wished she had better news to welcome him with. She crossed to join him and reached out to softly touch his hand. "Jennifer called."

"When?"

"This morning, about an hour after you left. She'll be in her room for the afternoon."

He nodded, rubbing the back of her neck. "Ice water first, I'm parched, then I'll call her back."

She was surprised when he rested his arm across her shoulders as he walked with her back to the kitchen. Something had happened that morning, enough to make him show the fatigue. "Can I get you something to eat?"

"I'd appreciate a sandwich."

"Roast beef and hot mustard?"

He held up two fingers. "I like your sandwiches."

He sampled one of her cookies as she fixed the sandwiches. "I hate to do this, but would you consider staying inside the house for the next couple days?"

She looked over at him. "Of course. Whatever you need me to do."

"We need to come up with a better plan for covering someone trying to come toward the house from the north."

She nodded. "Then I'll stay in the house."

He picked up the first sandwich and got to his feet. "Let me go call Jennifer back."

Shari thought about warning him to be prepared but didn't have the words.

He paused beside her, rested his hand on her forearm. "I talked to Tom and then her doctors late last night," he said quietly. "It's okay, Shari. I know what she was told this morning."

"You know?"

"One of the specialists from Mayo who first saw her was flying out last night to join her doctors, was due to get there midmorning. They are far from reaching the end of what they are willing to try. This is only a disappointing turn, not an end in the road."

"I wish you could go see her. She sounds really down."

"Shari, she's worried about you and your safety; it's one of her first questions when we talk. We'll be back east soon enough and I'll be able to see her then. Don't feel guilty about the timing of this. I made the choice to stay with this case. And my family was involved in making that decision. I've accepted that distance from Jennifer for a short time is part of it."

Shari heard the calmness and was surprised at it.

"Part of knowing how to lead the O'Malleys is knowing what to bring to the table that can help them. The doctor from Mayo can help as the next course of action is chosen. There are treatments that will help Jennifer; we'll find those ideas and people." He ran a hand down her cheek. "Trust me, we're only in the first round."

She relaxed. "Call her."

"Are you okay?"

She nodded.

"If you have a few extras, box some cookies. I'll arrange to get a package to her."

"I'd like that."

He selected another one and smiled. "Besides, these are good."

Marcus settled in the den to call Jennifer. He wasn't surprised when Kate answered on her behalf. "Hi, Ladybug."

"Marcus." He heard her smile. "Good timing, as always. Can you do us a favor?"

"Sure. What?"

"Arrange a delivery. We want Chicago-style pizza for dinner tonight. Two of them. Large."

He had to laugh. "I see your solution to this problem is starting with the fundamentals."

"Jen is eating like a bird and pizza sounds good to her. But it has to be good pizza."

"Don't worry, I'm already writing it down. I'll get two sent from Carla's packed in dry ice if you can find a place to bake them out there."

"Not a problem."

"It will have to be a late dinner."

"First flight you can arrange is fine. Jen takes a late evening nap so we can watch the late shows and get a good laugh."

"Ask her if Benny's cheesecake sounds good too."

"Hold on." A muted conversation went on. "Strawberry topped."

"Got it."

"Thanks, I appreciate it. You'll like the new specialist from Mayo Clinic; he joined us during lunch. He's from Louisiana, and he and Jen spent half an hour discussing hot Cajun cooking. Then they started talking about kids and he pulled out his wallet to introduce his favorite patients."

Marcus relaxed; a doctor, but also one comfortable being more than that. "I already like him."

"He spent over an hour with Tom and Jennifer going over the film from the bone scans of her spine." Her voice became serious. "They want to try radiation pellets around her spine."

He knew the details of that option; it wasn't his favorite, but he understood why it would be chosen over another chemotherapy cocktail. Jen would be looking at surgery around her spine, something that made him queasy, and then more radiation. "How did she take the news?"

"A lot of questions; she and Tom are still talking about the risks."

"I can't say I'm thrilled with them either." They would be taking the gamble that the radiation would destroy the cancer before it destroyed her vertebrae.

"I think she's waiting to talk to you before they make a final decision."

"Then pass me over and I'll add my two cents worth to this discussion."

"Coming up."

The phone at their end changed hands. "Hi, Marcus."

Marcus understood immediately why Kate had purposely stayed lighthearted and done the talking. Jennifer's voice was so weak he could hear her breathing easier than he could her words. The doctors had warned him to expect the weakness to continue until they were able to end this round of chemotherapy and give her body time to recover. "Hi, precious." He tried to relax.

"I worried Shari. Sorry."

"Jen, it's good for her to worry about someone else. She's thinking about you, not the mess here."

"Okay." There was a faint smile. "Let her worry."

"She was baking cookies to soften the word that you had called."

"Oh."

He laughed. Not every batch Shari had baked had been a success. "Relax. These were good. She'll send you some."

"Good." Her voice grew serious. "You sent a good doctor."

"A favor from an old friend," Marcus reassured before she could ask. The doctor was one of the best cancer doctors in the country, and his time was at a premium. Marcus had tried to offer compensation and had been turned down. "That bank robbery eight years ago where the kids were killed, I mentioned I got to know the local investigator quite well. Your doctor is his son."

"I liked him when I met him at Mayo; I like him even more now."

"I know he's suggested several options, recommended one. What do you want to do, Jen?"

"The surgery might cripple me."

"I know," Marcus said softly.

"And they'll need to do it in the next couple days. You won't be here."

"I know that too."

The quietness was that of twenty-year friends.

"Have the surgery," he said quietly.

"Will you carry me down the aisle if the worst happens?"

He moved the phone away so he could bite back tears and steady his voice. "Sure."

"I would ask Jack, but he would drop me; fireman that he is notwithstanding," she said with forced lightness.

"I'll walk you down the aisle or carry you. That's a promise."

"Thanks."

"You're welcome."

"No hair, so my wedding pictures will be interesting."

"Rachel will get creative. Trust me, you'll be beautiful."

"Of course. Besides, I've always dreamed about being size six for my wedding."

He had to laugh. The illness had not robbed Jennifer of her essential good humor. "Pick the dress out, and it will be my wedding present to you."

"That's charming of you."

"I'm a charming kind of guy."

Shari knocked softly on the doorjamb. Marcus was relieved to see her. He held out his hand and curled his around hers when she joined him.

"I'll tell the doctor yes."

Marcus's grip tightened on Shari's hand. "Do that, Jen. I'll talk to him in the morning for the schedule details."

"Would you talk to Rachel for me later?" Jennifer asked. "She's been too quiet."

"Sure, Jen."

"Tell Shari hi for me."

"I'll do that."

"Here's Kate back."

"Marcus."

He had to clear his throat. "I'm here."

"Call me after ten, okay?" Kate asked quietly.

"I'll call."

"Good-bye for now."

Marcus closed the phone, stared at it a moment, and took a deep breath. There was some relief just in knowing he didn't have to keep the carefully maintained calm in place for Shari. He had meant what he said earlier, about this being the first round of a long fight, but it was still an intense strain. He rubbed his eyes. "They're going to put radiation pellets in her spine."

Shari tightened her hand around his. "You'll be okay. All of you. How can you not go?"

He shook his head. "The other O'Malleys are there; I'm needed here."

She wanted to argue, then stopped and simply nodded. "Send her some orchids. Those you got for me last week were gorgeous."

He rubbed his hand across hers, then picked up the phone. "First things first. They want two Chicago-style pizzas and a cheesecake sent out for dinner."

"Do they?"

"Hmm." He was amused at Kate's request. "I think I've become their delivery man."

"I think they just want you to feel involved."

"Probably some of that too." He wrote down the number directory assistance gave him for the pizza place near Kate's home, then placed the call.

It never failed to amaze him what mentioning Kate's name could do in her neighborhood. Carla herself came on the phone to get the details and gladly volunteered to take care of the shipping arrangements. A brief second call took care of the cheesecake request.

"Unless you need to rejoin Quinn, why don't you come keep me company," Shari offered, tugging his hand.

"Doing what?"

"I thought I'd ice some of those cookies. You can watch, or do some too if you like. It will give you something mindless to do while you tell me what was going on this morning."

He didn't particularly want to be alone at the moment. He let her pull him to his feet. "Lead the way. As long as you promise not to make blue icing this time."

"But it's a guy color."

"I draw the line at blue food."

Marcus called Kate late that night after his final rounds, spent an hour talking with her about Jennifer's upcoming surgery, the details of the security arrangements he was making with Dave for the grand jury testimony, family schedules for the next two weeks. When he hung up, he walked to the window of his room to look out into the darkness, weary in his heart.

Two days from now his sister would be in surgery. He knew the pellets had a reasonable chance of killing the cancer, but the risks involved— he couldn't do anything to minimize them, that was what made the situation so hard to accept.

"Jesus wants you to choose to trust Him. He won't take that trust you place in Him lightly."

Shari's words echoed again. He wanted to be able to cross the hesitation and trust enough to pray, but he felt mute the closer he came to that line. He had believed and prayed for his mom and she had died. It wasn't logical, but thinking about praying for Jennifer brought a resonating fear that, in doing so, he would lose her too. The emotion wasn't rational. But it was powerful.

He had always thought in the mix of experiences each O'Malley shared from the orphanage that it was Kate who bore the worst scars from the past, that Rachel carried the most pain. He had never dealt with the reality of how strong his own memories still were.

"I miss you, Mom," he whispered as he traced a hand down the windowsill.

Jennifer would come through surgery strong, and this treatment would be effective. Shari was praying for her. That had to make a difference.

Why couldn't he just trust?

Because he'd made a deal with God so that his mom would live, and she had died. And inside his heart he was still an angry little boy.

Marcus sighed and forced himself to turn out the lights and turn in, trying to sleep. It did not come for a long time.

Nineteen

S he's out of surgery?"

"In recovery," Kate confirmed. "They gave her something to make her woozy and used a local so her system wouldn't have to fight off the heavy sedation. Marcus, she's reacting to it like she's drunk. She's trying to sing nursery rhymes at the moment. They said it would wear off, which is a shame. I would kill to have a tape recorder right now. She's never going to believe me."

"What did they say about the actual surgery? Was it successful?"

"Better than they hoped for. Even Tom was smiling when he saw the film results showing the placements."

Marcus could feel the building relief. "And the risks? Is she moving her toes?"

"The biggest problem at the moment is she wants to get up and go for a walk. The local has removed any concept of pain, and her foggy mind clearly does not remember she's just had surgery. They've got her strapped down to keep her back still."

"Thanks for calling me immediately."

"No problem. Let me call Lisa and Dave. I'll brief you again once she's been moved from the recovery room."

Marcus hung up the phone. Shari was waiting, impatiently. She had been pacing around the house ever since word had come that Jennifer was going into surgery. "She came through just fine," Marcus said, taking away the worry for them both. "She's got good movement in her feet, the pellet locations look good, and she's in recovery."

"I'm glad," Shari said simply, her smile sharing the emotions that were hard to fit into words.

Marcus crossed the room, leaned down, and gently kissed her. "Thank you for praying," he said quietly, from the bottom of his heart. Jennifer was in better shape than he could have hoped for. Shari's prayers had really mattered.

"Marcus," she studied his face, reached up, and cradled it in her hands. "You are very welcome."

Quinn came down the hall and the moment of privacy was lost. Shari tightened her hands around Marcus's as she stepped away, then turned. "Quinn, there's wonderful news regarding Jennifer."

Marcus reread the interviews of those who had seen Connor at the hotel and finally admitted defeat. He had been over these interviews until he could quote them. As much as he wanted to find something the team had missed regarding Connor, it wasn't there. He closed the folder and dropped it on the floor.

"No luck?" Shari asked absently, not looking up from the book she was absorbed in reading.

"No."

He had to smile as he watched her. She was sitting with her legs draped over the side of the deep leather chair, the side table light turned on. He reached down for his sketch pad and pulled out his fine pencil. She looked beautiful tonight, truly relaxed.

He took his time with the sketch. She was inspiring him to improve his art, so he could try to do her justice.

An hour passed as he worked and she turned pages in her book.

"Can I see?"

He glanced up to see she had set aside the book. He didn't want to show her, but only because it would be to admit she had been the subject on more than one occasion.

He closed the sketchbook and handed it to her.

Watching her face to see her reaction, he knew exactly when she turned pages and saw the first portrait. She turned the pages more slowly after that.

She looked up at him. The one time he didn't want her to hide what she thought, she did. She slowly smiled. "I'm flattered, Marcus. You're an unfulfilled artist under that badge and gun."

Come on, Shari…what are you thinking? I've got my heart on my sleeve in those sketches.

"My mom loved to draw." He hadn't told anyone that but family.

She flipped to a blank page. "May I?"

Not sure what she planned, he nodded. She picked up her pen. Her sketch was done fast, with a hand that didn't stop, her confidence showing. She was an artist and she hadn't said a thing. That turkey.

"My contribution to your greatness." She handed him the sketchbook with a flourish.

It was a cartoon. A baby panda bear leaning over an artist's palette getting paint on his paws, curious. "You're good."

"So are you. And Marcus…I'm not that pretty."

"You're beautiful."

"And you've been listening to my mother too much. What did she have to say this evening about London?"

A well-done tangent, he let her get away with it. "Afternoon tea. She is very impressed."

"She gave me the recipes for scones."

"Want to try making them someday?"

"Only if you volunteer to clean up after the disaster I leave in my wake. Two hours of cleanup for one batch of cookies. They were good, but not that good. I plan to let another month go by before I consider stepping into a kitchen again. I never did get very domesticated."

"Shari, some of the people I like the most are Quinn, Lisa, and Kate. Enough said?"

"You've got a high tolerance for clutter."

"I would rather have a case solved, a bad guy caught, a standoff peacefully concluded. If the clutter bothers me before it does them, I pick it up. Besides, you're smart. You could learn."

"Like I can learn to tell directions?"

"Well—that one might take some time."

"You're being generous. I think it's an impossible cause."

"How's the speech you were working on this afternoon coming along?"

She winced. "It's my nightmare of the month. I thought I was done with fiscal policy and it's back to haunt me."

"What's the problem?"

"John's legislation hit what I call the cement wall—the opposition in the senate finance committee. It's on its way to crashing and burning. So…the cycle starts all over again." She shook her head. "It doesn't help that I don't understand John's insistence on the positions he's taken. Personally, I would change the legislation. There's a compromise sitting there to be taken, but neither side wants to be the first to move to the middle."

"So why don't you just write the speech you think should be given and see what John thinks? Your strength is persuading someone to your point of view."

"I work for him. I'm supposed to be writing his speech, not mine."

"So call it a proposal," Marcus replied. "He'll love it when he sees it."

"You've got more faith than I do."

"More confidence at least."

"Ouch. And I'd hate to let it be said that I ducked a challenge."

Shari crumpled page five of the speech, the sound sharp in the quiet kitchen, the paper yielding to the pressure of her hand as she pulled it in with her fingers and crushed it into the center of her palm. The words were too bold.

She started writing again on the next sheet of notepaper.

"What are you working on?"

"The proposal for John you talked me so sweetly into writing." She didn't bother to look up at Marcus; if she did she would never get her concentration back. It was 1 A.M. and she still had several hours of work to do.

"It's not going well?"

She grimaced. "It's going fine. I just can't see John ever moving this far from his present position."

He pulled out a chair. "May I?"

He had shown her his sketch. She passed over the text. "It's still rough," she warned, nervous.

"Relax. What I've read of your stuff is good."

He took a seat and in doing so totally distracted her. Jeans, an old sweatshirt, barefoot. She forced herself not to stare. He started reading. "Okay if I make comments?"

She nodded and he reached for his pencil.

He made a few notes in the margins.

When he finished and got up, he squeezed her shoulder lightly. "Good job. I'll be back after rounds."

She nodded and accepted the pages of the speech.

She read his comments. The one at the bottom of the page left her stunned. *Why aren't you running for office?*

She spun around only to find with frustration that he had already left.

Run for office. It was her lifelong dream. One her father had always supported for her future. It was like having someone suddenly shine a spotlight and illuminate a hope, long resting dormant.

She had to wait forty minutes for him to return. She heard him talking to Quinn in the front hall. Gathering her courage, she poured two mugs of coffee and went to join him.

"Thanks."

"All quiet?"

"All quiet," he assured.

He nodded to the living room and waited for her to have a seat before he sat down nearby.

"Why did you say that? About running for office?"

"You're a good speech writer. But you're not going to be content there forever. You were made for something more."

"I've always dreamed of being a legislator in Washington someday."

"So why aren't you? What are you waiting for?"

"You need to be married to run for Congress."

He threw back his head and laughed. "Shari, that's a cop-out. You'd make a wonderful representative. I'd vote for you. Go for it."

"It takes money."

"No. It takes friends. And those you've got." The warm smile hit her in a wave.

"You're serious."

"Yes, Shari, I am. It's a dream. I'm not in favor of seeing dreams die."

"You really think I could do it?"

"Think about it. You've got a work ethic that would put most people in the ground after a day. You know the state of Virginia; you know the issues inside out. You've got good political skills and the Rolodex to match. What do you need that you don't already have?"

She wanted to seize the suggestion, found it incredible that he was so strongly in favor of the idea. Was he that different from Sam? Or didn't he see them having a relationship beyond friendship in the future so it didn't matter what her career was? She was suddenly not certain of anything. "I'll think about it."

"Do."

She got to her feet. "You'll be up for a while?"

"Yes."

"I left the coffeepot on. I think I'm going to head to bed."

"Sweet dreams."

Shari nodded and walked toward her bedroom.

When she curled up in bed, she hugged her pillow and looked at the ceiling. Marcus had dug until he touched her heart, snugly wrapped inside her passion for work. What she did for John, what she dreamed of some- day doing, it wasn't a job with her. It was how her heart beat. He had patiently found it and then watered it with a quietly written note at the bottom of a speech.

The hard part was figuring out how much of it he had done deliber- ately and how much of it was simply Marcus being who he was. She wanted to read into it something profound and hope it was true. Her heart was involved. She wanted this to mean something profound.

He had her heart in his hand. Did he even know that?

She loved him.

Marcus believes I can do it. The emotion was intense, the realization he was serious. To see that in his calm face, that confidence, it stunned her.

If I go for my dreams, do I lose a chance to have a future with him? He might not want a wife who is in politics. And I have to trust that someday he will change his mind and believe. I love him more than I do my dream. And I couldn't say that with Sam.

Jesus, I want a future with Marcus, and I want a political career. Are You telling me both are now possibilities on the table?

Tracking the private jet was only a matter of time and money and charm. Lucas had been a pilot since he was seventeen. He leased a piper cub and flew to New York, where he was just another pilot who liked to borrow a cup of coffee and chat. The private charter pilots and the maintenance crews liked to talk and they remembered planes like other guys remembered cars. Two weeks after Connor was arrested, Lucas had tracked the private jet the marshal had used back to Kentucky and from there west to Montana.

The chase was coming to an end. Lucas picked up the sniper rifle he had arranged to have modified, spent a day in the country sighting it, then he headed west.

Finding the plane they had used was a matter of searching the ranches in the corridor of the last known flight plan and locating the plane he sought. Most of the ranches had private airstrips, finding the right one was simply a matter of time. He found it on Wednesday, August 30.

He had changed planes, leasing from a private company the same plane the park service used to create their topographical maps. High-powered cameras mounted to the skids were recording every detail of the ranches far below. He flew high, straight, on a direct bearing to the next town, covering the airstrip and house in the morning, and that evening flew a straight return path mapping the approach roads, barns, and fence lines.

By morning the film was developed and tacked to the wall of the office he had rented. The hangar had been designed for privately flown twin-engine Cessnas, not the larger business jets, and the tail numbers were visible through the open hangar doors.

The dry summer and fall would make the trek in by foot slow but not particularly difficult. The security perimeter they had established was obvious from the air. Interesting. He studied the pictures and was pleased. This was not going to be all that easy after all. The cops guarding Shari knew what they were doing. He had always appreciated a good adversary.

He picked up the phone. "I've found her."

"The secret grand jury panel convenes on Saturday. Kill her before it convenes."

Lucas hung up the phone with a frown. Saturday. He'd just found them and they were about to abandon this place and fly back to Virginia. Wonderful. He would have preferred to have more time. Still, it could be done.

He looked at the maps. They did give him options. He would prefer to avoid that perimeter around the house. If they were going to be leaving, that meant the airstrip would be back in play.

He'd kill them at the airstrip. Kill them all so no one could interfere

Twenty

The dawn was brightening the sky. The trees around the ranch house were silhouettes against the blue sky. Marcus leaned his sketch pad against the corral fence as he sketched the nearby stand of oak trees with color pencils.

"Aren't you cold? It's chilly out here."

He glanced to his right. Shari's hair was tousled and her eyes still sleepy. She'd come to join him for a sunrise; Marcus didn't miss the significance of that. "Good morning. Hot coffee helps."

She moved to lean against the fence beside him. "The sketch is pretty."

He was drawing the trees, determined to know each one in detail so he would know instinctively when something out there was wrong. There was no need to tell her that. "Thanks." He leaned over and softly kissed her good morning, wise enough to keep his hands full.

She leaned against him and kissed him back. "Nice."

"Hmm." She settled into silence beside him as he resumed his sketch. She seemed peaceful enough, but he noticed her hands were tight against the fence. "Bad dreams?"

"Vaguely."

"You want to talk about tomorrow and the grand jury testimony, the security arrangements we've made?"

"Not really."

She had been ducking the topic for a week. It made him uneasy, that absolute trust she was putting in him to keep her safe.

"I suppose I should go pack."

They weren't coming back here, and her disappointment with that was obvious in the way she had been dragging her feet in getting ready to leave.

"A change in location is necessary, Shari."

"I won't be seeing you as much."

"No," he said softly. He was tucking her away at Quantico, the FBI academy, for the next several weeks. She would be living in the on-site housing with the next training class. An unusual move, but it was there or a military base. It would be hard for Lucas to reach her, that had to be the deciding factor. They would drive her there each evening after her grand jury testimony, and she would be living there full time after that until Lucas was located. Marcus would be around, but it would not be the same. He didn't like the idea any more than she did.

She sighed. "What time are Dave, Kate, and Lisa arriving?"

"Shortly after 4 P.M. We'll fly out around 7 P.M." He wanted them arriving in the middle of the night.

"Okay. I'll be inside."

Marcus watched her walk back to the house. In the next twenty-four hours the danger to her life would escalate sharply. Lucas not appearing here during the last weeks had been a relief, but now it only coiled the fear Marcus felt tighter. Lucas might have chosen to spend all that time studying the courthouse, preparing to act there.

He looked back at the stand of trees, closed his drawing pad.

Jesus, I figured something out last night. He had begun to pray again early of a morning, cautiously, feeling out the words to reestablish what he had once had. It was a slow reconciliation. *The anger of being abandoned as a child—I didn't know where to direct my pain; You were near. I knew I could hurt You, and I tried my best to do so. I rejected Your comfort.*

You sent it anyway. You sent the O'Malleys. Only You could have figured out the combination that is this family. I'm coming to see that You never left me. But I've been trusting only myself for so long…

It's come down to crunch time. I need Lucas stopped. I can't do it on my own. I'm trusting You, Jesus. Not only with myself, but with Shari. Tell me what I need to do. I'm depending on You.

Marcus felt the buffeting wind as he stepped from the truck and watched the plane line up with the airstrip to land. The weather forecasters had been wrong. The storm front that had not been expected until late this evening was coming through much earlier. On the horizon the sky was dark and lightning could be seen.

Dave was the first one down the steps when the plane stopped. "We've been tracking the front with the on-board radar. We can still get out if we get the plane turned around and prepped quickly. Get Shari and Quinn and go now. If we wait, we could be stuck until late tonight, assuming we can even get out."

Marcus turned to scan the sky again. Storms, weather. Was it just fanciful thinking to consider the weather change as a show of God's hand? Shoving them out early, or telling him to wait?

Lucas saw the plane arrive. He had hiked in during the night and reached his chosen spot before dawn. The location was even better than he had hoped for: the slight rise in the land, the perspective below. He drew a bead down on the airstrip to watch this new development unfold.

He saw the men talking. In the crosshairs of the scope each man came close enough to touch. He recognized Marcus O'Malley from the newspaper photographs. The weather must have caught them by surprise.

He did not see Shari. But where Marcus was, Shari was not far away.

He felt anticipation build inside. They would be leaving before the weather closed them in. This was it. His hands settled the rifle into stillness. He mentally began adjusting for the wind and distance. The first shot would go for the cop nearest to Shari, confirm his adjustments and remove the only person who could help her. Shari Hanford would be dead before the sound of the second shot reached them.

Marcus saw lightning flash to the south. Dave was right. They needed to move now. Once the storms arrived, there was no telling how long the rain would last. And the airstrip would have to be checked afterwards for tree limbs and other blown debris. That could put them leaving well after dark. And if for some reason they couldn't fly out, they risked the downpour from the storm cutting off the road by flash floods.

But he felt...queasy...with the idea. He didn't want to move Shari out of the secure perimeter on this ranch until absolutely necessary. Arriving in Virginia early was simply too dangerous. Lucas was out there somewhere...waiting.

He shook his head. "No. We wait it out."

"You're sure?"

"Yes. I'm sure." His gut told him it was the safe thing to do. "Let's get Lisa and Kate to the house."

Lucas watched two pilots appear from the plane, start walking around doing their post-flight check. Two more passengers disembarked. The marshal talked briefly with the group. Lucas was surprised when they gathered up their belongings and moved to the waiting vehicles. They were going to the house.

They weren't leaving immediately? They had time to beat the storm front. He glanced at the darkening horizon, then back at the plane. The crew was preparing to move the plane into the hangar.

Wonderful. He was about to get wet.

Lucas withdrew a stick of gum from his pocket and unwrapped it. He could tolerate the rain even though he disliked it. He had worked in worse and it would give him good cover. It wouldn't affect a bullet. A few more hours, and this job would be over.

Shari would be dead.

He hoped she had an enjoyable last meal.

Marcus was relieved to see Kate, to hear firsthand that Jennifer was reacting well to the latest treatments, to have a chance to say thanks again to Lisa for the work she had done in the last few weeks. He led them to the house.

Kate and Shari shared a long hug. Kate turned and looked at Marcus, her arm still around Shari. "I don't know about the rest of you, but I'm hungry. Let's fix dinner and talk afterward," Kate suggested.

"What sounds good?" Marcus asked.

Kate grinned. "Pizza. We girls will make it, you three guys go talk."

Marcus looked at his two sisters, then at Shari. He sensed a girl talk conspiracy forming. "I don't know about this—"

Lisa pushed him toward the door. "Go."

Marcus went. He settled in the library with Dave and Quinn. They spent an hour reviewing the security arrangements for Shari's testimony.

"We'll keep her safe, Marcus," Dave reassured.

"Lucas is out there somewhere. He's going to have found out when and where the grand jury testimony will be by now. Is there anything we are missing?"

"We're ready, Marcus," Quinn agreed. He glanced at his watch and got to his feet. "I'll be out on the perimeter."

Marcus went to check on dinner.

He walked back toward the kitchen, following the laughter. He stopped at the door, couldn't stop a chuckle. Susan had turned the kitchen over to them; the place was a mess. There was as much sauce on Kate and Shari as there was on the pizzas.

"I thought you said you were going to make pizzas? This looks like a war zone."

"We're being...creative," Shari replied.

It was enough to set Kate off into another peal of laughter; it was obvious they had both crossed into the giggle zone where everything was funny.

Marcus smiled, for the laughter was contagious. Shari needed a little relief; it was absolutely the best thing in the world for her. He paused beside her at the counter and snitched a sample of the grated cheese. "Put green peppers on my half."

"Half?"

"I'm hungry."

There were four pizzas in the making, she scanned them. "With or without mushrooms?"

"Without." He pointed to the pepperoni pizza. "That one."

"Kate, did you leave onions off one?" Dave leaned around the doorway to ask.

She scowled—she hadn't—and she began picking them off the pizza she had just finished. "Just because you dislike kissing me with onions on your breath..."

"Your breath," he corrected with a grin.

"I hope you recognize what a sacrifice this is. I happen to like onions."

Marcus, watching the interchange, stored it away as a memory never to be lost. He liked seeing Kate happy.

"What kind of cheese do you want, Marcus?"

He glanced back at Shari. She had both provolone and mozzarella grated. He leaned over and kissed her. "Both."

"What was that for?"

"No reason." He'd just left Lisa and Kate speechless. He didn't know if Shari would appreciate him saying that. "Call us when the pizza is done."

Dinner was filled with laughter.

When it finished, they moved to the library, and the mood changed, turning somber. Marcus tugged Shari down beside him on the couch. It was still raining out, and it was time to talk about the case. "Lisa, you've got the floor. Take us through what we know."

"Do you want me to argue for the prosecution or for the defense?"

It was a telling comment. "Both," Marcus replied.

Lisa leaned back in her chair, folded her hands, and settled herself as she organized her thoughts. "On Wednesday July 5 Connor checked into the Jefferson Renaissance Hotel to hold secret merger talks under the guise of attending the judicial conference. We know he came to the conference for more sinister reasons.

"On Friday night, during the evening program, he slipped into Carl's hotel room. He shot Judge Whitmore when he came back to his room at 10:20 P.M. He tried to shoot Shari, did hit Joshua and William. He fled up the stairs to the thirteenth floor and entered room 1323. There he stripped off the hairpiece he wore and changed his suit and his shoes. "We think his planned celebratory drink turned out to be one of anger instead, for he hurled the glass—he was drinking Scotch by the way—at the wall and then had to clean up the broken glass. The guard at the fourteenth telecommunication center saw Connor at the merger discussions shortly after 11 P.M. He checked out of the hotel the next day at 10:14 A.M.

"What we have for evidence—in Carl's room: the shell casings, a thread from the shooter's suit, bloody shoe prints, the fact the shooter is left-handed. From room 1323—we have a trace of Carl's blood on the carpet, threads that match the suit, and blood on the glass slivers."

Lisa sighed. "Arguing for the defense—I can find a reasonable way to explain away all of our evidence. Without the gun, the hairpiece, the shoes, there is nothing direct. Even the DNA can be shot down because, one, there is not enough to repeat the test by the defense making it liable to challenge, and two, it doesn't say if it was Frank or Connor and that means reasonable doubt.

"The fact that Connor is clean, not even a parking ticket, and Frank is known to work for Titus and is dead makes it too easy to pin him for the murder. And Connor has an airtight alibi for when Shari was shot at the church, so that says it was Titus and Frank acting alone. Connor can argue he cut himself off from his family ages ago, and the beautiful thing is, he has."

"Nothing links Frank to Connor?"

"No."

"Can we prove it was Titus behind killing Carl?" Quinn asked.

"Not without Connor. And beyond Shari's direct testimony, we've got nothing else we can use as leverage. The case is circumstantial."

Shari sat forward on the couch, for the first time entering into the conversation. "My eyewitness testimony is the difference in this case."

"Yes."

"No wonder he wants me dead." She squeezed Marcus's hand. "When do we leave?" The rain was still coming down heavy outside the windows.

"Two hours, maybe three."

She got to her feet. "I'm going to go finish packing."

Lucas had long since accepted being cold and wet. As time passed he considered his options from all angles. He had hoped to see the rain come to an end before sunset but it showed no signs of abating. The airstrip below was deserted; the perimeter patrols around the house were doing their best to cope with the rain. And while he could wait this out, they couldn't. Shari had to be in Richmond tomorrow.

Would they decide to drive out, take a commercial flight? He had to stop her here.

He slowly rose from the ground, a dark shadow appearing where there had been nothing before.

Twenty-one

Marcus leaned his shoulder against the doorpost of the guest room and watched Shari as she absentmindedly fingered a rose petal from the vase on the dresser. He tried to arrange for flowers to be brought in every week, partly because he loved to write the cards and partly because he loved to see that sparkle appear in her eyes. "You're welcome to take them with you if you like."

She turned and smiled, albeit slightly sad. "No, that's okay."

"Can I help with anything?"

She shrugged her shoulder. "I'm packed."

"Just not ready to go."

"No."

"You may get your wish. I came to tell you the storm appears to be getting worse." A rolling crack of thunder outside punctuated his words.

"I see what you mean."

"We may end up flying out at 2 A.M. I'm sorry for that. It will mean a broken night of sleep."

"Don't worry about it. I doubt I'll sleep much anyway. I'll need the distraction."

"Tomorrow is just another step toward justice. Don't be afraid of it."

"I'm not. I know you'll keep me safe."

He knew the words that would most reassure her. He meant them. "I'm also trusting Jesus to keep you safe."

She absorbed those words slowly, and then her smile blossomed. "That's progress, Marcus."

"Yes. Some." He let himself share her smile. "Ask me what I think in a month, by then it might have a little more confidence to it."

"It doesn't have to be a leap back, Marcus. Slow and steady is good too."

"Hand me your bag."

When she did, he closed his hand over hers and leaned down to gently kiss her, letting it linger. "Something to think about while you are tucked away at Quantico."

"Quinn should be back by now." Dave strode into the den where Marcus and Kate were watching the weather report. "He went out to walk the perimeter and he's not back."

Marcus instantly tensed and reached for his radio. "Quinn, come back." Only the static of the storm was heard. "Quinn."

He looked out the window to the darkness lit by the lightning.

He had made the same mistake at the church. It was a perfect night for a sniper. The house was lit up like a beacon. "Kate, kill all the lights except the living room and get everyone down in the cellar."

She was already moving, her pistol out and safety clicked off. "Where is it?"

"The breezeway built on behind the kitchen. Move aside the planters and you'll see the wooden doors of the old storm cellar. Dave, you're with me."

Marcus grabbed the dark jacket and cap still dripping from his last walk around the perimeter forty minutes ago. There were eighteen men on that perimeter. Quinn being off the air—he was down, or he was hunting. Marcus was heading toward the side door of the house, his nine-millimeter Glock in his hand, when he saw Shari in the hall walking toward him. The fear was intense. "Kate."

"She's covered. Go."

Marcus and Dave slipped out into the rain.

A cold hard driven rain struck his face. Marcus blinked and waited for his eyes to adjust to the night. On any other night they would be patrolling with night vision goggles, but wearing them when lightning struck would do permanent eye damage. They had pulled the perimeter in to compensate. Good move or bad? It was too late to second-guess that decision.

Dave pointed west and Marcus nodded, then turned east toward the fence line where he had been sketching that morning, where Shari had joined him.

Jesus, don't let me down. I've got serious trouble here.

He ducked under the railing.

Quinn materialized beside him. "He's here. I saw him with a sniper rifle silhouette for a moment down by the hangar. He's working his way around the barn to get line of sight to the house. The perimeter is pulling back even tighter to the house."

"Good. Don't let him get past."

Quinn squeezed his shoulder and disappeared.

Shari found the sound of thunder muted by the storm cellar eerie. Marcus, Quinn, and Dave were out in this, not to mention the other men of the security detail she had come to know and like.

"Where two or three are gathered together…this counts," Kate said softly.

"Keep them safe," Shari said.

"Amen."

"What are you two talking about?" Lisa asked, curious.

"We'll explain later," Kate replied, sharing a look with Shari.

"What was that?" Shari was determined not to be the most nervous one of the three of them, but she couldn't help it. Something had just brushed by her foot.

Lisa found a flashlight on the shelf by the stairs, illuminating the dark, dry earth out of the reach of the one bare overhead bulb.

Shari took a rapid couple steps back. "That's a snake hole."

"Too big," Lisa replied, discounting that suggestion. "And not large enough for a gopher. Besides, look how dry and packed the ground is. It's abandoned."

She went poking around behind the storage shelves where boxes of canning jars were stored.

"Lisa, if we have company down here I would prefer not to know," Kate remarked.

"It's probably just a mouse," Lisa replied, tipping boxes forward to look behind them. Shari was relieved when Lisa wasn't able to find anything.

Lisa turned her attention to shining the light back in the crawl space that went under the breezeway. "Well, hello there."

She found a pair of thick tough work gloves and pulled herself partway up into the crawl space, reaching back. A moment later she wiggled back, holding something in her hands.

"Yuck," Kate said flatly.

Shari found herself looking at a mole. It was horrifyingly fascinating.

"He just came inside to get out of the rain. His tunnels must be filling up with water," Lisa said, looking at the six-inch smooth furry animal, holding him firmly. "Did you know a cat would catch him but not eat him? He's too bitter."

"I can see why," Kate replied.

"I've never had a mole before."

"You're going to keep him?" Kate asked, then shook her head. "Never mind, of course you are."

Shari found a shoebox being used to store candles and emptied it out. "Lisa, will this do?"

Marcus's sister looked at her, grateful, then carefully put the animal inside. "Thanks."

"He is kind of cute."

Lisa grinned. "I think I like you, Shari Hanford. I'm going to name him Charlie."

Thunder rumbled overhead. The humor disappeared. "I sure hope this cellar doesn't leak. That rain is pounding down."

"It's dry. Just look at the cobwebs."

Shari turned a crate over and tested it, then took a seat. "Kate, could I tell you a secret?" She had waited for just the right moment.

"Sure. I love secrets."

"Did you know Marcus hates broccoli?"

Small rivers of water were cutting into the sun-baked land of yesterday, running across Marcus's boots as he moved through the darkness. The driving rain covered the sound of his movements...and those of his adversary.

He worked his way from the house east, slipping into the trees he had sketched that morning. The branches and leaves blocked some of the rain, transforming the storm into heavy raindrops and a deafening assault of sound. It was a dangerous place to be not only because of the lightning. Lucas would have to come this way in order to get line of sight on the living room and the one remaining light on in the house.

He reached the oldest of the oak trees and put his back against it, eliminating his silhouette, listening intently. Locating a man in this…

A shot rang out.

Kate surged from her seat, heading for the steps out of the cellar. "That was a gunshot, not lightning."

Lisa grabbed her from behind.

Kate tempered her instinct to throw an elbow since it was family, tried to break free, only to have Lisa literally try to lift her off her feet. "We wait," Lisa insisted.

"That was close to the house, now let me go."

Lisa just tightened her hold. "No. I can't keep Shari safe like you can. I'm not as good a shot. Dave is fine, Kate. Dave is fine."

"You don't know that," Kate whispered, breathing hard but stopping the struggle.

"He's too stubborn to get killed."

Shari tentatively touched her arm. "Marcus and Quinn…with Dave they're practically the three musketeers. They'll cover each other's backs."

"They'll try," Kate said grimly. Lisa let her go, and she paced away from the stairs. "I hate waiting."

Lucas was picking off their perimeter guards. As a tactic, it was an effective one. Marcus's heart pounded as he ignored the radio traffic over his earpiece. Others were helping the injured man. He focused on putting himself between the shooter and the man that had gone down. The movement made him a target, but it couldn't be helped.

Lucas was close. Already south of the house.

Marcus reached the edge of the trees. Lucas could pick them off; they could also pick him off. As a plan, it left much to be desired, but it would work. At this point, that was the only thing that mattered.

He needed a place to wait out Lucas. And this wasn't it. He wanted to be situated so Lucas would have to literally go over him to get to the house.

He stepped from the tree line. Lightning struck close, hitting and exploding a tree on the ridge. Marcus dove for the ground as another shot rang out.

That one had been meant for him.

At least he now knew with reasonable certainty that Lucas too had set aside using a nightscope because of the lightning. One man injured instead of killed, an actual miss…Lucas was using the lightning to establish his shots; he would have never missed otherwise. Marcus said a silent thanks for small favors as he spit mud out of his mouth. That had been too close for comfort.

He crawled toward cover. Lucas was directly south.

A single click over the earpiece alerted him to company. He cautiously turned his head, scanning, and a shadow behind him to the right lifted a hand. Dave had joined him.

Marcus pointed to the knoll ahead, his best guess. Lucas had moved to the high ground. Dave nodded.

Eighteen minutes. Marcus had counted every second. He knew where the man was; he'd actually seen the muzzle fire of the last shot. Patience. Lucas would move to change locations or he would try to shoot again.

Stretched out on the ground with his gun sighted on the knoll, Marcus waited. Water rushed in the front of his shirt, his body acting like a dam in the way of what was becoming a river. The wind was easing up, the intense storm cell drifting east, but the rain had intensified. It pounded on his back, his jacket now a heavy weight. There was not an inch of him that was dry.

They had triangulated on Lucas, Quinn taking the left flank, Dave the right. It would be possible to flush him out if Marcus were willing to use the other agents, but it wasn't worth another injury and possibly the first death.

He'd wait.

Because he wasn't going to lose.

If he made a mistake, he was dead.

There was nothing like a foxhole to focus one's heart and mind on what really mattered.

What was really true.

Jesus, please be my Savior again. You've waited a long time. I'm back, and I'm all Yours.

He relaxed, finally at peace.

Lightning spidered overhead between the clouds. The light illuminated a man lifting from the ground. Having sketched that face so many times it took only an instant for Marcus to confirm an identity. Taking him alive wasn't even considered. Protecting a witness came first. Protecting those he loved. Marcus pulled the trigger.

The shot knocked Lucas back and down.

Shaking slightly that he'd actually caught Lucas moving, Marcus rose from the ground and tightened his grip on his weapon. He held it in both hands in a shooter's stance as he walked forward with care, expecting to have to react. He didn't trust that stillness.

Quinn joined him. Lucas had crumpled on his side. They stood in silence as rain beat down on them. Quinn knelt and closed the man's eyes. "It's a shame he ever went bad," he said heavily. "Had he worked on the right side of the law, he would have been one of the best."

"He just about got through." Marcus holstered his Glock. He bent to retrieve the sniper rifle, carefully cleared the chamber. The hollow point would have been lethal had Lucas been able to draw a bead on Shari.

Jesus, it was necessary. But I'm sorry.

Quinn accepted the rifle. "Ask Lisa to join me with her cameras. Dave and I will put together the case scene notes then get your statement. You can't help, and Shari doesn't need to see this."

Marcus knew he was right. "I'll get them. The men?"

"Brad hit in the shoulder, Gary in the arm. They'll recover."

And Lucas Saracelli was dead. Shari was safe for now. Marcus wasn't sure what to tell her. It had been necessary to kill, but it hurt. Would she understand?

Shari started at the thud from above. Kate shoved her back against the dirt wall and the cellar shelves, her pistol coming up, sighted. Four knocks, a pause, and two more came sharp against the wood, and then the large wooden doors swung open. "Don't shoot me, Kate," Dave protested. "You ladies okay down there?"

"Fine," Kate replied dryly, lowering her pistol from a direct bead on Dave's face. "But Lisa has found a new pet."

Shari shook slightly as the relief settled across her. The wait had been horrible. They stepped out of the back shadows into the light of the one bare bulb as Dave came down the six wooden stairs. Kate was now acting as if it hadn't bothered her, and Shari silently shook her head at that even as she understood it. Lisa opened the shoebox lid so Dave could glance inside. "That is not flying back on the plane with us."

"He's just scared."

"Sure."

"I think he's kind of cute," Kate commented, coming to her sister's defense.

"Cute," Dave replied, doubtful.

Lisa moved to the stairs. "What happened? Is Quinn okay? Marcus?"

"Let's talk upstairs," Dave replied. He stepped back to let them precede him.

Shari was grateful to leave behind the claustrophobic reality of being underground. She found Marcus in the kitchen, wiping his face dry. His expression was grim. "What happened?" she whispered. "Where's Quinn?"

"He's fine." Marcus held out his arm, and she accepted the silent invitation, not caring that he was dripping wet. He wrapped both arms around her, hugged her close. "Lucas is dead."

She froze. "He was here?"

Marcus rubbed her back. "Quinn spotted him when he was making the rounds."

"Who killed him? Quinn?"

"I did."

Marcus had shot someone to keep her safe. She rubbed her cheek against his wet shirt, seeking to add warmth, seeking to comfort, knowing how awful that must be to deal with, and feeling ashamed at the relief she felt. "I'm sorry you'll have to carry that."

"I promised I wouldn't let anyone hurt you."

"I'm grateful. The others? We heard shots."

"Two injured, they are going to be fine." He eased back, saw her worry.

"It could have been much worse," he said softly. "Let it go."

Lisa had joined them. Marcus reached over and squeezed Lisa's shoulder. "Quinn needs your help."

"He actually asked for my help?"

"He did," Marcus confirmed, smiling slightly. "Go enjoy it."

"I will." She lifted the box in her hand. "Could you watch Charlie for me?"

"What did you find?"

"Another friend. Dave isn't so sure about letting him fly home with us though."

Marcus opened the lid to look inside, then raised one eyebrow. "Got your backpack?"

She nodded.

"Tuck the box inside. Quinn will smuggle him back for you."

"Think so?"

"Oh, I think so."

She sighed. "If he keeps this up, I may just have to change my mind about him. Then life will get boring."

Marcus took the shoebox. "Somehow I don't think that will happen."

"Let me go get to work." She kissed his cheek. "Shari, get him some coffee to warm him up. Unless you can think of a better way."

Shari blushed.

Marcus laughed and swatted Lisa's arm. "Go on. Quit embarrassing my girlfriend."

"Girlfriend?" Shari whispered as the kitchen door swung shut.

He carefully set the shoebox down on the table, his startled look confirming he hadn't meant to say it that way. "Got a problem with that?"

"Well—"

"Oh, now I'm getting that grin that spells danger. What are you thinking, minx?" He linked his hands behind her back, his hold light, his gaze frank and appreciative.

"Do cops have girlfriends who are politicians?"

"This one does."

"No, let's think about it."

"Honey, I have. And if you haven't, we've got to talk about your lack of thinking ahead. I hear it's a politician's greatest asset."

She rested her head against his chest. "Get me through this, Marcus. And you've got a girlfriend."

His hands rubbed her back and she felt the brush of a kiss on her hair. "Deal."

Twenty-two

The federal courthouse in Richmond had become a secure fortress. Shari watched Connor through the one-way glass of an interview room as Dave and Quinn faced off with him one more time over the shooting. She would go before the grand jury at 1 P.M., and unless Connor plead guilty, she faced at least a year of protective custody until the trial was over.

A year would not destroy a chance at a relationship with Marcus, but it added more uncertainty than Shari could accept.

Jesus, let this end. Let there be justice now, and strong justice. Against everyone involved. Please.

She watched as a series of photos were laid down on the table. Crime scene photos. Frank. The place his body had been found. The brutal way he had been killed.

"Tell us about your father," Dave said.

Connor's glaze flickered to the photos, then back up, his face remaining impassive. "Why?" He smiled. "You'll never convict me."

It was the cool confidence in his voice that pushed Shari over the edge. Before Marcus could grab her arm and stop her she had pulled open the door to the room and stepped inside. Her color was high, her pulse up, her anger hot.

"You look surprised to see me," she remarked, seeing the startled look on Connor's face as well as on Dave and Quinn's. She planted her hands on the table and focused on Connor. "Don't worry. That big future payment you thought you would have to make will never come due. Lucas is

dead. And I'll even tell you where I'm going to be from the grand jury testimony to the end of your trial. Quantico."

Dave grimaced, and Marcus took her arm. "Shari."

"No. I want him to know. I want him to try again. It will ensure he
gets a death penalty when the next fool sent to kill me gets captured alive.
Just try it, Connor."

Marcus pulled her from the room.

She paced, hot anger triggered at being a foot away from the man who
had killed Carl and her dad burning off.

"You shouldn't have done that."

She sent Marcus a frustrated glance. "He's so confident he's going to
walk."

"He won't. Your testimony along with what else we have will be
enough."

Marcus looked back into the interview room, where Quinn was stepping in to take advantage of the unexpected moment.

Quinn laid down photos of Connor's brother Daniel after the execution.
"You are going to join him for killing a federal judge. The only way you can
escape a death penalty sentence is to plead guilty and start talking. We want
to know about your father, about his involvement, about his business."

Connor moved the photos around on the table and finally picked up
one. "He didn't deserve to die."

"You do."

Connor set the photo down, then looked toward the one-way glass.
He looked at Quinn. "Titus ordered Frank killed."

Titus was working at his home office, very aware of the date, the time, and
ruthlessly keeping himself occupied. Lucas would strike, swift, like a
cobra, and the news would begin to come out in rumors—"The witness is
dead, the grand jury has been postponed."

The call came an hour later than he had expected.

Titus listened to the lawyer on the phone, his expression growing
cold, his fingers on his pen tightening. He didn't say anything, just hung
up the phone.

Anthony had joined him.

"Connor is talking. And I won't pay for his mistakes. Kill him."

‒‒‒∞‒‒‒

They were on the way to Quantico. Shari watched the countryside pass by along the interstate.

Marcus reached over and gripped her hand. "Relax. Frank is dead. Connor has turned against his father. We've got enough to bring down Titus. Once he's in custody the threat to you will be contained."

"I know. But I'm still stuck at Quantico until Connor and Titus go to trial. All Connor gave up was that Titus had Frank killed. He admitted nothing about Carl."

"Shari, we take it a day at a time."

She didn't know what to say. She didn't want to face a potential separation of several months.

The car phone rang. Marcus reached for it. "Yes?"

Shari looked over at him when the silence lasted. Something had happened. The distant look was there in his gaze. "How?"

She reached over and touched his knee. His hand came over and firmly grasped hers.

He didn't say anything after he hung up the phone. "Marcus?"

"Connor was just killed at the jail as he was being processed back into solitary."

She started. "He's dead?"

"It looks like an ordered hit: Titus just killed his son." Marcus leaned up to speak with the driver. "Tell our escorts to pull in tight. And get me every cop car in the area converging on us, now!"

Shari didn't think she would ever get accustomed to Quantico. After what had turned into a tense drive to reach the safety of the compound, she had found herself joined by a group of very grim bodyguards.

It was a fascinating if intimidating place. She had been there three days when she came down from her room to the cafeteria for lunch to find Marcus waiting for her. She didn't care who was watching. She wrapped him in a hug and kissed him.

He didn't let her go. "I think I'll show up for a welcome again."

"Thanks for coming."

"Feel like sleeping in your own bed tonight?"

Emotions washed over her—relief, hope, intense joy that this long nightmare was over. "You're serious?" she whispered.

"Titus has been arrested. The FBI came down on his organization like a hammer, and people beneath him are already rolling, giving evidence against him to get an easier deal themselves. There are strong rumors there is now a contract out on him. There are a lot of people in the world who fear what he might say. He'll cooperate eventually, if only to get the government's protection to prevent his associates from reaching through the prison doors to kill him."

"He's reaping what he sowed."

"Yes."

"Watch how fast I can pack."

They were on a private plane flying to meet her mom and brother who were arriving in New York an hour later.

"Who's this?" A rather beaten-up raccoon sat in one of the plane seats, a big red bow around his neck.

"Rugsby. He's about to reappear. I was dispatched to Rachel's home to retrieve him."

Shari picked up the raccoon, delighted with it. "No ransom?"

"It has to be paid next week. And you'll notice I just kidnapped you from Quantico to pay my part."

She grinned. "True. Kate mentioned there was an O'Malley dinner scheduled."

"I thought you might like to join me."

"I would."

She relaxed in her seat and watched the ground become smaller below them.

"What are you thinking about?" Marcus asked.

She looked over at him and went out on a limb. "The future."

He leaned back, folded his hands across his chest, and lazily looked back at her. "So...do you want to run for state legislator or go straight for what you really want, a congressional house seat?"

"You're determined to get me to go for it."

"It's your dream."

"You have to be married to run for congressional office," she reminded him.

He quirked a grin. "I guess that means you'll just have to marry me before the elections."

She blinked. *He just proposed.*

"I love you, minx, with all my heart."

"I love you too," she whispered back.

"I know." His warm smile curled around her heart. His foot nudged hers. "The O'Malley family thinks you should run for the open house congressional seat. Lisa wants to be your field manager; she sees it like running a military campaign. Kate will organize your volunteer staff so she can boss around Jack and Stephen, and Dave volunteered to handle transportation. Oh, and Jennifer thinks we should make the wedding be the event of the Virginia social calendar so everybody will love you, and they'll vote for you because they adore you."

His entire family was saying welcome. She loved them all. "What do you want to do?"

"Elope."

Shari laughed.

"But since the O'Malleys will never let us get away with that, a social event of the year sounds like a good second choice."

"My mom will love it."

"I know." His expression became serious. "Shari, I'm not threatened by the idea of a smart wife with great ideas and a passion for her job. You have to dream big if you're going to fit with me."

"You're serious."

"You're one of us now. So start defining your dream, and we'll help you get there. Kids, a political career—we are a family that believes in fulfilling dreams. And Shari…we don't believe in small dreams."

She knew that was true. She considered him. "What's your biggest dream?"

"I'll tell you on the honeymoon."

She blushed but didn't mind. "I'll probably convince you to sleep in." She laughed at the look he gave her. She was going to enjoy the permanence of a marriage with him. Just getting to tease him would fill her days with laughter. She picked up the aged raccoon. "I like your family."

"You're fishing for compliments. They love you."

"It's important that they feel like I'm joining your family and not taking you from it."

"They know it," Marcus reassured. "You want to surprise them at the family gathering?"

"How?"

He nodded toward Rugsby. "While he was gone, he found himself a lady and they had baby raccoons."

She burst out laughing. "He did?"

"Start thinking of names."

"I like the fact you encourage the silliness."

"It's called smart family management. The O'Malleys unoccupied just come up with trouble."

"Good try, but you're really still a kid at heart."

"Maybe true too."

She set down the raccoon, looked over at him, smiled, and came around to a subject she had meant to mention to him. "You know, I realized something the other day when I was sorting out what was in my purse."

"What's that?"

"I still have the slip of paper with the pager numbers you asked me to memorize. I never had reason to page you with my private code."

"You will in the future," Marcus noted, watching her.

"I think I'll have to. I noticed something about the private code you assigned me."

"Did you?"

"I should have noticed it before…"

He slowly smiled. "Yes, you should have."

"225-6469 spells CAL-MINX."

"Well, what do you know…" He laughed at her expression.

"I only saw it because I was bored and was doodling. You weren't going to tell me, were you?"

"Nope."

"You're terrible."

"I love you too."

They shared a smile. Shari tilted her head to one side, considering him. "I'll need a private code for you, for when I want you to call me back immediately…"

"Why do I get the feeling you thought of one?"

She had a hard time containing her joy. "484-8463."

He pulled out his phone, looked at the keypad, putting letters to the numbers. He laughed softly as he figured it out. "Minx, I like the way you think."

"Not too subtle?"

"I'll remember it," Marcus promised.

"Can you use the phone while we're flying?"

"Briefly."

She unclipped her pager from her belt to see the display. "Page me."

He smiled at her as he dialed. "Just wait until we get on the ground, Shari."

The numbers flashed on the pager.

HUG TIME.

Multnomah Publishers

The publisher and author would love to hear your comments about this book. *Please contact us at:*
www.multnomah.net/theguardian

Dear Reader,

Thank you for reading this book. I appreciate it. This was one of the most fascinating books I have written to date. I fell in love with Marcus O'Malley while writing *The Negotiator,* and I knew this man who leads the O'Malleys would have a powerful story. He blew me away with his story and surpassed my expectations. This is the book I look back on and think, I wrote that? Some stories are gifts. This was one of them.

Prayer is such a rich topic to explore, both from the viewpoint of someone strong in their faith and someone who walked away from faith years before. One has concluded prayer is answered by chance as much as by a caring God; the other believes God is answering prayer despite the fact the answers are hard to accept. But they are both struggling with the conclusions they've reached. I found myself able to defend the conclusions of each one of them. I think they both made rational decisions—yet only one of them made the right one. Understanding why was a rich journey through my own beliefs.

I have found in a lifetime of prayer that Jesus really does love me and know me, and best of all likes me. His answers eventually work out to my good. Even those I do not understand yet, I continue to trust will be good answers...

As always, I love to hear from my readers. Feel free to write me at:

Dee Henderson
c/o Multnomah Publishers, Inc.
P.O. Box 1720
Sisters, Oregon 97759

E-mail: dee@deehenderson.com
or on-line: http://www.deehenderson.com

First chapters of all my books are on-line, please stop by and check them out. Thanks again for letting me share Marcus and Shari's story,

Sincerely,

Dee Henderson

THE O'MALLEY SERIES

The Negotiator—Book One

FBI agent Dave Richman from *Danger in the Shadows* is back. He's about to meet Kate O'Malley, and his life will never be the same. She's a hostage negotiator. He protects people. Dave's about to find out that falling in love with a hostage negotiator is one thing, but keeping her safe is another!

ISBN 1-57673-819-1

The Guardian—Book Two

A federal judge has been murdered. There is only one witness. And an assassin wants her dead. U.S. Marshal Marcus O'Malley thought he knew the risks of the assignment...
He was wrong.

ISBN 1-57673-642-3

The Truth Seeker—Book Three

Women are turning up dead. Lisa O'Malley is a forensic pathologist and mysteries are her domain. When she's investigating a crime it means trouble is soon to follow. U.S. Marshal Quinn Diamond has found loving her is easier than keeping her out of danger. Lisa's found the killer, and now she's missing too...

ISBN 1-57673-753-5

THE O'MALLEY SERIES

The Protector—Book Four

Jack O'Malley is a fireman. He's fearless when it comes to facing an inferno. But when an arsonist begins targeting his district, his shift, his friends, Jack faces the ultimate challenge: protecting the lady who saw the arsonist before she pays an even higher price...

ISBN 1-57673-846-9

The Healer—Book Five

Rachel O'Malley makes her living as a trauma psychologist, working disaster relief for the Red Cross. Her specialty is helping children. When a school shooting rips through her community, she finds herself dealing with more than just grief among the children she's trying to help. There's a secret. One of them witnessed the shooting. And the murder weapon is still missing...

ISBN 1-57673-925-2

The Rescuer—Book Six

Stephen O'Malley is a paramedic who has rescued people all his life. But he'll never forget this night: a kidnapping, a storm, and a race to rescue the woman he loves…

ISBN 1-59052-073-4

<u>**Available April 2003**</u>

Available now from
DEE HENDERSON
THE NEGOTIATOR
ISBN 1-57673-819-1

Don't miss book one in this captivating new series!

Dave waited until Kate's brother Stephen disappeared up the stairs. "Why didn't you tell me yesterday? Trust me?"

"Tell you what? That I might have someone in my past who may be a murderer?" Kate swung away from him into the living room. "I've never even met this guy. Until twenty-four hours ago, I didn't even have a suspicion that he existed."

"Kate, he's targeting you."

"Then let him find me."

"You don't mean that."

"There is no reason for him to have blown up a plane just to get at me, to get at some banker. We're never going to know the truth unless someone can grab him. And if he gets cornered by a bunch of cops, he'll either kill himself or be killed in a shootout. It would be easier all around if he did come after me."

"Stop thinking with your emotions and use your head." Dave shot back. "What we need to do is to solve this case. That's how we'll find out the answers and ultimately find him."

"Then you go tear through the piles of data. I don't want to have anything to do with it. Don't you understand that? I don't want to be the one who puts the pieces together. Yesterday was like getting stuck in the gut with a hot poker."

He understood it, could feel the pain flowing from her. "Fine. Stay here for a day, get your feet back under you. Then get back in the game and stop acting like you're the only one this is hurting. Or have you forgotten all the people who died?" He saw the sharp pain flash in her eyes before they went cold and regretted his words.

"That was a low blow and you know it."

"Kate—"

"I can't offer anything to the investigation, don't you understand that?

I don't know anything. I don't know him."

"Well he knows you. And if you walk away from this now, you're going to feel like a coward. Just what are you so afraid of?"

He could see it in her, a fear so deep it shimmered in her eyes and pooled them black, and he remembered his coworker's comment that he probably didn't want to read the court record. His eyes narrowed and his voice softened. "Are you sure you don't remember this guy?"

She broke eye contact, and it felt like a blow because he knew that at this moment he was the one hurting her. "If you need to get away for twenty-four hours, do it. Just don't run because you're afraid. You'll never forgive yourself."

"Marcus wouldn't let me go check out the data because he was afraid I would kill the guy if I found him."

Her words rocked him back on his heels. "What?" He closed the distance between them, and for the first time since this morning began, actually felt something like relief. He rested his hands calmly on her shoulders. "No you wouldn't. You're too good a cop."

She blinked.

"I almost died with you, remember?" He smiled. "I've seen you under pressure." His thumb rubbed along her jaw. "Come on, Kate. Come back with me to the house, and let's get back to work. The media wouldn't get near you, I promise."

Marcus and Stephen came back down the stairs, but Kate didn't look around; she just kept studying Dave. She finally turned and looked at her brother. "Marcus, I'm going back to Dave's."

Dave gave in to a small surge of relief. It was a start. Tenuous. And risky. But a start, all the same.

THE TRUTH SEEKER

Lisa O'Malley was sitting on the side step of the fire engine, silent, one tennis shoe off as she'd stepped on a hot ember and burned the sole, her stockinged foot moving slowly back and forth in the soot-blackened water rushing down the street toward the nearest storm drain. Her gaze never leaving the dying fire. Her brother Stephen had wrapped a fire coat around her, and she had it gripped with both hands, pulled tight.

Quinn Diamond kept a close watch on her as he stood leaning against the driver's door of a squad car, waiting for a callback from the dispatcher. She was alone in her grief, her emotions hidden, her eyes dry. She'd lost what she'd valued, and Quinn hated to realize how much it had to resonate with her past.

Kate sat down beside her.

Quinn watched as the two sisters sat in silence, and he prayed for Kate, that she would have the right words to say.

Instead, she remained silent.

And Lisa leaned her head against Kate's shoulder and continued to watch the fire burn, the silence unbroken.

Friends. Deep, lifelong friends.

Quinn had to turn away from the sight. He had so much emotion inside it was going to rupture into tears or fury.

He found himself facing a grim Marcus O'Malley.

"Quinn, get her out of here."

"Stephen has already tried; she won't budge."

"No. I mean out of here. Out of town," Marcus replied grimly. "The killer goes from notes and phone calls to fire. He's not going to stop there."

Marcus was right. Lisa had to come first. "The ranch. She's going to need the space."

"Thank you."

"I'll keep her safe, now that it's too late."

"Quinn—we'll find him."

That wasn't even in question. He was going to hunt the guy down and rip out his heart.

"I highly recommend this book to anyone who likes suspense."

—Terri Blackstock, bestselling author of *Trial by Fire*

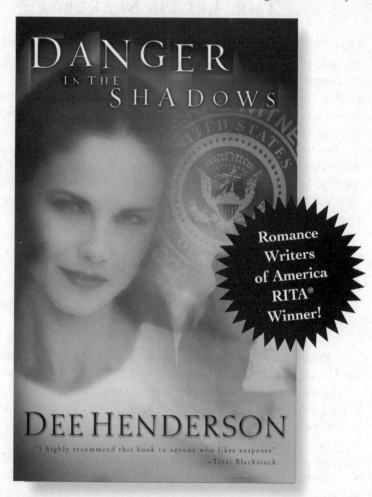

Romance Writers of America RITA® Winner!

Don't miss the prequel to the O'Malley series!

Sara's terrified. She's doing the one thing she cannot afford to do: fall in love with former pro football player Adam Black, a man everyone knows. Sara's been hidden away in the witness protection program, her safety dependent on being invisible—and loving Adam could get her killed.

ISBN 1-57673-927-9

DANGER IN THE SHADOWS

RITA Award Winner—the highest national award given
for excellence in romantic fiction
National Reader's Choice Award Winner
Bookseller's Best Award Winner

The summer storm lit up the night sky in a jagged display of energy, lightning bouncing, streaking, fragmenting between towering thunderheads.
Sara Walsh ignored the storm as best she could, determined not to let it
interrupt her train of thought. The desk lamp as well as the overhead light
were on in her office as she tried to prevent any shadows from forming.
What she was writing was disturbing enough.

The six-year-old boy had been found. Dead.

Writing longhand on a yellow legal pad of paper, she shaped the
twenty-ninth chapter of her mystery novel. Despite the dark specificity of
the scene, the flow of words never faltered.

The child had died within hours of his abduction. His family, the
Oklahoma law enforcement community, even his kidnapper, did not realize it. Sara did not pull back from writing the scene even though she knew
it would leave a bitter taste of defeat in the mind of the reader. The impact
was necessary for the rest of the book.

She frowned, crossed out the last sentence, added a new detail, then
went on with her description of the farmer who had found the boy.

Thunder cracked directly overhead. Sara flinched. Her office suite on
the thirty-fourth floor put her close enough to the storm she could hear
the air sizzle in the split second before the boom. She would like to be in
the basement parking garage right now instead of her office.

She had been writing since eight that morning. A glance at the clock
on her desk showed it was almost eight in the evening. The push to finish
a story always took over as she reached the final chapters. This tenth book
was no exception.

Twelve hours. No wonder her back muscles were stiff. She had taken a brief break for lunch while she reviewed the mail her secretary had prioritized for her. The rest of her day had been spent working on the book. She arched her back and rubbed at the knot.

This was the most difficult chapter in the book to write. It was better to get it done in one long, sustained effort. Death always squeezed her heart.

Had Dave been in town, he would have insisted she wrap it up and come home. Her life was restricted enough as it was. Her brother refused to let her spend all her time at the office. He would come lean against the doorjamb of her office and give her that look along with his predictable lecture telling her all she should be doing: Puttering around the house, cooking, messing with the roses, something other than sit behind that desk.

Sara smiled. She did so enjoy taking advantage of Dave's occasional absences.

His flight back to Chicago from the FBI academy at Quantico had been delayed due to the storm front. When he had called her from the airport, he had cautioned her he might not be home until eleven.

It wasn't a problem, she had assured him, everything was fine. Code words. Spoken every day. So much a part of their language now that she spoke them instinctively. "Everything is fine"—all clear; "I'm fine"—I've got company; "I'm doing fine"—I'm in danger. She had lived the dance a long time. The tight security around her life was necessary. It was overpowering, obnoxious, annoying...and comforting.

Sara turned in the black leather chair and looked at the display of lightning. The rain ran down the panes of thick glass. The skyline of downtown Chicago glimmered back at her through the rain.

With every book, another fact, another detail, another intense emotion, broke through from her own past. She could literally feel the dry dirt under her hand, feel the oppressive darkness. Reliving what had happened to her twenty-five years ago was terrifying. Necessary, but terrifying.

She sat lost in thought for several minutes, idly walking her pen through her fingers. Her adversary was out there somewhere, still alive, still hunting her. Had he made the association to Chicago yet? After all these years, she was still constantly moving, still working to stay one step ahead of the threat. Her family knew only too well his threat was real.

The man would kill her. Had long ago killed her sister. The threat didn't get more basic than that. She had to trust others and ultimately God for her security. There were days her faith wavered under the intense weight of simply enduring that stress. She was learning, slowly, by necessity, how to roll with events, to trust God's ultimate sovereignty.

The notepad beside her was filled with doodled sketches of faces. One of these days her mind was finally going to stop blocking the one image she longed to sketch. She knew she had seen the man. Whatever the cost, whatever the consequences of trying to remember, they were worth paying in order to try to bring justice for her and her sister.

Sara let out a frustrated sigh. She couldn't force the image to appear no matter how much she longed to do so. She was the only one who still believed it was possible for her to remember it. The police, the FBI, the doctors, had given up hope years ago.

She fingered a worn photo of her sister Kim that sat by a white rose on her desk. She didn't care what the others thought. Until the killer was caught, she would never give up hope.

God was just. She held on to that knowledge and the hope that the day of justice would eventually arrive. Until it did, she carried a guilt inside that remained wrapped around her heart. In losing her twin she had literally lost part of herself.

Turning her attention back to her desk, she debated for a moment if she wanted to do any more work that night. She didn't.

As she put her folder away, the framed picture on the corner of her desk caught her attention; it evoked a smile. Her best friend was getting married. Sara was happy for her, but also envious. The need to break free of the security blanket rose and fell with time. She could feel the sense of rebellion rising again. Ellen had freedom and a life. She was getting married to a wonderful man. Sara longed to one day have that same choice. Without freedom, it wasn't possible, and that reality hurt. A dream was being sacrificed with every passing day.

As she stepped into the outer office, the room lights automatically turned on. Sara reached back and turned off the interior office lights.

Her suite was in the east tower of the business complex. Rising forty-five stories, the two recently built towers added to the already impressive downtown skyline. She struggled with the elevator ride to the thirty-fourth floor each day, for she did not like closed-in spaces, but she considered the view worth the price.

The elevator that responded tonight came from two floors below. There were two connecting walkways between the east and west towers, one on the sixth floor and another in the lobby. She chose the sixth floor concourse tonight, walking through it to the west tower with a confident but fast pace.

She was alone in the wide corridor. Travis sometimes accompanied her, but she had waved off his company tonight and told him to go get dinner. If she needed him, she would page him.

The click of her heels echoed off the marble floor. There was parking under each tower, but if she parked under the tower where she worked, she would be forced to pull out onto a one-way street no matter which exit she took. It was a pattern someone could observe and predict. Changing her route and time of day across one of the two corridors was a better compromise. She could hopefully see the danger coming.

Sara decided to take the elevator down to the west tower parking garage rather than walk the six flights. She would have preferred the stairs, but she could grit her teeth for a few flights to save time. She pushed the button to go down and watched the four elevators to see which would respond first. The one to her left, coming down from the tenth floor.

When it stopped, she reached inside, pushed the garage-floor parking button, but did not step inside. Tonight she would take the second elevator.

Sara shifted her raincoat over her arm and moved her briefcase to her other hand. The elevator stopped and the doors slid open.

A man was in the elevator.

She froze.

He was leaning against the back of the elevator, looking like he had put in a long day at work, a briefcase in one hand and a sports magazine in the other, his blue eyes gazing back at her. She saw a brief look of admiration in his eyes.

Get in and take a risk, step back and take a risk.

She knew him. Adam Black. His face was as familiar as any sports figure in the country, even if he'd been out of the game of football for three years. His commercial endorsements and charity work had continued without pause.

Adam Black worked in this building? This was a nightmare come true. She saw photographs of him constantly in magazines, local newspapers, and occasionally on television. The last thing she needed was to be near someone who attracted media attention.

She hesitated, then stepped in, her hand tightening her hold on the briefcase handle. A glance at the board of lights showed he had already selected the parking garage.

"Working late tonight?" His voice was low, a trace of a northeastern accent still present, his smile a pleasant one.

Her answer was a noncommital nod.

The elevator began to silently descend.

She had spent too much time in European finishing schools to slouch. Her posture was straight, her spine relaxed, even if she was nervous. She hated elevators. She should have taken the stairs.

"Quite a storm out there tonight."

The heels of her patent leather shoes sank into the jade carpet as she shifted her weight from one foot to the other. "Yes."

Three more floors to go.

There was a slight flicker to the lights and then the elevator jolted to a halt.

"What?" Sara felt adrenaline flicker in her system like the lights.

He pushed away from the back wall. "A lightning hit must have blown a circuit."

The next second, the elevator went black.

UNCOMMON HEROES SERIES

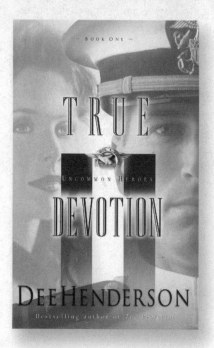

True Devotion, **Book One**

Kelly Jacobs has already paid the ultimate price of loving a warrior: She has the folded flag and the grateful thanks of a nation to prove it. Navy SEAL Joe "Bear" Baker can't ask her to accept that risk again—even though he loves her. But the man responsible for her husband's death is back, closer than either of them realize. Kelly's in danger, and Joe may not get there in time...

ISBN 1-57673-886-8

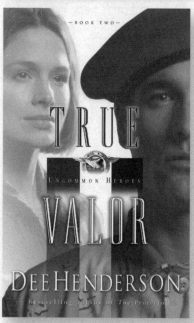

True Valor, **Book Two**

Air Force Pararescueman Bruce "Striker" Stanton spends his life rescuing pilots downed behind enemy lines. Grace "Gracie" Yates spends hers flying an F/A-18 Hornet for the Navy. With dangerous jobs, often away from home, they exchanged love letters. Now a fight between Turkey and its neighbors is spiraling into a confrontation. For the military deployed in the region, it's not just the occasional news headline—it's their daily problem. When Grace is shot down behind enemy lines, Bruce has got one mission: get Gracie out alive...

ISBN 1-57673-887-6

Available now from
DEE HENDERSON
TRUE DEVOTION

Uncommon Heroes—soldiers standing in the gap for
honor…and love.
Don't miss book one in this exciting new series!

Kelly slipped her hand into Joe's as they strolled down to the water's edge
then turned north to follow the beach toward the Hotel del Coronado
where their evening had begun. Music from the Ocean Terrace restaurant
at the hotel drifted toward them, the colorful lanterns lit around the
Terrace reflecting on the water. It was a festive mood.

"One of the last memories I had in the water before you rescued me
was from the last time we walked this beach."

"Really?"

She nodded. "Friday night after dinner. You indulged me with a walk
down to the Terrace to buy a frozen fruit smoothy. Remember?"

"I remember the smoothy—it gave me an ice cream headache."

"I had forgotten that."

"I haven't."

"What I remember is holding your hand while we walked, deciding
how nice it was not to be walking alone."

He squeezed her hand gently. "Thank you. You're welcome to hold my
hand anytime you like."

Kelly returned the pressure, communicating without words her pleasure, and they walked in silence along the shore. This was the best memory maker of the evening. The restaurant, the movie, roses, and the bear—
of all the images of the evening, this was the one she treasured most. She
had walked this beach with Joe before, but this time it was different. This
time in a new way she belonged beside him and it felt that way: special.

The evening was going to end eventually, and she didn't want that to
happen. Would he kiss her good night? There were already stars in her
eyes; that would certainly cap this evening with the best ending possible.

The moonlight flickered as clouds skimmed over the sky.

Joe stopped.

She looked at him, puzzled, and saw his eyes narrow as he gazed ahead.

There was only the dark shadow of the surf and the resulting white breakers. The sound clued her in, an odd interruption in the withdrawing surf as it pulled back to sea.

They both began to run.

A limp body was rolling in the surf, being thrown by the sea to the shore.

UNCOMMON HEROES SERIES

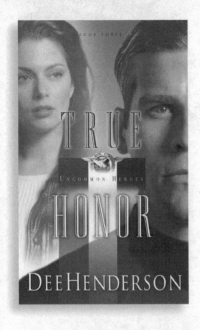

True Honor, Book Three

For CIA officer Darcy St. James, the terrorist attack on America is personal: Friends died at the Pentagon. She's after a man who knew September 11 would happen and who chose to profit from the knowledge. Navy SEAL Sam "Cougar" Houston is busy: The intelligence Darcy is generating has his team deploying around the world. Under the pressure of war, they discover the sweetness of love, and their romance flourishes. But it may be a short relationship—for the terrorists have chosen their next targets, and Darcy's name is high on the list…

ISBN 1-59052-043-2

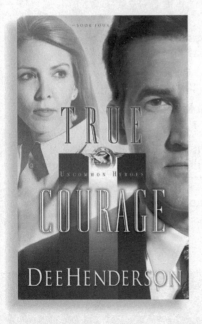

True Courage, Book Four

Someone snatched his cousin's wife and son. FBI agent Luke Falcon is searching for a kidnapper and sorting out the crime. He's afraid a stalker is responsible. He's afraid they're already dead. And he'll do anything required to get them back alive…but he didn't plan on falling in love with the only witness.

ISBN 1-57673-887-6

Available February 2003

A FREE "BEHIND THE SCENES" LOOK AT YOUR FAVORITE FICTION AUTHORS!

www.letstalkfiction.com

Let's Talk Fiction is a free, four-color mini-magazine created to give readers a behind-the-scenes look at Multnomah Publishers' favorite fiction authors. *Let's Talk Fiction* allows our authors to share a bit about themselves, giving readers an inside peek into their latest releases. Published in the fall, spring, and summer seasons, *Let's Talk Fiction* is filled with interactive contests, author contact information, and fun! To receive your free copy of *Let's Talk Fiction* get on-line at www.letstalkfiction.com. We'd love to hear from you!

Multnomah® Publishers   *Keeping Your Trust...One Book at a Time®*